Introduction to

The Jade Cross Trilogy

TOLBANE RETIRES

Harold W. Weist

Fulton Books
Meadville, PA

Published by Fulton Books 2023

ISBN 979-8-88731-961-2 (paperback)
ISBN 979-8-88731-963-6 (digital)

Printed in the United States of America

Let the other son of a bitch die for his country.

—Gen. George Patton in the movie *Patton*

PROLOGUE

Viet Nam, June 1966

Somewhere in the province of Quang Nam in the Republic of Viet Nam, after an hour and a half at the quick pace that infantry units were used to stepping out to, SSgt. Travis Tolbane, still waiting for his promotion warrant to gunnery sergeant to catch up to him, mentioned to his interpreter, Nguyen Van Ba, who was trudging along beside him, his muscles bitching at him, as was Tolbane's, "This humping all day sucks, know that, Ba?"

Tolbane's jungle utilities were dirty, wet, smelly, and salt-stained from the miserable heat. The temperature was probably 130 percent under his steel pot. Looking at Ba, he noticed that his garb was in the same condition. Sweat was pouring down from their hairlines and armpits. Even so, they kept up with the grunts step by step.

Their packs were heavy, but they were nothing like what the grunts were carrying. The grunts carried extra magazines and other items essential to accomplishing their mission: get close to the enemy and kill him.

Ba carried a .30 M1 Carbine while Tolbane wore his TO weapon, a model 1911 .45 ACP semiautomatic. There was a seven-round magazine inserted in the weapon's handgrip and a round in the chamber to make eight. There were also some in his holster and on his cartridge belt, along with two magazine pouches, one on each side of the buckle, with two magazines of .45 ammo each. He also had a first aid kit, four canteens of tepid water, and his favorite, a Ka-Bar.[1] On their backs were packs containing C rations, dry

---

[1]   A Marine Corps fighting knife.

socks, extra ammo, pencils, tablets, message books, and a poncho. Not much more was needed downrange.

"You, as you Americans always say, you can say that again," Ba replied. "It's too damn hot here to be alive in this place. My head is on fire. My feet are burning up. My back hurts, and my legs feel sore and tight and don't want to walk anymore."

Tolbane and Ba had only been at their team's CP and captive collection point in the Da Nang Air Base for three days after a temporary duty assignment with the Seventh Marines on the Chu Lai Combat Base for five and a half months. They interrogated two VCSs (Viet Cong suspects) that morning, who turned out to be VCCs (Viet Cong confirmed), and had just returned from lunch at the Marine Aircraft Group Sixteen's mess hall for their REMFs, commonly known as rear-echelon motherfuckers, adjacent to the captive collection point.

The team chief, Gunnery Sergeant Le Duc, already selected to be promoted to master sergeant, spotted them and called them to the CP hardback.

"Hey, you guys, the skipper wants to see you in here now. Not yesterday. Today!"

As the two entered, they saw the team commander, Capt. Joe Sledge, sitting beside the team chief's desk. The captain knew better than to sit behind the gunny's desk. All hell would break loose, and lightning would strike the CP.

The captain rose and said, "You are the very two ugly galoots I'm looking for today. And have I got a great deal for you!"

Tolbane groaned when he heard this. He knew he was about to get shafted one more time, sent out to one of the infantry units to be the duty target for the VC. He thought of BOHICA (bend over here it comes again). Oh well, he was used to getting shafted. What was one more shafting to a knight errant anyway? Each time he fell, he would rise again, and woe to the fucking VC.

The captain had a good sense of humor, and it kept him in good standing with his subteams' leaders and their personnel. Knowing this, Tolbane had a good response.

"So that means you are going out to some grunt unit with us, right, sir?"

"In your wildest-ass dreams, Staff Sergeant. It'll be just you and Ba going to do or die. If you weren't the best, I wouldn't send you two on to glory for Mom, apple pie, Stars and Stripes, and the Corps."

"Gee! Thanks a lot, skipper. I never thought you'd ask, sir," Tolbane chided back.

"I guess you know the drill by now. I hate to send you two, as we are shorthanded here with some of the other subteams already out with troops. It's out of my hands, as you well know. I have to be a good little boy and do division G-2's fervent wishes. I have sent Gunny Stoltz and his interpreter there already. You two will be going to Bravo 1/1/1, and the other two to Charlie 1/1/1.

"Your transportation will be here within the hour. The good Lord willing, the creek level doesn't rise up and the dried-out rice paddies fill with water and fish—from where, we can only guess. I don't know what the mission is, where it is located, or what dangers may be involved. But I'll be awaiting your safe return.

"You two will return safe and sound. That's an order. When I got this assignment as team commander, I had no idea I would have to send my troops into any danger period. I thought all of our work would be here at our CP. That's the way the card is dealt, though, I guess. Good luck to you, guys."

The captain returned to his office and paperwork, and the gunny wished them luck. They left to their respective hooches to load up their gear and stand by. Tolbane got his gear together rather quickly. He also included in his pack three message books and some sharpened pencils, three packs of C rations and some extra cans of C ration fruit, and cheese and crackers from his stash. He then lay back on his cot and waited, his eyes beginning to droop.

Tolbane was asleep on his cot when the gunny came in to let him know that two mighty mites, the Marine Corps's sorry answer to the jeep, were there to pick them up. Each one had a driver and a shotgun, ready to shoot at anything that didn't look right. He went to Ba's hardback and woke him. Then they moved to the front of the

CP's hardback and boarded the vehicles, Tolbane in the lead one and Ba in the second.

In a flash, they were headed, full speed, lickety-split, south, down the potholed Highway 1 toward Hoi An City, an old Chinese trading center that was originally named Fai-Fo. The vehicles always moved as fast as possible over roads and trails in case of an ambush or passing over a mine. In no time, they were at the enclave of the First Battalion, First Marine Regiment, First Marine Division, a few miles north of Hoi An City. Arriving, they were shown to a hardback, empty except for Gunny Stoltz and his interpreter, Lam. Tolbane and the gunny acknowledged each other.

Tolbane and Ba each chose one of the eight empty cots, four on each side, and dumped their gear on them. Tolbane sat on his wood-frame-and-canvas cot and asked Gunny Stoltz why they were there.

"What's up with this deal, Guns? Have you got any idea at all why we're here in this den of inequity? I'm hoping it won't be like the fiasco the last time I was down here with this bunch. That deal was the pits right from the get-go. If GI Joe had been here, he most likely would have shot the company commander rather than any VC."

"Damned if I know, Tolbane. When Lam and I got here, we were greeted by some corporal with a broom up his ass at the S-2 and who had a PFC guide us to this hooch. I guess we will find out tomorrow, as the S-2 officer and chief weren't there today for some reason or other."

"Gee!" Tolbane noted, tongue in cheek. "How about this? I always wanted to find out what it's like to camp out in a real Marine Corps hardback tent on a canvas cot. This is a great surprise, Gunny, and it's not even my birthday yet."

"Glad your wildest dream came true, marine. Maybe we can get a hint at the SNCO mess in about an hour or so. Look out the back door. Notice we are twelve feet from the sandbagged perimeter, about three and a half to four feet high. All we have to do is step out that entrance, and we'll be in the bunker we'll need to man if anything happens—you know, like shit hitting the fan. Slop, slop, slop, and more slop."

Tolbane looked out to the bunker. He thought it looked pretty good inside. It wouldn't be filled with trash and garbage like an RVN bunker. He thought Chesty Puller would say you could fire in all directions in it.

Then collapsing on an empty cot, Tolbane closed his eyes and uttered, "Wake me when it's chow time!"

In the blink of an eye, he was snoring. Gunny Stoltz just shook his head at him. Even so, he knew Tolbane was top-notch in his trade. He was a great friend and a terrible enemy to have.

*****

They were in luck at the SNCO mess that night, the last hot meal they would have for several days—grilled hamburgers and hot dogs, baked beans, potato salad, outside with all the trimmings, and peach cobbler for dessert.

"Wow!" Tolbane exclaimed. "Something different."

Tolbane had thirds on the cobbler on top of one more hot dog, two more hamburgers, and a ton of beans. The gunny thought about what kind of gas attack in the hooch was in store for him from Tolbane that night.

After eating, they went to the makeshift small staff NCO / officers' club, had three beers and one shot of Jim Beam, and then returned to their hooch to get ready to call it a night. They spoke of what they had learned about the morrow, but no one they had spoken with knew anything about it. When they turned in, they wrapped themselves in their ponchos and got as comfortable as they could, not knowing when they would have the luxury of sleeping on a cot again, if ever.

Ba and Lam had a similar experience visiting with a couple of the battalion interpreters who weren't in the field that day. However, their fare was rice, smoked fish, and nuoc mam sauce topped off with Ba Moui Ba (33) beer, warm. They had not learned anything either and turned in about the same time as the gunny and Tolbane.

The night was calm and peaceful. There was no harassing fire from the VC, and the mortars had no H&I fire (harassing and interdiction) mission to disturb one's sleep.

*****

The four awoke at about the same time and did their morning chores, and all went to the staff NCO / officers' mess and had a good breakfast. Gunny Stoltz wondered if Tolbane would turn into a strip of bacon, as he had fourths of it. They returned to their hooch, waited about half an hour, and went over to the S-2 desk at the huge command and control bunker.

No one was at the S-2 desk, so they just crapped out and waited for an hour before a First Lieutenant Boyton arrived and greeted them and thanked them for coming as if they had a friggin' choice. Shortly thereafter, the intelligence chief and the clerk came in. The clerk got the four's names, service numbers, and units and made the first entry of the day in the S-2's chronology log. Then the captain came in and sat at the desk.

When everyone was as comfortable as they could be, Lieutenant Boyton began the briefing while the captain listened.

"I know what's on your minds, guys, so listen up, and I'll give you the scoop as I know it. We have some reports of VC activity in two areas"—he pointed to the situation map—"about two klicks or so apart. In about two hours or a bit, Bravo and Charlie companies will begin to move into the two areas, then begin sweeping the areas. Tolbane, you and Ba will go with Bravo. And, Gunny, you and Lam go with Charlie. We have two LVTP-5s waiting to take you to your assigned areas.

"Our information indicates there are two small VC units, one in each area. They are going through hamlets and subhamlets, harassing the peasants, stealing their food, and forcing the young men to join them. We believe they have murdered a few peasants that refused to feed them and give up their stored rice. There may have also been a few rapes, beatings, and murder in those areas too.

"The task of our two companies is to collect information. That's your job. Capture or kill the enemy if he chooses to resist and fights. That's all I can tell you, as we're not in the entire loop on this one. The company commanders were briefed by the battalion commander, Lieutenant Colonel Frazor, last night, and they will fill you in as much as they can. Any questions for now? If not, your limousines await you by the back gate. The lance corporal here will guide you to them. Good luck, gentlemen, and God be with you."

They left the bunker and moved to the extreme northeastern edge of the enclave. There was a break in the sandbagged barrier with a framework and a barbed wire gate with two guards posted there, who challenged them. On the other side of the barrier sat two LVTP-5s, engines running, smoke rising from the exhausts, and a staff sergeant hustling them to the top of their appropriate vehicles, which were sandbagged on the top. He waved, along with the lance corporal.

The vehicles took off like a turd of hurtles.

CHAPTER 1

A sunbaked plains area, Quang Nam

MGySgt. Travis Tolbane had just received his final discharge paper, a large document thanking him for his thirty years of meritorious service to his country and the United States Marine Corps and an original DD214 to go with his other DD214s.[2]

Sitting in his car, unaware of future adventures, he tilted his head back against the headrest and began dreaming about the years and events that really made his career interesting and formed him into the man he had become.

*****

The top of the LVTP-5 had two long doors over the cargo/seating compartment that could be opened or closed. In this case, they were closed and had two layers of sandbags atop them. All passengers sat atop them, not in the compartment. This was protection for passengers in case the P5 struck a mine.

SSgt. Travis Tolbane and his interpreter, Nguyen Van Ba, sat atop the sandbags, along with six other marines. They were not really enjoying the ride; each weapon was locked, loaded, and ready in case of an ambush by the VC. It wasn't a real smooth ride either, as the tractor was following in the deep-rutted tracks made by the passage of amtracs moving to and from supplying ammo, C rations, etc. to the troops in the field. The route took them through treed areas, parched, level areas, and now and then, small hedgerow areas.

---

[2] All veterans are issued a DD214 upon discharge to verify their service history.

"You might have known," Tolbane mentioned to Ba. "Here we are at our assembly area, and it's level, hard-packed, and parched like hell and just as hot as ever. So it looks like we'll find out how hot hell is once more. It's not even noon, and I'm already a roasted jungle bunny."

"Me too!" Ba replied. "If you got some eggs, we could fry them on the metal parts of this metal dragon. We're going to burn our asses getting off this hot metal monster."

Getting down, they walked over to a group of five marines standing by a radioman. Tolbane reckoned it was the company commander and his cohorts. It was the company gunnery sergeant and three second lieutenants, who were the company platoon leaders.

Tolbane and Ba approached the captain directly and introduced themselves to him and the group.

The captain introduced himself as Captain Booker, company commander, and said, "Good. You're finally here, and we'll be off to see the wizard shortly. Which one, I don't know. Company gunny, get the command group saddled up. And, you three"—he pointed at his platoon leaders—"get to your platoons.

"The order of march is as follows: second platoon in the lead, then the first platoon behind the command group, and third platoon will be forward, back, and flank security. Now move into your positions."

The marines, with an "Aye, aye, sir!" moved to their assigned jobs. The captain told Tolbane and Ba that he would update them on the mission when they reached their first break area. When all were in their assigned order of march, the captain gave the order to move out. It was not forward ho.

The area was arid, dry, hard-packed, and dusty. The unit was moving in a generally southern direction. Tolbane knew that a ways to the left was the South China Sea. Far to the right, it looked like there were periodic small hedgerows having sparse vegetation; and farther on from there, he could see the tops of treed areas. Even though he could not see them, he was aware that there were dried-out rice paddies intermingled with the terrain and that here and there were thatched hovels where the families who tended the paddies lived. Maybe there were fields of vegetables too.

He had no idea where they were headed or, for that matter, how far. His main problem, along with Ba, now wasn't so much as the physical but the intense heat bearing down and sapping an individual's strength from his very soul.

Finally, after a backbreaking pace, the captain called a halt to the march to have a rest break; and immediately, certain marines broke from the company command group and took up security positions automatically. Then he instructed his radio operator to call his three platoon leaders to come to his location ASAP.

Within a couple of minutes, the three approached the group at a run, huffing and puffing and sweating profusely. Their uniforms were more soaked with sweat than Tolbane's and Ba's together. Tolbane felt kind of sorry for them. They would get no respite this day. At the three's arrival, the captain waved Tolbane, Ba, and the company gunny sergeant over; and all seven sat on the ground in a circle. The captain looked each one in the eye and smiled. Then he took his map out of the cargo pocket of his trousers and began his briefing.

"Gentlemen, I don't know what to expect up ahead. The intelligence and orders we have been getting on activity in this one large area is, at best, conflicting. A recon team reported heavy activity in two parts of the area. The team estimated about fifteen to twenty well-armed VCs in each of two separate groups, and they were moving from sub-hamlet to sub-hamlet.

"They are stealing rice and vegetables, beating some of the stubborn elders. They've raped a few young women and killed some men. The kids who are just old enough to fight are being sent off to be forced to become a VC and fight. Needless to say, that's a very bad situation. The recon team also felt there could be more VCs than their conservative estimate. If so, maybe it's a village guerilla unit. Could be fifty or sixty of them between the two groups.

"The conflict comes from the ARVN's district headquarters in that area. Their intel claims that there is no VC activity in the areas. I tend to believe the marine recon team."

3

One of the second lieutenants shouted at this juncture, "Ooh-rah!"

The captain gave him a dirty look and continued.

"Our mission is to capture or kill them if they resist, find the young men, and return them to their sub-hamlets, along with any rice, bread, or vegetables we may find. The brain trust believes that the VCs in both areas are from the same unit and will most likely link up when their job is done. It's believed they will link up somewhere between the two areas.

"That's where we and Charlie company enter the scene. We move in from the east, and Charlie moves in from the west. If the two VC units merge and are much larger than is thought, the powers that be will want to make it a vertical envelopment. We and Charlie will contain them as a blocking force, and an ARVN unit will chopper in and assault the VC.

"Now you see where the conflict in the operation order comes in. I think someone wants to make brownie points with someone upstairs. Company gunny, see that the word is passed to take a couple swallows of water and saddle up!"

Three to four minutes later, the company was once again on the march.

*****

A half hour later, the overheated, leg-weary, backs-hurting company turned to the west and began moving inland. An hour later, they had moved into an area among a stand of trees surrounding a few dried-out rice paddies. The captain told the command group that this was their home away from home for the night.

The company gunny immediately set the encampment security in place. The platoon commanders were notified to find a good spot to settle their platoons into the treed area and set their security. Tolbane and Ba found a small spot that seemed to be kind of level, put their packs on the ground and sat beside them, and breathed a sigh of relief that they could rest their weary bones at last. Within a couple of minutes, they were lying down, nearly falling asleep.

They both noticed at the same time and commented on a pagoda about 150 yards into the tree line. They could see a couple of marines cautiously approaching it with their weapons at the ready. They went in and soon made their exit. Nobody was at home at this time. Tolbane hoped it would stay that way during the night.

He and Ba heated their C rations by heat tabs for their early supper. Ba had the grease-laden canned hamburger patties, pouring half a can of grease from it, and Tolbane had his favorite: ham and motherfuckers (lima beans).

By the time they were done eating, a resupply amtrac came clanking into the area. It contained water cans, cases of C rations, ammunition, and two cans of Olympia beer per man. He and Ba each refilled their canteens and grabbed a couple individual C meals and two cans of beer, which they drank while the troops ate. When the troops were done eating, Tolbane saw something that absolutely disgusted him.

The amtrac also brought out service record books on a few of the troops. The captain stacked up a few cases of Cs in two piles to use as a desk and a seat. He actually held a captain's mass in the field. He berated a few troopers and gave them a sentence, which would begin once their company was out of the field for a rest. Tolbane and Ba could not believe their eyes and ears. This was crazy shit. Those troops had enough problems being in danger day and night in the field without being given something else to worry about. Tolbane wondered what kind of ass this company commander really was.

Darkness had finally arrived, and the troops were wrapping up in their ponchos and trying to get some sack time. It was also mosquito time on their faux home front. Being surrounded by a treed area, they were bad at night. They were big enough to land on an air strip and get refueled. Everyone had a small bottle of mosquito repellent held in place by a strip of inner tube around the base of their helmets, and they applied a liberal amount to their exposed skin.

The problem was being wrapped up in their ponchos. As the temperature dropped some, condensation formed inside the ponchos, and suddenly, poof, the repellent would be washed off, and they would be sharing their ponchos with gobs of unwanted Draculas.

*****

Around 0200 hours, the first round was fired from the pagoda. Then it seemed like there were three rifles firing from it. It didn't take but a few seconds of massed fire from the marines in the command group to gain fire superiority over the situation. Ba and Tolbane capped a few rounds too.

After a few minutes of chaos, the massed fire, sounding like hundreds of strings of fireworks going off at once, the cease fire command was given. All was suddenly quiet, an eerie silence. No sound came from the pagoda. After a few moments, all was back to normal, and the rest of the night was quiet and uneventful, and they slept soundly.

*****

The next morning, bright and early, the captain sent a four-man patrol, a fire team, to check out the pagoda. They found a lot of blood inside and blood trails leading from it. A decision was made by the captain not to follow up on the blood trails. He gave the command to saddle up after eating. The command group would move out to the east; Tolbane and Ba would be in line behind the Radio Operator.

A nice target position for Ba and me, Tolbane thought.

C rations were passed out again for all to eat before moving out. Luck of the draw, Tolbane and Ba both got canned scrambled eggs.

Both commented, "Ugh!"

After eating, the company moved out as directed, back to the arid area, and once more headed south. The sun was not too high yet, but that didn't delay the heat of the day. The troops were already soaked with sweat and taking occasional sips from their canteens.

The day was uneventful, just miserable. Then another move into the tree lines for the night. The captain performed the same routine with the troops. Then after another day and night, the company found itself at the target area and made contact with Charlie company. Both units began their sweeps and patrolled their areas for two days without having any enemy contact.

A few native captives were taken by Bravo company, whom Tolbane and Ba questioned and released. The captives were mainly old men and women, as the VCs had taken their young men with them as usual, and they really didn't have much information to give, except what the VCs had done to people in their sub-hamlets and what the VCs made them do, such as make punji sticks, ladder-like deals to carry the wounded to underground hospitals, aid stations, etc.

Two disappointed rifle companies then, humping as usual, returned to their regular operating areas. The only good thing from the fiasco was, there were no WIAs or KIAs during the operation. Foremost in his mind, Tolbane wondered why the companies weren't choppered into the target areas. They might have been able to have contact before the enemy fled the area. As long as it took a while to get the companies in position, the VCs would have plenty of time to leave the areas at their leisure.

Bravo and Charlie companies arrived back at the enclave at about the same time. Bravo dropped the gunny and Ba and continued to move to the east. It was Charlie's time to rest at the CP while the able company moved out to the west.

Tolbane, Ba, the gunny, and Lam were hoping to get some clean jungle utilities from the battalion supply; take a good shower; and feel like a million dollars again. But it was not to happen. Murphy's Law was in effect once more.

On arrival at the enclave, they were informed that there was a 6x6 waiting to take them to their Da Nang CP pronto while it was on a supply run.

CHAPTER 2

Tolbane was taken aback as the four of them walked into the CP's hardback.

The first thing the captain said was, "Wow, and damn nation, you four clowns stink to high heavens and back. You guys been swimming in a landfill? Go get yourselves a shower, put on clean jungle utes. And, Tolbane, get your ass back here ASAP! The headquarters battalion commander wants to see your sorry ass. Why aren't you back?"

Tolbane, shocked, a tingle running down his back to his ass, said "Yes, sir!" and scooted for the exit and moved to his hooch at the double time. The captain laughed watching him.

*****

Never in his life had Tolbane ever showered, shaved, and dressed so damned fast. He couldn't fathom what the hell he had done wrong now. He had never harmed a captive, except the one who attacked him a short while back—the guy got his ass kicked upon his shoulders—nor had he given any of his seniors any undue grief. He only knew he didn't want to make the battalion commander wait any longer than need be.

Within eighteen minutes, he had completed his task and met the captain, who was standing beside a team jeep. The captain instructed him to drive; he got behind the wheel as the captain climbed in, and they were off.

The drive up Freedom Hill (Hill 327) seemed to take forever for Tolbane, but he finally pulled up in front of the battalion HQ's CP hardback. He wasn't sure if he should shit or go blind. He and the captain entered the hardback and approached the counter separating the admin section. Immediately, a warrant officer told them to stand by, and he would notify the colonel they were there.

When the warrant officer returned and nodded the okay, the captain addressed Tolbane.

"SSgt. Tolbane, march in at the position of attention."

Tolbane squared and rolled back his shoulders and marched into the office at attention, stopping about two feet in front of the colonel's desk.

He announced, "SSgt. Travis Tolbane reporting as ordered, sir!"

Colonel Mark "the Bear" Jordon eyed Tolbane very closely, then asked the captain if the staff sergeant had been informed as to why he was there.

"No, sir! I felt the battalion commander could explain the circumstances to the staff sergeant much better than myself. Also, he'll listen to you. He's pretty stubborn at times."

Tolbane, hearing that from the captain, felt that something must be serious, and he felt very nervous.

"Well, Staff Sergeant," the colonel said, addressing Tolbane, "do you understand that you could be in serious trouble here?"

"Yes, sir!"

"Are you feeling a bit nervous?"

"Yes, sir!"

"Do you realize this situation will affect your career as a marine?"

"Yes, sir!"

"Don't you have anything to say except 'Yes, sir'?"

"Sir, if I knew why I'm here, I could respond more positive."

"Well, Gunny—"

"Begging the colonel's pardon, but I'm a staff sergeant."

"Not anymore, Gunny!"

The colonel opened his middle desk drawer and pulled out a document.

"Marine, I have here your promotion warrant to gunnery sergeant signed by the commandant of the Marine Corps, precedence number 1256."

9

The colonel stepped in front of his desk, read the warrant to Tolbane, and congratulated him.

As the captain reached out his hand, Tolbane took it, grinned, and said, "Captain, you son of a bitch."

The captain grinned, saying, "Back at you, Guns. Congratulations, Gunny, but don't forget, the beer's on you tonight."

"Gunny," the colonel said, "on your way out, the gunner will give you a packet with cloth and metal chevrons. Now take those one-rocker things off your uniform and make sure you're in proper uniform when you exit the hardback. Now"—he smiled—"get the fuck out of my office."

Tolbane, with his head above the clouds, turned and made for the gunner at the double. The colonel and the captain waved at each other. Shortly, a captain and a new gunnery sergeant left the battalion headquarters' CP.

Arriving at the team CP, Tolbane received congratulations from the team members on-site, got his stripes tacked on by the two gunnies, and—"Surprise, surprise, Sergeant Carter"—steaks were grilled out behind the CP, along with a tub of iced beer.

After a little ceremony and after everyone had their fill of steak, the three gunnies got into one of the team's jeeps and headed for the US Army's Take Ten Club in Da Nang. The newly promoted always had the privilege of buying the beer, and those of equal rank and above had the privilege of drinking the beer.

After a couple of hours, the two gunnies poured Tolbane into the jeep, took him back to the CP, and dumped him on his cot. There was no doubt about Tolbane's state of being the next morning: Headache City with a rumbling stomach and trembling ribs.

*****

That afternoon, the captain sent word for Tolbane to come in and see him at Tolbane's convenience. When Tolbane entered the captain's cubbyhole, the captain popped the tab of a Falstaff beer and handed it to him.

"Gunny, let's sit on the bunk. I need to catch you up on something. I got a message from HQ Marine Corps this morning. In about two months, we'll be losing the other two gunnies. They'll be rotating stateside. It looks like you'll be the team chief. Replacing the two, we'll be getting two staff sergeants, a sergeant, and a corporal just before the two rotate. That's all I know about the situation.

"I know you've spoken out about the lack of a proper indoctrination to our situation here for the FNGs,[3] as you didn't have any idea what was happening with the troops on their arrival here and with the Vietnamese people and their customs. I want you to be prepared to see that the new bees get schooled properly on what they need to know about those things before they get turned loose from the hive.

"There is a bit of sad news about me. I love it here. But alas and alack, I must rotate too. I'll rotate about a week after the gunnies. My replacement won't be here until about two weeks after I leave. The captain you're getting has been in admin and supply each for two years and one year of Vietnamese language school. Good luck with on-the-job training with that one."

"Captain, I have realized that the two gunnies would be rotating. However, I never considered you leaving. You'll be sorely missed. You've been a good leader for us. You understand people and can relate to anyone. I've never been around any officer as astute as you are. You'll be missed by everyone here. I'll do my best to keep this the good team you have molded. We have some good young men on this team, and I'm sure they will be of great help working with the new bees."

"I know you will do it right, Gunny. I hope we can serve together again sometime."

"The feeling's mutual, sir!"

"One more thing, Gunny. You'll have to make the commanding general's morning briefing every morning until the FNG captain reports in and maybe a couple with him until he feels comfortable there."

---

3 Fucking new guys.

"Oh, joy, skipper! I always wanted to sit up on high."

"Glad you approve. I got things to do now. Go do your gunny job, whatever the hell that is."

"Aye, aye, sir! See you around."

"Get the fuck going!" the captain joked with a smile.

By the time it was said, Tolbane was gone out of the hardback.

*****

Three days later, Tolbane was given a TAD (temporary additional duty) to the MP's criminal investigation section. He had been called up to the division headquarters' G-2 section. He was shown into the G-2's office. The G-2 was absent, but there was an individual in a suit and tie. (*In Viet Nam?* Tolbane thought.) He greeted Tolbane by name and stated he was with the NIS (Naval Investigative Service). However, he would remain nameless to Tolbane.

"Here is a set of TAD orders for you. Don't read them until you're back at your unit and alone. Do not share the content to anyone even if you are ordered to. I can't offer you any answers to any questions you may have. I can only say that you will be involved in something important. Although I can't give you any answers, I am bound by regulations to ask you if you have any questions. Do you have any questions? If not—"

"Oh, I do have one major question! Where the hell is the head?"

"As I'm not allowed to answer any of your questions, so cross your legs, go out, and ask the 2-chief where the freakin' head is, if you can wake him up."

Tolbane took the orders, turned, went out to the 2-chief's desk, crossed his legs, and asked, "Is that guy in there for real?"

"I'm afraid so, Gunny. The head is through that door."

"Thanks, Top. See you later."

Then Tolbane was gone. He found the outhouse, did his business, and returned to his jeep. He stood beside the team jeep, contemplating and not believing what had just happened.

"Are they going to make me a superspook? Will I be another James Bond? I can just picture myself saying, 'Tolbane! Travis

Tolbane! I want my martini shaken, not stirred.' Would that not be a blast? I wonder if there will be any gorgeous blondes there."

He shook his head, climbed in the jeep, and drove back to the CP.

Entering the hardback to walk through to the team area, the captain was the only one there at the time.

"Hey, Guns, guess we won't see you for a while."

"Sorry, skipper, my lips are sealed forever and a day. I sure don't want to sink any ships today or yesterday!"

"That's a good marine, marine."

Tolbane passed on through and went straight to his bunk in the staff NCO hardback. Everyone billeted there was out working with captives in the several interrogation huts. He sat on his bunk, opened the envelope, and read and reread the orders several times. They made no sense to him, but the gist was that he was ordered the following:

1. Where to go.
2. To arrive two days hence at 1300 hours.
3. Speak to no one of these orders.
4. Bring his gear.
5. Be prepared to stay seven days.
6. A jeep would pick him up one hour before reporting time.

Those were the orders in a nutshell. He had never had such orders in his entire time in the Corps. Must be from some high-level spook.

Tolbane lay back on his bunk and wondered, "What the hell will I be getting into this time?"

A minute later, he was snoring up a storm. He awoke half an hour later, shook his head clear, and decided it was chow time. So he managed to get to his feet and trudge to chow and, no surprise, ate more than his share.

*****

As prescribed in the orders, a mighty mite[4] was there in front of the team's CP to pick him up at precisely 1300 hours on the nose. He put his gear in the back and climbed in the passenger seat. The driver, a corporal, gave no introduction and no conversation and wasted no time in getting on the way, so quickly that Tolbane was rocked back into his seat.

After about ten minutes of the bumpy-ass ride, the jeep pulled into the middle of a ten-vehicle convoy, and the convoy began moving north, driving as fast as the lead vehicle could take them. All the troops were on high alert for ambushes and mines in the road.

Nearly half the distance from Da Nang to Hue City, the convoy slowed some and took what seemed to be a new dirt road to the left almost too fast and nearly capsized and then headed due west. Half an hour later, they came upon a small enclave with about ten hardbacks, a mess tent, a couple of shacks, a COC bunker, and the usual sandbagged perimeter with fighting bunkers spaced about fifteen yards apart and with barbed and concertina wires strung high above the sandbags. The foliage and trees were cut back to about five hundred yards in all directions.

Tolbane's only thought about this desolate outpost was, *What the fuck kind of place is this, and what the hell am I doing here?*

Before getting out of the vehicle, the corporal reached over and grabbed Tolbane's shoulder and said to him, "Gunny, my orders are to tell you to remove your metal chevrons at this time and put them in your pocket before entering this hardback. Also, you are not allowed to use your rank in any conversations with those inside or ask anyone else for their rank or branch of service. I'm supposed to ask if that's clear, but I don't think I need to. Good luck, anonymous guy! I'm going to chow."

With that, Tolbane thanked the driver for the info, calling him Corporal Anonymous, removed his chevrons, placed them in his pocket, exited the jeep, and grabbed his gear. He stood looking at the hardback for a few moments, wondering what secret lay beyond the screened door. After working up his nerves a bit, he then entered the

---

[4]   The Marine Corps's version of a jeep.

hardback, which contained six desks, a large map board, a couple of bookcases with several books in them, and a few typewriters; and the space was topped off by a field table set up with a coffee urn, coffee cups and condiments, half a sheet cake, powered sugar doughnuts, paper plates, and napkins.

All the way in the hardback, he could see three men and one woman, all wearing jungle utilities like his. The woman, an Asian type, was standing in the rear and drinking what appeared to be coffee from a canteen cup. One of the men had broad shoulders and needed a haircut and a shave—sure signs he must be a civilian—and he was about six feet tall. He looked Tolbane in the eyes and spoke the following as a greeting:

"Hark! What evil demon doth appear from yonder dark portal? Could it be he who seeks the balm in Gilead?"

Tolbane couldn't believe his ears.

Without thinking, he said, "Excuse me all to hell and back, people! Am I in the right fucking place? And pray tell, what the hell is this balm and Gilead shit? Does this have anything to do with an asshole raven knocking on your doors?"

The four broke into laughter, nearly splitting a gut, and the one whose statement had befuddled Tolbane nearly split a bigger gut.

"Well, I guess we got a live one here, folks. Welcome into our inner sanctum. I think you'll fit right in with this weird and disorganized group very well."

CHAPTER 3

The woman, presumably a Vietnamese lady, maybe in her midthirties with long black hair and a superb body—not too bad looking for her age—walked over to Tolbane, took his hand, and greeted him in Vietnamese.

"Chao ong."

He replied in kind. "Chao ba."

In English, she addressed him, smiling while doing so. "Welcome to the group, Tolbane. I understand you don't use your first name, Travis. I'm Troung Thi Phuoc. I guess I'll have to be the official greeter to this conglomeration of misfits and malingerers."

Tolbane could not help but notice that she spoke impeccable English.

He commented so, and she answered, "I won't say which one. However, I have a master's in literature and another master's in linguistics from a major university. That being said, at this time, let me introduce these three clowns to you.

"The one who thinks he's a poet and don't know it is Marcus Boeling. He has a doctorate in psychology. As you can tell, he needs to see a psychiatrist."

Marcus gave Tolbane a half-assed salute and said he was glad to make Tolbane's acquaintance.

"Next, with what you Americans used to call a butch haircut is Prof. Joe Morrison. He teaches Asian history at Stanford University."

Joe nodded a greeting.

"And last but not least, the six-foot-five monster over there is Charles Du Pont. He is an expert in the art of interrogation. Ha ha! He can't even interrogate himself out of a wet paper bag."

Charles stepped forward and clasped Tolbane's hand and welcomed him. The other two guys followed suit. Tolbane sized them
up during the introductions. He needed to watch his uneducated ass
and step. These were high-powered people.

Charles then spoke to Tolbane. "I'm sure you'll have a lot of
questions about why you're here with such an amazing assortment
of brainiac weirdos out here in some god's dung field. Join the club,
my man! You are not alone. Perhaps we will be able to enlighten you
sometime tomorrow, the next day, or even the day after that. We are
not quite sure ourselves at this time as to what's happening here. But
we need to get you situated in our hardback first off. So grab your
gear and follow me, and I'll show you to our quarters, and you can
get situated."

They left the makeshift office and went to the nearest hardback.
There were empty cots, and Tolbane dropped his gear on one of
them. Charles motioned him to go outside, then showed him where
the head was, as well as a washstand and a shower stall.

"Travis—if I may call you that, sir."

Tolbane nodded.

"This situation is a very curious thing to me. It really has me
baffled to hell and back. I have absolutely no idea why we're here,
but it seems strange that two top-notch interrogators, you and I, are
needed in this oddly formed group. Must be something really big
going on as opposed to something little happening in this man's war."

"Charles, I must say, I'm snowed under here too and have no
idea what to think either. I think, like you do, why two interrogators and all the secrecy? I, too, wonder why I was selected to be sent
here in this heavenly paradise. Frankly, Charles, my man, like Rhett
Butler didn't say, it's damned weird, my dear. It sounds super spooky,
it seems to me. Maybe Mike Hammer could make sense of it and
blow somebody's head clean off their shoulders."

"You can say that again," replied Charles.

Tolbane did.

"Travis, since I've been here, I've read good things about you in
your dossier. Yes, we do have one on you. I look forward to working
with you. Whatever lies ahead of us, I hope we don't bump heads."

"I don't think we will, Charles. I'm looking forward to learning from you. I didn't expect, after being introduced to the other two, to be introduced to an expert in my field. My experience is only what I've learned during this tour of duty."

"Well, then, rookie Tolbane, let's wander over to the chow hall and get a cup of coffee and maybe a piece of pastry. It's still a couple of hours till chow time. I'll catch you up on what I've observed about the others here."

Charles placed his right arm around Tolbane's left arm and guided the way. They drank three beers—Tolbane was surprised the mess hall served beer—then gossiped about events and whatever subject came up till it was finally chow time. The two egressed the makeshift clubhouse section of the mess hall and partook of the evening meal of spaghetti, meat sauce, meatballs, sautéed green beans with bacon chunks, mushrooms, onions, tossed salad with French dressing, and chocolate cake. Tolbane even managed to wheedle two more pieces of cake from one of the cooks.

Back at the hardback, Charles offered further, "We hit the sack early here. For some unknown reason, God forbid, the powers that be feel that it's taboo to sleep late in the mornings, like 0630 hours. Someone will be disturbing our slumber about 0530 dark hours. We break the fast at 0630 hours. After that, who knows what the day will bring to us? We just while away the time till someone finally decides to spill the beans as to why the hell we're here. By the way, that Phuoc is a pretty good-looking gal for her age, isn't she?"

"To be truthful," Tolbane replied, "I really didn't take a real good look at her. I had too many things on my mind. However, since you mentioned it, I'll make it a point to check her out tomorrow. Abstinence is not the most agreeable thing during these situations. I'm going to put up my gear, get a shower, and hit the sack. See you in the a.m."

*****

As Charles had predicted, a lance corporal came around at 0520 hours, waking everyone up. As Tolbane was stretching, he noticed that Phuoc had slept in the same hardback. She was actually wearing a nightgown. He couldn't tell much about her body because of it. She quickly exited the hardback, carrying her clothes and a towel, heading for the shower that had been built for her.

Tolbane performed his morning toiletries, dressed, and headed to the makeshift mess hall with the three guys. As he walked, he made it a point to observe and listen to the three guys. He still couldn't fathom why he was here, who and what these three and Phuoc really were, and whatever they represented.

CIA maybe! he thought.

After breakfast, in the hardback, which also seemed to be a communal office, the group sat around, enjoying a hot cup of coffee. Phuoc was drinking her hot Vietnamese tea. Tolbane was checking her out when they heard the rumbling and clanking of tracked vehicles.

They stepped outside to see what was up and were surprised to see an armored convoy entering the compound. In the lead was an M48 Patton tank, then a deuce and a half truck with a reinforced squad of marine riflemen aboard, a mighty mite with a driver and three officers, an LVTP-5 amphibious tractor, another duce and a half with another reinforced squad of marine riflemen, and then followed by another M48 Patton.

When the convoy stopped, three officers left their vehicle and approached the mixed group. The one in the lead, a captain, spoke.

"It's best if we go inside before we conduct any business."

Everyone complied, entering the hardback at a quick pace. With all seven inside, the captain continued.

"I'm Capt. Jim Arnold, this is Colonel Winslow, and last but not least, Maj. Les Dumbrosky. We call him Dumbass." He turned to the colonel and stated, "Your ball game, sir!"

"Thank you, Captain! I can imagine what you all may be thinking about this conglomerated lash-up." He giggled a bit. "Believe me, I'd be curious too about what was going on if I were in your shoes. Happily, I'm not!"

"Before I enlighten you all, if you haven't been told so already, you're here because of your skills, your work habits, your tenacity, your loyalty, your trustworthiness, and all that bullcrap people tell you when they want you to kiss their ugly behinds. You have been specifically chosen to perform the most important duty you may ever encounter in your present careers.

"First, shut up inside that LVTP-5 is a very important prisoner. Yes, I'm aware we are not to call anyone a prisoner in this theater of operations, but I personally think that's a bunch of crap, especially since he's not Vietnamese. He will be guarded and tended to by the contingent of troops with this convoy. There is a Gunnery Sergeant Beaumont in charge of the guard unit, and he will see that anything that needs to be conveyed to the troops by either of you will be done posthaste.

"As we speak, the prisoner is being moved to his quarters. And the guards posted, all their equipment will remain here. I and my aides will be choppered out in about an hour in an army Huey, not our UH-34s.

"Gentlemen and lady, I want to empathize that this is not a piece of overkill whatsoever. The tanks and troops are here to reinforce this command and for your protection while the prisoner is here. There are inimical forces who would like to rescue this prisoner, so if word as to this location should be leaked somewhere, it is plausible you could come under attack at any time. If so, air and arty support are already on standby and have this area registered. Is this clear to everyone?"

The group nodded their ascent silently.

"Now as to your mission at this heavenly island of godforsaken pleasure. To our knowledge, MACV headquarters, Saigon, has no idea that we have this particular prisoner in our custody. Otherwise, he would be on his way to Saigon, and any of his information would be lost to us. This is a very sensitive situation that could easily backfire on us, so please, please, ply your trades to him carefully.

"I hate to tell this to a group like you, but alas and alack, I must. This is hush, hush, hush! Under penalty of the law, for the rest of your lives, your lips are sealed forever like they're sealed with superglue. You may never talk of this place or of anything that transpires here. It's top-secret, need-to-know only period! Got that? I hope so."

The colonel received the same nod of understanding from all.

Looking over at Captain Arnold, the colonel inquired, "Captain, can you get the major and I each a cup of that coffee?"

The captain turned to the field table, where the coffee was.

Taking a couple of sips of the hot brew, the colonel continued.

"We believe this prisoner is a Chinese general and possibly has information on Chinese activities here in South Viet Nam in addition to NVA activities close to this area but also information as to possible Cuban and Russian activities happening north of the DMZ and possible plans for them to commit to hostile operations here in the South.

"We are limited by time for any long-term, intensive interrogation, so whatever information you may extract in a short amount of time here will be much appreciated. We'll have to get this dude to the MACV grand pooh-bah real soon. Well, I wish you luck, people. I do not envy your duty right now. I know you'll do your best, and I hope you will surpass that.

"The gunny will bring you reports and whatever as soon as he can for your enlightenment and edification, as he has the prisoner secured, troops fed, and defensive positions in place. Thanks for the coffee. It's not too bad. I like it. It's hard to get a good cup of it in most godforsaken places I wind up in. Once again, troops, good luck in your endeavor!"

He and his aides departed the hardback and moved to their pickup site. The five new team members stood looking from one to the other and back again, dumbfounded, to say the least. You could have heard a pin drop for a few minutes.

Finally, the guys looked toward Phuoc, and she didn't hesitate to speak up.

"Well, now, guys, it looks like we are now a new and super talented interrogation team in this war of—will wonders ever friggin' cease? I hate to ask this question of you, but just how many of us here in this very room at this very time speak any friggin' Chinese dialects at all?"

Marcus Boeling didn't skip a beat and chanted in a singsong tone what he hoped sounded like Chinese.

"Confucius says if you don't speak Chinese here and now, you all fucked."

They all nearly doubled over with laughter.

CHAPTER 4

Tolbane decided to give Phuoc a once-over as the five pulled chairs into a circle and began a round table discussion as to how to begin their task. He approved of her looks. As they started to pass ideas back and forth, there was a knock at the hardback entrance, and a commanding voice spoke up.

"Cpl. WoJin Tang requests permission to enter, sir!"

Tolbane spoke out. "Enter at attention and report, Corporal!"

Entering and standing at the position of attention, the corporal sounded off.

"Sir, Cpl. WoJin Tang reported as ordered, sir!"

Tolbane, without asking, took the lead.

"Stand at ease and relax, Corporal. One thing for you to remember, we do not stand on any ceremony here. We will come and go as if we are civilian friends. No ranks or positions will be mentioned or spoken to anyone. Grab a cup of coffee and pull up a chair, put your butt on it, and tell us what's on your ever-loving mind this day."

The corporal's mind was totally blown. He had never in his life expected to be treated as an equal.

"Yes, sir!"

"Look, Tang, no sirs either."

After getting coffee and a chair, Tang joined the circle and informed the group as to why he was there.

"Sergeant HoungBo Ming and I are Chinese interpreters, and we are here to serve you in any way we can. We will be alternating the duty and are at your disposal anytime you need us for conversations."

Once more, Boeling was in true form.

"Hallelujah! We are saved! Thank you, Buddha!"

Before Tang could react, Tolbane informed him, "You wouldn't understand him at all, Tang. It's a mental midget thing."

Tolbane made a circling motion with his index finger pointed at his head.

"He's touched in the head."

Everyone laughed.

Boeling retorted to Tang, "See, nobody loves me anymore."

More laughter.

Phuoc, who seemed to Tolbane not only an extrovert but also the ad hoc leader of the group, spoke to Tang.

"I understand that this is unusual military procedure for you, but believe me, the informality has a reason, but we cannot speak of it to you. None of us speaks any Chinese. Hence, you and your sergeant are here. You and Ming enjoy yourselves as much as possible with us. One caution. The informality does not include your unit out there. You still need to comply with military regulations with your unit. We are glad to have you two, as we do not, I reiterate, speak a word of Chinese. Therefore, you two are our lifelines and career savers."

Phuoc finished with a grin, "Maybe you're even saving our butts."

"Yes, ma'am! The corporal hears and understands."

She responded, "Tang, it's Phuoc, not ma'am, and no rank."

He answered, "You got it, Ms. Phuoc. I'll inform Minh."

He dashed out the door, and Phuoc giggled after him.

"Looks like we are in good hands, and it's not even Allstate."

When Tang was clear of the door, the five retook their seats in the circle. Phuoc took the lead. Somehow, Tolbane was not surprised at that. He had gotten the impression that she might be the boss.

"With no more than what the colonel related to us, I think we must organize ourselves to cover the various administrative tasks before us. Marcus, I think you should be our admin person. Wait! Don't put your hand up yet. With your experience, you will be able to evaluate our reports as you type and log them in. You're the psychologist. Maybe you can pick up on any nuances the subject has that we might have missed or even be able to give us a better profile of the prisoner.

"Charles, you and Joe will be interrogation team 1, and Travis and I will be team 2. That gives us a bona fide interrogator on each team. We can alternate working on the prisoner in three- to four-hour shifts. That way, we can evaluate the information we've obtained from him and plan our team's next shift approach and have a catnap. Is everyone, as you Americans say, cool with that?"

The four guys all nodded and replied yes in unison.

"Well," she commented, "that went smooth. Let's hope the rest of this journey does the same. Somehow, the morning has passed us by. Since we can do nothing else right this minute, I suggest we dismount this hardback and head to the chow hall for the noon meal."

Marcus, the first to rise to his feet, announced, "Phuoc's motion is seconded, no discussion, is carried, and approved. Let's go eat."

They filed out of the hardback and moseyed down to the chow hall.

After eating noon chow, the group went about doing their own things for a couple of hours before having another meeting. Tolbane took the opportunity to walk around the encampment to familiarize himself with the area and see what kinds of defenses were protecting the compound and the everlasting, better part of his anatomy. He was really impressed. It looked like everything—from the old adage—from soup to nuts was well taken care of.

While walking in and out of hardbacks and along the sandbagged perimeter, he remembered walking with Ba to the PX CONEX box at the Seventh Marine Regiment headquarters under the monsoon rains in Chu Lai a while back. They had caught a clown impersonating a gunnery sergeant and stealing from the PX's CONEX box.

Tolbane had taken him down in the mud and rain, rubbing the guy's face into the mud, infuriating him. Captured, he was turned over to the enclave commander and the MPs and was given a court-martial with brig time and dishonorable discharge. What made him remember was that this compound was laid out similar to what the Seventh Marines enclave had, only smaller.

He finished his walking round of the compound, arriving back at the group's hardback quarters, lay down, and dozed off big-time until Charles slapped him on the foot a short time later. He shot up like a rocket.

"Time to rise and shine in the midafternoon, cot-jockeyed sleepyhead."

Tolbane arose a little further, shook the fogginess from his head, and finally stood; and the two walked to their makeshift office.

Phuoc began in earnest.

"I talked to the gunny. He should be here in about forty-five minutes or so, bringing us documents on the prisoner, then briefing us on what he knows about him. Afterward, Tolbane and I will talk to the prisoner first, no more than an hour and a half or less. We'll brief team 1 afterward.

"Team 1 will decide what time tomorrow to get started with the guy and how to approach him. Then we'll all get together and debrief our shifts. By then, it'll be chow time, and Tolbane and I will do our thing."

Marcus snickered at that comment, and Charles giggled, but Joe remained silent. Phuoc gave Marcus a dirty look that burned into his soul.

"We'll debrief after that, then set up a regular round-the-clock schedule. Everyone in agreement?"

She received four strong yeses.

"That sounds like a plan to me," Charles commented. "I like the idea of feeling the guy out before we really get down to business. We need some insight as to what makes him tick before we begin. After you and Tolbane are done and brief us, I have arranged, after my worldwide travels and amazing feats and discoveries, a tub with iced-down Ba Moui Ba to be delivered to our quarters after this evening's chow."

Four groans and moans were heard at the words Ba Moui Ba being mentioned. Their palates were not too excited either. At least it was not that Biere Larue crap.

The three guys left, and Phuoc and Tolbane remained to plan an approach technique with which to begin their interrogation.

But before they settled on any approach, there was a rap on the screen-covered door.

"Permission to enter!"

Tolbane, in his best imitation of a marine drill instructor, spoke out, "Enter and be recognized."

The knocker entered, came to the position of attention, and spoke out. "Gunnery Sergeant Beaumont reporting as ordered, sir!"

"Come on in, stand at ease, cut the military crap, grab a cup of coffee, and sit your butt down, Gunny. No formalities here, nor are there any ranks here. This is Ms. Phuoc. I'm Tolbane, Travis Tolbane! I like mine shaken and not stirred. To reiterate, we have no ranks, so the formalities are lost on us. Our names are plain Tolbane and Phuoc."

Phuoc was surprised and pleased by the way Tolbane took charge. She decided there was more to this man than what met the naked eye. The gunny was also surprised by this. He had no idea he would be dealing with a bunch of superspooks. Then he did as was suggested—got a cup and took a seat.

The next unexpected thing from Tolbane's lips nearly caused Phuoc to break out laughing. She pretended to cough into her hand to cover up her surprise. He was a number one bullshitter too, she was now finding out.

Tolbane addressed the gunny.

"You know, Beaumont, I envy you. I had always wanted to be a marine. However, I was turned down because of a recurring medical problem as unfit for combat. So guess where I ended up. Vacationing here in the sunny south of the Republic of Viet Nam. Isn't that something? This lying around, sunbathing and drinking martinis, shaken not stirred, all day long is just the cat's pajamas. Almost makes you want to jump up and turn somersaults."

Beaumont replied, "I hear you! It really does beat going to war at any time. However, I do not have that luxury at this time. On a more sober note, Tolbane, I do have some documents I understand you all need plus what I've observed of the prisoner. I need to pass this on to you so I can get back to my troops."

"I quite understand your position here, Beaumont. It's real important to the success of our mission here. Now let's put our heads together and get down to business. Ms. Phuoc, if you would, please sit here between us."

She took the seat.

Phuoc couldn't believe her good luck. Tolbane, whether on purpose or accidently, gave Beaumont the idea that he was in charge. The less anyone knew as to why she was chosen for this assignment and what her orders really were suited her to a tee.

"In this folder," Beaumont began, "is what little the MP HQ at Dong Ha could find on the prisoner. Since he was brought in by a patrol while he was reconnoitering their base camp, I have been in a position to observe him almost constantly. He had on a soft-billed cap with a red star on it when captured. Besides his obvious Chinese clothing, the only gear he had was a Chinese handgun, a semiautomatic, a pair of binoculars, and a notepad with Chinese scribbles and drawings that look like our Dong Ha compound on a few pages. The two Chinese interpreters can expand on that.

"Observing him, he seems very docile, but I do not think he is docile, and he is very composed. He shows no fear openly. He is very respectful to his captors, knows when to butter his bread. He appears not to understand a word of English, but I have my doubts about that too. He is a very good actor, and he hears and understands what's being said. His eyes do not miss a thing, working all the time. The eyes tell the story.

"He is a dangerous man. I do not trust him one iota, and I do believe he is a flight risk. That is about all I have on that. Whenever you need the prisoner brought here, we will have two guards and one of the interpreters with him at all times. We cannot be too careful with this bird."

"Wow, Beaumont! That is a great assessment. You have missed your calling. I could not ask for or do a better profiling myself."

Tolbane then looked to Phuoc and opted, "Don't you think so too, Phuoc?"

"Yes, I do think it is great. We will have to keep an eye on him."

"Those are my thoughts exactly, Phuoc. Great minds think alike without a doubt. Well, Beaumont, we appreciate your observations. They are very good. The observations will help us to establish a rapport with him. Just keep us posted on anything he says and does no matter how minuscule."

"I sure will. I need to get back to my troops now. If you need anything, just whistle."

"Ha ha. This is just like Bacall to Bogie in *Key Largo*. We do know how to whistle, do we not, Phuoc?"

"You bet, you number ten non-GI."

They laughed till Tolbane thought they died.

"Beaumont, we would like to have the prisoner and the interpreter Tang here in about forty-five minutes, if that's convenient for you. In fact, you can send Tang over now."

"You got it, Tolbane. You will see them in forty-five. By the way, great coffee."

Beaumont was out the door quickly.

Tolbane waved ta-ta at Beaumont's back and quipped, "Alas and alack, parting is such sweet sorrow."

"You're something else, Tolbane, you know that? You are really good at this shit, aren't you?" Phuoc commented. "I love it to pieces. You really gave Beaumont a good line of bullshit. Now let us put our heads together and decide how to start with the subject."

CHAPTER 5

Tang opened the hardback door easy and slowly entered the room, testing the edict of no formality. Phuoc noticed him and waved him in. He felt more at ease at her waving, making him feel more comfortable about not knocking. It was just like being at home, only not quite.

"Get on over here and sit with us, Tang. Tolbane and I were about to decide how to begin our first session with the prisoner. We don't want to upset or alienate him right off the get-go. Since you've been around him quite a bit, do you have any suggestions we can consider to kind of break the ice with him?"

"Well, if I might comment freely, I know what I'd like if I were a prisoner being brought in here the first time. A cup of coffee and something sweet to eat just might get my attention big-time. Oh, and maybe smiling faces to disarm me, you know, cause me to relax. As for what else, I don't know."

"Phuoc," Tolbane commented, "he's got a good point. We both know that once you've played the bad guy, you can't change up and be the good guy, except in extreme circumstances. We'll put his ass at ease right off the bat."

"Well, we have got the coffee, but no sweets right now. Tolbane, what do you suggest?"

Tang spoke up. "If I may interrupt, Phuoc, the mess hall has some leftover sheet cake from last night's meal. I could go down there and get some for us. One of the cooks told me earlier when I made arrangements to feed the prisoner rice and meat during his stay that anything we needed in the way of extra chow or whatever, let him know."

"You're not gone yet, Tang," Tolbane said, laughing.

Phuoc and Tang joined in the gaiety. Then Tang was out the door in a jiffy.

"I'm glad he's on the team with us, Tolbane. I think he will prove to be very valuable to us."

"I say amen to that, Phuoc. I've a hunch that barring anything bad happening, this kid will go far in the Corps. So we do the wine and dine without the wine thing. We can use the approach of just getting some background information, as we are admin people, not information collectors, like when and where he was captured, where he's from, and that sort of crap for our administrative report."

"That's good. We'll just talk about what the weather's like, does he need anything, we don't know why we're with him, yadda yadda yadda! We'll just make it like old home week for him."

"Yessiree, my two-legged deer, Ms. Phuoc. We should be able to place him in a psychological trait category, after which team 1 can begin in earnest tomorrow. If he's real hateful of us, he'll just be the usual hostile/antagonistic creep we usually end up with. Who's that tap, tap, tapping at our hardback door? Could it be the raven? Quote a dumbass bird somewhere, Evermore. I'll get it."

He opened the door, and there stood Tang, holding a sheet cake pan with half a chocolate sheet cake with white icing and a bag with paper plates and plastic forks.

"Well, I swan, Mr. Tang. You're just about the cat's meow!" Tolbane commented in a high, singsong voice.

Tang laughed so hard he nearly tripped and dropped everything. Phuoc liked to split a gut. Tolbane took the cake from him and placed it next to the coffee on the table. Meanwhile, Phuoc dumped out the stale, bitter old coffee, filled the pot from an excursion can of water, and started a fresh pot to brew. Just then, one of the marines on mess duty arrived, bringing a folding field table, which he leaned against a desk.

"Compliments of the chief cook, sir," the man said and departed.

"Tang," Phuoc stated, "we'll need about fifteen more minutes or so before we're ready for our star performer to arrive. So when you get back to your area, wait fifteen minutes, then bring him here. Tolbane and I should be ready for him by then."

Tolbane pulled out the legs and set the table up, and Phuoc arraigned the cake, plates, cups, and forks on it.

"Phuoc, I was just remembering something from a few years ago, from when I was in the interrogation course."

"I wasn't aware you could remember your own name from a few years ago," she said, giggling. "Was it Mr. Mudd, by any chance?"

"Ha ha! In the early sixties, there was a women's perfume that was named Arpège. It was advertised on TV in a real catchy way. It told the guys giving perfume to women, 'Promise them anything, but give them Arpège.' One of our interrogation instructors at Fort Holabird, Maryland, used to tell us to do the same to our interrogees. You just promise them anything in the world they want, but give them Arpège. I think that should be our goal with this guy to start with. We make sure he gets plenty of Arpège."

Giggling, Phuoc responded, "Tolbane, you are something else. Maybe I promise you a kick in the best part of your body, and I'm just the gal to do it."

She swatted him on the rear. Then she took a portable tape recorder from a desk, put a new tape in it, checked the batteries, and placed it on the desk.

To Tolbane, Phuoc explained, "This is supersensitive and voice-activated. When we see the prisoner nearly to the door, I'll turn it on and put it in the desk drawer and leave it partly open. We'll seat him as close to the desk as we can. I guess we're ready for the big show. Look!"

Gazing through the screened door, she added, "Here comes Johnny!'"

Tolbane looked out the hardback door. The formation was Tang in the lead, the prisoner about three paces behind him, and then two marine privates at port arms three paces behind the prisoner. His hands were tied in front at the wrists, and there was a cord tied just above his knees, just long enough for room between them for him to walk but not run.

When the group entered the hardback, Tolbane stationed the two privates outside at the front and back doors to the hardbacks.

He sat the prisoner in the chair he wanted him in. Then he turned to Tang.

"I see no reason for these restraints on this man. Please remove them. If it's really necessary, you can put them back on him when you leave here."

Tang did as he was ordered. When the restraints were removed from him, Tolbane addressed the prisoner directly with Tang interpreting for him.

"We are civilians assigned here. My name is Tom, and this is Ms. Linda. She takes notes for me—you know, like a secretary does."

Phuoc bowed to the prisoner, and he nodded to her. She took a chair and sat upright, still with her tablet being held on her right knee. The prisoner told Tolbane, through Tang, that it was good to see the woman knew her place among men.

Tolbane replied, "Yes, it is good. I always make sure my woman knows her place and also that my secretary knows hers too."

Tang interpreted to him. The prisoner smiled and nodded his head in agreement. Tolbane was sitting facing the prisoner from the front, and Tang was sitting to the right, halfway between the two men.

"Now that we're a little more comfortable here, sir, would you like some coffee and cake?"

The man nodded. Then Tolbane turned to Phuoc.

"Ms. Linda, please get our friend some cake and coffee now!"

She did her duty, bowing to the prisoner when she handed him the items. The prisoner was doing the same as Tolbane and Phuoc. He was studying their every move and wondering what kind of game was being played.

Tolbane addressed the prisoner.

"I don't know why I was selected for this job, but I've been requested to ask you some important administrative questions. No hard questions, just little things someone somewhere needs to put in their reports to make themselves look good. My first one is, what is your name, sir?"

"Xinwei Tam."

"How old are you?"

"Do you want to know if it was the year of the horse, rat, pig, or in gaijin years?"

"I believe gaijin years would be best for us."

Ah! thought Tolbane. *The game begins.*

"I'm forty years old in your years, born in 1926—in May, I think."

"So where were you born?"

"In my mother's bed."

"That is very refreshing to know. In China, what town and province would your mother's bed be in?"

"To be truthful, I'm not really sure at all. I only remember growing up in the Cho Lon District, Saigon, Cochinchina. My parents moved there from somewhere in China while I was too little to know what was happening, and they never spoke of from where to me. I've always been curious about it, but I never tried to find out."

Tolbane recognized the game.

The prisoner would give up some truths to gain our trust.

He would learn later it did not work very well.

"So did you live your whole life in Cho Lon, Saigon?"

"My mother died when I was about fourteen, and my father took me to live in Beijing."

"Is your father still living?"

"He went to his ancestors five years ago."

"How did you end up in the Chinese military?"

"My father put me in a local monastery to study the martial arts. When I was sixteen, an army proselyte came to the monastery and took the top twenty of the students for military service, of which I was one, to serve in the People's Liberation Army. Our country was at war with the bastardly Japanese horde at that time."

"What did you do in the Army?"

"I was just a foot soldier. By the time the war ended, I had been wounded twice, hospitalized about a month each time."

"Sorry to hear that. I'm glad you made it okay. War is terrible. What kind of rank did you have when the war was over?"

"I was a senior private when I left the Army."

Tolbane decided to drop the military bit for a while.

"Did you ever marry? You look like the kind of guy a woman would want to take care of her."

"Yes, I did marry for a time. Two years after taking a lovely young lady for my wife, her and our child both passed away during childbirth. I was very devastated. Depressed for a while. That's why I went back into the Army. Soldiers experienced in combat were needed at that time, and I was made an officer. It raised me from my doldrums."

Score one for the good guys, Tolbane thought.

"How well did you do in your new position in the Army?"

"That's not a good question for me to answer. It is not administrative."

"Oh, I'm sorry! I just got caught up in the moment, wanting you to be successful. Do you like it here in Viet Nam? It must be very different from China."

"The people and places are very similar in both countries. My stay in Viet Nam has been very nice, especially the Vietnamese ladies, such as your beautiful secretary."

This was said with a leer at Phuoc.

"Do you enjoy the favors you receive from your secretary there? She looks like she'd be good sex."

"Sorry to disappoint you, Tam, but I never do anything with my hired help, especially females. They are nothing less than trouble," Tolbane answered. "This one is lazy and a pain in the ass to deal with at times."

Phuoc, with her head tilted down, remained stone-faced the whole time. She was thinking that the right woman could get to Tolbane. She also felt she couldn't wait to get at this asshole Chinaman during a later session.

"Ah, so!" the prisoner replied. "You must be what is called a puritan. Or is it a virgin? Is that not so?"

Tolbane was just as quick as the prisoner.

"That is not so. I just don't mix business with pleasure. So where do you live here in Viet Nam? Your normal residence, not military billeting."

"I did live in Cho Lon when I was married. After that, just any-place the Army sends me. You can report that I've lived all over Viet Nam. It's been a long time since I have had what you would call a place of residence and a regular bed for a night."

Tolbane thought for a second.

"I don't envy longtime service members who have no real home to go back to. You must long for that, I presume."

"Yes, sometimes, I think it would be nice to settle down, have a family, and not worry about war. Right now, that's not my fate."

Tolbane looked at his watch.

"Oh, I'm sorry. We've run out of time for today. We have to conclude our session for now. We can catch up later. I do have a few more questions to ask. Right now, I have to attend to another stupid duty. You know how that is. With all these soldiers around here that don't know whether they're coming or going, I never get to finish anything I get started with."

"Ah, so! You are so right. I think all armies are like that all over the world. We always have to stir around and wait until some com-mander decides to issue orders, if he ever does. It's so boring."

The session over, Tolbane, the prisoner, Tang, and Phuoc all stood. They kind of bowed half-assed to one another. Then after being called, the guards secured the prisoner's wrists and legs once more and marched off with the prisoner between them.

"You played that session pretty well, Tolbane," Phuoc stated. "Tit for tat. This guy will be a hard nut to break down, but I think we have a good start on establishing rapport with him. Team 1 will be the bad guys to him for sure. I thought I'd puke when he gave me the eye."

Tang spoke up before Tolbane could comment further.

"Did you happen to notice the extra chatter between the pris-oner and me? He thinks I may be on his side to an extent since I'm Chinese. He likes Ms. Phuoc's body and would like to have all kinds of weird sex with her. He thinks you have a hidden agenda, Tolbane, but he can't figure it out yet. I think he was very honest about several things, but he's playing it close to the vest. I think he's very, as we say, street smart, like he's been there before."

36

"Thanks, Tang!" Phuoc observed to him. "That's good observing on your part. Keep him thinking you may be partial to him. But be very careful, though. He will try to use you in any manner he can. If there is anything, day or night, you think we should know about him, please let us know even if you have to wake us up."

"Aye, aye, mon capitaine. Can you believe they sent a Chinaman to French language school? I can play the game, and personally, just for the hell of it, I'd love to wake your ass up at o'dark hundred hours," Tang kidded.

"Tang, get the fuck out. You're too much like me. I don't want to rub any more on to you."

That was said with a grin from Tolbane, and Tang grinned back and hauled ass out of the hardback to catch up to the guards and the prisoner.

"Well, Phuoc, what are you thinking? You're awfully quiet sitting there."

"I'm thinking that I should have one of those new kind of skirts the women wear back in the states. You know what they call them: miniskirts. I could really keep him distracted wearing one of them. I could tell he had the instant hots for my body right from the start. It could work in our favor big-time."

"It would probably be a big distraction to me too, a real big one!"

Tolbane's face got a little red as he blushed.

"Why, Tolbane, you're blushing! It makes you look so cute."

He reddened a little more and tried to change the subject.

"You know, if I were Mike Hammer, I would have already gotten all this dude's info. I'd smack him upside the head with my 1911 .45 ACP and then shoot the guy in the knee a couple of times. Good old Mike Hammer knew how to collect information."

Phuoc laughed at him.

"Hey, Mike Hammer, or whoever you are, let's go to chow. My sexy body is hungry."

Tolbane believed he knew how to feed that sexy body.

CHAPTER 6

After chow, Tolbane and Phuoc walked over to a sandbagged, empty bunker about six-by-ten-by-four deep. It was one that would only be occupied during an attack. They climbed in and sat on some sandbag seats and discussed the afternoon's session with Xinwei. The task at hand for them was twofold. First was to try to establish more rapport with the subject's hots for Ms. Phuoc, and second was to assign him one of three personality traits. They felt that Xinwei had tried to project different images of himself to them, and the rapport with him was minimal.

As to the personality traits, at times, he was (1) friendly, cooperative at others, and (2) neutral, nonpartisan. They finally agreed that in the long run, he would most likely be (3) hostile, antagonistic. Now that they had decided on these three, they would go to their quarters and brief team 1 on the afternoon's session and their and the interpreter's observations. It would be up to team 1 to decide on an approach technique and what time to start the next day.

Additionally, both felt they were thirsty enough by now that they could drink an ice-cold Ba Moui Ba or a couple or three or…

Entering the hardback, Tolbane and Phuoc found the three guys sitting on one cot, facing a tub of iced-down beer. They greeted Tolbane and Phuoc.

"Hey, guys! We thought you'd never get here. We've been waiting on you, and we're all thirsty as hell."

Joe handed Tolbane and Phuoc each an iced-down Ba Moui Ba and then announced, "Let *la fiesta* or whatever the hell you call it begin."

It did. By the time they were on their third or fourth beer, the briefing was over, and the comradery had begun.

*****

Having mild hangovers, the early reveille came too soon for the previous night's revelers. Ba Moui Ba had the distinct pleasure of causing the worst hangovers imaginable. Tolbane thought his head would explode any minute, and his stomach never wanted anything to ever enter it again, except for bacon maybe. That was topped off by the proverbial sour, cottony taste in his and the other's mouths. He did manage to get up and take care of his morning toiletries without actually dying.

When Tolbane finally made it to the chow hall, the others were already there, eating big plates of food. He thought of barfing when he saw the food but settled at the table for a couple of cups of coffee. Then he went to the chow line and got a big plate full of greasy bacon and some almost green-looking powdered eggs and toast. He wondered how the others were able to cope so well. Phuoc clued him in later that it served him right, as he had drunk about four or five more beers than the others had. He groaned and moaned and swore off the stuff until the next time.

Since there was nothing pressing for him at the time, he crashed on his cot and dozed off, hoping to feel better later on. He woke up about an hour and a half later, feeling a little better. Phuoc was sitting on her cot, and when he awoke, she started to giggle at him, then gave him a ragging about drinking too much and having the granddaddy of hangovers. He took it in the spirit in which it was offered.

Tolbane told her that as far as getting a super hangover again, he was going to be like the raven dude: "Nevermore!"

"I have a request, Mr. Tolbane. Can I call you Travis? I think it sounds better than calling you Tolbane all the time."

"Sure thing, ma'am! I also answer to *Dien Cai Dau*"—which meant crazy in the head or dummy—"after last night."

"Good. I've an idea to pass by you, and I want to know how you feel about it. The guy really thinks I'm the downtrodden and abused female. I've got an old pair of trousers I've been thinking about throwing out. I could cut the legs off, making a pair of shorts. Do you think it could be distracting enough to work on our horny guest?"

"Seriously, it would probably distract me more than him."

"Yes, I know, Travis. You're one *ba moui lam gi*."

This meant horny as a goat.

"A numba one thou GI. I no lub you long time."

"Wow, you really know how to stick it to a guy, don't you, Phuoc? You sure you don't work in a bar in Hoi An City or some-place like that? Yes, it will distract the ass, and I might even forget my questions."

"Travis, you're a jewel. I could never get the truth out of the others if I ask the others the same question. It's refreshing to be around someone so true to himself. I really wouldn't want him gloating over my legs, but I wouldn't care if you did."

Embarrassed again, red-faced, and kind of stuttering, Tolbane said, changing the subject, "Do you think they'll be done working with the prisoner very soon?"

Phuoc nearly fell off her cot laughing at his misdirection. Tolbane had to laugh too.

"Travis, you are so cute when you're embarrassed. I'm glad we're teamed together. This kind of thing we're doing here can evolve into boredom and get more and more tedious day in and day out. If there is not good rapport between the players, it can become a disaster for all parties involved."

"I agree. So far, it's been interesting. But if yesterday is a blue plate for success, we have a long way to go."

"I know you have the patience to see it through, Travis. I know of some of your extended interrogations and the success you've had since you arrived in Viet Nam. I chose you to team with because I knew about you and felt you can be trusted. I don't really know much about the others at all. I do have many questions about one of them."

"Phuoc, with all due respect, who and what are you? I'm at sea. I can usually get a handle on whom I'm working with, but you are an enigma to me. I just can't figure you out. I do like you, though. You seem to be a very nice person."

Phuoc thought for a moment.

"Travis, I like you too. However, I wish I could tell you a few things that's happening here, but I can't right now. Maybe later, I'll be able to tell you the whole thing. All I can do is ask you to trust me for now. Believe in me please, Travis. I am one of the good guys."

"I do feel I can trust you, and I will unless I find something to the contrary. Since you seem to be seeking honesty, I'll be honest with you. You are a gorgeous fox, and you do make me so horny with that fine body of yours!"

She fell back on her cot, laughing hysterically.

*****

It was nearly lunchtime, and team 1 entered the hooch. Both Phuoc and Tolbane were sound asleep on their cots. Marcus kicked the legs of the cots, waking them. He was going to make a smart-ass remark, but seeing the look on their faces, he figured he best leave it alone.

"Well, my good friends—and I add those words loosely—we had an interesting morning with a perfect Chinese asshole. Confucius would never be able to find a quote for this guy," exclaimed Joe, who had always been kind of quiet. "Charles and I both found out what we were to do with our mothers and how we could have intercourse with our female ancestors and each other. It was really educational and enlightening. Marcus sat at his desk, smirking at Charles and me the whole time."

"Amen, Brother Joe!" Charles retorted. "The guy is a classic piece of work. Let me give you the rundown. He answered very few questions. He kept trying to question us one minute and berating us the next. Imagine that. The only thing we accomplished was that his rank is probably equal to our lieutenant colonels and that he has been with VC or NVA units during some attacks. Other than the additional fact that he'd like to get into Phuoc's pants there, we didn't accomplish much."

Marcus injected, "The fact that he is a prisoner doesn't seem to faze him. He seems to feed on his captivity. I got the feeling that he's sociopathic, along with being a narcissist. When Charles was asking about how many people were slaughtered during the attacks he had participated in, I got the feeling there was a little pathological spark there. It seemed to me he enjoyed the killings, whether he participated in the killings or just watched them."

"I had the same feelings as Marcus," Charles said, not looking too happy about the session.

"I don't envy you two being with him this afternoon. This guy can be a real animal in my estimation," Joe reckoned. "Nope, don't envy you two at all," he added, mostly directed to Phuoc.

She replied, "Never fear, dear. Our dear Mr. Travis Tolbane and I have a plan. Don't we, Travis?"

He blushed and turned his head toward the door and commented, "Come on, gang. It's howdy doody chow time."

He exited the hardback. Phuoc suppressed a smile. She had his number big-time.

*****

After Phuoc was finished eating, she excused herself while the others drank coffee and told stories. She returned to the hardback, got out the old pair of trousers, cut the legs off, changed into them, and waited for the guys to return. She was interested in what the responses from them would be when they entered, and she was posed like a supermodel. She thought one of them wouldn't be too happy to see her this way, although he would try to fake it, and another might swoon.

When the guys returned and saw her, her suspicions were right on. One guy was displeased. It was the one she had in mind. The others' responses pleased her to no end.

On the way to the office hardback, Phuoc stopped Travis.

"Travis, I've been teasing you about my legs. I hope I haven't hurt your feelings any. You're such a nice guy. I don't mind you checking me out. I do have a reason for doing this. So far, it's working. I hope it won't affect our working relationship. Just promise me one thing. During the sessions, make the guy know I'm just your servant more or less, maybe even bitch at me a bit. Make him dislike you and let it build his desire for me. It'll work for us. You'll see!"

"I had gotten the feeling that Charles was the master interrogator, but I was dead wrong. I was meant to get the impression that no one was in charge here, but I've changed my mind. You really are the boss and the master interrogator, aren't you?"

"Hey, rosy cheeks, just keep believing in me, okay?"

"Okay! Shall we enter our den of iniquity and prepare to greet our subject while I scope out those gams? I love 'em."

"We don't have a yellow brick road, but let's continue."

She hooked her arm on his elbow, and they kind of skipped the rest of the way.

Ten minutes after they entered their office / interrogation area, Tang arrived with the prisoner and the guards. Everyone took the same positions as the previous day, and Phuoc got more coffee and cake for the prisoner. Xinwei let it be known right away that he noticed the gorgeous pair of legs on the secretary. He stared at them and, smiling, licked his thick lips. Phuoc pretended to be a little offended and turned slightly away from him. Tolbane gave him a dirty look.

"Xinwei, my secretary is off-limits to you. I don't know why she wore those shorts today anyhow. Now where were we when we had to quit the other day? Okay, first question of the day. We really do need to know if you do have any living relatives, and how can they be contacted by the Red Cross about your capture?"

"Look, Mr. Whatever You Name Is," the prisoner said in a kind of slurred and broken English. "What kind of fool are you guys trying to play me for?"

Tolbane saw no facial or physical changes in the chainman's demeanor.

"I'm no fool, mister! You're playing a cat-and-mouse game with me, and I don't like that at all."

"You surprise me. You do have a little grasp of my language. But we'll continue to use our interpreter. Let me say this to you. Don't piss me off! I don't know what you are referring to. I and my secretary were pulled from our office in Da Nang and told to be kind to you and obtain whatever background information from you that we can.

"I have no idea what the hell went on with you and those other guys. We don't work for or assist them in any fucking manner. I'm just doing what I was ordered to do, and fuck them and the boat they came over on."

The last part brought a smile to Xinwei's lips.

Tolbane continued. "I am an administrative man, and all I do all day long is push papers here and there and gather background information on stupid things the brass wants to know. Is that clear to you? Also, I don't like you ogling my secretary's body. I distinctly told her not to wear those shorts today, but no, she said the trousers were too hot to wear. Now back to the question at hand! What about relatives?"

Tolbane made sure that he came off as really angry. Phuoc made herself look frightened at the discussion and held her head down. Xinwei smiled at her, and she kind of blushed a little.

"Wow! You are serious about this. To my knowledge, I have no living relatives. My last uncle went to his ancestors around the middle of last year. When I go, so does the family name."

"That's better," Tolbane answered. "It's a shame when an entire family chain is gone forever. All the family history will never be known. What happened to your uncle?"

"He was in an auto accident was what I was told."

"I'm sorry for your loss. I know what it's like to lose a loved one. At this time, do you have a mistress or some young lady you have your eye on?"

Xinwei glanced down at Phuoc's legs before he answered.

"Not really at this time. We move around a lot. The VC does offer comfort girls to the leaders of their units from time to time. It is a nice, temporary pleasure but has no real meaning like a wife or girlfriend would have for me. Is your secretary married?"

"I'll say this one more time only. She is off-limits period."

"Okay. I get the hint. But she is very attractive."

"I get your point. Is there any special place where the comfort girls are brought to you?"

"No, there has never been a special place. They just pop up from time to time. I don't know where they come from, where they've been, or how they just seem to know where we are. Sometimes, we even have a feast and entertainment in our camp when they arrive. Lots of good food and warm beer. The ladies perform hero skits with ancient weapons and do patriotic dances before we leaders grab the lady we want and do our thing. It really helps our morale a lot. It gets lonely moving from place to place and fighting and seeing your comrades die. When they die, it weakens our unit."

"I have heard that same comment from some of the GIs I talk to sometimes at our club. After a night of revelry, do you go into combat the next day?"

"Usually, one or two days later. The fighting spirit is usually higher after one of these nights of sex."

"Moving on," Tolbane said, noticing the prisoner checking out Phuoc's legs again. "Do you ever know in advance where you're going to do battle before the comfort girls come?"

"Very seldom. We normally find out just before we move out to our target."

"I don't want to get into your military movements, but I am curious. How do you feel when you are on the move to engage your enemy?"

"It depends on a few things. If it seems like a small engagement, my spirit is kind of high. If it seems like it will be a big and long engagement, I feel a little fear and hope I survive."

"That's understandable. I know I would feel scared shitless. I'm glad I'm not a soldier. It's scary enough just being over here. Can't wait for time to go back home."

Tolbane looked at his watch, stood up, and walked over to the coffee urn to get another cup. He knew that while his back was turned, the prisoner would be scoping out Phuoc big-time, especially her legs.

Turning back to the others, he said, "Well, I guess we've used up our time for today. Those other clowns don't even want us to talk to you at all. They think we'll spoil you for them or something or other."

Tolbane turned to Tang.

"Take him back now, but keep a check on him. If there is anything you can do for him, please do so. We are obliged by our rules of engagement to see that he is adequately fed and cared for and secure in his being."

Tang snapped up but not to attention and said, "I have already received those instructions from the gunny, and I'll do my best to apply them."

Xinwei took a last glimpse of Phuoc's legs before he turned to go. She blushed this time and, without turning her head, looked him straight in the eye.

After he left, she commented, "Damn, I'm glad he's gone. He gives me the creeps and willies all over."

When the prisoner was gone, she shivered a bit and threw her arms around Tolbane's neck and spoke elatedly.

"Travis, you are the greatest bullshitter. I think he actually believed you—somewhat anyway. I almost did. You showed the right amount of emotion and honesty needed and changed back to being mild at the right time. I think you are the master interrogator here."

She gave him a peck on the cheek and released her arms.

"I was amazed. Your conversation did get some information from him, although he probably knows it's already known. But he is talking and gaping at me. He's just about where I want him."

"I feel it went well. It's a start. We'll just get a little at a time. Oops! I mean a little information at a time."

"I know what you meant, Travis, both of your meanings," she said with the look of the Cheshire cat. "Now let's go brief the others."

They left the office hardback, and she took his arm once more. Tolbane still could not understand what her motivation was, but he enjoyed her company nevertheless.

*****

After briefing the others on the afternoon, the five went to chow and took their time eating, except for Tolbane. He appeared to eat the way a vacuum cleaner sucked, making the chow disappear like a vacuum by sucking it up. That included seconds and seconds on dessert too.

As they were leaving the chow hall, Phuoc mentioned to Tolbane, "Wow, you were really a hungry boy, weren't you? Don't you answer that. I know what you'll say. 'I'm a growing boy.' It's all right. I love to see a man chow down that way. I also know what you're hungry for."

She got him blushing again.

"Well, Phuoc, you know how it is."

"Travis, I have to check on something important right now. I'll check with you later."

She walked away, back in the same direction they had come from. Tolbane thought nothing of it while he watched her buns in motion. He continued on, jumped on his cot, and went to la-la land, dreaming of scantily clad ladies in a *Playboy* magazine.

Phuoc assumed that the guards at the front and back of the hardback where Xinwei was kept in knew that she was one of those who had access to the prisoner. They knew she was granted entrance, and she entered, having a sheepish "I shouldn't be doing this!" look.

Xinwei looked at her with a mild smirk on his face and asked her in Chinese, "Well, now what did I do to deserve a visit from one so fair?"

Phuoc answered him in his Chinese dialect, seeming shy.

"I wanted to see if you were being properly cared for."

"Well, my little lotus blossom, what else about you do I not know?"

"My father was part Chinese, and he taught me the Chinese way. I'm not really good at it, but I can manage."

"Very nice. I am being well taken care of considering the circumstances. It is nice for you to be concerned about me. Does your boss know you're here?"

She tried to look shier, turning her head to the side.

"No, he doesn't, and I asked the guards not to tell him."

"I guess you must like me, huh? You want me to bed you?"

"I'm sorry. I must go!"

She got a look of fear on her face and ran out the door. The sentry asked her if everything was all right. She smiled at him.

"Everything is going perfectly. Remember that I was never here."

She leaned over and gave him a peck on the cheek.

"Ma'am, I never saw nobody who was never here, if that makes any sense."

"You're my hero," Phuoc chided him.

She was already walking away while the guard checked out her shorts and that fantastic rear end. She then took a slow walk around the perimeter on the small enclave, letting her mind wander through several scenarios, considering or dismissing them.

By the time she returned to the hardback, she believed she had all her t's crossed and her i's dotted. When her plan went down, she would be ready for any changes she might have to make.

When she entered the team's hardback, she smiled at the group and, to no one in particular, commented, "It's wonderful just walking around, enjoying the walk, and clearing one's mind. I feel renewed. I'm ready to take up where we left off today. Travis, are you ready to go after him tomorrow? I've a new plan for you to consider."

"I'm always ready, Your Highness. Mine is but to serve and do or die, my sovereign."

Everybody got a laugh from that. Up till then, it had been quiet in the hardback, but Tolbane's comment got the gossiping and storytelling started.

By the time taps (at 2200 hours) would have been playing in a noncombat zone, the whole group was asleep. One member quietly slipped out of the hardback, then got back to his cot and resumed his sleep an hour later.

*****

The next morning, everyone seemed to be bright and chipper and ready to meet the day on a good note. They felt really good after breakfast, as the best SOS (shit on a shingle)—actually, it was creamed beef on toast Marine Corps style—they had ever consumed was served that morning. All five had seconds. Tolbane even managed a third plate, visibly upset that there was no bacon. A baconless man was not properly fueled for the trials and tribulations of the day.

CHAPTER 7

Team 1 worked the prisoner for three and a half hours without any new results. The prisoner was absolutely hostile, antagonistic, and insulting to them. Joe in particular was ready to drop-kick Xinwei's ass from there to the moon by the time they terminated questioning for the day, letting the prisoner know they would have more questions for him later.

Tolbane and Phuoc weren't too happy to hear that the morning had been a bust. They had hoped for some success they could capitalize on. During the morning, they had planned a different approach to Xinwei. Tolbane was a little leery about it but agreed to give it a try. He hoped Phuoc knew what she was doing. He would be glad if Tang and the guards were in the office with them. Their little plan might just set the prisoner off, causing him to become violent and to attack Tolbane. He would definitely tip Corporal Tang off as to what would be happening during the questioning.

When Xinwei was brought in, he grinned at and ogled Phuoc more than he had been. She managed that shy look of an abused woman, hoping to send the right message to him. Tolbane took Tang aside and clued him in on the plan of the day.

When everyone was seated, Tolbane spoke to Xinwei.

"Hey, jerk, you need to look at me, not her. This isn't a cathouse, where women are lined up for you to choose. Now where did we leave off yesterday?"

Of course, Xinwei had something to say.

"You seem to insult the lady. She's not your slave. If she wanted to, she would tell me she didn't want me to look at her. I think you need to be a little more kind to her. It's plain on her face when you tell me not to look at her she feels insignificant."

"I can't worry about what she thinks at any time. That's her personal problem. We are here to get background information from you, not to hook her up with a date. I believe you commented about having some fear and concern when you're headed for a big contact with your enemy. What about when you are in contact? Do you still feel the fear?"

"I think once the first round is fired, I think only of what is happening at the time. When the last round is fired, I feel a little shaky but glad to be alive."

"Is that the same way the other members of your group feel too?"

"Yes, I think everyone who survives feels elated they aren't dead or wounded."

"You mentioned wounded. What do you do with the wounded? Do you have a special place to take them?"

"It depends on the area we are in and how close to an aid station we are. If we are too far from one, we treat them as best we can and bring them with us."

"Where would these aid stations be?"

"That is a question I can't answer!"

"Sorry!"

Just then, Tolbane looked at Phuoc, as they had planned. She was smiling at Xinwei big-time.

"Damn it, you fucking whore!" Tolbane spoke to her in an incensed manner. "I told you not to pay any attention to that man!"

He reached over and knocked the notepad from her hand.

Xinwei leaped at Tolbane, screaming, "You don't treat her that way."

Tang grabbed him and shoved him back into his chair, nearly tipping it over. The prisoner was shouting and cursing at Tolbane, wanting to kick his ass from now to Sunday.

Tolbane shouted to Xinwei, "It's none of your concern how I treat her. She works for me, not you! I didn't want to be here in the first place, and I won't put up with any crap from either of you. Pick up your notepad and get ready to take notes."

"It won't do you any good to ask more questions. I'm not answering any more of your questions today, asshole."

Xinwei looked at Tang.

"Take me back to my prison, my good man."

Tang and the guards marched him out.

Laughing, Phuoc said, "Travis, you are wonderful. You should be in Hollywood. You didn't over or underplay your part. He's going to be putty in my hands."

She put her arms around him and hugged him tight. Tolbane stood silent for a couple of minutes, looking into Phuoc's eyes, and then explained why.

"Phuoc, so far, I like and respect you. I like working with you. You've got good instincts, and you're smart but very devious. You're playing some game that I can't figure out. I don't want to get burned and harm my career because of it. What is it you're trying to accomplish?"

"Travis, I feel for you. It's like what I said the other day. There are things I'd like to tell you, but I can't, not now anyway. Soon maybe, but not now."

"Phuoc, just tell me you're on the up-and-up. Promise me I'm not headed for a downfall, and you have my undying support."

"I promise you, Travis, you will not regret this. I do know what I'm doing. In the next couple of days, you will know everything I know now, and you will understand why I couldn't say anything to you. I would never forgive myself if I cause you any problems."

They walked side by side back to their hardback and briefed the others, then listened to them bitch about how their morning with Xinwei went. Then it was chow time again.

*****

Later that evening, after darkness fell on the enclave, Phuoc motioned to Tolbane to meet her outside.

"Travis, let's take a walk."

She took his hand in hers, and they strolled around the compound. They came to the empty bunker, and she pulled Tolbane into it.

"Travis, I go from place to place doing my job. I meet a lot of guys, most of them horny and lusting for my body. I've not been interested in them. The moment I saw you, I felt you were different from them. You didn't even seem to notice me. Charles had to comment about my body to you. Yes, he told me. I liked the way you scoped me out after that.

"And you are attracted to me, but you have respect for me as a person, and you don't make it so obvious. You have a mental and physical strength most men lack. To make a long story short, I've been horny too long. I know you are too. This is the only offer I'm making, so you best take advantage while you can."

In an instant, Tolbane's lips were on hers, and their biological instincts took over.

Afterward, on the way back to their quarters, they were arm in arm, each telling the other what an exceptional experience they just had. Just before entering the hardback, Phuoc had the last word.

"Travis, I feel bad that we will most likely never see each other again. A shame it is."

During the night, one of the guys snuck out of their quarters again, thinking he was in the clear, but Phuoc noticed and followed him. She was right in her assumptions. The guy did exactly what she thought he would do. Then she returned to her cot, pretending to be asleep when the guy returned. Then she let herself drift off to a satisfying sleep.

*****

The next day was status quo. After the other three left for the makeshift office, Tolbane and Phuoc, without any mention of the previous night, had their usual brainstorming session. Once more, they decided on how to play Xinwei. Tolbane had to admit that Phuoc was a genius at being devious. They couldn't wait to put it in play.

During the noon hour, team 1 felt they had had a breakout session with the Chinaman. They learned how the VC and NVA proselyted villagers to either join with them to fight or at least assist at various times prior to and after an operation. The team even got a list of many things the villagers had to do while assisting the VC. Phuoc and Tolbane congratulated them and promised to find out more about it. All five were still at odds with themselves that they had not found out why a Chinese was operating with the unit he was captured with.

When Phuoc went to the afternoon session, Tolbane remained in the hardback for more than half an hour. Phuoc went to the office and waited for the prisoner to be brought in. When he was led in, his first observation was that Phuoc was alone and looking sad and dejected. She asked Tang to wait outside, as had been arraigned, leaving just her, the prisoner, and the guard. The guard didn't speak Chinese, so the two could converse freely in that language.

"Phuoc, where is your shadow? You look very sad today. Has that jerk done something to you? You can tell me!"

With teary eyes, in a wavering voice, she stated, "Last night, he pulled me into a bunker and raped me repeatedly. It was horrible. I am dishonored. I had never had a man before. I hate him. I wish I could kill him and get out of here. I'd do anything if I could."

"I'm sorry you had to endure that. Are you serious about wanting out of here?"

"Oh yes! I can't stand it here with him anymore."

By now, she had tears flowing.

"I think I must kill myself. I've been defiled and don't want to face the world anymore."

"If I could take you away from here, would you go with me? I would treat you like a woman should be treated. I would show you that sex can be glorious. You would be a very happy woman."

"If only you could. I heard that once the Americans have all of your information you can tell them, they intend to shoot you and bury you out there someplace."

"I'm one step ahead of those American pigs. I'll be getting out of here tonight. Will you come with me?"

"Yes! Wait! You're a prisoner. How are you leaving here?"

"I have a plan. It will work, as I have help to do it. You'll be safe with me."

She looked at him with hope in her eyes.

"Oh yes, I'll come with you. I can't stand it here anymore."

"Tonight, pretend to be asleep and sneak out when everyone is sleeping deep, and come visit me. About one in the morning, we'll be leaving this place. Don't bring anything more than you need with you. We'll have a long, hard trek to where you'll be safe."

Just then, Tolbane and Tang entered.

Tolbane's first remark was, "Wipe those tears off your face, woman, and let's get to work."

Xinwei spoke first.

"I'll let you off the hook about yesterday's treatment of Ms. Linda, even the rape. Maybe I'll even tell you something to make you look good to your superiors. Just don't demean her today."

"That's an offer I can't refuse," Tolbane replied. "I just need her to do her job. So what is this something you wish to tell me?"

"If you must know, I guess it's all right. The unit I was with will be moving to join a larger unit close to the Dong Ha combat base within the next week for a mass attack on the marines there. I don't know what day they will link up or the day of attack, as I've been away from my unit for a few days, so I have not all the details. All I know is that it is supposed to be big and ferocious, driving the marines back to Phu Bai and, of course, killing as many as possible."

"Are you sure about this?"

"Yes! I'm telling you this because I'm pissed off I won't be in on it. I was looking forward to killing a bunch of you guys."

"What is your role in all of this?"

"My current job here in Viet Nam is to train my unit's commander in leading his men in preparing for battle, figuring the number of men that will most likely be killed or wounded, and developing the procedures and logistics to handle the situation. I also tutored him in several other areas of leadership, such as administrative, training, and communications during battle, etc."

"You must be a very well-trained and experienced individual. Why would you be wasting your time in this kind of position?"

"I shouldn't tell you this, but all of the experienced leaders in the group I was working with were either killed or wounded. The individual who was put in charge has very little experience, so he needs a mentor."

"Interesting. So what is the unit designation?"

"I will not tell you that."

"Where is the unit supposed to join the larger group?"

"Won't tell you that either."

"Why won't you tell?"

"Because we had not been briefed yet on the operation before I was captured. I give you credit. You ask good questions, whereas those other asses have no clue as to how to question a subject. Would you like to come over to our side?"

"Surely you jest, sir. I studied the great Chinese detective Charlie Chan! I learned a lot about people and how to question them."

"Who's he? I never heard of him."

"He was a great man with the Honolulu Police Department. He solved many crimes and murders there. He was so great they made movies about him and his sons."

Tolbane checked his watch.

"It's that time again. I guess I'll see you again tomorrow."

"Yeah, right."

"Okay, Tang, you may take the prisoner back."

He turned to Phuoc.

"Good! You've stopped your crying. Hope you didn't get the pages in your notebook wet."

Xinwei gave him a dirty look as he was led out the door.

"Damn, girl, you really know how to do crocodile ears. If I hadn't known better, I'd have thought they were for real."

"Boo-hoo, Travis, you raped me last night," she quipped.

She grinned and grabbed Tolbane around the neck, pulling him into a big lip-lock.

"I am for real as far as you are concerned. I really enjoyed our time in the bunker. To me, it wasn't just the sex. There was an intimacy I had not felt in many a moon. I was married once, and I had a nice man. The VC conscripted him into a village guerilla unit, and he was killed during his first battle. You gave me something missing from my life for a long time."

"Phuoc, I felt something too. I'm not sure what it is I'm feeling right now, but all I can think about is that you were magnificent. I'll never forget last night as long as I'm alive. I hate to change the subject, but did our ruse work on the man?"

"Oh, brother, did it ever. Tomorrow, you will know everything about this operation. I hope you can find your way to our hooch on your own. I have to attend to something right now. Ta-ta!"

And she was on her way. She needed to talk to Gunnery Sergeant Beaumont ASAP! She found him, and they spoke for a few minutes about the situation, and she left. She returned to her hooch and helped Tolbane brief the three guys.

The three guys didn't actually know about any interaction between her and the prisoner, because she and Tolbane made it a point to keep it out of the briefings. The guys would be surprised tomorrow, one of them especially so. Now she had another pressing item to ponder. She wondered if she could get Tolbane into the bunker again before the shit hit the ceiling.

CHAPTER 8

Phuoc realized that unless she could get Tolbane into the bunker right as darkness ruled, she wouldn't get much sleep. Suddenly, the light bulb went off in her head. Just before darkness came, she invited Tolbane to go to the little club and have a beer with her. He agreed. They had one beer, and then she maneuvered him to the bunker. They were like wild savages in their sex.

When they were spent, they returned to the hardback and wasted no time at all hitting the sack. After a couple of hours of sleep, Phuoc arose and quietly left and walked down to the prisoner's hooch. She managed to convince the guard to let her in to see the prisoner. He was asleep, and she nudged him awake.

"I didn't think you'd come," Xinwei stated while trying to shake the sleep from his head. "I guess you really do like me."

"Yes, I think I do like you. I'll stay with you as long as you treat me right."

"Don't you worry your pretty little head. You will be well taken care of."

Looking at his watch, he told her, "I'd start showing you right now how I'd take care of you. However, I'm expecting someone that's going to help us get out of here."

They heard a commotion outside. A figure had stealthily snuck up on the guard and coldcocked him and entered the tent.

His first words were, "What in the fuck is she doing here, Xinwei?"

"She has been mistreated by that ass she works for and wants to escape."

"You stupid ass. Her and that dumbass marine have been playing you like a fucking piano. She's conned you real good."

"Is that true, Linda?"

"I don't know what he's talking about, Xinwei. He is another one of those brutes that want my body. He's number 10."

"Look, Xinwei, you need to tie and gag her, take her with you, and dispose of her on the way to your unit. Believe me, she's played you the whole time."

"You are sure about her?"

"Damn right. Come here, bitch."

"You'll never get away with this, Marcus. The powers that be know all about what you've been doing, helping important prisoners escape. Your days are numbered. You'll probably be executed."

Marcus reached for her, but she was quicker than he and put a side kick into his groin area, and he fell, holding himself and groaning. Before Xinwei could make a move toward her, Gunnery Sergeant Beaumont burst through the door with three armed guards, Tang, and HoungBo Ming. Marcus and Xinwei were immediately handcuffed and thrown down on empty cots.

"Phuoc, I was starting to think we wouldn't get in here in time to save your butt. I guess you had the situation under control."

He addressed the two prisoners.

"There will be guards inside here tonight."

He looked at Marcus and Xinwei.

"After breakfast in the morning, both of you will be transported to MACV headquarters in Saigon. As for you, Phuoc, you go get some sack time. I'll notify the colonel for you. I must say, you did a damn good job."

"Thanks, Gunny!" She turned to Marcus and then to Xinwei and commented, "I just wish I could cut your balls off, both of you. But if I did, it would piss off someone up the line, and I might lose my job, so you're lucky in that respect. Xinwei, you are a disgusting individual. I'd love to shit on your head."

She turned sharply and left the hardback.

When she got back to her hooch, she gently nudged Tolbane and whispered in his ear, "How would you like to take me to the bunker and fuck the hell out of me again, big boy?"

Before she could blink an eye, Tolbane had grasped her hand and was pulling her out the screen door.

*****

They woke up in the bunker just as dawn was breaking and hurried back to their hardback, snuck in, and sacked out before the others awoke. They had not been asleep for long when it was reveille time. Phuoc told Charles and Joe that there would be no interrogation session that morning and that she would explain to them later. She and Tolbane made sure they got their showers first. The showers really woke them up. The water was warm during the day and became chilly at night due to condensation. Afterward, the lovers went to chow.

Tolbane tried to roll with the status quo, but he finally asked Phuoc what was going on while they were eating. She bade him to have patience until after breakfast.

"We'll take a stroll around the compound, and I'll spill the beans. I don't want to sound egotistical or narcissistic, but I hope you'll be proud of me."

"Phuoc, I'm sure I will be. This silence is driving me crazy, but not as crazy as I am for you and that fantastic body."

They took their time chowing down, and of course, Phuoc had to wait until the food vacuum was sated. Then they went for a walk and started the long-awaited narrative.

"Travis, my name is Phuoc, but it's Nguyen Thi Phuoc. I am a marine captain, and my duty is with the NIS. Gunnery Sergeant Beaumont is one of my troopers. I was on a mission here. There have been important prisoners being shot while escaping. The three guys—Marcus, Charles, and Joe—were each a suspect. We were not sure which one was guilty of arranging the killing to protect important information from getting to MACV. This foray was to discover which one it was."

She continued. "We caught Marcus last night. He was the one. He was going to maneuver Xinwei into being killed going over the sandbagged barrier. I got to Xinwei and agreed to go with him over the barrier. Marcus showed up and would have had me killed too. Once Marcus got into the hardback, the gunny and a few guards came in when the situation became too tense. So we got our man. He and Xinwei will be going to MACV. All of what little we elicited from him will accompany him."

"Damn, girl, wow! You're something else. Oops! Oh, I mean Captain!"

"Cut the crap, Travis. I'm serious when I say I really do have the hots for you. I was not faking anything, but regulations do forbid our relationship. If we ever meet again in the Corps, I'm only Captain if others are around. I want you to always remember me as the Phuoc you knew here. Just in case we do meet again, I may just end up getting banged again.

"When we go back to the hardback and I brief Charles and Joe, they will not be told of my rank and duty. Only the gunny, you, and I know it. I may need the alias again sometime. The colonel and his aides will be here this afternoon to debrief us. I'm sure he will compliment you. Before we part, I'll tell you why you were chosen for this. Let's go check in with Charles and Joe. I'll explain while we walk.

"Why did I select you for this mission? We wanted to have someone not connected to the three guys. Someone suggested to check with the division about their interrogation team, so I contacted division G-2, and they mentioned you. I checked some of your interrogation reports. Checked with your captain, who gave me a glowing recommendation of you. I masqueraded as a Viet Cong suspect and questioned some of those you interrogated.

"I also got the chance to observe you in person. I liked what I saw—a staunch individual that doesn't compromise his principles, very good at working with his enemy, a top-notch interrogator, and a stud. There were other things too. I decided I wanted you aboard for this mission. I hoped having you would keep the three guys feeling the mission was legit. I'd be remiss if I didn't confess that I kind of got the hots for you while checking you out."

"Hot damn, ma'am! I don't really know what to say. I also have to admit one thing. After Charlie mentioned it, I had to scope you out. I liked what I saw. I really loved our time in the bunker."

"That's because you horny numba one thou GI, and I lubed you long time."

Tolbane laughed at her impersonation of a Vietnamese short-time girl.

"Are you sure the NIS is your job and you're not a camp follower? Seriously, I believed the mission was legit. You know I had questions. However, I felt you were going to surprise Xinwei by taking over the interrogation after you got to him, which you did. You are really good at your job. Your instincts are right on. The sex aside, I'd work with you anytime you might want me to. I feel so humbled that you selected me for the job and happy you did at the same time. Thank you!"

"You are very welcome, Travis. I'm glad I chose you. You're very good at your job too. You do bunker time really good too."

The pair walked arm in arm back to their quarters.

Before entering, Phuoc reminded Tolbane, "Gunny, don't forget to get those chevrons on!"

Then Phuoc briefed Charles and Joe, only with a slightly different version.

*****

The colonel arrived with his aides by chopper. Phuoc and the gunny were there to greet him. He instructed the gunny to get the prisoners ready for transport and form the convoy. Then he and Phuoc went for a walk for the colonel to get a brief on the operation's success. Tolbane sat in the hardback, drinking coffee and eating cake the mess hall had sent, along with the major and the captain.

If one listened closely to the conversations, one thing would have become clear: most of the anecdotes began with the phrase "You ain't gonna believe this shit, but..." It was like the three had been bosom buddies forever.

When the colonel and Phuoc returned from their walk, the colonel held a small ceremony. He complimented Tolbane for a job well done and presented him with the Navy and Marine Corps Commendation ribbon for his participation. Tolbane thanked him while thinking that his real reward had been in the bunker. Everyone shook his hand and congratulated him. He kind of felt like he was on display. A quarter of an hour after the colonel had some cake and coffee, the group said their goodbyes.

When no one was looking, Phuoc gave Tolbane a peck on the cheek, told him a chopper would be there to take him back to his team in about an hour, and walked sexily out to the convoy and out of Tolbane's life. Tolbane felt empty and sad watching her leave. He knew there would be a vacuum in his life for the rest of his tour. The chopper finally came, and it wasn't long before he was lying on his cot at the team's CP, wishing bunker time had never ended.

During the rest of his tour in Viet Nam, he did his job by rote. He and his interpreter, Ba, had a few close calls while going on patrols with a prisoner who knew of booby traps or punji pits in their operation area. On one of those patrols, they uncovered a beautiful jade cross encrusted with precious gems. After admiring it, it was reburied where it was found.

He did a short period as the Third ITT commander, then as team chief. His rotation date finally arrived, and he found himself relaxing on the big bird, a C-130 again. This one only had a small load and lots of leg room. Once again, it took him and some troops to Okinawa, landing them at MCAS Futenma, Okinawa. The take-off from the Da Nang airstrip was memorable.

The group he was flying out with arrived two hours early at the airstrip. It was dark and very foggy. They were told after an hour and a half that the flight had been cancelled due to fog throughout the area. The troops were disappointed, to say the least. Before buses could arrive to take them back to the transit area, good news arrived. It seemed the plane crew didn't want to disappoint the troops rotating home after their tour filled with trials and tribulations, so the crew decided to come to Viet Nam anyway. After it landed, the troops were boarded, but they were a little leery and not cheering, as troops rotating usually did on takeoff.

There was a mountain located directly in front of the takeoff pattern, and it could not be seen from the airstrip due to the fog. The big cargo plane's four engines revved up real high, and the plane took off down the runway with a great jerk to the passengers. Suddenly, it stood on its tail, flying nearly straight up. Then the craft leveled off above the fog, and the cheering began from the troops. They were finally leaving hell behind. They were on their way home. The plane captain welcomed them aboard the flight they would always remember.

Tolbane leaned back as much as the strap seat would allow him to, closed his eyes, and thought about things he and his interpreter, Ba, had experienced during his tour, two times in particular. One was bunker time, and the other was finding a jewel-encrusted jade cross. Sometimes, he wished he had kept it. It was magnificent.

CHAPTER 9

Tolbane began daydreaming about an incident he was involved in. The VCS had indicated that he knew where there were booby traps and punji pits east of the enclave of the First Battalion, First Marine Regiment, First Marine Division, a little north of Hoi An City. Tolbane planned for him and Ba to take the VCS to the battalion and have a patrol take them out to the area and destroy any traps they could find.

All had gone well until the patrol was on its way back to the enclave. The patrol returned on a different path, alongside a wooded area, and was ambushed by an ARVN[5] platoon dug in along the trees. As the scenario unfolded, the two sides finally got together, Tolbane giving the ARVN platoon leader hell. Then they discovered a bejeweled jade cross buried by an abandoned, run-down hovel by accident. They reburied it and moved along.[6]

Tolbane finally fell asleep and awoke when he heard the grating of the lowering of the landing gear and the plane captain announcing for everyone to fasten their seat belts. After landing, he and the troops were loaded into a cattle car and taken to Camp Hansen for processing and acclimating to a new existence and awaiting orders and transportation back to the real world.

Being a gunny, Tolbane was not restricted to Cinderella liberty (at 2400 hours, liberty was over), as it was for the lower-rated troops. He found the Japanese sake and Asahi beer great, and the ladies in the bars were charming as well as beautiful, well-stacked, and available for the night. So he indulged in their feminine charms for three

---

[5] Army of the Republic of Viet Nam.
[6] *See* book 3, *The Jade Cross*, of *The Jade Cross Trilogy* by Harold W. Weist, 2020.

nights in a row, feeling like he was on cloud nine or higher, but not higher than where Phuoc could take him.

Then on the morning of the fourth day, he was notified that he would be flying back to the continental US, boarding at 1800 hours that late afternoon. This time, it would be a nonstop ten-hour flight to San Diego, California, in a Continental Airlines 707. He was in seventh heaven, enjoying the flight, knowing he had left hell behind. No more fears, bullets, or monsoon rains.

After landing in San Diego and processing out, he had a major dilemma on his hands. He had not given a thought about where he wanted to go when he returned. His parents and brother were no longer living, and he had no real home to go to. He felt like the biggest ass and loser ever.

Since his hometown was not to his liking because of his memories and having no one to share them with, he decided to go to Washington, DC. He would get a hotel room for a couple of days, visit memorials and museums, and think about where he would like to be, someplace he could use as a home of record for the Corps.

While there, he bought a white 1964 Chevy four-door sedan from Capital Motors. He ended up staying for five days and left for Camp Lejeune, North Carolina, his next duty station. He took two days poking along to get there, and on arrival, he checked in at Second Force Troops headquarters, mainside, and was assigned to a room in the staff NCO quarters.

The next day, he checked in with the G-2 section and learned he would remain in that billet, but he would be stationed with one of the interrogation/translation teams at Montford Point, a few miles from mainside. He was officially still on leave, so he just drove to the team's site just to see what the area looked like. The area didn't look too awfully bad to him.

He drove back to the staff NCO club mainside and had a beer, then went to the main PX, bought a couple of books, and went to evening chow. After chow, he changed into civvies and drove into Jacksonville, North Carolina. It looked pretty much the same as when he was stationed there before. He found a place to park and found a bar that looked decent. He went in, noticing the sour smell of stale beer and smoke that many bars had, and ordered a beer. That was when shit hit the fan.

The place was a little noisy and about half full. Tolbane grabbed an empty seat at the somewhat crowded bar. Just as the bartender set the bottle of Bud in front of him, a couple of guys at the table behind him started throwing punches. One bumped into Tolbane, nearly knocking him off his stool. Tolbane stepped back from his stool and confronted the man.

"Don't you think you should excuse yourself?"

The guy, nearly Tolbane's size, replied, "Shut the fuck up, asshole!"

The man took a swing at Tolbane with his left fist. Tolbane grabbed the guy's left wrist in his right hand and pulled the guy to his right and across his body and kicked him behind the left knee with his right foot, driving him to the floor.

It so happened that one of the three-man MP patrols was just coming into the bar to check on things. Seeing Tolbane put the guy down, two of the MPs grabbed him and cuffed him while the other MP helped the guy up and handcuffed him too. The third man melted into the background. The two combatants were seated roughly at a table.

The staff sergeant in charge didn't ask any questions. He immediately called for a vehicle to pick the two up and take them to the military lockup to await the periodic checks of a Second Marine Division officer of the day (OD). The OD would decide whether to charge them and lock them up, order them back to the base, or just turn them loose.

Tolbane was smart enough not to open his mouth, but the other guy started cursing the MPs and threatening them. The corporal pulled out his night stick and nearly pushed it into the guy's nose, warning him to keep his mouth shut. The guy took the hint.

While they were waiting for transportation, the staff sergeant checked the two prisoners' military ID cards and entered the information in a notepad he had, as well as the unit they belonged to. He kind of had half of a reaction when Tolbane informed him of his outfit, which he had not checked into yet. The transportation arrived, and they were off to the lockup.

About an hour later, the OD, a Major Cantrell, whose ribbons reflected he was both a Korea and a Viet Nam veteran, arrived at the lockup. He read the report from the check-in and decided he would talk to the gunny first. He introduced himself to Tolbane and explained what the outcome of this interview could lead to.

"All right, Gunny, explain to me why you were cleaning that guy's clock and why you have a unit you have not checked into."

Tolbane held nothing back. He gave straight answers and answered the OD's questions.

He also added, "I'm pissed at that creep. I didn't even get a sip of my beer, caused by that ass's major malfunction of his brain housing group."

The major had to laugh at that.

"Gunny, I don't doubt your story one iota. That clown has been here in the lockup a couple of times before for fighting. The turnkey recognized him and tipped me off. You're free to go, but your nemesis will go straight to the division brig from here. I'll see to it he gets a court-martial this time. Some of these guys never learn the lesson. They never take the easy way of life.

"Anyway, glad to see you made it back to the world in one piece, Gunny. I was medevaced to Guam and then to the States a month before my rotation date. I had two bullets in my right leg. They missed the bone and femoral artery but caused a lot of muscle and tissue damage. I'm in good shape now, run five miles daily."

"Sorry to hear you got hit, sir, but glad you're doing all right. Too many of our guys got really fucked up for life. I saw too many marines and ARVNs shot up or missing body parts. Enough mutilation to last a lifetime. I came close a few times, but my dumbass luck protected me."

The two said their so longs, and Tolbane left the lockup. The major had one of the drivers take him back to the bar.

Tolbane got another surprise when he entered the bar. Some of the guys hailed him and told him they were glad to see someone fix that ass.

The bartender set two ice-cold Buds in front of him and said, "One is for the one you didn't get to drink, and the other one is for getting that clown out of our hair."

Tolbane hopped up on the same stool he had left, took a big swallow, lifted the bottle to the ceiling, and toasted everyone.

"Hey, marines! Here's to heat—not the heat that burns down the shanties but the heat that brings down the panties."

He was an instant hero! For the next couple of minutes, all he heard was ooh-rahs and semper fis from all the jarheads in attendance. Needless to say, he didn't pay for another beer the rest of the night. After a while, a guy—about five foot nine; built like a bull with an unshaven look; wore a ragged white T-shirt, worn-out jeans, and jungle boots; and looked like he had been in the Corps for 150 years—sidled up to him.

"So you're Gunny Tolbane. I'm MGySgt. Richard Head. They call me Dick Head. You won't believe this shit, but I'm the team chief for the Second ITT. The team heard you would be joining. We heard good things about you. I guess we'll formally meet whenever you get around to checking in with us. I liked the move you put on that friggin' maggot. From watching you, I guess we'll finally have someone to liven things up at the team."

The two drank and gossiped for the next hour and a half, then parted and went on their merry ways.

For the next couple of days, Tolbane lolled around his quarters during the day and caroused around in J-Ville during the evenings. But then he began to tire of this regimen, so he decided to come off leave a few days early. He rose early, did his morning routine, and drove to Second Force Troops duty office to check in officially. He then went to morning chow, had his fill of bacon, and then headed for Montford Point and his new team.

When he arrived at the team, Dick Head was already there. He sure looked different. Not only had he cleaned up, but he and his uniform were squared away. He was a sharp-looking marine. They sat in the team's office, drinking coffee, telling war stories, and waiting for the team commander, Capt. Tim Tyler, to arrive.

When the captain showed up, Dick said, "I damn sure ought to put your young ass on report, sir. You're three damn minutes late."

"Up yours and the horse you rode in on, Master Guns."

Looking at Tolbane, the captain continued.

"Is this our FNG, Dick? He looks big enough to whip your ass."

He reached his hand to Tolbane to shake.

"I'm Tim in here, Captain D. J. Tyler around the troops. Happy to make your acquaintance, Tolbane."

"Likewise, skipper. I'm looking forward to my tour here. Can't say the same for the place I just came from."

"I hear you, Gunny. Let's get a fresh cup of coffee, and the three of us will sit on our butts and go over what we've been doing here and what is expected of you here."

An hour later, the three went into the troops' area. There were seven marines of various ranks sitting behind desks, either reading foreign language books or listening to language tapes. They all stood as the captain entered a few minutes after Dick and Tolbane did. However, they had an unwritten rule of not jumping to attention for officers in their space unless it was a senior officer to their captain.

The team was comprised of SSgt. Jack Daniels, Sgt. Bill Durban, Cpl. John Bracken, LCpl. Harold Brown, and three private first classes. Tolbane shook hands with and introduced himself to all seven of the marines. He explained that they should not expect him to remember their names right off the get-go because he was brain-dead from Nam.

The captain offered that the next two large rooms belonged to the Fourth and the Sixth ITTs respectively and that he could meet their troops later. He was shown to a desk, a larger one than the others had, that would be his and told him that he was the first subteam chief. Staff Sergeant Daniels would be the second subteam chief. Tolbane would have Bracken and two PFCs. Daniels would have the rest.

The captain then said, "Dick and Travis, let's go back to my office."

The door was closed. The captain took a bottle of Beam's Choice and three glasses from his bottom desk drawer. He poured three glasses half full. Then he and Dick toasted the newest member of the team.

CHAPTER 10

Everything went well for Tolbane the first three weeks. He met the members of the other two teams, and all seemed cool. Early the next Monday morning, he was called into the captain's office.

"Tolbane, I know you were on a classified operation for NIS in Nam. It seems that NIS wants you for another one. It would entail taking your subteam with you. It could be dangerous. You and the guys would function as an ITT subteam as a cover, but you and the subteam would have a clandestine mission. I can't tell you any more than that, as I'm not cleared for the need-to-know for anything additional.

"You can let Bracken but not the other two in on what's happening. There will be a time when you'll tell the other two. However, I have no idea when that will be. As I understand, within the next few days, you'll be contacted by NIS for a briefing. It won't be here at the team headquarters.

"Get Corporal Bracken, and you two take a long walk. Just let him know your subteam will be deploying in the near future, and it's hush-hush. He needs to know that you'll only be able to tell him what NIS allows you to pass on. He can get the other two troops ready for the deployment. He can use the ploy of practicing emergency deployment or whatever. You'll inform them later that you will be on standby for deployment. Don't know what else I can say about it. Any questions, Gunny?"

"I can't think of any right now, skipper. I'll let you know whatever I can after I get the briefing."

Tolbane felt that because this was Marine Corps business, he needed to show military courtesy to the captain.

He requested, "By your leave, sir!"

"Dismissed!"

"Aye, aye, sir."

Tolbane took one step backward, executed a sharp about-face, marched out of the office, and went to his desk. He sat and contemplated for a few minutes and called Corporal Bracken over.

Tolbane requested, "John, let's you and I go for a long walk."

Bracken looked at him quizzically, then nodded. They left the building and began walking toward the main entrance road and the PX/barbershop complex. Tolbane explained the situation as well as he could to Corporal Bracken, emphasizing the need for sealed lips and the reason he was recently upgraded from a secret to a top-secret security clearance.

"I can tell you from my own experience, John, that when we get the word not to spill the beans, it is meant, and any security breach is serious and has serious consequences. I presume you understand. Am I correct?"

"I do understand, Gunny," John replied. "Operations get compromised, and guys die. You got my word, not a word passes my lips. I'm not the one that's going to sink ships with my lips. You got my word on that."

"Good! While we are here, over there's the barbershop. My treat on the haircuts. You know, I remember when they were $00.10 here. This $00.50 for a haircut is highway robbery."

John Bracken thought that was funny.

He grinned and said, "You got that right, Gunny."

Returning to the team HQ, Corporal Bracken went to work with the PFCs. Tolbane sat at his desk, tilted his chair back, put his feet on the desktop, and slipped into dreamland. Beautiful women in the tiniest bikinis were parading before him in a continuous mile-long procession. His mouth was salivating over the bountiful bevy of beautiful broads when he awoke with a jerk, his desk chair nearly tipping over.

"Wake up, sleeping beauty," boomed Dick's voice as he slapped Tolbane on his feet. "It's club time, youngster. We can down a couple before chow."

"Aye, aye, sir!" Tolbane blurted out. "I hear and obey. I hear an ice-cold Bud calling my name and shouting, 'Drink me! Drink me!'"

He and Dick moseyed on over to the staff NCO club. After the pair had downed a couple of brews, Dick began speaking in earnest to Tolbane.

"My compadre, I brought you here to kind of clue you about your upcoming mission. I can't say what I know, but I can give you a warning. Make sure you watch your ass and your troops' asses too. This deal could end up being the biggest can of worms to come down the pike in a while.

"I got a few reasons for the warning. I don't want to see anything happen to you guys. You just got here, and we need the warm bodies. The third reason is that you will most likely be team chief in about a month and a half. I'm retiring about then. Long live the Corps without me!"

"Thanks, Top. It'll be dull here without you to shoot the bull with. I wish you luck in your retirement. Thanks for the heads-up. I know you can't say too much about the mission. However, without disclosing any info, do you think there could be some life-and-death situations with this deployment?"

"You didn't hear it from me. You just bring your candy asses home safe and sound. I got to have some useless-ass gunnery sergeant to step in for me. It's a fucking shame. The Corps will never be the same."

"Once again, I hear and obey. Just remember one thing before you retire. You need to introduce me with a recommendation to your sources. I don't want the team to suffer from a lack of info."

"You got it, marine! Now let's down another Bud quickly. My gut's telling me I'm hungry."

"You got it, Dick Head."

CHAPTER 11

Two days after the impromptu club outing with Dick Head, Tolbane and Corporal Bracken were called to the Second Force Troops G-2 office, mainside. The G-2 intelligence officer, Colonel Dusty Donner, and the intelligence chief, MGySgt. Dorian Jones, greeted Tolbane and Bracken with a "Welcome aboard!" and a handshake. Then the colonel pointed to a door on the opposite side of the office and invited the two junior marines to enter.

"We won't waste too much of your time this morning. Let's go into the conference room and get down to business. After you, gentlemen."

There was an amtrac crew already in the room. The colonel entered last. Tolbane nearly fell on his ass upon seeing the woman sitting at the conference table, eating a doughnut and smiling at him with pouted lips.

"My God, woman, what the hell are you doing here?" he exclaimed.

"Hello, Travis. Nice to see you again. You're a great big hunk, you know, and you'd be a sight for sore eyes, if I had them," commented Truong Thi Phuoc as she greeted Tolbane.

She gave him a bear hug and planted one big, sloppy kiss on his cheek.

Tolbane looked at the colonel and stated, "Shit, sir, it looks like I'm fucked again!"

Colonel Donner laughed.

"Sounds like you've got a personal problem, Gunny. You and the corporal get some of the coffee and doughnuts and have a seat. Yes, you, Gunny, may sit by the young lady if you care to."

He did. She grinned.

"I understand you two have a history together in our Marine Corps. Later, you may have some catching up to do, but not at this particular time, okay?"

"Well, Colonel, believe me, it's a tough job keeping up with her, but someone has to do it," Tolbane quipped as he took a seat beside his paramour in Viet Nam, with his four doughnuts and two cups of coffee, and gave her a big smile.

With everyone seated and filling their faces with doughnuts and coffee, Colonel Donner began his briefing.

"In order to begin this briefing, let me bore you with the old, corny gag. I see you all are in wild anticipation, and I guess you all are wondering why I called you here."

Everyone groaned loudly on cue.

"People, I won't soft-coat anything about this deal. This assignment can be a breeze, or it could go south like shit hitting the fan. Plop, plop, plop in an instant. That means there could be a serious element of danger to your physical well-being. You have been selected for this operation not because your leaders want to get rid of your ass for a while but for your record of dedication to your job and the logical and professional way you approach each and every one of your assignments.

"As to this mission, you are expected to carry yourselves in the highest tradition of the United States Marine Corps. If it goes south, all bets are off, and you may get as down and dirty as need be with my complete blessing. Any questions so far?"

The group voiced noes while shaking their heads.

"You amtrackers will be briefed separately at your unit. Good! Now to get to the nitty-gritty of the details. First, you, Ms. Phuoc and Tolbane with your subteam, need to be at the MCAS Cherry Point, NC, at 0900 hours two days from now. Flight time is 1100 hours. You will be joining the Third Battalion, Sixth Marines, at Gitmo, who are there for familiarization of the post while they are the Caribbean-deployed response unit, the Sixth MEB.

"Except for the CO and his exec and S-2, no one knows of your mission at this time. The rest of the headquarters unit will be told you are there for your subteam training or in case your subteam is needed in a tactical situation and nothing else. The CO will make sure you have everything to complete your assignment, including logistics, transportation, and some equipment.

"One thing I must make absolutely clear this very instant is, if you or any member of your force is killed or captured, the US will disavow any involvement in the situation, and the tape will self-destruct in five seconds. As far as we know, there is just one rogue American trying God knows what in some South American country.

"If the mission goes off like we hope it will, no one will even know you have been there or that anyone was extracted from the area. Once you have been inserted into the promised land, you will have three days before your transportation arrives and leaves the area with or without you and your team aboard. Are we all clear on this aspect of the operation?"

There was a round of "Yes, sirs!" in response.

"Good! Now let me move to the mission. You will meet a man who has a prisoner and some documents. You will receive the documents and interrogate the prisoner. Before your mission is launched, you will be given a sealed envelope with specific questions to ask. Any information you may obtain beyond those questions will be gravy for us.

"Make no mistake about it, you will be in hostile territory. If things go south, if at all possible, bring the man you meet with you, but don't worry about the prisoner unless you're certain you can bring him out too without endangering yourselves more than the situation calls for. As an afterthought, let me state that all of you will be locked and loaded at all times.

"I'm not sure, but I believe the man you are to meet will have three or four guards with him. Your two PFCs, Gunny, and the guards will provide security while you're engaged in your duty. I have nothing more to say on the subject officially. Unofficially, I am concerned for your safety and welfare. Between now and the briefing you will get at Gitmo, things can change in a heartbeat. I have no knowledge of what your briefing will be about.

"This having been said, good luck, marines! Hang around here as long as you please, have as much coffee and as many doughnuts you want, and toss around ideas. Once you leave this room, your lips are sealed for eternity. Good day, marines."

The colonel exited, and the marines snapped to attention and replied, "Aye, aye, sir!"

Before either Phuoc or Tolbane could say a word, Corporal Bracken asked, "You two actually know each other?"

Beating Tolbane to the punch, Phuoc spoke up.

"We sure do. Best sticking I've ever had to date, Corporal!"

Tolbane's face turned a bright red, and he groaned. He slyly changed the subject quickly.

"So tell me if this sounds like this mission is going to suck to hell and back!"

Phuoc and Bracken laughed out loud. Then Phuoc turned to Bracken and introduced herself.

"I am Phuoc, and I'm happy to meet you. If I didn't introduce myself to you, we probably would wait for an eternity for this Neanderthal dummy standing here to do it for us. Yes, Travis and I do have a history of working together, in more ways than one. But don't worry, he can get the job, whatever it is, done properly. He and I can work together without his hanky-panky getting in the way of our mission's objective."

Bracken responded in kind.

"I'm glad to meet you too, Phuoc. I guess I'm proud as all get-out to meet one of Tolbane's friends. I didn't know he had any. Ha ha! I hope you won't take this wrong, but I can see how the Gunny could get sidetracked by hanky-panky with you."

It was Phuoc's turn to get a little red in the face even though she agreed and laughed.

They feasted some more on the free doughnuts and coffee, tossed around what little they knew about the upcoming mission so far, and then left. Outside, after parting ways, Bracken looked at Tolbane, who was watching Phuoc's rear end walking away, and chided him.

"Gunny, you sly old dog, you."

Tolbane smiled as he got behind the wheel.

CHAPTER 12

Tolbane lay half-awake on his Marine Corps-issued metal bed, wondering what fate had gotten him into this time. The briefing really didn't tell him much. Going through his mind were adventures of GIs on film and in books. All had missions going south at one point or another, good guys getting wounded and killed and whatever. Would his group have to improvise to save the mission and their lives? Finally, he drifted off into a restless sleep.

Waking the next morning, he felt like shit warmed over. He managed to do his morning toilet and went to chow at the staff NCO mess. He felt a little more like facing the world after three eggs over medium, buttered toast and blackberry jam, enough bacon to feed an army, and of course, three cups of coffee.

Arriving at the team headquarters, everything seemed normal as usual. He gathered his subteam outside under a sprawling and leafy tree. They spoke about deployments in general, things that the Navy always expected on embarking or debarking—from the time you started up or down a gangplank, saluting the flag and deck officer, or climbing up or down a cargo net and keeping an eye on the rise and fall of the LCVP below, rising and falling with the rolling sea, and the potential for serious injury when dropping into the LCVP[7] when the boat suddenly rose and broke your knees, legs, or ankles or a combination thereof.

He informed the two PFCs that they would be deploying soon but not when or where or why and for them to make sure they had everything about their lives in order, especially a will, and to notify their family that they would be going on a Caribbean deployment for

---

[7] Landing craft vehicle personnel.

ITT training. He gave them his final word of the day and turned the rest of the briefing over to Corporal Bracken.

"The corporal will work with you two some more on predeployment preparations and what we as an ITT subteam need to deploy with and what our duties would entail. I'll see you dudes later."

He went to the team office to speak to the captain for his men. He knew exactly what he wanted. He wanted Bracken promoted to sergeant and the two PFCs to lance corporals before they were deployed. If any member of his team needed to assert authority, their rank would really count.

Entering the office, Tolbane's first sight was a weird-looking man in civilian clothes—a wrinkled gray suit coat, scuffed shoes, a pale-blue shirt, and khaki trousers. Captain Tyler greeted Tolbane warmly.

"Gunny, I was about to call for you to come over here ASAP. I want you to meet local NIS agent Bill Moyer. Bill, this is GySgt. Travis Tolbane, our first subteam commander."

The two shook hands as Tolbane looked him up and down, wondering what in the hell kind of creature he was looking at.

"Gunny, this NIS agent is here to see you on some matter relating to some deployment you were on in Viet Nam."

Agent Moyer began.

"Gunny, I'll get right to the point as to why I'm here. I'm here to get some vital information from you about a situation that happened in Viet Nam. I understand you know a Nguyen Thi Phuoc, aka Troung Thi Phuoc."

"As a matter of record, what is it to you whether I know some woman named Phuoc or not?"

"Let's not beat around the bush here! I need to know if you know her."

"And I need to know why the hell you want to know."

"If you are going to be stubborn about this, it could be very problematic for your career in the Corps!"

"Look, Agent, whoever you are—and I personally couldn't give a flying fuck who you are—I wouldn't make threats to me if I were you. I don't take them lightly, and I might respond to you in a manner you wouldn't like, no way, no how. How about that, shithead?"

"I don't make threats I can't back up."

"Let me explain one thing to you, and you need to listen up, hear it loud and clear, and you best understand and heed it. This is one thing your mental midget mind has no control over you, shit-for-brains. As to whether I do or do not know this woman you're asking about, there is something you best understand, and that is you are not security-cleared high enough for any information I may or may not know about her. You do not have the proverbial need-to-know clearance.

"Now if you want to know about something you are cleared for, I'll be glad to answer your questions. If you have no questions, I suggest you fuck off at the double and find your ass going out that door without letting the door hit you in the ass. Don't worry, I will be checking to see if you are legit."

Agent Moyer turned red in the face and stomped out the door, stating, "Just you wait, asshole. You'll answer my questions sooner or later."

"Gunny," the captain said to Tolbane in a soft voice, "I didn't like that fucker either. I don't know what his game was, but it sucked. He wanted to know if I knew this woman too, whoever she is."

"Captain, I really wish I could explain some things to you. However, I'm not in that position at this time. It's pretty high up the food chain, and I don't want shit to come tumbling down on us any way, shape, or form. Whatever did or did not happen or regardless of who I may or may not know, my lips are sealed forever."

"Don't fret about it even a little, Gunny. We all in our field have many things we can't discuss under penalty. I want to get something straight between us. As I said, I didn't like that clown either. If you hadn't sent his ass packing, make no mistake, I would have, and not as kindly as you did. I thought he was an asshole from start to finish."

"Thanks, Tim. Roger that!" replied a smiling Tolbane as the captain took a bottle of Beam's Choice, a good sipping bourbon, and two glasses from his bottom desk drawer and poured a good two fingers in each glass.

The two clinked glasses and had a quick nip, and then they went about their business after Tolbane convinced the captain to look into promotions for his troopers. Tolbane had one thing in his mind, though. He needed to find out how to contact Phuoc ASAP, and it should be sooner than later. He decided to call the G-2 chief to see if he knew where she was staying. The chief did.

He called the base's female marines' quarters and left a message for her to meet him as soon as possible at the main PX. He checked out and went to mainside to the main PX as quick as the traffic would let him drive.

By the time Tolbane had driven to mainside and had made the long drive from the main gate to the main PX, Phuoc was waiting for him in front of the facility. She was wearing her female marine uniform and her captain's bars. Approaching, Tolbane saluted her, and she returned it. Then in a low voice, he spoke quietly.

"We need to talk, Captain, like, right now. Let's go over to my car. It will be more private."

They moseyed slowly to his 1964 Chevy, the one that never made it to the levy when the levy was dry. Once they were both seated and comfortable in the vehicle, Tolbane turned to her.

"Phuoc, do you know an asshole NIS agent named Bill Moyer?"

"Do I know him? I sure do! He's a regular pain in the ass—my ass, in particular—a real fucking dud. Why do you want to know?"

"I walked into our team office today to see the captain about getting some of my subteam members promoted, and the creep was in there, waiting to pounce on me."

"You got the creep part right. He gives me the chills just thinking about the fool. What was he sticking his nose into this time?"

"First, he asked the captain if he knew you. Of course, the skipper doesn't. Then when I got there, he wanted to know if I knew you by either of your names. He knew the name you used in the operation we were involved in, in the Nam. I asked why he wanted to know. He became a little demanding. I let him know he doesn't have a high enough security clearance or the need-to-know and that he could fuck off. He did. He stomped out at quick time, all pissed off to the brim, but not like Maxwell House coffee."

She laughed.

"That's one thing I like about you, Travis, straight and to the point. Good for you. That guy is a pain in the ass."

"Mind telling me why he's such a pain?"

"It started long before I went to duty in Viet Nam with his professional jealousy. Then it turned from jealousy into a real obsession for him. We were both being considered for not only a certain covert operation position but for promotion to captain too with only one slot available in NIS. He didn't get either one, because he would stab anyone he could in the back or elsewhere just to get what he wanted, just to further his own career.

"He keeps digging into my past assignments to find some dirt I'm involved with so as to take me down and, in his mind, get his just deserts: the coveted position and a promotion. Since you evidently pissed him off today, we'll both have to watch our backs for an incoming knife. He'll be investigating you now too. He is one sneaky bastard."

"I got that sneaky impression about him too. I also thought he had a broomstick up his butt. I felt like twisting it a little while and jamming it up a bit further. I've met a few asses like him before. Damn shame they exist at all."

Laughing once again, she replied, "That's him all right. I need to do some checking on this crap. Come to think of it, how the blazes does he know what name I used in that Viet Nam sting operation? That's highly classified information. The other two guys were never told what I revealed to you there."

Tolbane spoke up.

"I'm going to change the subject right now, as we can think on this situation later. My question is, is it permissible for a captain in the United States Marine Corps to have her gunnery sergeant aide with her when she goes from here to a nice steak house, leaving the gunny to pay the bill?"

"Damn right it is, Gunny."

She chortled.

"I thought you'd never ask."

And away they went. The steaks, wine, dessert, coffee, and intimate conversation were great. Tolbane's only complaint was, there

82

was no bacon to be served. He was hoping Phuoc would be served on a mattress later that night.

Later on that night, Tolbane entered the staff NCO quarters, bent on getting some sleep. In the little reception area, a tall gentleman in a sharp, well-tailored blue suit with a matching tie complementing the yellow dress shirt he was wearing was waiting for Tolbane's return. He introduced himself as the local NIS agent in charge, named just Cramer. They shook hands.

"Gunny, if you don't mind, can we go over to the SNCO Club? Walls are notorious for having ears."

They left the quarters and walked to the club, talking about the weather and nothing important. As soon as they were seated at a far table with a bottle of Bud in each hand, the agent in charge began.

"Gunny, let me be clear about this situation. I know everything about you and Captain Phuoc in Viet Nam. Phuoc let me know all about it when she was chosen for the upcoming operation, except I don't know what the mission in Nam was. I don't care what it was. I don't even want to know about it period. As far as I'm concerned, whatever happened in Viet Nam, no matter what it was, stays in Viet Nam forever. War changes a lot of things on-site, especially military regulations relating to certain covert operations."

"I appreciate that, Cramer. The last thing I'd ever want to do is to hurt Captain Phuoc in any manner. She's one terrific marine. Right now, I'm concerned about one of your agents—one asshole clown named Moyer, to be exact."

"That's exactly why I'm here, Gunny. Phuoc is one of our best NIS agents when it comes to overt and covert operations. Sometimes, she's a little unorthodox, but she gets great results. Right now, I'm concerned about how some idiot found out what name she used on a covert operation in Viet Nam. Even in my position, I can't access it. All of that info should have been closed off to any and all inquiries due to its classification.

"Someone has breached confidentiality and compromised the mission information. Someone may get off the hook for some serious charges as a result of the mission if the leak has not been found and eliminated. I can assure you that I will find out how that idiot Moyer has learned her identity there and how much more about the mission he knows. His ass is grass when I find out."

"I understand, Cramer. Mow over his grass ass with a dull-bladed lawn mower. When he asked me about knowing her by both names, a red flag went up, and it pissed me off. I damn sure wasn't going to tell him crap. I even felt good when I told him to fuck off. He wasn't happy about it. Even threatened me. I threatened him back."

"I bet you did. He came to me and said you weren't cooperating with a classified operation and wanted to have you taken into custody until you decided to cooperate. I told him I'd check into a warrant. He didn't know it, but I already knew there had been a compromise but was unaware of what he was into until Captain Phuoc called me from the restroom while she and her gunnery sergeant aide were having medium-well steaks.

"I've already talked to your team commander about the situation. He was proud of your reaction to the clown. We'll keep this quiet. You two won't have to worry about it. Moyer doesn't know about your upcoming deployment as far as I know so you will not be bothered by him ever.

"He'll just have to boil inside trying to find you two. No one knows a thing as far as he's concerned. He'll be banging his head against a brick wall. I'll bet you two to one he'll try to nail you two as AWOLs. He was chomping at the bit and wanted a piece of your assess big-time."

"No bet on that one. It wouldn't surprise me either. He seems like a very vindictive asshole, not to be trusted. By the way, will Captain Phuoc and I be allowed to talk about this development while we're deployed?"

"You bet, as much as you want. I'm tired of his sorry ass too. Hopefully, you two will learn more about the situation when you return. Good luck on your new operation and its success. I'll be looking forward to your safe return. See you later, Gunny."

Then Cramer was up and gone in the blink of an eye. Tolbane was caught off guard by the agent's rapid departure. He didn't get a chance to say thanks. Thinking about everyone wishing them a safe return, he wondered what the hell they knew about the operation that he and Phuoc didn't. It made one wonder what kind of crap lay before them.

CHAPTER 13

Tolbane and his subteam met at 0530 hours at the team headquarters.

His comments at the time were, "We'll go to the mess hall for chow, meet back here no later than 0630 hours, and pack our gear in the team's three-fourth-ton pickup. A member of the Fourth ITT will be driving to MCAS Cherry Point for our airlift. Let's hit it, guys!"

They were on their way to Cherry Point by 0700. Forty-five minutes later, they were checking into the terminal. A lady, a Spanish interpreter named Phuoc, was waiting for them and introduced herself to all, as the two newly promoted lance corporals had no idea who she really was. At five minutes to 0900, they were loaded aboard and airborne minutes later in a four-engine C-130 transport plane, headed toward Guantánamo Bay, Cuba.

The flight was like a local. It made a couple of stops before reaching its destination. Sitting in the plane at the stops with the cargo ramp down, it was hot as hell and uncomfortable, whereas it was cold as hell while in the air. All five of them were glad to deplane and stretch their legs after sitting in those fold-up bench seats made of interwoven cloth.

The team, upon debarking the plane, was met by a Colonel Radcliff, the Sixth Marine Expeditionary Brigade commander. He personally shook hands and introduced himself to each one of them and bade them a semper fi welcome to the Sixth MEB. The colonel waited patiently for them to retrieve their gear from the aircraft and led them to a waiting deuce and a half truck and waited patiently until they and their gear were aboard the cargo area with the sides up. The colonel climbed into the passenger seat, and they were off to the unit's headquarters and billeting area, a regular tent city.

The colonel mustered them into his small office like a can of sardines and briefed them, but not before he offered coffee and cookies. The lance corporals still had no idea what was going on.

The colonel began.

"I'll be taking you over to our MEB G-2 office momentarily. They are expecting you. However, as you already know, they think you are with us for a training exercise for your MOS. They know nothing more about the situation than that. Before you deploy from us, you will be briefed by pertinent individuals on the operation. I do not know what you will be doing on your mission once you leave us, only that I wish you success in whatever your endeavor might be.

"All I know is that it must be pretty important to be so hush-hush. Just remember to reply to people that might ask that you are playing aggressor and good guy for your quarterly interrogation training. Please finish all those chocolate chip cookies so I won't be tempted. I need to go out and see one of the admin clerks for a minute. Indulge yourselves. Please."

Before the lance corporals could ask, Tolbane spoke up.

"Don't even ask questions right now, troops. I'll let you know what's happening tonight when we have a subteam meeting. You've been kept in the dark for good reason."

The colonel returned with a Corporal Boreman, an admin clerk, and introduced them.

"The corporal will take you to your billet, let you stow your gear, and then will take you to the MEB G-2. Good luck, marines. You too, Ms. Interpreter."

They left with the corporal driving the truck and were taken to their quarters, where they stowed their gear in a GP tent. Then they walked back to the headquarters area, where they were guided to the G-2 office. The corporal left them there. The G-2 officer wasn't in, but they were greeted by a Major Hernandez.

They all shook hands, and Phuoc went one step further. She greeted the major in perfect Spanish. He thought she must be Cuban. After a few minutes of small talk, the major asked the now sergeant Bracken to take the interpreter and the other two back to their quarters.

After the troops were gone, the major addressed Tolbane.

"Gunny, the colonel regretted he couldn't be here to greet you. He was called back to Camp Lejeune for some kind of a staff meeting and won't be back for a couple of days. I've been asked to make you and your team comfortable and help with anything you need. I must admit, I was surprised when I learned that the Corps was giving some on-the-job training to its ITTs.

"Our task force will debark the day after tomorrow around 0800 hours, as our training cycle here is completed by noon tomorrow. As I understand it, you and your subteam will receive a mission briefing tomorrow in the afternoon. By whom and where it will be held, I have no earthly idea. I can only assume that you will be notified in a timely manner of time and place. Otherwise, the colonel and I are completely in the dark on this. That's all I have to offer you at this time. I wish you and your subteam a successful training exercise."

Tolbane thanked the major and wandered back to the tent area with Phuoc after finding out from one of the G-2 clerks where the mess tent was. He informed the team about what the major had to say and added his own thoughts.

"I believe he's not comfortable not knowing why we're here. He's the type who'll have and keep his secrets but gets upset when someone else has a secret he doesn't know about and can't find out. Ms. Phuoc, will you please step outside with me for a moment?

"Phuoc, we'll get our final briefing tomorrow afternoon, the time and place to be announced. When I brief the subteam tonight, mostly for the benefit of the lance corporals, do I tell them anything about who you are and why you are with us? With everyone wishing us a successful mission and safe return, I'm not sure what we're walking into. I'd hate to see anything happen to those guys, them not knowing the status quo."

"Travis, think of it this way. They each have an interim top-secret security clearance, and they will be performing with us regardless of what happens. I, too, think they should know what's what. Tell them, but remind them of keeping everything secret about me. There is only one thing that should be held back: that I'm a woman marine and an officer. Knowing I'm NIS is no problem, and I'm only here as an interpreter, as the subteam has no Spanish interpreters from the Sixth ITT."

"One other thing. I didn't know you spoke Spanish, and like a native no less."

"My man Travis, there is a lot you don't know about me yet. So for now, please just live with and learn a little bit about me a little at a time. You will not regret it at all, I promise! Well, Travis, my stomach is growling big-time, big boy. I know yours is too, and I hope you know where the mess tent is. Let's get the others in formation and go.

"Oh, before that! Before I forget to tell you, if you should in any way get a chance to whisper sweet nothings in my ear while we're deployed, please call me Em.[8] That's a little more intimate for us."

Tolbane leaned over and said, "Em."

Then he stuck his tongue in her ear. Laughing her butt off, she pulled away, a chill running up her spine, and gave Tolbane a light slap on his cheek. Then they gathered the crew and made for the mess tent.

At 1630 hours, Tolbane finally addressed the group.

"First off, I apologize to you two, lance corporals. Sergeant Bracken and I attended a briefing where we met our interpreter, Ms. Phuoc, and were given a mission and instructions not to discuss this mission with anyone at that time. As long as you are in the intelligence field, there will always be things you will not be informed about or things you participate in that you cannot talk about.

"And to further your knowledge, neither Ms. Phuoc nor I have any idea as to what this mission entails right now, how it may come out, only that it's important and maybe a little dangerous. We will get a briefing on it sometime tomorrow afternoon. You will then know exactly what we know at that time. We sail the morning after that. I must remind you that this mission is classified, top-secret. You will only discuss it among us five and never ever to anyone else. Is that clear?"

He got yeses.

---

[8] *Em* is a collective Vietnamese term for daughter or a young single lady and is also a term of endearment.

"Secondly, I was just informed by her that I could tell you that Ms. Phuoc, while being our interpreter, is also an agent with NIS, the Naval Investigative Service.[9] Our team has no Spanish linguists, so she is on lend to us as an interpreter. At this point, she is not aware of what we will be doing either, so please don't feel all alone and left out.

"No matter what, we are a team together, and we will work together like the team we are. We will have each other's backs at all times, do or die. Semper fi, motherfuckers. I've been there myself, so I know you might not like what you're asked to do at any time. So for the sake of all our lives and the mission's success, please do it without question. You can question things when we are back in a safe area. Any questions here and now?"

There were none, and the meeting was concluded. They made their way to chow.

*****

That evening, an armorer came to their tent to check their weapons. He detail-stripped the two lance corporals' M14s, making sure they were serviceable. He checked the 1911 .45s of the other three. He then issued M14s to Tolbane, Phuoc, and Bracken. He gave each five twenty-round loaded magazines and a bandoleer of ammo to each for the M14s. The three with the .45s received three loaded magazines and one in weapon for their handguns.

He instructed them to keep the magazines and bandoleers hidden in their gear until they were in their amtrac's cargo area a couple of days hence and away from the ship. Then they were to lock and load their weapons, unlocking only when the ramp went down on their amtrac. The team thanked him, and he was gone.

This was one more thing of concern for Tolbane, the lock and load. This operation felt shittier each time he thought about it. The good Lord up above was probably the only one who really knew what was going on.

---

[9]   NIS is NCIS today.

Tolbane didn't sleep well that night. He woke from bad dreams on three occasions. In the dreams, the whole subteam was wiped out by Hispanic belligerents, along with Phuoc. He hoped this was not an omen of what was to be.

CHAPTER 14

The Sixth MEB's task force had been at sea for three and a half days. No one except the big wheels upstairs knew where they were or what they were there for. At evening chow time, Tolbane and his subteam were taken to a small dining room in the officers' mess, where they were met by the task force commander, ADM Jake Coventry, and the MEB commander. The admiral was tall, slim, and gray-haired and seemed to have a great disposition.

After each team member was seated at the fabulous table setting, the admiral spoke.

"It has been a tradition to feed the troops a steak meal before debarking on an amphibious assault. We are serving you here with me tonight not only a traditional predeployment steak dinner but with all the trimmings. I am glad to say, you won't be debarking on an amphibious assault or sailing into hell. I don't know where you're sailing to, only that someone with the Sixth MEB knows, I hope, but I wish you all luck.

"I have to admit that I was taken aback when I was informed that I would have an elite interrogation team aboard for, for lack of better words, a secret mission. We have accommodated SEAL teams in the past but never an interrogation subteam such as you all. I know you are curious, but I can tell you that sometime tonight, you will go down the cargo net into an awaiting amtrac. Usually, you have to change ships to board one. Tonight will be a first, and to do it at night is mind-boggling. I think you'll do fine, though."

The two lance corporals looked a little green in the face.

"Under the circumstances, I thought, rather than you having a send-off meal in the mess hall later, I would have you here to wish you fair winds and following seas. You two younger marines, feel free to ask me questions or give me sea stories. I know the others won't hesitate to do so.

"As for chow—that's what you call it in the Corps. We call it mess in the Navy. Sometimes, the crew thinks it's a mess. My own personal chef will prepare whatever kind of steak you'd like and how you'd like it cooked. A waiter will be here in a moment to pour water and fill your wineglasses and take your steak orders.

"Besides the steak, there will be garlic mashed potatoes, a rich and thick brown gravy, buttered peas, buttered corn, garlic bread, and a tossed ship's salad. Our intelligence sources tell us that you, Gunny, like gobs of honey mustard for your salad. We have gobs of it and also an order of bacon to go with it. My chef told me that even though I run the ship, the dessert was top-secret, and I didn't have a need-to-know basis of what kind of concoction it is."

The waiter appeared and began filling the water glasses and taking the steak orders. After the first wine pouring, a nice Riesling from the winery at the Vanderbilts' Biltmore estate, the admiral proposed the first of a few toasts of the evening.

"Here's to the United States Navy and Marine Corps, the finest air, sea, and ground forces the world has ever known!"

Tolbane and Phuoc answered with "Hear! Hear!" and the first glass was tasted. Tolbane then explained to his troopers about "Hear! Hear!" at toasting.

The meal was finished, the last toast was proposed, and the group was sated. The admiral shook each hand and wished them all fair winds and following seas. The team returned to their quarters and began to get their gear together and await the command to debark. Phuoc, who had been billeted in the woman officers' quarters without revealing her rank, was on edge as much as the rest of the team was. Eventually, all five drifted off to sleep.

*****

At 2300 hours, one of the master-at-arms woke the four, and a female third class woke Phuoc. The team mustered on deck by a railing that had a cargo net attached. They could hear the mummer of the amtrac's motor and its occasional bump into the ship's side. Tolbane was surprised when an unidentified marine captain appeared with two PFCs with M16s with the automatic selector switch, plenty of ammo, and full combat gear.

The captain stated, "I've been instructed to give you two of my men for your increased security. This is PFCs Johnson and McCormack. Have a good trip, and do us proud."

He was gone before anyone could say a word. Tolbane welcomed the two PFCs and once again warned his crew to gauge their drop into the amtrac as it hit its highest point and going down and not while it was coming up.

As he looked down at the craft, he noticed that an amtrac crewman was holding the net away from the ship and into the cargo hold for them. Tolbane then ordered them to saddle up and begin their descent, as each individual was ready. Eventually, all seven were safely aboard in the cargo hold. Then the overhead doors were closed, and the craft moved along, being mildly tossed by a slightly rolling sea.

Tolbane pointed out where the barf bags were. Bracken and the two younger marines had never been in an LVTP-5 amphibious tractor before. They looked the worse for wear during the ride but did not get seasick, though they would have felt better if they did. Two and a half hours later, the team could feel it when the tractor entered surf, and it hit the slope of the land and moved up the gradient leading onto the back beach and a small open area for embarking/debarking.

When the tractor stopped and the rear ramp was lowered, the team left the sterile white of the cargo hold and moved into the moonlight. A sergeant, the crew chief, came around and met them and spoke.

"Hope you all had a great trip in our classic P5 limo."

He laughed. Then he gave Tolbane and Bracken each a small laminated sketch map showing mostly trails, a directional north arrow, and an arbitrary grid. He informed them that this was the twenty-second day of the month, and he would be back at this same time on the twenty-fifth of the month. He would then wait for two hours. If they weren't back by then, he had orders to leave and return to the ship without them, and they would be on their own.

His driver appeared just then and gave one of the lance corporals an AN/PRC-25 radio, known as the Prick 25.

"This radio is my idea. You can use this if you are close to us and time is running short. If you're a long way off, we'll have to leave, as directed. Call signs. I'm Red Dog Alpha, and you're Red Dog Bravo."

"Sergeant," Tolbane answered, "we understand completely. We'll do what we are ordered to do, and you follow your orders to the letter. I don't want to put you guys in any harm's way. We could be in real deep doo-doo before you return."

The crewmen climbed back into the tractor, put the ramp up, and disappeared into the sea.

Tolbane looked at his team and said, "It's a fine mess you got us into now, Stanley."

After the blank looks he saw in front of him, he had to explain Laurel and Hardy to his brethren. He and Bracken took out their flashlights with the red filters and their compasses and oriented their maps. They worked out which paths to take to get to the X on the maps and their rendezvous.

Tolbane looked at McCormack and Johnson and asked, "Either of you two ever walked point?"

"I have, Gunny!" Johnson said. "In fact, I even like it."

"Good."

Tolbane looked at the rest of the team.

"Okay, Johnson will walk point for us and set the pace. Sarge, I want you next in line with your map handy to help the point man." He pointed at the lance corporal without the radio and said, "You're next, and you need to watch both flanks as much as possible. Then Ms. Phuoc, me, and you other two bring up the rear. If we come under fire, you two will move up to assist. Everybody clear on our order of march?"

"Yes!"

"Good. Point man, look over the map with Sergeant Bracken, and when you two are ready, we make like we are going up a yellow brick road, without our arms linked and skipping. But we do have brains, a heart, and courage."

Five minutes later, they were moving along on the trail at a pace similar to what a grunt unit would use. The flora was near junglelike. However, the trail seemed to be much used until they had to branch off into a narrower one, one that was not as well-traveled. It was hot and sultry, and after about forty-five minutes, Tolbane called a halt when they came across a very small clearing. He set up his security, and they sat or lay down to rest for a few minutes.

When they were ready to continue, Phuoc whispered something in his ear, and Tolbane passed that bit of information to the group.

"The people we are to meet will make contact with us somewhere along this trail. We have a code for them to ID themselves to us. If you hear someone call out Ina-gadda-di-vida, that's our contact. Don't shoot."

Once more, they were on the march. Half an hour later, they heard a voice with a heavy Hispanic accent hollering, "Hey there, jankies! In-a-gadda-da-vida, baby! You know I love jou!"

Tolbane responded with the countersign.

"Born to be wild."

Tolbane wondered which stupid ass came up with this sign and countersign. Then a weird-looking Hispanic guy with a big grin and a long, drooping black mustache down each side of his mouth came out of the brush.

"Jou made good time. Jou got here early."

He moved to Tolbane, grasped his hand, and shook it.

"I was told the tall man would be in charge, no? I am Pedro. Not my real name, of course, but you can call me Pedro."

"Glad to meet you, Pedro. We were a little worried about getting lost around here. It's a load off our minds," Tolbane lied. "I'm Tolbane. This is our interpreter, Phuoc. Have you been waiting here for us very long?"

"No. I follow jou from the clearing where jou rested. Jou guys move really good, real quiet, and fast. Jou protect jourselves pretty well too. My yob was to find you and make sure jou got to the meeting place safely."

"Thank you, Pedro! We are glad you were looking out for us. We're ready to go whenever you are."

Pedro turned, waved, and moved into the brush; and the team followed. In ten minutes, they were at a campsite with four American general purpose tents. Pedro showed them to a large tent and told them to rest there.

"Jour man will not be here for a few more hours. We have guards out, so jou guys can relax."

He pointed to the tent entrance, and he left. The tent had ten cots, so there was no problem finding a place to crap out. Having been up most of the night, they all fell asleep.

*****

When they awoke some hours later, the sun was up, and they were hungry.

Pedro saw them exit the tent as a group, approached them, and offered, "We got coffee and boiled rice yust waiting for jou. Help jourself. Boss be along shortly."

The team all thanked him and made their way to a campfire. They grabbed cups, bowls, and a spoon-like thing; got coffee and rice; and returned to their tent. After Tolbane and the others ate, finished, and drank the overly strong coffee, Tolbane gathered his lance corporals and PFCs.

"Look, guys, we don't know what the hell we're into here. It just doesn't seem right to me. I want two teams, each with one lance corporal and one PFC. You guys decide who's with who on your own and create some kind of schedule. Hang around the camp guards, and if you can, try to learn what you can from them. The sarge or I will wander around and check on you periodically. If you learn anything important, let us know without alarming these guys. We'll lock and load, then go on out and figure a game plan.

"The troops are going to set their guard," he explained to the others. "For some reason, I'm not a fan of Pedro. He seems too good to be true. We need to be vigilant. Phuoc, I've been thinking. What do you say about a disgruntled female interpreter that's not happy about being here but had no choice in the matter at hand?"

"GySgt. Travis Tolbane, why did you drag me here, you Gila monster?"

Phuoc was even able to get watery eyes.

"How's that, Travis? Does it float your boat?"

"I've said it before, and I'll say it again, Phuoc. You're something else. Your boat floats really well with me."

Looking at Bracken, Tolbane said, "Do you believe this shit, Sarge?"

"Gunny, I got no choice but to believe this shit. Phuoc, you're really good at it."

"Ta-ta! Guys, see you in a bit."

And she left the tent with a wiggle of her butt.

"Sergeant, there is only one way to while away the time for us. It's been Marine Corps tried, tested, and approved since Tun Tavern. We just crap out on our cots and crash big-time."

They both did exactly that.

*****

About an hour and a half later, Phuoc came in the tent, excited. "Hey, guys."

She woke the two up.

"There are people coming into camp. Looks like a really big American—bigger than you, Travis—two armed guards, and a prisoner, hands bound behind him with a blindfold, a gag, and a rope leash around his neck."

The three left the tent and went out to where the campfire was laid out. The American was removing the blindfold and gag from the man and sat the man on the ground. Then he looked up and saw the three. The man, maybe two inches taller and broader-shouldered than Tolbane, glanced directly at the three.

"Well, well, what have we here?" the American said in a booming voice. "Is it a welcoming committee just for me that I see? I'm Lucious Dupont, adventurer par excellent or whatever you'd like to call me. To whom do I have this distinct pleasure?"

"I'm GySgt. Travis Tolbane, United States Marine Corps. I'm glad to make your acquaintance, Lucious. This is Sergeant Bracken, my next in command, and last but not least, my lovely interpreter, Ms. Phuoc. I presume you are the one we are to meet here. If not, take a fucking hike!"

Laughing, the big man said, "I thought the code was, 'Dr. Livingston, I presume?' Seriously, you have presumed correctly. I need not take a hike. I think we'll get along."

He looked at his two guards, told them to keep an eye on the prisoner, and motioned to the two marines.

"Leave your interpreter here, and let's go to your tent."

"I'm sorry. My interpreter goes with me wherever I go."

"Fine. I won't quiver over the small stuff."

Tolbane led the way. Inside the tent, Tolbane and Phuoc sat on one cot facing the other two on the next cot.

Dupont began.

"I need to know right off the bat, do you have any instructions about taking me back with you? I rather hope so. My name has become mud in certain circles here, and there are those looking to cook my goose in hot oil."

"My instructions are to do just that and also bring the prisoner along, if the situation allows for it."

Speaking in a more natural voice now, Dupont began.

"Good deal. I've been undercover here for several months with a bunch of cockeyed outlaws and terrorists or what have you, far too long. I'm tired and exhausted. There are a bunch of bad dudes looking for me and the prisoner back up the trail right now. They'll most likely be here sometime in the morning. My guards I can trust right now, because they have not been made aware of my situation and have no idea we're being pursued or why. I don't think the ones in this camp know about it yet either. I've got very little time on my side, and I'm not ready for a pine box yet."

"Look," Tolbane said, "just what the hell is going on here? We don't even know what country we are in or what danger may be imminent for us, and exactly what information are we supposed to elicit from the prisoner? Seems as though the list of promised questions was never given to us. We know jack shit about this operation, because it's been draped in secrecy from day one. If you want to get out of here with us, I suggest you come clean, or you can stay here and take your chances."

"The information this guy was supposed to have was to be vital to some of our operations going on in South American countries. Supposedly, this guy was some grand pooh-bah in operations run from Cuba and was on a visit here to get orders for a big op. The idea of the mission was that you people would interrogate him for any information of immediate nature and bring us both out.

"Well, wouldn't you know it? It was a counter operation against me. I had no idea they were on to me. This guy doesn't know did-dly-squat. He's a useless plant. He's still playing the big man part, though. He may be useful for some background information, but tactically, that's a big no-no! There is that part of it."

"What's the other part of it?" Bracken asked. "Oops, Gunny, I wasn't thinking."

"Hey, knock it off, Sarge. You were in the right asking the question. You're part of this lash-up too and second man on the totem pole. Something happens to me, you're it, my friend. This is a kind of round table for us. Remember, the worst question is the one not asked. Feel free to ask questions if you feel the need anytime. It could save our bacon. You never know."

Tolbane had set Bracken's mind at ease. Then Dupont began again.

"I've got to level with you, Gunny. If they catch me, I'll be tortured like no man has been before. I'd hold out as long as I could, but I could hurt a lot of our operations and agents. If they should make contact with us, don't let them take me prisoner. Shoot me in the head if you have to. I beg of you."

Tolbane was quick at the last comment.

"Look, we're going to get your ass out of here, along with ours, no matter what. Put that in your fucking pipe and smoke it. What gives with this Pedro character?"

"He'll be all right until he hears about me. Then he'll be dangerous."

Tolbane looked at Phuoc.

"You find out anything from those dudes out there?"

"A little. Like me, as I told them, they weren't really happy about being here. They would rather be in some cantina, drinking rum, dancing, and fondling the women there. They don't seem to know the why or wherefore of themselves or us being here. As long as they are not told differently, they'll protect us."

"Dupont, as far as the guards here know, Ms. Phuoc, my interpreter here, is disgruntled and regrets being here. However, she is loyal to me and completely trustworthy, but I can't tell you how I know her loyalty. Do you know anything at all about this area, like a place for us to hide out for around twenty-four hours?"

"I've been through here a time or two, but I'm not very sure."

"Sarge, show him your map."

Bracken handed it to him.

"If we could sneak out of here in the middle of the night and hide, we might just be okay."

"I see one place we might hide out, but Pedro knows this area like the back of his hand and could find us easily. Then, Katy, bar the door."

"There are seven of us. You and your two guards make ten. We'll make that turd prisoner of yours fight too if necessary. That makes eleven of us. We can set up a defensive perimeter with no problem. Could we move out of that area under fire to get to our rendezvous in the dark? Look at the map again. We need to formulate a plan."

"I don't know for sure. We'd have to hack through all that brush and growths."

"Crap. We need something better than that. Everybody, think on it."

They all sat there thinking for about ten minutes. Then Sergeant Bracken spoke up.

"We might be thinking of a place too far from the pickup spot. We got a radio to the LVTP-5, right? It's got a Ma Deuce in that turret. If we set on the other side of the pickup site and we're taking fire, we call the P5 and have them land, turn right, and let Ma Deuce spray a bit while we load through the back ramp and hightail it."

"Damn, Sergeant Bracken," Tolbane interjected, "we need to promote you to General Okay instead of General Screwup. I think we can refine that a bit. Phuoc and Lucious, what do you think of our boy wonder's suggestion? I think it's great."

The two agreed with him.

"Okay, let's check the map again. We may just have a winner here."

After checking the map again, they decided to set up adjacent to the pickup point. Next, they checked the C rations in their packs, then made it a point to make sure they refilled their canteens and picked up any other foodstuff or article they could use on the QT. Next, they needed to find a way to get past the guards.

Tolbane sent Sergeant Bracken out quietly to inform the other four of their plans. Now the next step was to make it seem like they were performing their duty. They set up an area behind their tent to feign an interrogation of the prisoner. Tolbane, Phuoc, and Bracken took turns questioning the dude for about five hours until the prisoner was exhausted from the constant harassing.

While the questioning was going on, Tolbane made sure his troops got some shut-eye. The rest took catnaps during the day. When they started out early the next morning, they needed to be as fresh as possible and able to move over the trails quickly and quietly.

During the day, Phuoc came up with a way to use a couple of the camp guards by letting them feel she needed to escape. They would help her if needed. When wandering around the compound, each one picked up anything they thought would be useful and filled their canteens.

After eating boiled chicken, bread, and rice for the evening meal, they sat around the fire and talked among themselves and Pedro. He was interested in what kind of information they had obtained from the prisoner. Phuoc told him in his language that it was mostly useless crap he gave out, and they would have to take him back to the States with them for some enhanced interrogation. Pedro agreed it was a good idea to take the prisoner with them.

Finally, at about 2100 hours, the team pretended to tire and retired to the tent. Tolbane set up a fire watch, two at a time for an hour. That way, they had a warning of anything changing, and those not standing it could get some shut-eye. At 0145 hours, Dupont woke his guards and got the prisoner ready. By then, everyone was awake and saddled up, and the order of march was set.

They moved silently to where the two guards closest to their trail were. Phuoc informed the guards that there had been a change of plans, and they were to escort them to the pickup point. She duped them really well, and they led the way.

Along the way, they set a false trail toward the clearing they had first considered. By 0420 hours, they were taking up positions about thirty feet on the other side of the pickup area. By now, Phuoc had performed more of her magic on all four guards. If they helped the teams' defense, they would take them back to the States with them, and they would receive a reward for their help. All four guards sucked it up. They now had a thirteen-man position in a semicircular defense. Tolbane set a guard schedule, and those not on guard could sleep.

*****

After sunrise, Tolbane stepped into the pickup area. He couldn't see any of their positions due to the foliage and bushes. *This is great*, he thought. It would be a short while before they would be missed. Pedro would be going nuts when he found out they and two of his guards were gone.

Hopefully, the bunch looking for Dupont and their men would show up before Pedro launched a search party. Maybe they would eat before beginning the search. Tolbane and the rest felt that after following the false trail they had laid, the Hispanics would not be sure of just where the subteam was positioned; and hopefully, they would just set up an ambush close to the pickup area to get them before they arrived and could get to the LVTP-5.

The whole group was in good spirits as they lay around talking softly or napping.

CHAPTER 15

As the sun came up and moved across the sky, it became hot and muggy in the team's positions. At least with the kind of flora they were in, the sun didn't hit them directly. Just before noon, the search party reached the clearing where the LVTP-5 would come the next morning. There was a lot of jabbering and pointing around the area going on between Pedro and some other dude. Tolbane hoped Phuoc could understand them.

The search party then turned and faded back into the jungle-like area. So far, that group was acting the way Tolbane hoped they would. He could hear them setting up their positions. They were really noisy in doing it. Finally, they seemed to have settled into their positions, and it got very quiet.

Phuoc crawled up to Tolbane and told him what was being said. Pedro and the other guy both wanted to be in charge, and Pedro lost. He wanted to press forward, but the other guy did not. He wanted to set a trap. Phuoc then crawled to each position, except the guards who spoke the language, and let each know exactly what had just happened. Then she made sure she warned everyone to be silent.

Tolbane made sure at lunchtime that some of the C rations were given to the guards with the tactical can openers. The guards had seen these openers before; they fared well with them. The worst part was eating the rations cold. Time dragged on, and the team got more miserable as the day got longer. Lying in one spot and only being able to squirm a little at a time sucked.

The sun was setting finally, and some of the mugginess eased up. When night finally came, the team felt a relief from some of the heat. They were hoping it might get a little cool or breezy out, but it didn't happen.

Before it was completely dark, Lance Corporal Carter, their radioman, had made a little path behind their position to a spot where he could whisper on the radio without the other side hearing him. Tolbane had instructed him what to say. When they heard the P5 moving up the beach, they would do what the army units did at night: have a mad minute.

They would open fire into the area where the bad guys were. When the P5 arrived, it would turn, drop the rear ramp, and spray the bad guys' area with its .50 while the team rushed to the ramp, firing all the way. When the last one entered the cargo hold, it would up-ramp, keep the Ma Deuce talking, and back the hell out of there and sail away.

When the P5 could be heard in the surf, Carter crawled to his spot and radioed the LVTP-5, giving Tolbane's instructions. As the P5 moved close to the small clearing, a couple of the bad guys opened fire prematurely, so Tolbane did his best imitation of a marine firing line at a rifle range.

"Ready on the right. Ready on the left. Unlock. Targets."

The team began firing as quickly as possible every round they could. They heard screams coming from the search party. The P5 moved into the requested position, and the Ma Deuce began to wreak havoc on the bad guys, eliciting more screaming.

Several of the search party began firing at the team. Tolbane heard a couple of screams, and then they were running for their lives to the P5's rear and up the ramp. The ramp came up, and the P5 went into reverse, but the Ma Deuce kept firing. The P5 did a turn, its passengers getting bumped around. Then they were in the surf and moving out to sea.

Tolbane took a head count. All were present and accounted for. However, one of the guards had caught a round in the leg, just missing the femoral artery, Carter had a right shoulder wound, and Johnson had been grazed in the side. They broke out the personal first aid kits each had on their cartridge belts and tended the wounded. When the wounds were taken care of, Tolbane addressed the team.

"I want to thank you all for the job you've done, especially the guards and the prisoner. I'm proud to have led you."

Phuoc translated for him.

"I never doubted you guys for an instant. Together, we out-thought, outsmarted, and outfought the enemy. That's what we do as marines, and you guys were terrific at doing it. Now I'm going to shut up and see if I can get some shut-eye in this bouncing behemoth."

He got a round of applause as he sat back on the bench and closed his eyes, his body and everyone else's moving with the gentle rolling up and down, side to side, of the LVTP-5 with the oceans swells.

*****

By the second day back aboard the command ship, the wounds had been treated, and Tolbane and his team were finally done with debriefings. Tolbane was lying on his fold-up bunk, sound asleep, when Dupont came up and jostled him.

"Wake up, you sleepy-headed jarhead."

He waited till Tolbane seemed to be conscious and shaking his head. He took Tolbane's hand and shook it.

"I still can't thank you and your crew for saving my ass. Yes, I know, it was just part of the mission. Let's face it, the mission could really have gone to shit without you and your good team. I was amazed that you delegated things to your troops, and they performed admirably.

"My name is not really Dupont. However, you can still call me Lucious. I can't tell you much, but I was deeper into things than what I told you, and the information I have is vital to things I cannot talk about with you. You weren't told, but the mission was really to get me out of that place period. During my limited debriefing, I offered some very good comments about you and your troops."

Just then, in marine utilities and the gold leaf ornaments of a Marine Corps major, Phuoc came into the crew area. Dupont couldn't take his eyes off her collars, and Tolbane was taken aback, jumping up at attention. Phuoc looked at him and commented with an old Corps adage.

"At ease, disease. There's malaria in the area. Guess what, guys? I got promoted this morning."

Both men congratulated her with a hug.

"Yes, Lucious, I was in charge of the operation. I trusted Travis because we had worked together in the past. Plus, he had experiences I had not yet encountered. He didn't disappoint me. I apologize, Travis. I did know a little more about the operation than you."

"I figured as much, and it didn't bother me in the least. I knew if I needed to know something, you would have told me. We're square."

Dupont commented more.

"Damn, Major, you had me fooled. I really thought you were an interpreter, and Tolbane was protecting you. You guys really work good together. Well, I have to get along for now. A copter will be here for me shortly, so thanks again. I'll see you two again the good Lord willing."

They shook hands, and he was gone. Tolbane started to reach for Phuoc's hand, but she pulled it back.

"Travis, be still a minute. I have some news for you and your crew. The two marine PFCs that was with you from the Sixth Marines will be promoted to lance corporal and get a medal. As far as your team, there will be five Armed Forces Expeditionary Medals, one Purple Heart, one Bronze Star, and five Navy and Marine Corps Medals for your crew, the Star for you. You now have two corporals and a staff sergeant on your crew, Master Sergeant Tolbane. That's how important this mission was. My congrats to you too!"

Tolbane couldn't believe his ears.

"Wow! Master sergeant? I don't know what to say. You did this for me and the team?"

"To be truthful, I was asked for input. It seems the powers that be wanted to offer something in appreciation for you guys. Since I had been told of my promotion, I felt you guys deserved one too. After all, you and the team made me look good. You guys will get your rewards at 0800 hours in the admiral's office in the morning."

She took Tolbane's hand in hers.

"Travis, I'm going to miss you after this. I'll have a different job now, so we may never see each other again. I have to admit, you've stolen this marine's heart."

"And you've definitely stolen mine," Travis replied. "No other woman has ever meant so much to me. I'll truly miss you."

They hugged.

"Master Sergeant Tolbane, attention! You will report to my quarters at 2000 hours this night for my nonjudicial punishment throughout the night. Is that clear, top?"

"Aye, aye, sir."

She pivoted and left the crew area. Tolbane watched her derriere with a feeling he could never remember having.

CHAPTER 16

At 0800 hours, Tolbane and his team were in the admiral's office. They received the appropriate documents, ribbons, medals, and metal and cloth chevrons from the marine liaison officer after the admiral performed the honors. After the honors and handshakes, the team left. The now Master Sergeant Tolbane walked Maj. Nguyen Thi Phuoc to the fantail area where the helicopter pad was located, and one was waiting for her.

"Travis, I wish I could take you with me. I'll never forget our adventures together, especially last night's nonjudicial punishment. You're quite a guy. I'll miss you day and night."

"And I'll miss you too, Phuoc, and not just the sex, which is marvelous. I wish we had more time together."

"Master Sergeant Tolbane, I know this is not appropriate for a major, but…"

She threw her arms around his neck and kissed him passionately on the lips, then broke away and ran to the chopper. They both had watery eyes.

*****

Tolbane had returned to his bunk in the crew quarters until he could compose himself. He was just getting ready to go address his team when a third class boatswain's mate came and informed him to grab his gear, as he was being moved into a room with a navy chief. Tolbane followed him to a two-man room. After the third class left, he stowed his gear and left to round up his team.

"Okay, guys, in my best John Wayne demeanor like good old John W. does. Anyhow, I need you to heed my words. I knew when

I asked the captain about getting promotions for you guys since we may be going on an operation that could be dangerous that there would be questions from your teammates and those on the Fourth and Sixth teams when we return. I was a little ahead of the game. The Sixth team is mostly Hispanic dialects. You'd think that, that team would have been selected. I know why ours was selected, but I cannot tell you. It's another secret.

"I think there will be more questions asked, what with your additional promotions. Remember, this operation is highly classified. Any questions that are asked of you about the operation, there is only one answer: 'I'm sorry, but you do not have the need-to-know.' Is that clear? As for your promotions, just say you heard the admiral wanted to do something to thank the subteam. It'll look good for him when he goes up for another star."

He received a "Yes, sir!" from each of the men.

"It won't be too hard for Staff Sergeant Bracken to fit into his promotion. However, you brand-new corporals have very little time in the Corps. You need to study and learn what you can about leadership and the responsibility of being an NCO. Read your *Guidebook for Marines*. Staff Sergeant Bracken and I will help. Anytime you have questions or need guidelines for your rank, just ask. Always remember, I quote once more, the dumbest question is the one not asked. Any questions?"

One new corporal spoke up.

"Top, we want to thank you for your coolness. The other guy and I were very apprehensive, some nerves, and never been on anything like we just did. It felt good that we had you in charge. We could have had some guy with a broom up his ass, but we had you. Your always being so cool and levelheaded allayed much of our fears. Your confidence in us to do the job made many fears go away too, especially when that first round was fired. I was chosen to thank you from us corporals. We'll go anywhere with you. Thanks once more, top."

Tolbane felt a tear trying to form in one eye.

"I thank you guys for not letting me down. Staff Sergeant, do you have anything to add?"

"I could only say what the corporal said. Thanks for being our leader. We didn't know much about you when you joined the team. We hoped you weren't another asshole, but you're number 1 asshole in our books now."

"Thanks to you all! There is one more pressing matter we must address for all new promotees. It is a Marine Corps tradition to have pinning on the stripes and have wetting down parties on promotion day. At the first opportunity when we get back, there will be one for Second ITT for us, I have deemed. We'll invite the Fourth and Sixth and have a big cookout—plenty of beer and sodas, hamburgers, hot dogs, baked beans, and potato salad.

"Since it's also tradition for the promotees to pay, we will all pay, only it will be prorated by rank so you corporals won't get stuck paying more than you can afford. I'll pay the largest share. Welcome to the history and traditions of the United States Marine Corps—not born on a mountaintop in Tennessee but in Tun Tavern in Philadelphia, Pennsylvania. Ooh-rah!"

A chorus of ooh-rahs followed.

"Is that all for now, top?" Staff Sergeant Bracken asked.

"Yes. You guys enjoy your all-expenses-paid Caribbean cruise for now. We dock at Gitmo tomorrow morning. See you then. Staff Sergeant Bracken, I need to see you for a minute."

When the others went on their way, Tolbane addressed Bracken.

"Welcome to the SNCO[10] ranks. First, you'll see more respect for your rank and different treatment from the higher- and lower-ranked members than you've had up to now. There could be some resentment by others to your rapid promotions. If you catch any flack, send them to me. I'll damn sure inform them what's what. Just be cool, relate to the troops on their level, and don't be an instant ass like some dudes.

"Number two, when we get back and unload and check in, we'll gather your gear, and I'll get you checked into the SNCO quarters mainside. You can ride with me to and from the team until you can

---

[10] Staff noncommissioned officer.

get your own ride. Then we'll go into town and celebrate. Is that clear?"

"You got it, top, especially the celebrating part."

*****

The ship dropped anchor just off the Cuban coast the next morning. Tolbane and his team were taken ashore in an LCVP.[11] After debarking and putting in a GP tent once more, they were informed that they would fly out to MCAS Cherry Point, North Carolina, at 1500 hours that very day. Then the flight was cancelled due to weather off the Carolinas. They got a good night's sleep.

They flew out at 0700 hours the next day. The flight was the same as always in a C-130 cargo plane, and finally, they reached touchdown, and all felt a release of tension to be back on US soil again. Captain Tyler, Second ITT commander, was waiting with a six-ton truck. He greeted them, and they loaded up and headed for Swamp Lejeune, North Carolina.

After checking the unloading, checking into the team, and getting welcome backs, they went their own way till 0800 the next morning. Tolbane was as good as his word. They collected Bracken's gear, and Tolbane got him checked into the SNCO's quarters in no time.

After they cleaned up and changed into civvies, they took off for J-Ville, the marines' name for Jacksonville, North Carolina. They went to the same bar Tolbane hit his first night and were not surprised to find MGySgt. Dick Head already there, clad in a T-shirt, jeans, and boots, partway into his cups. He saw the two and waved.

"Here's the wayward dudes. Back from an infamous operation, I presume?"

He signaled to the cute barmaid.

"Hey, you guys, grab a damn stool and fall on your asses and drink a few beers. And you, you newly promoted staff sergeant, can

---

[11] Landing craft vehicle personnel.

you guess who gets to pay? I'll give you four guesses, and the first five of them don't count."

He got off his stool, bear-hugged the newly promoted Staff Sergeant Bracken, and exclaimed, "Welcome back to the living, and I hope you have many successes as an SNCO! Congratulations are in order. Hey, barkeep, three Buds and a thing of popcorn for us, and charge this young dude."

Bracken had a shocked look on his face. Then Dick Head roared with laughter, and the regular patrons laughed with them.

"Tolbane, you got the next round. Then you two promotees alternate fucking paying."

*****

The next morning, Tolbane was early, already in the office at his desk when the captain came in.

"Congratulations on your promotion to master sergeant, top. That makes things a little easier for both of us right now. You do know that Dick Head's retiring soon, and you've got his slot. By the way, he won't be in today, maybe not even tomorrow. Seems he got pretty well-snockered downtown last night at some watering hole. You wouldn't know anything about that, would you, top? No, of course not.

"The other thing you need to know is that I received orders to FMFLANT at Norfolk, Virginia. I'll be leaving next Friday on leave. As far as I know, the new skipper for Second ITT will be arriving the following Monday. I have no idea what his qualifications are or who he is. All I know is, he's a captain.

"I'll sure miss this place for sure. I don't know anything about your recent mission or what happened on it, but the general now thinks that Second ITT walks on water. Whatever you guys did, it made him look good. Any questions?"

"None that I can think of. I do know one thing, skipper. The team will miss you, and we wish you the greatest success in your next endeavor in our ever-gloriest Marine Corps."

"Thanks, top. Right now, you need to get in your area and get the wetting down party arranged. Now scat."

"Yes, sir, on the double."

Tolbane was gone.

*****

The wetting down party had been a success. Dick Head, being so close to retiring, was seldom there, and Tolbane eased into the team chief slot. Captain Tyler left. The next Monday morning, the new team commander, Captain Holt, was in at 0800 on the button. He had checked in on Saturday and Sunday. He found MSgt. Travis Tolbane sitting at the team chief's desk and introduced himself.

"Top, this will be my first time being in an ITT. Don't really know what the hell it is. I got orders to Arabic language school, got promoted to captain there, and then orders to here. Three days from now, I'll be leaving for Fort Huachuca for some intelligence course. Believe me, right now, I'm at sea about any of this. Wednesday, I understand, a First Lieutenant Proust, a Viet Nam veteran, will be checking in. As far as I know, he'll be your team commander in my absence."

The captain walked behind the team commander's desk and sat down.

"I was told not to sweat the petty stuff, as you had everything under control. Glad to hear it. I need someone I can depend on. The next couple of days, I need you to clue me in as much as possible about this assignment. Wow, didn't mean to run off the head. I hope I won't be a pain in the ass."

"Skipper, I am a marine, and I have landed, and the situation is well in hand. Welcome aboard. You'll never be a pain in the ass to this team if you can relate to the troops. Right now, we have nothing pressing going on, so briefing you on who and what we are will be my utmost pleasure.

"First thing right now is to introduce you to the Second Interrogation Translation Team. If they pop to attention, tell them to carry on, as we are very informal here unless big brass visits us. Step right this way, sir, and enter our den of iniquity and see little Elmer shimmy and shake! She walks, and she talks, and she crawls on her belly like a reptile!"

"It's true what I was told about your sense of humor. That was a good one."

Introductions were made to the team members. Then Tolbane and the captain returned to their office. Captain Tyler left his bottle in the bottom drawer. A welcome drink was had.

"I won't discuss any classified info with you since it would most likely change and be useless to you by the time you return. I'd better ask, you do have a top-secret security clearance, don't you? I presume you do."

"I just received my secret clearance last month. For some friggin' unknown reason, the background investigation took a long time, so I only had an interim secret clearance till then. I guess they needed to find out if I was an enemy spy or something."

"I recommend you go up to the Second Force Troops G-2 in the morning and begin the process for an interim top-secret clearance. Do you have a copy of the paperwork you filled out for your secret?"

"Yes, I do. I try to keep copies of everything I do."

"Good, because you have to fill in the same information with absolutely no changes and then update it to the present. NIS is very picky about that stuff. Any change and you'll have to do the mile-long paperwork all over again. At the same time, ask one of the clerks to verify your clearance to me. Now let me screw up your head about ITTs. I presume you understand the term *interrogation*."

*****

First Lieutenant Monroe reported in finally, and the captain was gone to Fort Huachuca, Arizona, for school. Tolbane believed he would be comfortable with the lieutenant as acting team commander who had been on the Seventh ITT in Viet Nam. Sometimes, they would tell war stories or have a beer at noontime together at some sloop-shoot in J-Ville. Things were slow and undemanding at the team at the time, which pleased both of them to no end.

Then Tolbane received a new set of orders. He called Bracken into the office and broke the news. Tolbane began the conversation.

"When Staff Sergeant Daniels left the team, you became the man. Hate to break it to you, but you're about to become a bigger man."

"Holy batshit, bat top! Are you in one of your delirious trances again, top?"

"Heaven forbid, boy wonder! You are about to become—drumroll—a team chief."

"You're shitting me!"

"I wish I were, but you know the Corps. I just received orders to the—one more drumroll—Third MAF,[12] Republic of Viet Nam. Who would have thought that? What kind of billet will I be in? I have no earthly idea what it will be. I might even become one of the shit burners for a four-holer. Who knows? As far as I know about my replacement, there's none scheduled right now. How do I know I didn't have a brainstorm and called our MOS monitor in DC? So you got tagged. You're it for a while."

"Wow! I never expected that. I hate to see you go, but I don't know the first damn thing about being no team chief."

"Once again, grasshopper, you have the world's greatest ITT team chief ever to tutor you for your future endeavor. Seriously, Sarge, the time we've been together here has convinced me that you'll be good at the job. When it comes time to get that second rocker on your sleeve, it'll look good on your record. Some may think you're a slow thinker, but you're levelheaded and don't jump to conclusions without thinking things through, not like a lot of NCOs and SNCOs I've come across."

"Thanks for the compliment, top. I appreciate it. I'll have no choice but to work my butt off to be a better team chief than you."

"That's the right attitude. Don't forget, you already know a lot about our operations, having been there. Now go on back to your desk and cry for the next hour. Then we'll go have a beer down at the club."

---

[12] Marine amphibious force.

There was something Tolbane could not get off his mind. Then he had a sudden revelation. He had not heard anything from that NIS asshole. Great!

"You're on! Ta-ta!"

*****

The two had gotten comfortable at a table in the SNCO Club, a pitcher of beer on the table before them beside frosted glasses. They had been talking about intelligence. Bracken confessed to Tolbane that he didn't know what intelligence really was.

"My man, it's like the fisherman carrying a cooler of beer, a can of peas, and a ball bat to his dingy with a two-horse outboard. Once he motors out to his favorite fishing spot, he drops anchor. He gets comfortable. Then he pops a top on a can of beer, guzzles half of it. He then opens the can of peas and dumps them in the water. When a fish comes up to take a pea, he clubs it."

"Oh, crap, Guns. For a minute there, I thought you were going to explain something."

"I will. Everything that has any recorded information on it is a document. There is a thing called the intelligence cycle. First, it's decided what the commanders in the field need besides beans, bullets, and bandages. That's all of the available, processed information on the enemy, the weather, and the terrain. Follow me so far, grasshopper?"

"I'm with you."

"First, decide what information needs to be collected. Then the task is passed on to units, such as interrogation, recon, aerial recon, troops in the field, etc. Secondly, the information is collected. Then the information is processed through evaluation and interpretation into usable intelligence. Lastly and most importantly, it's disseminated with timeliness and propriety to the appropriate commanders. That's intelligence in a nutshell."

"I think I get it now. You explained it nicely."

Tolbane stood and took a bow to Bracken. SNCOs at other tables wondered if this dude was sane or insane.

"One other thing, grasshopper. While processing the information, one thing looked for is indicators—things that point to a pattern or would point to possible enemy operations. Make sure your young troopers understand these things. In our S&C room, there are a couple copies of a confidential army field manual that will give you more info pertaining to our field. Check one out each day and devour the contents until you can teach it in your sleep."

"You got it, top. Thanks for the guidance. I'll make sure all of my team is familiar with the manual.

CHAPTER 17

A month and a half later, Master Sergeant Tolbane checked into the Third Marine Amphibious Force (Third MAF) headquarters in Da Nang, Quang Nam, I Corps, Republic of Viet Nam (RVN). The Tet Offensive was long over. North Vietnam was defeated. However, support was waning for the war, and there was a great disrespect for the veterans of the conflict in the US by the progressives. Even so, there was still a job to be done in the RVN.

Tolbane, due to his rank and experience, was assigned as the team chief for Third MAF's headquarters for the combined interrogation teams on Hill 327, Freedom Hill. The main duties of the office were to check interrogators in upon arrival and assign them to a team, then check them out when rotating back to the States. The office also monitored the teams, compiled interrogation reports, disseminated information, and kept master files.

After a couple of months in-country, Tolbane went down to the US Naval Hospital in Da Nang to check on the interrogator working with wounded North Vietnamese captives. He received a pleasant surprise. His interpreter Ba from his first tour was interpreting there. They had old home week. After returning to his office, Tolbane pulled some strings and had Ba transferred to his office to work as his own interpreter.

Periodically, Tolbane would go to different enclaves to check out the teams and subteams at the various camps. Ba became a great source of information on the members and operations of these small units by talking with the interpreters assigned to them. Things were going great guns.

Tolbane, after four months in-country, managed to get himself and Ba assigned to a Combined Military Interrogation Center in

Saigon. They mostly worked the Saigon Chieu Hoi Center in Cho Lon and the National Chieu Hoi Center on the outskirts of Saigon. Ba could go to his mother's house in the evenings for meals and sleep. Tolbane had his own room at the Montana BEQ and could party at night if he so desired. He got to know several girls working at the higher-class bars and clubs. He was in seventh heaven. He was also able to solicit information on VC activities in the area without the girls becoming suspicious.

On occasion, he would go to Ba's house for an evening meal. Sometimes, Ba's mother would cook for them if she didn't have to work at the market all day. Then the group—Tolbane, Ba, his mother, and Ba's ten-year-old stepsister, Mai—would sit around drinking tea. Tolbane and Ba would teach mother and daughter English words and phrases, and Tolbane would learn more of the conversational Vietnamese language patterns.

One afternoon, they left the interrogation center a little early. As Ba was just opening the door to his home, they heard his little stepsister screaming. Tolbane pushed past Ba into the room. An ARVN soldier whom Ba knew was trying to pull down Mai's pajama bottoms. The soldier already had his pulled off and had an erection.

In two giant strides, Tolbane was just close enough to knock the asshole soldier over tin cups with a looping right-hand roundhouse punch, leaving the ARVN out cold, maybe breaking his jaw too. Mai jumped into Tolbane's arms, sobbing and trembling and thanking Tolbane in her native tongue over and over. After a moment, she kissed him on the cheek and then turned and hugged her stepbrother.

Several minutes later, Tolbane looked at the ARVN, who was still out cold, and he thought the guy's jaw was broken. He and Ba carried him and his pants outside and dumped him in the street. Ba's mother came home a little later and couldn't thank the two guys enough, hugging and thanking Tolbane especially for coldcocking the guy's ass.

After a meal was cooked and devoured, they sat around as usual, except for one thing. Ten-year-old Mai climbed on Tolbane's lap, put her arms around his neck, and placed her head on his shoulder and lay there and stayed quiet the rest of the evening. Little did Tolbane know at the time that in over two decades, he and a very beautiful Mai would have the adventure of a lifetime chasing a madman who murdered Ba to Viet Nam over a jade cross icon and would then be married and have children. Ten-year-old Mai had fallen in love with her hero forever and a day from the timing of the roundhouse punch on the chin of the sorry-ass ARVN.

All through this assignment he was on, it was beginning to seem to Tolbane that he had the luck of the Irish. He knew he wasn't Irish at all, but it seemed to follow him wherever he went. One day, shortly after he saved little Mai, as he wandered from shop to shop on the streets, he got hungry, which was not unusual for him, so he went to the huge cafeteria at the US Embassy for lunch.

Suddenly, a beautiful Vietnamese lady wearing one of the new-fangled miniskirts, a three-inch spike heels, and legs all the way up to her derriere stepped in front of him. He recognized her instantly. It was none other than marine major Nguyen Thi Phuoc.

She threw her arms around his neck, kissed him, and then whispered in his ear, "No one here knows I'm a marine."

Tolbane couldn't resist. He grabbed her tighter and planted the kiss of all kisses on her sweet lips.

An American woman with Phuoc said, "Well, honey child, I guess you must know this guy pretty well, huh?"

Phuoc released him and introduced the two.

"Ginger," Phuoc, quick on her feet, never one to blush or mince words, said, "back when I worked in Da Nang a couple of years ago at the First Division of the ARVN headquarters, he came in one day. We got to like each other, so Travis and I shacked up a few times whenever he could break away from the war. He's great in the sack, and he had a great appetite for my body."

Tolbane, not one to mince words either, said, "Ginger, this gal is about the best stuff you'll ever find at bedroom gymnastics—very agile, spry, and with fluid motion unparalleled. She's so fantastic when she…"

Phuoc put her hand over his mouth firmly and calmly stated to Ginger, "I think it's time to grab a tray and get some of that good American food."

They got in line, got their chow, and sat at Tolbane's table.

After eating, Phuoc asked Ginger, "Ginger, would you mind going back to work alone? I'd like to relive some of Travis's and my adventures together. We always found a way to have lots of fun in the bedroom."

"Sure, Phuoc. Just looking at this hunk, I bet you two had some real wild-ass orgies. See you back at work."

She left the two sitting at the table, looking passionately at each other. Phuoc broke the staring first.

"Travis, I'm so glad to see you, but would you make yourself useful to us for a change and get us a cup of fresh coffee from the big urn over there? Please, my darling dumpling," Phuoc said, adding, "I want to devour your eyes and grin."

"Well, Phuoc, if I really have to."

"Travis Tolbane, get your ever-loving ass up to the coffee urn and get us some coffee right now, or you don't get dessert tonight!"

"I'm on the way, Your Royal Highness!"

She threw her wadded-up napkin at him. He was back in quick time.

Phuoc explained, "Travis, you know what I do in the Corps. I can't tell you what I'm doing here right now. However, there is one thing I do know and can tell you. You could, if you feel the same as me, be a part of my cover, as I'm working alone. I'm going to give you my address, and we can be reunited lovers from Da Nang.

"I want to make it clear that I want us to be lovers, but if there is ever an emergency, I may need your help. It could be dangerous for us both. I know you want to bang me all day and all night long, and I feel I want you too, but I don't want to put you in needless danger if things go south. The decision is all yours. I know what I'm hoping for, but I want not only the decision to be fair to you but that you want it too."

"Phuoc, tell me truly, have I ever kicked you out of bed over some petty crap? I'm in like Flynn, or should I say into Phuoc? Shakespeare had it right. Lovers cannot see the petty follies themselves commit or something like that. I'll be your cover. Plus, I'll cover you from top to bottom."

She smiled and nodded a few times.

"Travis, I get off at 1600 hours. I have some shopping to do. Then I'll go on home and cook something for you. Can you make it by 1800 hours?"

"I'll be there like stink on a skunk's butt, like jelly on toast."

"The jelly sounds like a good idea since we don't have whipped cream. See you then, big boy."

She gave him a piece of paper with her address, blew him a kiss, and was off. Tolbane finished his coffee and walked slowly back to his jeep, back to the war. His head was in the highest clouds just thinking about what the night would bring.

CHAPTER 18

After eating Phuoc's *pho ga*,[13] three bowls filled to the brim, Tolbane pushed back from the table and rubbed his stomach.

"Damn, Phuoc, that was the best *pho ga* I've ever slurped. The chicken and the noodles were perfect. The fried rice wasn't bad either. You can cook for me anytime, anyplace, clothed or naked."

"Thanks for the compliment, Travis. I was hoping you'd like it. Growing boys need their nourishment, lots of it. I seldom cook for me. This is the first time I've ever cooked for a guy. I really felt good doing it for you."

"It's well-appreciated, believe me. I feel a ton overweight now."

"Well," Phuoc replied, "I just guess we must go work some of that weight off of you that I just put on you."

They did just that. Afterward, before he decided to take a nap, Phuoc took a couple of pictures of him, headshots in particular.

*****

At Phuoc's request, Tolbane was not to contact her until the third day. He didn't ask why. On the third day, before she fed him, she handed him an ID card.

"This ID card is legal, and it is authorized by the US ambassador, the only one who knows my mission here. I used one of the pictures I took of you the other night, and the ambassador knows I forged your signature on it. Pretty good job, if I do say so myself. It will pass muster on the street. It gives you the right to carry your

---

[13] Similar to chicken noodle soup (white meat).

military weapon anywhere in Saigon or a concealed weapon if you're in civilian clothes."

Tolbane really enjoyed the meal that night. She served medium rare *thit bo bit tet, rau dau, sua, dao*, and *ca phe* (beef steak, vegetables, milk, peaches, and coffee). She explained he should thank one of the cooks she knew at the embassy.

"The cook is Vietnamese too, so we see eye to eye, especially since she is the romantic sort. I've one more thing important before we hit the sack. I'll give you a hint tonight, and tomorrow night, I'll brief you on a project you are going to help me with. Okay?"

"Okay, my Oriental princess. To hear is but to obey you!"

With that, Tolbane picked Phuoc up and carried her into the bedroom, where he savored her many delights, and she indulged in his many feats of glory.

*****

The following night, they went out to a Chinese restaurant for supper. When they returned to her place, she began explaining what she had planned for the next night.

"Don't answer till I'm done, okay? First, I hope you have some civilian clothes. If not, I can get you some tomorrow. Just give me your sizes. I'll have a holster for you to conceal your .45. We are going visiting. There will be some danger, but that's what you thrive on. The person we'll be seeing is very important, if he shows up. More on it tomorrow. The ambassador has arranged for you to be absent from the center for the next two days, so you can stay here tonight if you can stand being in the same bed with me. Ha ha! Any questions, my perverted hunk of junk?"

"I've got civvies, my lovely. My only question right now is, when do we hit the sack, woman?"

She grabbed his hand and guided him to the location, without GPS, of the sack. The rest was up to him.

*****

The next morning, a while after Phuoc went to the embassy, Tolbane went to his quarters and cleaned up, put on his civvies, went down to one of the open-air markets, and in American terminology, window-shopped, but without buying the windows. When he returned to Phuoc's place, he plopped down on the bed and immediately fell into la-la land, dreaming of Playboy Bunnies on the beach, naked to the bone and all of them attempting to jump his bones at the same time, Tolbane reveling in the Bunnies' melee.

Returning home and seeing her sleeping paramour in dreamland, Phuoc swatted his foot on the bottom and hollered, "Reveille, my big hunk. It's party time, and your party girl is here."

"Oh, you lub me long time. How muchie you chargee?"

"More than your ever-loving ass could afford."

Tolbane grabbed her hand and dragged her onto the bed, where their clothing disappeared from the bed to the floor like magic. Afterward, Phuoc fixed a light meal; and after they ate, Phuoc sat her man on the side of the table beside her and started her premission briefing.

"I'm here because I must make contact with an important man from the NLF for whatever reason. The ambassador would not tell me in case of my being killed or captured. I am to retrieve certain information from the man which could be very beneficial to our side. I was to go do it alone till you, the thief of my heart, suddenly appeared. I convinced the man that a bit of security wouldn't hurt the op. It will take place on the outskirts of the Cho Lon District, a very dangerous area. It's my understanding that the man's family has been spoken to by an armed propaganda team made up of Hoi Chans, or returnees. Okay so far?"

"Sure. Please continue."

"Someone with an overwhelming brainpower decided it would be safer to have one person make contact as a whole team with some firepower. Then maybe a Vietnamese woman would be less noticeable in the area. That's where I come in. Me and the ambassador came to the conclusion that with you, we can look like a lady of the night taking her client to her home for an all-nighter, hence you and me, my dear customer, client, or whatever you are."

"Your client who is overwhelmed by your luscious, sexy body and your superior intellectual brainpower that has so often overwhelmed me."

"You're so full of bullshit, Travis Tolbane, but I love it. You got something else I love too."

"Likewise, my dear. So what other surprise do you have for me?"

"Well, before we look at a city map, nothing else, except that the VC rules that territory every night. Two houses down from the one we want is a cathouse. If it looks like it's not kosher at the house we want, we'll just go to the brothel and pretend to make out there and then leave to meet our transportation. He will take us about a block and a half from our target and wait for our return. He won't go any farther because of a VC roadblock about a block from our target. On the way back, he'll cover us if need be."

"Thanks a whole hell of a lot, my dear. It was good knowing you before our demise this glorious evening before us. Before we go to that demise, you need to do one more task. Wrap those gorgeous thighs around my face."

"Pervert! You're entirely welcome, my dear paramour. Now where did I put that map?"

She found it under her silken panties in a small chest of drawers. She unfolded it and placed it on the table, then sat next to Tolbane to point out some features. Before she began with the map, Tolbane had a couple of questions.

"Do we have to question the man? Do we just accept documents? What do we do with whatever information or documents we receive, like I make it and you don't make it?"

"We can discuss those questions on the way there. Let me show you some things on the map. Then we will have to look around for something to do before it's time to go. That is if your manhood is still in place and your face needs washed and squished between my thighs."

"You never know, Phuoc. We might just break the bed to smithereens this time."

CHAPTER 19

Phuoc had made arrangements for the night's operation with the ambassador. They would be in civilian clothes, and she would be dressed more like a hooker with the new style of miniskirt and pumps. He provided two Astra 300s and 9 mm Parabellums with three ten-round magazines with each one and a *xich lo* and driver for the evening's foray.

The driver would let them off about a block or less from their destination and would await their return with the subject. Because of the delicate situation, there would be no backup available. If they were captured or killed, the embassy would have no idea of what they were doing there and disavow everything.

Phuoc explained all the ins and outs of the operation to Tolbane and apologized for putting him in this kind of situation. She assured him it was only because she trusted no one else to have her back. It was soon time to go. Tolbane was dressed in a loose-fitting shirt and Phuoc a button-down blouse to cover up the fact they were armed. They left the apartment and went to meet their driver and what fate awaited them. She introduced Tolbane to him, and he reiterated his role in the operation.

Besides not wanting to drive into the VC-controlled area at any time, it was customary for the drivers' safety to let their fares walk into the VC-controlled area on their own, as there was a VC checkpoint and roadblock at night to go through, and they would await the customers' return and take them back to where they were picked up. Then Tolbane and Phuoc would be off to the far corner area of the Cho Lon District.

As prearranged that night, the driver left them off a block from the VC checkpoint, parking and waiting on his fare's return. Phuoc and Tolbane got out, then strolled slowly and a little wobbly toward it, playing kissy-face and Roman hands and Russian fingers in the same manner as the prostitutes bringing their marks to the brothel. The two VC guards, not too swift on the cognitive side, questioned them and were easily convinced they were legit, a boom-boom girl and her inebriated customer. They walked on down about four houses, and there was a woman sitting on an open-door stoop, looking like she was enjoying the night air.

Phuoc waved and told the woman she had a live one with a lot of money in Vietnamese dong and walked Tolbane two more houses down and entered a brothel. It had a hallway with five rooms on each side. The girls would pay at the office in the first room on the right when leaving with their marks. They found that the last room on the left was unoccupied, and she pulled him into it.

She whispered in his ear, "I don't like the look of things, Travis. That woman shouldn't be there or the door open like that. Our target was to be the only one at the house, and I had a special knock for the door. I'll bet my bootie they are waiting for contact to be made. Let's get out the back door here and see if we can get around the checkpoint."

"Lead the way, my dear Phuoc. I'm just here for the show. What's showing?"

She gave him a weird look and a gentle slap behind the head and put her index finger to her lips, opened the door slowly, and peeked up and down the corridor. Then she motioned for Tolbane to follow, and they slipped out the back door. She led him into a treed area behind the houses. They paused, looked and listened for a few minutes, and then started to move on. As they took their first step, they heard a commotion from the brothel.

Phuoc whispered, "They're looking for us. Let's move it."

They got past the target house and were nearing the checkpoint. They heard a couple of VCs running up the walkway, shouting that the spies got away out the back door. Phuoc and Tolbane took out their handguns, checked to make sure there was a round in their chambers, and moved on. The guards from the checkpoint started toward the area they were in, spotted them, and began firing, one round striking Phuoc in the mussel of her upper-right arm. She groaned but kept moving.

Tolbane returned fire, putting one of the guards down. The other two cut toward the street on an angle. For some reason, the guard did not pursue them, but those on the street were still rushing toward them, stopping to fire their rifles a couple of times and running some more, then firing again.

Tolbane and Phuoc were almost to the *xich lo* when a round caught Phuoc in the left hip, shattering it and dropping her to the ground. She begged and ordered him to leave her and save himself, but he disobeyed. He picked her up in a fireman's carry, still shooting behind him. The *xich lo* driver climbed out and returned fire with an M1 Carbine, hitting both VCs. They got Phuoc into the vehicle and took off.

The driver took them quickly to an ARVN hospital, where the ER doctors took Phuoc in to immediate surgery. Tolbane was treated for a couple of slight dings on the side and arm but nothing more serious than a need for small bandages. He cared nothing about himself but was so afraid for his paramour, Phuoc. She had lost a lot of blood from both of her wounds. The worst was the hip. It looked totally smashed to him. While he paced, the driver called an emergency number at the embassy.

An hour later, Phuoc was still in surgery, and the driver had a hard time explaining to Tolbane that he had to get him to his own quarters ASAP to keep him out of trouble. Reluctantly, he finally agreed to leave Phuoc. Arriving at his own pad, he took a long, hot shower and finally collapsed on his cot, and his fatigue couldn't be put off. He fell into a deep asleep and didn't awake until someone was beating on his door at 1330 hours the next day. It was a corporal from his unit.

He was instructed to be at the ambassador's office at the embassy at 1600 hours in the uniform of the day. After the way things got fucked up the night before, his initial feelings were that he really had it now. He wondered just how much trouble he was in and what the outcome from the night before had to do with it. He did as he was ordered.

*****

Two minutes before the appointed time, Tolbane gingerly approached the ambassador's office, being at sea as to what was happening. The door was open, and he could see the army colonel in charge of his joint service unit. The ambassador bade him to enter and close the door. He did and reported as ordered. He was told to be at ease, and he assumed the position and waited.

"Finally, Master Sergeant Tolbane, please assume the position of attention," the colonel began. "This will have to be quick, as I was just informed of a situation I have to respond to immediately. On behalf of our country, I present you with this Silver Star for rescuing a wounded Vietnamese female civilian who was being attacked by VC while under fire. Here is your medal"—he pinned it on Tolbane—"and a Purple Heart for the wounds you incurred during the rescue."

This medal was also pinned on him.

The colonel handed the citations to Tolbane and stated, "Congratulations, Master Sergeant. Sorry, Master Sergeant and Ambassador, I must leave. Duty calls."

And he was gone. Tolbane stood dumbfounded by the situation. He wasn't expecting to be rewarded like this.

"Stand easy, Tolbane," the ambassador stated. "Phuoc told me you prefer to be called by your last name. Take a seat on the couch, and I'll sit beside you. This morning, we found out that your target had been captured, tortured, had given up the info on your operation last night, then executed. I know, a day late and a dollar short.

"We lost a good operative last night. Let me clarify. Agent Troung Thi Phuoc was lost in a firefight last night. Maj. Ngo Bui Tri, USMC, was critically wounded in a fierce fight north of Saigon last night. She has been medevaced to Guam for further treatment. It seems she will be medically retired after her healing and rehab.

"I'm sad to say, I have to inform you that you are forbidden to try to locate her ever, or there will be consequences. I know you and her were close. War has a way of separating people, but sometimes, it's for the best. I shouldn't say anything, but she has enemies out there who would do her harm if they could ever find her.

"I am arranging for your immediate transfer back to the States as soon as we can get you checked out of your unit and a flight arranged. You are a target here now. Plus, there's a five-thousand-dong reward on your head by the local VC also."

"I thank you, Ambassador, for the update on Phuoc as I know her. I didn't know her real name, just as Phuoc. I'll miss her a lot. We had some good times together. I really respect her, and I can assure you, I will do nothing to put her in jeopardy period. I have way too much respect and special feelings for her than to cause her any more hurt or grief. I only wish I could have said so long to her. Sir, I'm all right here. I'd like to finish my tour if it's acceptable."

"I'm sorry, Tolbane. It's not acceptable to me. The local VCs are already looking for you. They didn't like losing a few of their men in that melee last night. Also, you have a lot of information on things they'd like to have answers to, information we do not want compromised, especially that deal up north on your first tour with Phuoc. When you return to your quarters, pack up your gear, but stay in your civvies. Someone will pick you up later and take you to an undisclosed location to await transportation stateside. Good luck!"

"Thank you, sir! I won't disappoint you."

Tolbane left the ambassador's officer and stopped at the embassy's cafeteria and sated a stomach growl, having not eaten since the previous night at Phuoc's. He arrived at his pad, got his gear together, and waited. After all that had happened in the past twenty-four hours, he was lost at sea for sure. He didn't know whether to shit or go blind.

He knew Phuoc used different names. This new one must have been fake too. He was sad that he would never know who she really was. He wished her a short and wonderful recovery. He dozed off, and an hour later, a marine captain came knocking at his door.

When Tolbane answered, the captain said, "Let's grab you gear and get going on the double, guy. We can talk in the jeep."

They split the gear between them and left the building. When they were in the jeep and on their way, the captain introduced himself.

"I'm Jim Reed. I've been instructed to only refer to you as Tolbane. I've never had a hush-hush assignment like this one before."

"Glad to know you, Jim. I've had too many of them, enough to last me a lifetime."

Tolbane decided to play the game.

"Much obliged for the transportation. The wings I had got clipped last night but good."

"You got it. I was told you are a pretty important package and not to fuck it up, so how am I doing so far?"

"You're spot on, dude."

"I'm glad there's no traffic to speak of tonight, so we should get to our rendezvous in plenty of time. I know I'm not to ask, but you must be pretty important to rate this trip that never happened."

"You could say that, Jim. I appreciate your service. I think Charlie's on my tail, and he'd like to clean my clock. By the way, where are we going? I don't even know that."

"I'm not allowed to say, but I think there's a big bird awaiting you."

Shortly, they pulled into the Saigon International Airport, and the captain drove to a remote area where a C-130 transport was warming up its engines. The back ramp was down, and the crew chief was standing on it, waiting for Tolbane. The captain helped him put his gear aboard, saluted Tolbane, and was back in the jeep and gone.

The crew chief saluted Tolbane and informed him that he was the only passenger on board and that as soon as the ramp was up and he was buckled in they would be moving down the runway. He put the ramp up, and the craft began to taxi to the turn onto runway. It must have already had clearance for takeoff, because the engines suddenly roared to life, and with a jolt, the craft was moving down the runway. Tolbane felt the steep climb of the craft and the grinding of the wheels retracting.

When the craft attained cruising altitude, the crew chief came back to the cargo area to brief Tolbane.

"We were instructed not to tell you our destination until we were airborne and cruising. We are headed for Marine Corps Air Station Futenma, Okinawa, Japan. We'll be there in about five hours or so. Don't know if you've ever been there, but it's a nice place."

"I know. I was with MAG-16 when they opened the new base there. Flew with HMM-163 a few times in YP14. I liked it there. The girls were great. First time I went to Nam, I flew from there, only in a crowded and large, crate-packed C-130."

"Sir, if you will notice, there is a large urn of coffee and cups over there. Just help yourself. We'll have a box lunch for you in about two hours. What's in them? Your guess is as good as mine. We get some real surprises at times, either good or bad. I guess the cooks have a warped sense of humor at times. If you need anything, just press that buzzer over there, and I'll make like McArthur and return."

"Thanks, chief!"

When the crew chief left, Tolbane put this last part of his life in a separate compartment in his soul, then stretched out on the framework folding bench and was instantly asleep right after he said a prayer for Phuoc.

CHAPTER 20

Tolbane, having returned stateside once again, found himself stationed on the East Coast. His assignment this time was different. He was to work in a different genre of the intelligence community. He was to be the intelligence chief of the Sixth Marine Regiment, Second Marine Division, Camp Lejeune, North Carolina. Due to the Viet Nam conflict, the regiment only had one full and combat-ready battalion, the Third, and only a small cadre of staff manning the First and Second Battalions.

His job was really easy this time. His intelligence officer had other duties and was never around. He would read all the classified messaging going to and from the regiment and pass it on to the next section, attend and brief the regimental commander at his daily meetings, forward applications for various classified levels for certain troops, and laze around in general. He was in pig heaven. He couldn't have felt better if he was rolling in mud and shit.

One would never have known a war was going on by watching him. Whenever his clerk, driver, and head scout was not in the office, he could close the door with a sign stating a classified meeting was in progress, then kick up his feet on the desk, lean back, and go to dreamland. Sometimes, it backfired on him. He would dream of the hip wound, picking up Phuoc, and carrying her to the *xich lo* and would snap awake in a mild sweat. Even after several months, he still missed her most of the time.

One day, the regimental sergeant major, Jim Simpson, stuck his head in Tolbane's doorway and motioned for him to come. The regimental commander wanted to see the two of them ASAP. With a groan, he put down the document he was studying and complied, wondering what was up this time.

The sergeant major knocked on the office door, and the commander bade them to enter. They marched in at attention and stopped in front of the commander. The sergeant major reported them as ordered. The commander told them to be at ease. There were two other people in the office. One was the assistant regimental commander; the other was not known to the two enlisted men.

Tolbane thought, *Déjà vu.*

Whenever Tolbane was in this kind of situation, he always found himself in some type of covert operation. He felt that maybe he should have screwed things up the first time he was on one. Maybe then he would have been ignored.

"Gentlemen," began the commander, "allow me to introduce the individual sitting there. He is Mr. Strange from the State Department. Except for his name and department, I know absolutely nothing about him."

Mr. Strange stood and shook hands with the two and thanked them for their service.

Continuing, the commander said, "You will now accompany Mr. Strange to the conference room. You're excused."

The two marines left the office with Mr. Strange and moved to the conference room with him.

"Sergeant Major, I first want to address the master sergeant, but you guys go ahead and get a cup of coffee and get comfortable."

When the two had coffee and were comfortable, the man began.

"I can't ask you to address me as anything but Mr. Strange. I will address you two as Jim and Travis. Travis, I understand you have participated in a few operations that were a little hairy, especially the last one you had in Saigon, RVN. I have to ask you if you have had any adverse effects to the stress of those situations, such as freezing up during a stressful situation. So what say you?"

"To be truthful, Mr. Strange, I am presuming you know something about the last one, so let me say this. Certain aspects of the operation were stressful and somewhat personal to me, but I have moved on and put it behind me. I do think of my partner on the last one on occasion, but the memory does not affect me. Maybe later on in life, it might, but not at this time. I can still function under stress as well as Mike Hammer or Sam Spade could."

"I'm glad you aren't having stress problems. I was told you have nerves of steel. You may need those nerves in the future. One can never know."

"Mr. Strange, the shadow knows!"

"Haven't heard that one in a while. I was also told you have a weird sense of humor. You may need that too. Jim, if you take notice, the Purple Heart and the Silver Star Travis wears are from his last mission. It was a complete disaster. No fault of his, though. The intelligence was somewhat faulty, but he came through with flying colors. Now to get to the nitty-gritty as to why I'm here.

"I want to send you two on a weird assignment—here in the States for a change. There is a former field agent, disabled from a war wound, that needs some protection from the bad guys. The agent definitely has a big target on the backside and is not fully capable of self-defense. That's where you two come into play. This assignment will be in civvies, and you will be armed with weapons of your choice. We're hoping they won't be needed."

The sergeant major spoke up.

"With all of the government's assets, why would you assign two senior marines to be bodyguards?"

"The agent in question has some connection to the Corps, and the powers that be do not want to compromise any part of the agent's previous operations, as they were pure classified military ops. Besides, you two have been under fire in certain situations, have returned fire, etc. If something happens, we do not want someone who has never had the stress of exchanging fire in a position for which they have not developed an instinct yet. Besides, I think the agent would be more comfortable with military bodyguards."

"How long will this operation last?" Tolbane queried.

"As long as it takes some others to take down some bad guys is as close as I can call it, Tolbane. My answer is and has to be as long as it takes!"

Looking at his watch, Mr. Strange added, "I need to go. I've got someplace to be. You two need to be here in this conference room at

0800 hours tomorrow. You will receive further briefing and sent on your way shortly thereafter. Good day, guys!"

And he was out the door and gone. The two marines gave a puzzled look at each other.

*****

The next day, at 0800 hours, the two marines were grumbling about their new misfortune and what kind of shit detail they would be given to defend. They were in the conference room, scoffing up coffee, doughnuts, and coffee cake that had been placed there before the guys arrived; and they were telling war stories and cracking jokes from soup to nuts. Most of the stories began with, "You won't believe this shit, but…"

About twenty minutes after the hour, a man entered the room, all dressed to the nines.

"Sorry I'm late, guys. There was a minor fender bender holding up traffic on the way here. I see they put out some goodies for us. Let me grab some, and we'll get started. I love frosted doughnuts and coffee. Now where were we? Oh, wait, we didn't start yet, did we? I have no name to give you. However, I know yours and your histories in the Corps. The assignment you have been chosen for could be dangerous, or it could be a cake walk in the park. I have no idea whatsoever.

"Later this morning, you will go to the provost marshals and get a government concealed gun carry permit ID to make you legal. From there, you'll go to an armory to receive weapons and ammo, then to the disbursing office to receive travel pay, a month's advanced pay, a gasoline voucher, and a civilian clothes voucher to fit your cover. You'll then go and pack your necessities and await further orders at your quarters.

"Then you will each receive a set of sealed orders to be read when you're over fifty miles from here, then destroyed. Now that's a mouthful. Actually, you will each drive your own car, but there will be a two-hour difference in departure time between you so you do not look as though you're together. These doughnuts are good. I'll have another. Any questions?"

This time, Tolbane beat Jim to the first question.

"This agent we will be guarding must be pretty important and has invaluable information. Is there anything you can tell us about the asset, a name or anything else, so we can get a handle on what our responsibilities may be? We're in the darkest of dark here."

"I wish I could tell you. You're Travis, I guess. I don't have any idea myself. I'm as blind to this mission as you are. I only know what I'm to instruct you. Yes, Jim?"

"How high up the food chain does this op go? What can we expect if we fail not because of our own fault?"

"I only know it goes way up the chain. As far as consequences go, I have no idea. I only have one more thing to relate to you. There is a mighty mite and driver waiting outside for you. The driver will take you to your appointed places. Good luck, guys. And I need to take a couple of these doughnuts with me."

He grabbed a napkin and a couple of doughnuts and left the room.

Travis and Jim were chauffeured around all morning to take care of their appointed duties and then were returned to their quarters after noon mess. They packed up what they would need on the trip, put on their civvies, and waited. Finally, they were each approached by a major in their individual rooms. Each was given their sealed orders. Each was told that there was a map in each packet giving directions to the target area as well as orders.

Tolbane was to leave first, making sure he was well away from the base before stopping for chow. Jim was to eat in Jacksonville an hour and a quarter later, then head out. They would both head toward Wilmington, North Carolina. After that, they were on their own till they reached their destination.

*****

On the south side of Wilmington, Tolbane pulled into a gas station to refuel and checked his orders. He read them, then checked the map. He was to follow the directions to a tee to arrive at his destination in a timely manner. He eventually left the main highway and began traversing county roads and what seemed like cow pasture lanes heading up to foothills.

He felt a little sleepy, so he pulled into what looked like an over-grown path and slept for half an hour. Then he continued to a little one-stoplight berg and, as the instructions indicated, got a room at a prescribed B and B for the rest of the night. He breakfasted the next morning but didn't leave until 0900 hours per his orders.

Tolbane drove up and down roads once again until it was time for lunch at a roadside diner. He continued down the road for one more hour, finally finding the one vehicle lane he needed. He turned left onto it and drove another quarter of a mile. There he saw the journey's end: an old Victorian mansion with pillars in the front and gardens and hedges that had seen better days and needed a lot of TLC. He pulled into a small parking area in the front, and by the time he exited his vehicle, a man was coming down the long walk-way. It was evident that he was holding his weapon down alongside his leg.

He approached Tolbane in a stern mood.

"Who the fuck are you?"

"Nice to know you too, asshole! I'm Travis Tolbane, and I'm here as directed by the Lord only knows who and reporting for duty, if it's any of your fucking concern!"

"Let me see your ID and gun permit."

Tolbane produced them. He couldn't resist pulling the guy's chain a little more.

"See? That's me all day long, the savior of the days to come in full size and living color for those who give a shit."

"Okay! I was told I would be relieved by a smart-ass. I guess you fit the bill. I'm Jake Ballard. Glad to meet you and even happier that you're here. You're my immediate relief, and I get to go back to being normal."

"Jake, everything has been so hush-hush about this assignment. I really don't know what or why I'm here, only to protect a disabled agent as far as I know. But I am ready to relieve you here. I hope you can get back to normal as quickly as possible. Anything you can tell me about what's going on—or off, for that matter?"

"Thanks, Tolbane! Let me take you in to meet your charge. Best you get your answers there. After that, I am but a whisper in the winds."

Tolbane followed him into the house, where he reported as ordered to the target individual with a deadpan face.

CHAPTER 21

After reporting to the agent, Tolbane remained quiet while she introduced herself as Maj. Ngo Bui Tri and waited until Jake had grabbed his gear and was gone. Then he broke his silence.

"What the hell is going on here, Phuoc? My God! Are you okay? I've been going crazy wondering if you're okay, if your wounds healed, and a whole lot of other crazy things."

"Travis, my dear one, I've got a lot to tell you, but let me tell you first that I am in danger. As you can see, I still need crutches for my hip, which is not quite done healing. In another month or so, I should be able to get by with a walker or a cane and then hopefully later full use. I'm going to wait and brief both you and your friend at the same time. Until then, I want you to know you're my hero for saving me.

"I expected to die! I was hurt so bad. Then you picked me up, and I knew I'd be all right. I owe you my life, my love. I know you were ordered to stay away from me by the ambassador, but he doesn't count anymore. We can't be lovers anymore because of other damage to my body right now, but it doesn't mean we can't cuddle on occasion or even a passionate kiss once in a while. So what have you been doing for yourself lately?"

"As you know, I was sent back to the States right after they gave me a couple of medals I didn't want or need. I was assigned as a regimental intelligence chief at Swamp Lejeune with not much to do on the East Coast. It's been really boring for the most part. I had a lot of time on my hands until this gig came along. Before Jim gets here, maybe you can't say, but is this your real name? I always wondered."

"I can't even tell my favorite marine one way or another. This one will just have to do for now. I may need to change it again in the future, but you won't know that either."

"Okay! I won't ask again. I take it you must have had some operations that were more important and dangerous than what we were on together. You must have been in pretty deep cover. That being said, we did work together well. I never expected to see you again after that night. I was so afraid when you got hit. I wished it had been me.

"I want you to know one thing before Jim gets here, Phuoc. I'll die before I let anyone hurt you again. I'll do my best to make sure I don't let my feelings for you put you in any danger. As much as possible, I'll keep this as professional as I can."

"I know you will. That's one reason I wanted you to be part of my security detail. I know I can trust my life to you."

"I'm glad you did want me. I'll wait till Jim gets here before I go out and check the grounds. I don't want you left alone."

"I don't want to be alone either, but hiding here, I have been feeling so alone. It's been maddening. Travis, I don't feel alone now with you here."

"I'm glad! Is that a car pulling up here?" he wondered while looking out one of the front windows. "Jim just got out of his car. I'll wave him in."

Once Jim was in the house and introductions had been held, Jim commented, "Damn! I thought I'd never get to this place, Travis. What a convoluted route to drive. I wonder who the intellectual mental midget was who concocted this route. Now that I'm here, what's the deal with this detail, ma'am?"

"Well, Jim," Tri began, "to start with, I have worked with Travis a few times before, and I trust him completely. He even saved my life once. I do not know you, Jim, but someone in NIS highly recommended you for this mission. If you are as good as I heard, I'm really in good hands with both you and Travis.

"I have been in deep cover in North Vietnam and in North Korea. I can't explain why or how, but word somehow got out that I was a traitor to them and was now crippled and couldn't get around much, i.e., a sitting duck. Both countries have a contract on me.

"Someone in DC found out that I had been compromised to them and that a couple of hit teams, one from each of the countries, are looking for me high and low. As we speak, there is a major operation that is in progress to find these teams before they find me, if at all possible. Are you with me so far?"

"Up to a point, Tri. There are only two of us here. You make three. I know you can still shoot. It sounds like we would be outmanned and outgunned if you were found here. Shouldn't we have some more guards here in the house than just us two woeful asses?"

"Good news, my new friend. There is a reinforced marine platoon camped about a half mile or less back in the deep woods behind the house. The area is so thick it's hard to even move in there, so we don't worry about a threat from that direction. We have radio contact with them if needed, and it wouldn't take them long to get here in an emergency.

"We radio-check four times a day. We would be expected to hold off any threat until the unit could get here. Hence, it was decided to just have only two guys in the house. We don't want an observer to see too many here in the house."

"Do you think we could get a couple of their best shooters placed in upstairs rooms to assist in a pinch?" Tolbane asked.

Tri explained the security precautions already in place.

"We have sensors placed around the perimeter in addition to some hidden cameras. We have a control room to monitor them. I'll show them to you later. Also, there are watchers in town that will inform us of any Asian strangers in the area. I'm hoping that's enough. We could always ask about a couple of sharpshooters if you think we need them, Travis."

"What you have in place sounds good. I'll reserve judgment about getting shooters until Jim and I look over all the precautions and discuss it. Oh, while I think about it, Tri, what if the phone line from town is severed?"

"They have a PRC-25 radio. Telephones can be tapped."

"That's great thinking. You got any questions, Jim?"

"I'll wait until we can assess what is now in place. So far, it doesn't sound too bad. I would like to ask, who's manning the cameras?"

"I guess it would be you two. Oh, shit, no way you guys can do that too."

Tolbane asked, "Do you think you could get the officer in charge of the troops up here for a confab before we do anything else?"

"I'll call him right now. Good catch, Jim."

*****

Late that afternoon, 1st Lt. Ralph Pike, USMC, slipped into the house quietly through the back entrance. He announced himself and reported to the major in the proper marine tradition. She instructed him to stand easy and introduced Travis and Jim.

"Ralph, these two men are now in charge of my security here. I've been assured I can rely on Jim, and I trust my life in Travis's hands. In fact, he has saved it once before. There are no secrets about our security here with them. They have several important questions, and I hope you have the answers! We'll start with Travis."

"Ralph, I understand you have a reinforced platoon. How is it reinforced?" Tolbane inquired.

"I have assigned to me an additional rifle squad, one engineer, two snipers, an additional M60 team, and lo and behold, a second lieutenant for an assistant platoon leader. Dear Lord, help me with that."

The others had a good laugh over that. Then Jim entered the conversation.

"I'm sorry about the second lieutenant, Ralph. Seriously, what troops can you spare? I'd like to have either the snipers or two good shooters on call upstairs for observation or firepower and three good men to monitor the camera room, each an eight-hour shift. They would all stay here in the house, and they would live and dine and whatever with us."

Ralph, after thinking for a couple of minutes, suggested, "I might be able to do you a couple men better. You get the camera operators and a radio operator. I'll put two good shooters and a sniper upstairs. The sniper can work with the shooters. Of course, the seven-man subteam will need a team leader. You get the second lieu for that."

Everyone groaned at that.

"That gives the major ten plus herself. I hope that would be satisfactory to you."

Tolbane continued. "Damn, that's good. My last question before turning it over to Jim is, why wasn't the house reinforced before this?"

"The guy that was here before you, whatever his name was, felt he could take care of all things here all by himself."

This set off an alarm in Tolbane's brain. He would address it with Phuoc later.

"I had even offered him any support he needed, but he just laughed it off, saying we were too paranoid."

Jim began. "I'd like you to get together with all your comm men and set up passwords for us, the camera room, and the shooters first thing. I'm sure you know your response time to the house. I have only two questions right now. My first question is, why so far away? Number two, can you deploy your unit closer?"

"Jim, once again, it was the conclusion of the previous agent where we should bivouac. We can set up a little closer. I will take care of that on my return. As an afterthought, how about if I rotate troops in the house every two days?"

Tolbane jumped in.

"That's a good idea. Keeps the troops happy. I have some serious concerns about our predecessor's major decisions. When you get all the posts and watches set up and manned, I think we need to test all cameras and sensors and their angle of approach. The things you related just don't sound right to me. Could this guy be trying to set the major up for a big hit? If so, we got our work cut out for us. We can expect an attack at any time."

"Ralph, now you see why I trust Travis," the major commented. "I never considered any of this. If we find any discrepancies in the security functions, I have a secure line to report to. I really wasn't that enthused with that guy either, but he was all I had here at the time."

It was growing dark when each post was manned; and the two lieutenants, Jim, and Tolbane had checked all the infrared cameras and the ground sensors on the approaches to the grounds and house. They found that three different lanes of approach had been compromised. All camera adjustments were made and sensors replaced, restoring the original coverage. When everything was done, Tri had a meal ready for them.

After eating, she informed them, "I ordered more supplies on the secure line today. Shortly, there will be a chopper bringing in more food supplies and a military cook for the house. It's really needed with the troops eating with us now. I'll be notified of its approach so we don't get trigger happy. I also requested a few extra weapons and ammo for us. It's like having a dish of ice cream around here. There's never enough in a bowel."

An hour later, the chopper, an old CH-46, landed. It brought another refrigerator and another freezer, a lot of frozen meat, packages of frozen vegetables, and onions and potatoes and other fresh vegetables, along with flour, baking needs, and plenty of Folgers Coffee. One cook, an army specialist six aptly named Cook—James Cook, to be exact—was assigned to them.

In addition, they were sent twice the number of M69 grenade launchers and four times the number of M16s, each with a case of ammo, and a case of fragmentation grenades and a case of baseball grenades for the household. Then the copilot passed on an envelope marked Top-Secret, Maj. Ngo Bui Tri's Eyes Only.

The cook was busy arranging the foodstuff, and Tri was briefing the lieutenants, Jim, and Tolbane.

"The envelope addressed to me contained some interesting information. I reported your findings on the security arrangements. The clown that was here will be investigated thoroughly. I'll be updated as needed.

"Next is kind of alarming to us. However, we are better prepared for it now. It is believed that both factions after me are attempting to merge for my demise. As Travis might say, the families that play together might just die together."

CHAPTER 22

Tolbane's response to Phuoc was typical for him.

"Good! Now we can handle the situation the Marine Corps way. Hurry up and fucking wait. Semper fi! Eat the apple and fuck the Corps. Now as Chesty said, we can fire in all directions."

Everyone giggled to no end.

Laughing, Tri responded, "Travis, you are the perfect big dork and a half as usual."

Now everyone laughed, or maybe roared would describe it better.

"Ralph, from now on, we're on full alert day and night."

Just then, SPC Cook entered the room and introduced himself.

"Which of you is the major in charge?"

Tri introduced herself as the major, then introduced the rest to him.

"James, please join us while I finish my briefing. Then I'll catch you up-to-date. Ralph, get your troops set up in your two-man positions and on alert. Lieutenant Jones, alert your subteam positions. Both of you, establish comm security. Travis, Jim, and I expect to have periodic security updates from you two. Let's get shaking, guys."

The two lieutenants turned to leave.

James asked, "I hope this is not one of those silly questions, but this a serious thing, and it isn't an army operation, is it?"

Tri smiled at him.

"I'm afraid it is serious, and no, it's not Army, strictly USMC. Let me ask you. Can you handle a rifle, James?"

"You bet I can! I was in the infantry my first three years in the Army. Then I don't know how the hell it happened, but I suddenly found myself in cook and baker school with a white chef's hat and an apron. Been a cook for seven and a half years now. I never got into combat. However, I think I'm about to."

Jim answered, "That would be a very good surmise on your part, James. Travis and I both have combat experience and have both worked with army personnel before, so you are in good hands, just not with Allstate. We may need your assistance. We won't call on you, though, unless we need you."

SPC Cook looked at the major.

"I'm not sure how to address you, but I'm here and in for a penny, in for a pound. No way could I ever sit around here listening to gunfire and not participate. I'd damn sure like to do my share against any bad guys."

"May I interject?" Tolbane inquired. "James, we pretty much have the posts covered. Let me suggest that you can do a couple of things. If we get into it, we may need someone to pass ammunition to us, take the place of a wounded one, maybe help patch up one of us, cover for one while they relieve themselves, maybe make sandwiches, or any number of things. No one will argue about it if you happen to take some potshots at some asshole out there. You can be a very valuable asset to us if and when shit hits the fan. I think I speak for the rest of us when I say, glad to have you aboard."

"When you put it that way, Tolbane. Thanks! Glad to be of service."

"Jim and Travis, go check on things, and I'll bring James up-to-date on our situation here. James, come sit on the sofa with me."

He complied.

*****

Nothing happened for two days. The troops in the house were rotated, and everyone was on half-alert. SPC Cook demonstrated his skills as a top-notch chef. Then Tri received a call on her secure line. She understood the urgency of it. She called everyone together.

"I got a secure message today that confirms our worst fear. The two factions, the North Vietnamese and the North Koreans, have joined forces, and according to what has been learned, tomorrow is the target date for us. No time is available for when it would begin. It could be after midnight, in the morning, afternoon, or night.

"It's not known exactly how many to expect. Estimate is around twenty-five to thirty. One thing is in our favor. They probably do not know we have changed our security arrangements. We need to place ammo and weapons where we'll need them and be ready.

"I was updated on the previous security guy I reported. Seems his family was threatened if he didn't comply with screwing up the security here. Now the investigation is to find out just how the enemy knew about his assignment here and how to get to his family. That's not our problem. Let's get our butts in gear and get ready. Once we are ready, we need to get some shut-eye in shifts."

Everyone turned to their assigned tasks. When all was at the ready and while some were catching some zzzs, Tolbane sat on the couch with his arm around Tri's shoulder.

She admitted to Tolbane, "Travis, for the first time that I can remember, I'm having a hard time confronting my fear. I guess it's because I'm disabled now that I'm really scared. I'm glad you're here for me. It has helped a lot. I really needed you to help me cope.

"Feeling sorry for myself, I never checked that sorry-ass guy. Maybe I shouldn't really be mad at him under the circumstances, but I did trust him to an extent. Thank God I asked my handler to make a change and bring you here. Best decision I ever made, except for the one where I led you to that bunker and got laid."

"Tri, I haven't forgotten that first time. I'm sure when this is over, I'll never see you again. I think it's in the wind you'll get a name change and a new location. It'll be sad not being able to see you, but I know it's for the best. Your safety is paramount to me."

"Thanks, Travis. You're my rock! Now I'm going to bed. There's a couple of pillows and a couple of blankets in that closet over there. You crap out on the sofa here. I need you rested and alert tomorrow. Good night."

She shuffled off slowly, using her walker instead of her crutches, and Tolbane got a pillow and blanket, then drifted off into his dreamland once more, dreaming of the good times he and Phuoc had together. Morning came too soon for him.

*****

SPC Cook had a sumptuous breakfast ready and was feeding everyone in shifts when Tolbane was awakened by him.

"Hey, Travis, I heard your favorite breakfast is waffles and bacon. Guess what? If you don't get them on your plate in the next few minutes, they will disappear, and you'll go hungry!"

"Get out of my way, then, James. No way do I lay waste to such morsels except to my stomach!"

He made a beeline to the kitchen.

Two hours later, the sniper spotted some movement in the far tree line in front of the house. He reported that someone was reconning the situation. The camera operator reported the same. When Tri, Jim, and Tolbane were informed of the matter, Tolbane got his two cents in again.

"'It won't be long now,' Cyrano de Bergerac said when he stumbled into the fan."

Jim said, "Travis, you're too much to take. Now let's get everybody on full alert and get ready to rumble."

Word went out to the platoon, and each marine locked and loaded his weapon and made ready to get some. For most, it would be their first time under fire. Explicit instruction was given to hold fire unless directed to fire or fired upon. The situation did not need some trigger-happy grunt cranking off any rounds prematurely. Fire discipline was an essential part of the defense. It was presumed the bad guys didn't know of the changes that had been made. Surprise, surprise, Sergeant Carter. It definitely was not on the good guys' side this day. They were ready.

The day was nerve-racking, wondering when the attack would begin. Shortly after dark, the infrared cameras picked up a couple of individuals, most likely scouts, appearing at the edge of the tree line and moving along both edges of it, peering through binoculars at the house, which was dark with light only in a couple of the upstairs bedrooms to simulate that the occupants were there and were not expecting, just the situation the assault group hoped for. When the scouts returned to the unit, their leader began moving his men to the edge of the tree line.

The sniper and camera operators both reported about thirty-five men lined up at the trees' edge, simultaneously notifying the marine platoon to take their positions. Five of the enemy moved out of the trees, a good spacing between them, and began slowly moving quietly toward the house in a semi crouch.

Jim cleared the sniper to take out two or three of the guys to see what response they would get. He didn't want the two shooters to open up yet. The sniper took out one on each end; the other three hit the deck and crawled back to the tree line. The battle was now on, and those in the house were waiting. It was the bad guys' turn now to react.

CHAPTER 23

Two shots rang out, and two enemies went down from headshots. This caught the leader, North Vietnamese captain Nguyen Tam, completely by surprise.

What is that fool Jake Ballard's replacement doing? the captain thought. *Maybe he is just trying to make it look good. He'll probably surrender when we go in force.*

The three men crawled back to the tree line. Tam then ordered the sixteen North Koreans to charge the house. As the group moved out of the tree line, the sniper, the two shooters, and the two off-duty camera operators began firing; and two of the marine positions, one on either side of the house, one having an M60 team, began firing also.

Several of the North Koreans fell immediately. Only three made it back into the tree line. The groans of the fallen not killed outright were heard all the way to the house. Also heard was someone shouting at them in what must have been Korean. Tolbane and the others felt that the wounded were being told to shut up, or else…

Captain Tam had to reassess his situation. He was completely caught off guard. There were only twenty men left to do the job. Those wounded would not be in any shape to help. The captain was aware that they had hand grenades, but they had no rocket launchers.

With the fire from the house and the two marine positions, though he didn't know they were marines, he needed to find another angle to attack. He had to succeed. Failure was not an option for him. He might die while failing here, or he would die later because he failed. What a dilemma he was in.

After about ten minutes, he sent a couple of scouts to find a way around the positions they had received fire from. He moved the rest of his men to the edge of the trees and began firing at those two positions and at the house, drawing attention from the two scouts.

Inside the house, everyone was caught off guard by the volume of fire coming from the tree line into both floors. They lay flat on the floors, fearful of the bullets that were breaking up the windows and going through the walls and over everyone's heads. The occupants could hear the rounds going overhead, tearing up the furniture and destroying everything in their path. A few minutes later, the firing stopped.

Everything was still. It was an eerie and deathly quietness to them. In checking the positions in the house, they found out that no one was injured. Just for the hell of it, to send a message to the clowns, Tolbane coordinated a mad minute of fire at the tree line. A couple of yelps could be heard, along with the thump of bullets hitting the trees and of branches breaking.

He thought out loud to no one in particular, "Those asses don't know who they're screwing with. GI Joe and his troops will prevail with Mike Hammer's help."

The others looked at him as though he had a screw loose. Now the waiting for the main event began again. Soon, they heard a short volley of shots coming from somewhere behind the house. They didn't know that the gunfire was the North Vietnamese scouts going on a permanent visit to their ancestors at that very moment.

Captain Tam presumed as much. He just lost two more men. Three wounded had crawled back to his position. The fusillade from the house had wounded two more. Now he had twenty-one men, five of whom were wounded. Maybe four of those could still fight. He posted a couple of guards and advised the rest to try and get some sleep until he was ready to begin his assault on the house anew later on.

If only he had a plan. He was at sea as to what his next step would be. He did know that whatever he did, the grenades would have to be part of it. He decided to take a nap to refresh. Maybe he could reason a little better if rested. He informed a guard when to wake him up.

After it had been quiet for a while, the decision was made to go on 50 percent alert, allowing the troops to rotate getting some sleep.

Tolbane and Jim had determined that the assaulters would rest for a while, then regroup. They would have to rethink their tactics and come up with some different way of attacking. Ralph crawled up to the back and entered the house, announcing himself first so as not to meet Mr. Bullet.

Ralph began.

"I've got an idea that might work if you'd like to hear it."

Everyone nodded their okay.

"I've got a bunch of raggedy-ass marines back there that's just hungry to dip their wicks in some kind of shoot-'em-up. I think we can move in on the turds from two sides and clean their clocks. What say you all?"

"From two sides, you may be subject to friendly fire," Jim stated.

Tolbane followed up with, "If you got behind them and attacked on angles, it might work. Your fire would form an X, which would keep rounds from hitting the house too."

"I got it! An interlocking field of fire. That would tear their ever-loving asses up big-time. It's a good plan, if I do say so, Travis. Is everyone in agreement on this?"

Approval was voiced by all.

"Good. Let me get back to the troops. Just in case, when you hear the first round crank off, hit the deck. Let me go get my gunny and do some quick planning with him."

He left the house on the double. Then James Cook asked a question.

"Tell me, do you guys get into this kind of shit all the time?"

Tri answered, "James, we have been in a few hairy situations, but no, we don't do this all the time, only when it becomes a necessity. We do prefer the peace and quiet of normal duties at all times."

James Cook, after looking around at everyone in awe, addressed the major.

"I'm really glad I got assigned here now. I was not too happy about the assignment to begin with. It is really something to see how the other half lives when the stuff hits the fan. I don't suppose I'll be able to tell the guys about it, though, will I?"

"As long as you mention none of our names, I don't see why you may not tell of your experience with us. It is unique by any means. By the time you return to your unit, we'll have all faded into the woodwork anyway, and you'll have lots of 'You won't believe this shit, but…' stories," Tri answered, smiling.

"Hey," Tolbane suddenly exclaimed. "I've an idea. James, why don't you take one of the ARs, go upstairs, and relieve one of the shooters at the windows? When the shit hits the fan over there shortly, some of those guys may try to escape toward the house. If so, whether you get to take a couple potshots at the enemy or not, it's part of the grandiose experience of your very being at this time and space. Watching, waiting, waiting, and watching and then executing are part of the game. It will add to your story line too. The troops will be adoring you. You'll be the king of the camp."

"Damn! Thanks, Travis, for the pep talk. I'll never forget you guys. This is really the thrill that comes once in a lifetime. To do it with a group of warriors such as you all is a real privilege. I really consider myself lucky I was chosen for this fiasco."

*****

Nearly an hour after Special 6 Cook manned the upstairs window, all Billy Hell broke out in the treed area. The trees and foliage were so thick that the orange tracers could hardly be seen from the upstairs windows crossing in their X pattern. As Tolbane surmised, two of the Vietnamese came running out of the tree line. James got one, and the other got it from the marine shooter.

The firefight was over in about five minutes. Captain Tam was wounded, and he and four others who were wounded were captured. Ralph immediately came to the house and gave a sitrep to Tri. She called in on her secure line that the threat had been neutralized, that a medevac was needed for the wounded prisoners, and that body removal was needed for about thirty enemy KIAs.

Ralph's troops were relaxing until morning, when they would clean up the target area, gather weapons and equipment, and stack the bodies in the clear area in front of the house for the removal crew.

When the tasks were done, they would go back to their positions and relax until further orders from up on high came down.

As it happened, the troops were not removed from the site for two days. They were promised a terrific meal on return to their company area. Then they would receive a five-day liberty pass, no distance requirement.

It would be on the fourth day before Tolbane and Jim would be ordered back to Swamp Lejeune. James cook was asked to stay and cook for the three and would leave the day after Tolbane and Jim. The four of them had a lot of good conversations and kidding and playing games to while away the time. James had a few private conversations with Tolbane while taking walks around the campus.

James was so enthused about his time with this group. He never imagined that things like this ever happened in the good old USA. He additionally confided to Tolbane that when he fired on the fleeing guy, he felt no elation from the guy going down. However, since then, he had been a little ambivalent about taking a life even if it was the right thing to do.

Tolbane advised him that it was common for those feelings to emerge the first or second time you took a life. It was never a good thing to take a life, but sometimes, it had to be, especially when it was to kill or be killed yourself. James felt a little better about it then.

"One more thing, James. When you tell your stories, you have to begin with, 'You guys aren't going to believe this shit, but...' Also, if you lie to it, I'll swear to it."

Tolbane and Tri did have a few minutes alone each day. They would hold hands, hug, and kiss a bit. She confessed that if she really let herself go, she would fall deeply in love with him. He reckoned that he felt the same way about her.

She made him promise, "When you think about me, I don't want you to think of me as Maj. Ngo Bui Tri. I want you to always remember me as your one and only lady Phuoc and the wonderful things and the hardships we went through together."

"Phuoc, I've already decided that very thing."

"Travis, I don't mean to change the subject, but I've arranged for a letter of appreciation to be placed in James's service record and some kind of medal issued to him. I really enjoyed him being with us. His meals, I'll damn sure miss them. He's a great cook and a great Cook. Damn it, I'm getting as bad as you."

The departure day came too soon. The new security team for the major arrived. Tolbane and Jim stowed their gear in their cars and would eat their final lunch in the house. After lunch, the four went out front, watching a crew work on the damage to the house from the firefight.

Saying goodbye was really hard for all, especially to Tri and Tolbane. Neither one could hide the tears forming in their eyes knowing they would never see each other again. That final minute came, and Phuoc and James waved goodbye. Then Tolbane slowly and sadly got in his car and followed Jim down the road.

James Cook looked at Tri and commented on his duty with the guys.

"Jim's a good guy, but that Tolbane dude, wow! I've never met anyone during my military career like him. He's like Superman on steroids. I don't know of any army staff NCO that would have let me man that window. I hate to say it, but it was exciting. I think that will be the highlight of my career, never to be forgotten or topped."

"James, you've only seen a part of Travis. You'll never know how great he really is. I've never known such a fearless and levelheaded hero. I'll miss the ornery dork and a half the rest of my life."

Tolbane was maudlin the entire way back to Camp Lejeune, North Carolina. He really felt that life had decided to make disappointment his lifelong fate. This was the third time he had had to leave Phuoc. This time, it really was for real. He smacked the steering wheel with the flat of his right hand. He surprised himself that he didn't break it or the steering wheel.

He made it a point to try to think of something he had enjoyed, like the time in Saigon when his interpreter Ba got a tattoo of Snoopy on his bicep saying, "Happiness is a warm pussy." But that kind of thought didn't last long. He still missed the hell out of her.

CHAPTER 24

"Wow, I can't believe this shit. What have I ever done to deserve this?" he wondered aloud to no one in particular.

He had just left the battalion commander's office and was standing outside the Sixth Marines headquarters. When he and Jim returned on Friday night, the officer of the day instructed them to take the weekend off and report to the commanding officer's office at 0800 hours on Monday.

The battalion's commanding officer welcomed them back. He presented each a letter of appreciation for their recent assignment. Jim, the battalion sergeant major, was directed to reassume his interrupted duties and return to his office. The CO then addressed Tolbane.

"Top, your position as the S-2 chief has been replaced by another marine. You may go there and retrieve any personal items you might have there. Take the rest of the day off and report to the Second Marine Division's G-2 officer, Col. Roger Picket, at 0800 hours tomorrow. I can't tell you any more than that, but let me wish you well on your future endeavors and the rest of your career in our wonderful corps."

Tolbane was dismissed, and he walked outside with his head in the clouds. He had no idea what might evolve from the next morning, but he considered it a privilege to be assigned to a division regardless of the position he would be assigned to.

At 0800 hours on the dot, he knocked on the division G-2's door. He was ordered to enter and report. He did. The G-2 bade him to stand easy, then to take a seat on the far side of the office. The colonel didn't ask if he wanted any but said the coffee would be there shortly. The colonel then took a seat beside him.

"Master Sergeant Tolbane, I'll refer to you as Top. Well, Top, I'm overwhelmed by your career. Very distinguished service. Indeed, I am awed. It reads like a Dan Daly, a Chesty Puller, or a Smedley Butler saga. Maybe I'm stretching it just a bit, but I need you to know you are appreciated. Very few men, regardless of service, have had the opportunity to distinguish themselves as you have. Now before we begin about why you're here, are there questions you'd like answered besides 'What in the fuck am I doing here?'?"

Tolbane had been feeling a little tense; now felt a little more at ease.

He smiled and replied, "Sir, outside of being fucking curious, I can't think of anything. I just go where I'm sent and try to do the best job I can."

"That's why you're a master sergeant. You are very diligent in performing your duties and fearless in the pursuit of overcoming difficulties and making a success of your missions. You come highly recommended from other channels than the regular administrative hierarchy we deal with on a continuous basis. That's why you are the new Second Marine Division G-2 chief. What do you think of that?"

"My turn to be awed, sir. What an honor, Colonel! I'll perform my duties to the best of my abilities. All I can say is wow again."

"I have faith in you at this point, something I don't always have until a guy proves his worth. Anything else, Top?"

"Sir, if I may speak freely?"

"You have the floor now, Top."

"I really want to do this job to the best of my ability. However, my heart still yearns to be with the interrogation teams, my original duty in the Corps."

"I understand. I felt you may feel that way. Right now, the teams do not have slots for E-9s. Maybe when they do, you'll have the opportunity to return."

"Sir, I don't mean to correct the colonel, but I'm only an E-8."

"I hate to say it, but that's only for a few more days. The Marine Corps promotion list will be out in a few days, and I have it on good authority you'll be on it. I guess you'll just have to accept it and change chevrons when it happens. I don't know what your precedent number will be. What day you'll receive the promotion on, I can't say either."

"A promotion too? Wow! I really am overwhelmed now, sir. I never expected that. I've been so lucky promotion-wise. I've been jumped over some very good marines. It's mind-blowing to me."

"Top, believe me, from our researching your career, you've deserved every one of them in the finest tradition of the United States Marine Corps. So suck it up, Top, and welcome aboard. Now since you just got back from one of your escapades, you probably need a few days off.

"Monday morning, there will be an 0800 briefing with the commanding general, etc., so come in about 1000 hours and get with the intel chief, Master Gunnery Sergeant Dobrosky. He'll be snapping you in. Now get out of my sight until Monday. Enjoy yourself, because when you come back, I'm going to work your ass off. Enjoy!"

"Aye, aye, sir."

Tolbane stood, took one step backward, did an about-face, and marched out of the colonel's office. Once outside the division headquarters and heading to his vehicle, Tolbane wished he could jump up and click his heels. But even if he could do it, he probably should not try it where he was at the time. It wouldn't do too well for passing troops to see a master sergeant performing gymnastics. His Marine Corps career was now solidified. As good as he felt about this new phase of his life, he still missed Phuoc.

*****

The next Monday morning, he entered the Second Marine Division G-2 office, smiling at those he passed, and he noticed they were looking at him rather strangely. He noticed the intelligence chief's office, which would soon be his, and was met by the intelligence chief with a broad smile and a warm handshake.

"I've been anxiously awaiting you, Tolbane. You're a welcome sight," the chief began. "I'll be retiring after thirty years in two weeks. Haven't made any plans yet. Just gonna do a lot of fishing for a while before I try to decide. I don't think I'll have to worry about this office going downhill after I leave. For the record, I think you'll be the best replacement I could have."

"Thanks for the compliment, Master Guns. I'll damn sure do my best to live up to your standards. I've nosed around a bit and have been informed that you have been the best ever to sit in that chair. I'll do my damned best to keep this section up to your standard."

After the introductions, Tolbane's training for the position began in earnest. He soon realized it sure was a lot different from being a 2-chief at a battalion or a regiment. The scope of operations was nearly mind-boggling. He was finally catching on when three days before Dobrosky was supposed to retire, Tolbane was made the new division G-2 chief.

Tolbane had asked the office staff to come in half an hour early that morning to say a Marine Corps goodbye to Dobrosky. He had coffee, tea, and a sheet cake set out on tables. Everyone shook Dobrosky's hand goodbye. The female marines hugged him goodbye with tears in their eyes.

After Dobrosky left, Tolbane held his first meeting with his office staff to explain his rules.

"I've been informed that I inherited the best G-2 shop crew in the Corps. After being here nearly two weeks, I firmly believe that. I'm not making any wholesale changes like some dumbasses do when they take over an operation and want to show off their newfound power and screw everything up. You all know your job, and you perform it well, better than I could at this point in time. Keep up the good work. This office will continue to function in its day-to-day operations without change unless directed by the powers that be. Should any situation make such a demand, I will address it at that time.

"My office is always open to you anytime you feel the need, operational or personal. As a final note, before I chase your ever-loving butts back to work, I can tell right now there will most likely be times I'll be asking some of you what the hell I am supposed to do in certain situations. Right now, I'm at sea here. Anybody got questions, now's the time to put my dumbass on the spot."

All the staff came forward to welcome him to the office, then peeled off and went to work. Tolbane was nearly moved to tears. He had not ever expected this kind of support to the FNG.[14]

Somehow, Tolbane got through his first day as the division intelligence chief without screwing up. He had been a little apprehensive about starting his first day, as he should have. But as he left for the day, he felt a little more confident.

On Mondays and Wednesdays, he would attend the commanding generals' briefing. On Fridays, he would meet with the G-2 to find out what was desired of him during the briefing. He understood it would mostly be order of battle intelligence relating to marines from other units deployed in hostile areas. He wondered if his knees would collapse when he arose to give his presentation. Right then, he wondered where in the hell he would find the data.

*****

Things went well for Tolbane. Six months later, his promotion warrant arrived, and he became one of the youngest master gunnery sergeants in the Corps. A year and a half later, he was transferred to the G-2 section of the First Marine Brigade, Marine Corps Air Station Kaneohe Bay, Oahu, Hawaii.

It was a great tour of duty for Tolbane—sand and surf and all the good stuff. It wasn't nearly as demanding as it had been at the Second Division G-2, just enough happening with the job to keep it from becoming a bore. He only had to worry about a reinforced Third Regiment and MAG-24 air wing unit instead of a whole brigade.

He enjoyed an affair with a couple of island girls, but nothing really as serious as with Phuoc. He took up scuba diving and joined the base scuba club, the AKU Marines. (It was kinda like Tuna Marines.) He made thirty-two dives during his two years there.

When his tour of duty was up with the brigade, he got a great surprise. He was transferred to Fleet Marine Force, Pacific (FMFPAC). What was so surprising was the fact that FMF Pac was on the other

---

[14] A Viet Nam veterans' slang that stands for fucking new guy.

end of the island, atop Halawa Heights, Camp H. M. Smith, over-looking Pearl Harbor more than a few miles away. He couldn't believe he would be in paradise for two more years. It was hard to believe he would be spending four years in sand and surf. What a place to spend his twenty-something years in the Corps before he left the island.

His duties were somewhat different from his previous duties as an intelligence chief. He, along with a couple members of his staff, would accompany the FMF Pac G-2 throughout the Pacific to inspect the various marine installations and, for him, their intelligence sections. He and his staff members would audit various units of intelligence operations. Only on occasion would he have to make suggested changes to their routine. One thing he really loved about inspection trips was that red-carpet treatment was always the order of the day at each unit that was inspected.

When his FMF Pac tour of duty was completed, he hated to leave Oahu. He had begun to believe he was a Hawaiian islander for life. So far, the FMF Pac gig had been the crowning glory of his Marine Corps career.

When he was boarding the aircraft at Honolulu International Airport to return stateside, he really had mixed emotions about leaving. He wanted to look forward to his next assignment, but at the same time, he was loathe to leave his personal paradise.

He thought he would probably go to a duty station he had never been to before, but lo and behold, he was going back to the Second Marine Division, Camp Lejeune, North Carolina. He was at sea because his orders did not specify a particular post there. It was all up in the air. He decided he would do as he did once before. He would check in but would stay on leave status so he wouldn't lose accrued leave days.

He fell asleep as soon as the aircraft reached its cruising altitude. He awoke because of the screech and grinding of the wheels coming down. He noticed the flight attendant had secured his seat belt, and he never woke up. He reckoned he must have been tired.

CHAPTER 25

Swamp Lejeune, North Carolina, hadn't changed a bit. After checking into the Second Marine Division duty section the night he arrived, he was put up for the night in the transit facility, along with enlisted privates up to his rank. The next morning, he was assigned a better room at the senior staff NCO billet than he was last time he was at the swamp.

Stowing his carry gear, he walked to and checked division supply to see if the seabag and footlocker he had shipped a week before leaving Oahu had arrived. It had. The supply chief had a lance corporal transport him and his gear to his billet and help him take it inside. He brightened the lance corporal's day by insisting he take the two twenty-dollar bills Tolbane offered him. The kid was elated.

"Master Guns, if you ever need a lackey for something, you know where to find me!"

He left with the biggest grin ever.

Tolbane stowed part of his gear, then took a nap so he would be fresh to catch a ride into Jacksonville later that night. First thing on his slate was to get a vehicle and auto insurance. It would probably be a day or two before he could pick it up. Then he would go to the first bar he went to years ago as a gunnery sergeant.

*****

After hitching a ride into town, he hired a cab to take him around to three different car dealers. He bought a four-door light-tan 1978 Plymouth Volaré with an all-velour interior. It was too late in the day to get insurance, so he planned that for the next morning.

He then headed to what had been his favorite watering hole a few years before.

The same bartender still worked there. He greeted Tolbane and introduced him to the new breed of customers, one of whom drove him back to the base and poured his inebriated rear end into his room, where he crashed on the floor until morning. The bartender had given him some sad news. His old boss Dick Head had a seizure and passed away nearly a year before. Tolbane was really touched, as he had liked that old bastard.

Waking up with the mother of all hangovers, Tolbane cleaned up and changed into clean clothes. Being too late for chow, he hitched a ride into town, got his insurance coverage, and picked up his car. Being hungry as a bluetick coonhound, he found a small café and vacuumed down a huge breakfast. Finally sated and feeling less hungover, he decided to drive around Jacksonville, North Carolina, to see what was still old and what was new. Not sure what to do for the next few hours, he decided to go to a movie. He couldn't believe it when he read the marquee: *The D.I.* It was déjà vu.

He thought out loud to himself, "I'll be damned."

He had seen the movie starring Jack Webb the first time he went to town from Camp Geiger in 1957, so he bought a ticket and watched the film for the fifth time. After the movie, he graduated to his favorite watering hole once more. He made it a point to only have three beers, then drove back to base. Even though he was no longer hungover, he felt wasted from the previous night's indulgence and needed a good night's sleep. He did exactly that.

*****

For the next two weeks, he did whatever he felt like doing, making it a point not to drink in excess. He would eat, sleep, drive around, and carouse around a bit. One night, he thought he had met a nice girl, but he soon found out different from a couple of new drinking buddies. He finally decided he was ready to bite the bullet once more and checked into the division S-1 section from leave. His first question to the admin officer was about the fact that he was not assigned to any MOS billet. He had no idea what type of duty he would be assigned to.

The captain greeted him, and after checking Tolbane's orders, he remarked, "Well, Master Guns, I really don't know what MOS you'll be working in. However, I do know where I'll be sending you, but not down there even if you do deserve it. Please don't ask me what you'll be doing where I'm sending you, as I have no friggin' idea what goes on there either."

"Sounds kind of hush-hush scary to me, Captain."

"I agree with you 100 percent. I've sent a few others there too, but it's well beyond me that with my rank and position here, you'd think I might be given even the smallest hint as to what's happening there. Really strange crap. Hold on just a minute longer. I need to get something from my desk."

The captain took out a key from his pocket, opened the locked center drawer of his desk, and pulled out a single sheet of paper with the official Marine Corps logo at the top and with some typed instructions on it.

"This document has all the info you'll need to get to your assignment. After reading it, it won't self-destruct after five seconds, so take good care of it."

"I'll guard it with my life, Captain. Maybe I'll even chew it up into a wad. Then I'll bury it out at Onslow Beach under a ton of sand."

With a grin, the captain laughed a bit.

"Well, do bury it as deep as you can or swallow it. We wouldn't want the axis to get wind of what's going on. After all, loose lips sink ships. That's all I need with you today, Master Guns. I hope you have good luck with your super-duper spook job, whatever it is."

"Thank you, sir. By your leave, sir!"

Tolbane came to attention, took two steps to the rear, performed an about-face, and left the office.

"Damn, what in the hell kind of shit am I in for this time around?" he spoke aloud to no one, as he was wont to do on occasion.

Tolbane climbed in his car and sat there for several minutes in a kind of stupor, wondering once more what kind of shit he was in for this time, before he remembered the typed instructions he was given. He reckoned he should read them. As he began scanning the document, he knew he was probably going to be in deep doo-doo. One of the instructions was to tell no one where he was going and to turn the letter in when he arrived at his destination.

He followed the driving instructions to a tee and arrived at his destination, a small complex of old Quonset huts in a far-out and remote and isolated corner of Camp Geiger. One hut had an American flag and a Marine Corps flag flying on twenty-foot poles in front of it, so he presumed, with his superior intellect and logical mind, he made the deduction that, that was the office he needed to repot to. He parked in front of it and entered hesitantly, still leery of what was waiting for him inside the place.

CHAPTER 26

The office was pretty standard for an office in one of those type of buildings. The rear was sectioned off with a door in the center. A railing running to the walled section with a gate was to the left as one entered. There were four desks. The first desk had a PFC, the second a sergeant, the third a staff sergeant, and the fourth a first lieutenant, all wearing the Marine Corps utility uniform with their duty belt and .45s.

All four marines looked up at Tolbane when he entered. The staff sergeant and the lieutenant both stood and bade him to enter the gate.

The lieutenant said, "We've been waiting on your arrival. Thought you'd never get here. The staff sergeant will check some things with you. Then we'll get to know one another before I take you in to see the skipper."

The staff sergeant motioned him to his desk, shook hands with him, and introduced himself as Bob Styles. He pulled out a folding chair and handed it to Tolbane, who unfolded it and sat down beside the desk. Then he handed Tolbane a double sheet form.

"Master Guns, I need you to fill out this form before we can get started with anything. Any questions for me, just ask."

He also handed him a clipboard for it and a black ink pen. Before writing any answer on the form, Tolbane gave the two-page document a quick scan.

"I'll tell you one thing right now. I can't believe I have all the answers to these questions at this time."

"Just answer what you can. That will be fine for now. The important ones have an asterisk beside them."

Tolbane finished checking some blocks and writing sentences on certain lines and whatever, then handed the clipboard back to Styles.

"Your answers look good for now, Master Guns. I'll do a little research and see if I can find a few of the answers you missed. Lieutenant, I'm through here for now."

"Good! Okay, Master Guns, come on over and have a seat."

Tolbane moved his folding chair to the side of his desk and said with his usual silly-ass grin, "Reporting as ordered, sir!"

"Don't tell me. I know. We got another smart-ass around here. Seems we're plagued with them nowadays," the lieutenant said, laughing. "Actually, we're fortunate to have a little humor around here, or we'd go buggy."

"That's good to know. I do get carried away at times. Comes with the territory, I guess."

"We're glad to have you aboard in any case. As long as the major's not around, I'm Clyde, not Clyde the camel, and I'll call you Travis, if that's okay with you?"

"I have answered to worse epithets. Be my guest."

"I'll bet I know exactly what's on your mind at this very moment. 'What in the fuck am I doing here?' Am I correct?"

"You got that right. Give the man a cigar and a Kewpie doll."

"As long as it's Cuban cigar, I'll accept it. The major will tell you about your position here and what your assigned duties will be. For now, I can only say that we are a small group, and we're semiformal, more or less kind of a loosey-goosey unit. Being as small as we are, we can be a little more informal than most units in the Corps.

"We work close together as a team and strive to support each other to the max. I do know of your what some call heroic exploits, and without a doubt, I'm sure you'll have our six,[15] as well as we'll have yours. Anything you want to ask before I take you to the man?"

"Can't think of anything offhand. I'm curious as hell as to what's going on, and I'm ready to face the music and dance, if I could dance."

---

[15] To have one's back.

170

"Good. I'll just let you dance right into his office. As I said, we are a little informal. So when you go in, just say, 'Good afternoon, Major.' Forget 'Reporting as ordered, sir!' The major will take it from there."

They stood and walked to the door. The lieutenant knocked and heard the major answer with "Enter."

Tolbane opened the door and entered the office and nearly fell on his face when entering. He knew the major.

"MGySgt. Travis Tolbane, wipe that dumbass look off your face, close the door, and get your ever-loving ass over here."

As Tolbane closed the door, Phuoc got up and met him with a big hug and a deep kiss. He returned her amorous greeting in kind.

"My God, woman, I've missed you so much! What in the hell are you doing here anyhow? I thought you were medically retired and hidden in some obscure place for the duration."

"It's a very long story, my dear Travis. Right now, just let me get you briefed a little on your assignment here. Tonight, we can talk, and I'll catch you up on everything then. Travis, we are an experimental unit with a company-sized team concept, incorporating a few specialized jobs to see how our team may blend in with and support deployed units in contingency areas.

"You are now the team chief and the interrogation instructor. You'll need to set up a curriculum for that phase once we decide how deep we'll be going into the various MOS skill training we'll be doing. We'll begin conducting meetings on that and several other things in two days. We need to get you billeted here today and complete a security attachment to your top-secret clearance so you may operate with us. That's what the form you filled out was for. Questions?"

"None pertaining to this."

"Okay! We'll go get you a billet here, then go pick up your gear and get you settled. Then I know this nice little restaurant that serves great steaks, good salad and hot bread, and great wines. And we can have a quiet two-people booth and talk about our situation. Ready to go, my handsome dork and a half?"

"I'm as ready, willing, and able as you are, my dear Major. Lead me to that medium rare New York strip steak."

"I know you're ready to chow down, and you'll want plenty of bacon bits and honey mustard on your salad."

"How did you ever guess?"

"I'm psychic that way, my man. Let's get out of here."

Phuoc let the lieutenant know what they were going to do, all except for the restaurant, and they were gone.

*****

After getting Tolbane checked out of his quarters mainside, they got him a billet at Camp Geiger, stowed his gear, and went to Phuoc's favorite place, this time in her Cadillac convertible, a little hideaway restaurant a ways up from the Second Front.[16] The cute female waitress smiled at Tolbane and showed them to a two-person booth in a small dining room off the main dining area.

They both ordered New York strips, medium rare, baked potatoes with all the trimmings, house salads, and a pitcher of Bud draft. They decided to just have small talk between them and save the good stuff for later until they were done with the meal. They mostly talked about how some things had changed in the area, especially how things in the area had run down during Viet Nam due to lack of troops stationed at Camp Lejeune and how they had recovered to be even better.

After the meal and enjoying a steaming-hot cup of coffee, Phuoc began her story.

"Travis, after your foray on my behalf while I was recovering, Uncle Sam secluded me in a beautiful but secret mountain area retreat somewhere out west where I was safe. There were two surgeries on my hip. If you've noticed—I'm sure you did while checking out my butt—I recovered well enough to walk nearly as well as before the wound after a couple of years of therapy and exercise. I did a lot of hiking and other things. I began to feel brand-new. We can talk more about that later. I also missed you, but that's another story."

---

16 The bar and entertainment area across from Camp Geiger.

"I'm glad you are pretty well back to normal. Your butt is still as nice as it ever was, and I missed you too."

"Somewhere way up the totem pole of the military hierarchy, someway, somehow, someone got ahold of the reports of our little excursion to rescue that dude and decided that we needed small, clandestine units combining many different MOS skills. All members of the unit would be cross-trained in the basics of all the skills needed for covert operations. Instructors from each skill would be made available to initially cross-train a test unit.

"Some brainiac decided that since you and I had led a successful mission, we are experienced and should be the ones to head up this group. Once we are fully trained, an operation would be found for us to prove the concept is successful. Now although I don't want to, I do have to remind you that this is a highly classified program."

"I understand, Phuoc. I thought you were medically retired. It seems to me this is unfair to you after the things you went through during your time on active duty."

"This is only a temporary recall to active duty for me, then back to retirement when the project is over. In about two weeks or so, I'll get my silver leaf collar emblem, and that means you'll have to make love to a lieutenant colonel in the United States Marine Corps. How about that shit, Master Guns?"

"Wow! That's great. Congratulations! I always wondered what it'd be like to screw one. Hopefully, I'll get the chance in two weeks. Meanwhile, a major is fair game."

"If you play your cards right. Back to the Corps. There are some troops being checked out as instructors and some as students. The qualifications are pretty stiff. You won't be involved in that phase. First and foremost, you're the NCOIC.[17] Secondly, you'll set up an interrogation syllabus. You needn't worry about that until we know exactly how much of each skill is to be taught. As these teachers and students are selected and arrive, you'll interview them and begin their evaluation, which will continue throughout the course."

---

[17] Noncommissioned officer in charge.

"That won't be difficult to set up an evaluation process. I'll get Staff Sergeant Styles to set up a file system on each one, maybe even design an evaluation form for us. So until the personnel begin to arrive, what do we, not as individuals, do in the meantime?"

"We'll play it by ear as we go hippety-hop along."

She tweaked her ear with her index finger.

"We do need to set up an exercise regimen for each morning for the troops, and we, those of us here, need to start doing some conditioning hikes, starting with a mile and increasing that incrementally. By the time class is over, we'll need a couple of twenty milers with the whole class. We'll be expected to be combat ready at course's end. We might even get in some target practice with different weapons.

"Time-wise, the course could end up being six to eight months or maybe even shorter. That duration will be evaluated as we progress through the course and how competent and adaptable the students are. Hopefully, we'll get top-notch students and not unit castoffs."

"Looks like we'll have our hands full once we get underway. I don't feel right toasting with coffee. Waiter!"

When the waiter got to the table, Tolbane ordered, "Two large snifters of your best white."

The cute waitress returned with two flutes of a white wine, a Liebfraumilch, set them on the table, and then winked at Tolbane and wished them to enjoy. Tolbane looked Phuoc in the eyes and toasted.

"Phuoc, my beautiful lady, I toast to you the greatest of success in this new endeavor, and may it be the pinnacle of your career."

They clinked snifters and chugged them dry.

"Thanks, Travis. I think right now we have some unfinished business at my rental home and in my bedroom. Let's pay the bill and get the hell out of here, Travis."

CHAPTER 27

The next morning, Tolbane and Maj. Ngo Bu Tri, Phuoc to Tolbane, was using her retired name, and Tolbane toured the large area. Besides the headquarters hut, there were eight more. They discussed three of them being set up as classrooms, half of one for staff NCOs and the other half partitioned for officers, three for troop quarters, and the last as a kind of rec room for the troops.

The major would contact the Shore Party Battalion for an engineer unit to get help in designing and remodeling the Quonset huts to her specs, maybe even put in two more for good measure. They checked out another section of the compound by a tree line and considered putting in a mini obstacle course of some type there. PT was a must.

Another section of their compound that they looked at was heavily wooded. The major wondered if they could get aerial photos of it to see if there was anything on the other side of the trees that could be harmed by live fire. If not, they could put in a couple of berms and have a two-hundred-yard firing range for rifles, machine guns, etc. and a pistol range of twenty-five yards. From what the major knew, they would need plenty of live fire training. Another thing she could put in there would be a hand grenade range.

Returning to the office together, Tolbane happened to get a thought while looking around.

"I have a question, Major, that only one of your superior intellect and IQ could ever answer for me. There are four desks here manned by four marines. Not too much room left for me having a desk, is there?"

"Not to worry yourself, Master Guns. The situation is well in hand. I have another desk and desk chair coming for you. It will be placed in my office. When it gets here, we'll move things around to make it fit. Okay?"

"Your every wish cannot but be my every command, Your Highness!"

"You're so full of shit you'd need a full fifty-five-gallon oil drum in the shitter, you know that, Tolbane?"

The office crew who had been watching and listening to the two marines had to stifle their giggles while trying to keep straight faces. The major opened her office door, and they entered, and she closed the door. She slouched in her desk chair while he plopped on the fold-up chair.

"Travis, your desk should be here tomorrow. Once we have you situated in here, you need to start looking at ordering training manuals. I have a complete listing of all DOD[18] manuals you can use. Pick out ones you know we'll need, and as the instructors arrive, review the list with them. We'll submit the order when the last one reports in.

"The first two instructors are due to arrive day after tomorrow. The last one should be in by next Monday. The highest rank among them is master sergeant. All should be tops in their respective fields. Tuesday morning, we will go as a group to First ITR.[19] Supply and draw our personal equipment and weapons. The troops will draw theirs on checking in. Also, schedule a two-mile hike, full pack, and weapons for next Wednesday morning at 0630 hours."

"Good! That will give me something to get started with."

"Look, I have a long and important meeting to attend this evening. Can't tell you about it. I'm sure you have some things you need to do this afternoon and evening, so take the afternoon off to get squared away and drink a couple cold ones for me tonight, and I'll see you in the AM."

She walked over to him, kissed his cheek, and ordered, "Now get the hell out of here before I jump your bones!"

---

[18] Department of Defense.
[19] Infantry Training Regiment.

"Aye, aye, sir, ma'am, or whatever. I'll just go do or die. Semper fi and all that gung ho stuff even though jumping my bones sounds good too."

She threw her stapler at him, just missing him as he closed the door, bouncing off the door. He was smiling like the Cheshire cat. The four marines, hearing the stapler hit the door, looked on, wondering what the fuck was going on as Tolbane walked out the door, smiling and whistling, no less, the Marine Corps hymn.

Tolbane used the rest of the working day to get personal items from the Geiger PX, putting his gear in its place in his quarters, and taking laundry to the base cleaners as well as some items needing only to be pressed. He then decided it was naptime USA.

After naptime, he got spruced up and went into town. He parked in a lot and was walking around looking for a place to eat that suited him. He was walking past a jewelry store, and what to his wondering eyes appeared but the lieutenant from the office exiting the premises.

"Well, fancy meeting you in a town like this, Lieutenant."

"Oh, how about that. Are you slumming tonight?"

"Only if I can find the right slum to dine in."

"Come on with me. I think I know the right ptomaine palace. I remembered after you left today I never formally introduced myself to you. I go by Clyde, but my name is Josh Goodnight—Josh off duty, Clyde at work."

They shook hands, making it official.

"Glad to know you, Josh. Call me anything except too late for chow. We got quite a lash-up going on here, don't we?"

"I could win money on that bet. Let's wait till we fill our craws and sating our guts and then talk over a couple of cool ones."

"Best offer I've had today. You're on!"

Later after their dirty plates were removed from the table, they were served a Bud for Tolbane and a Miller Lite for Josh by the waiter. Then their conversation began in earnest.

"Travis, I'm sorry to say this, but having just arrived here, you don't know the real half of it yet. The major argued up and down against this very concept to no friggin' avail. Her position on it—and rightly so—was, if there was a specific clandestine operation to man, build an operational unit by drawing skilled personnel from different units, tailoring the personnel to fit the mission criteria.

"She knew it would work, as she had participated in such an operation before, and to highlight her presentation was the cost factors of billeting, training, and maintaining a unit's integrity, such as this one. However, the powers that be decided differently. They know everything there is to know, where mere majors don't know diddly-squat about squat. That's how it stands now. It really is a big bag of worms."

"It definitely makes *Hogan's Goat* seem like great MIT material. These mental midgets all come out of the woodwork during peace time."

"I'd say, you can say that again, but I have the feeling you'd say it again just for the hell of it. As for the major, she is not too thrilled at all to be here. She told me that if they hadn't offered her the Silver Leaf for full retirement, she would have told them to stuff it in their old kit bag. As far as being recalled to active duty temporarily, she really had no choice.

"That's it in a nutshell as far as my knowledge of the situation. We just have to continue to march and see where it takes us—success or failure."

"I know that feeling all too well. She'll continue to perform to the best of her ability, you can rest assured of that."

"I don't mean to pry, but she told me that you and her had some hairy adventures together, and you even saved her life once."

"I can't say much about it, highly classified, except that her serious wounds were due to a mission being compromised at a high level. We were both lucky to get our asses out alive that night. It was, as you say, pretty hairy. I was surprised to see her in the office and was happy to see her disability is less severe now."

"I might also add that she warned us about your sense of humor, which we saw firsthand today. It was a welcome scene. Things have been pretty dull around the office. We need cheering up sometimes."

"Since my flawless and fabulous reputation precedes me, I'll try not to disappoint."

"That's all we ask. What are you going to do now? I'm going to my quarters and do some reading."

"Don't tell a soul, but I'm going to my favorite watering hole and quaff a few."

"Okay. See you at work in the AM."

They each went on their own way.

*****

Half an hour after Tolbane arrived at the office the next morning, his desk and chair were delivered. He and the major rearranged the office to accommodate both desks. As soon as the desks were in place, Tolbane, since the door was closed, propped his feet up on the desk and leaned back, thinking about how nice it would be to drift off and have a nice nap. He opened one eye and saw the major giving him the evil eye; therefore, he thought it would be in his best interests to get to work.

Except for chow time, he kept busy with going over the training manual list and making some notes about what he needed to teach in an abbreviated interrogation course. He didn't notice the major didn't even mention her meeting the night before. She left early again, but she gave him a note indicating what time she would be home that evening. He was licking his chops.

*****

The course was nearing completion. The instructors and the students were exemplary. They were outstanding in their individual fields and readily adapted to the intense training they received. The unit was now in position to field three individual reinforced platoons, or a full company.

Each man was trained in explosive devices, interrogation techniques, radio communications, and hand-to-hand combat and skilled with several weapons, night operations, reconnaissance and reporting, and other tactical and combat skills. An additional bonus was, each reinforced platoon had native Arabic, French, German, and Spanish linguists who would be an asset in whatever region they were deployed in.

Tolbane and Phuoc only saw each other on rare occasions, as they did not want to arouse suspicions among the troops. Fraternizing between officer and enlisted personnel was definitely frowned upon in the Corps, a real no-no. One morning, Phuoc approached him with what she had been informed of the previous afternoon after he left the office.

"Close the door please. Thanks, Travis! I have no idea what is about to happen. I have to report to the G-2/G-3 FMFLANT[20] in the morning. I'll be gone at least two to three days. Something is happening up there. I don't know what yet. I don't know if this lash-up is being terminated or if we are about to be deployed in some manner. You and the lieutenant will have to keep things rolling for the next few days. I'll keep in touch as much as I'm allowed. I'd love to have you over tonight. However, I have a lot of paperwork at home to prepare for the meetings, and I need to leave for Norfolk, Virginia, this afternoon."

"I understand. I hope everything will turn out okay for you and for the unit. I'm beginning to feel at home here. I'll miss you while you're away, which means we'll have a whopping whoopee spree on your return."

"You're crazy as shit, you know that, Travis Tolbane? Of course, if you didn't have my pussy on your mind at all times, I'd damn sure dump you for a dildo. Come here and give me a kiss. That's an order from Maj. Ngo Bui Tri, MGySgt. Travis Tolbane. Then I need to leave."

Tolbane gladly took care of that order. Then he bade her fair winds and following seas, and she opened the door and was gone, leaving the office door open. Tolbane missed her already.

Tolbane walked into the office common, stood tall and erect, and announced, "I think it's that time. Everyone, lay your head on your desk and have a nappy time before we have recess on the playground."

---

[20] Fleet Marine Force, Atlantic.

The crew looked at him as though he had a screw loose, but they were getting used to his humor. This one took the cake, though. He grinned at them and walked back into his office space, closed the door, put his feet up on his desk, and was in dreamland in no time flat, dreaming of Playboy Bunnies romping on a beach, naked as a jaybird. He jerked awake when there was a knock on the office door.

Tolbane put his feet down, picked up a paper, pretended to be reading, and said aloud, "Come on in. It's unlocked."

Staff Sergeant Styles wasn't fooled, but he played the game.

"Hey, chief, a courier just dropped this top-secret document off. You need to read it posthaste. It's probably why the major had to go to Norfolk. The lieutenant went down to supply. He'll need to read it when he gets back too."

"Thanks! Oh, by the way, did everyone have a good naptime? I hope so!"

"Not as good as yours was, chief!"

Styles walked out the door laughing, closing the door behind him.

Looking over the document, Tolbane was frowning. There was a big coup attempt in one of the South American countries. It was believed to be funded by one of the other South American countries. "Shit" was his only oral comment to no one in particular. He hoped that this didn't mean that they would have to go into one of those screwed-up countries to rescue or capture somebody. Their troops were good, but the ramifications of their going in could be bad for Uncle Sam if they fucked up! He walked out and laid the file on the lieutenant's desk.

Tolbane looked at the three marines present there and said, "I hope to hell this document doesn't mean what I think it does. If so, we could be in for a rough time before long. If it does, you better write home and tell Mama to sell the shithouse, because your ass belongs to the Corps in some crappy country down south for a spell."

He went back to his desk, opened a drawer, got a pencil and paper, and began noting some of the things that would be needed on such a deployment. Fortunately, the troops already had most of what gear would be needed. Paramount would be plenty of ammunition for the various weapons they had, and plenty of individual rations would be needed, as well as batteries for radios and flashlights and medical supplies and a ton of etc.

He hoped that if they were deployed on a Mickey Mouse deal, there would not be any compromise of the operation to get them into the shit.

CHAPTER 28

Returning on Monday morning after three days at Norfolk, Lieutenant Colonel Ngo, having finally received her promotion in Norfolk, entered the hut immediately upon returning and gathered the whole office crew together for a preliminary briefing.

"I can't tell you much at this time, as the sorry, lame-brained asses up at FMFLANT don't know much about this either. What I don't like is the fact that if we are deployed, it will not be a surreptitious entry, which could put us in deep doo-doo right off the bat."

She looked each one in the eye and continued.

"Why would we be landing in a foreign country in full combat regalia in broad daylight, I have no earthly idea. I don't even know what area we may have to enter. As news anchors are fond to say, more to follow at 0800 hours. When I find out what the hell is going on, you all will find out. That's all I have to pass on today, so for now, it's business as usual. Tolbane, I need to see you in my office ASAP."

Before she could go to her office, the crew all approached her and congratulated her on getting her Silver Leaf. Once in the office with the door closed, she hugged Tolbane, and he gathered her close in his arms.

"Travis, I couldn't say too much out there, but between you and me, I think we went from the frying pan into the shit pile."

"It's that bad, Phuoc?"

"I wish I could tell you how bad, but"—she paused—"I'm not allowed, which sucks to high heaven."

"I understand, babe. Don't kick yourself in the butt. Just let me tap it one time. I wouldn't want to see such a thing of beauty bruised."

"That's the one thing I can always count on around here, Travis, some stupid, inane statement from you to make me feel better. You always do cheer me up. Now, MGySgt. Travis Tolbane, USMC, I think a new lieutenant colonel needs a congratulatory kiss."

He gave her a good one and copped a feel at the same time.

For the next half an hour to forty-five minutes, they discussed some of the minor things from her briefings in Norfolk. Most were just administrative changes to daily reporting and what additional things needed to go into their daily reports, as well as increased reporting being needed on the daily progress as opposed to the previous weekly reporting of their training cycle.

"Just two more things, Travis. First, tomorrow, I'm going visit that numbskull major over at the ITR supply who thinks a woman's job is in the kitchen."

"Well, if I may say so, you do pretty good in a kitchen if I remember correctly, my dear."

"Screw you, Travis. Number two—drumroll—I need you, but not tonight. I'm beat, and I really need you to understand that after the last few days, I need a good night's rest. I promise, we'll celebrate all to high heaven tomorrow night, and that's an order."

"I hear and obey, Your Highness. Your every wish is my command as usual."

"And as usual, you're still full of shit as a Thanksgiving turkey, but you are my cow patty."

"That's good to know. I'd be so disappointed if I weren't high on the list."

"Yeah, you're high on the list okay, but not the Christmas list. Now I need another smooch before I shove off. That was nice. See you in the AM. Ta-ta!"

Tolbane checked out the undulations as she walked out of the office. He realized he was one lucky bastard. Then he gathered the troops in the office and made a proposal.

"Wednesday is grab-ass afternoon, so why don't we plan a party for our recently promoted commanding officer and make it for the whole group? Beer, hamburgers, beer, hot dogs, beer, baked beans, beer and the whole menu, and beer."

The lieutenant jumped right in.

"First, we need beer. I can get it from the O club. Staff Sergeant Styles, you get the chow from the staff NCO mess. Sergeant, I need you to go to a bakery downtown and get three large sheet cakes decorated for a promotion party. No one but no one rats out the party. Our lieutenant colonel doesn't have the need-to-know, as we say in the hush-hush circle. Don't tell either the instructors of the troops either. It's classified, top-secret."

"Good deal, LT. I want to tell you guys, I know a few of the places and the many difficult and dangerous things she's gone through that you couldn't dream of, so I know she'll be happy as a double-cunted cow pissing on a flat rock to have the celebration," Tolbane offered to the others, who moaned and groaned at his quip.

After quitting time at 1600 hours, Tolbane went through his usual routine. But instead of going to his favorite watering hole in Jacksonville, he went to one of the small bars at the Second Front, directly across Camp Geiger. He drank the first one slow and the second one even slower, lamenting about his life and feeling rather stoic for some unknown reason.

He turned in early. He dreamed of him and Phuoc being shot at and her being hit a few times during the night, each time waking in a sweat. Come morning chow time, he felt pretty bedraggled. He knew then he would have to take the afternoon off if he was to be worthy of Phuoc's attention that very evening.

*****

Wednesday came, and Lieutenant Colonel Ngo was summoned to the G-2 shop at the Second Division over at mainside, not knowing it was a ploy arranged by Tolbane to get her away while the celebration was being set up behind the office hut. When she returned, the office crew surrounded her, blindfolded her, and led her out to the party. The three platoons were lined up, rank and file, standing at attention, when her blindfold was removed.

She looked around in amazement. There was an old M100 Jeep trailer filled with beer, sodas, and ice; a chow line set up, and what looked like some cakes on a separate table. She didn't know what to think until Tolbane guided her to the front of the formation, gave the troops at ease, and addressed them.

"Let's have three cheers for the newest lieutenant colonel in the United States Marine Corps."

The troops gave the three cheers, and then as they had been instructed, they headed for the beer trailer. Just then, the lieutenant handed her an ice-cold Bud and welcomed her to the party.

Later on, after chow, touch football, and other games, everyone gathered around Ngo; and once again, congratulations were given. Then Tolbane cut the first piece of cake and presented it to her. She took one bite, set it down, and then she cut the rest of the cakes and began serving it to the troops, occasionally wiping a moist eye. As she handed a plate of cake to a trooper, she received congratulations from the man.

When each marine was served, she addressed the unit.

"I don't know what to think or say right now. This will always be one of the most cherished and remembered days of my life, not just my Marine Corps career. I'm sure your NCOIC, MGySgt. Travis Tolbane, had something to do with this shebang. Something you all have no idea about is that this man and I have served together in some complicated situations that we cannot talk about.

"One thing I can say is that I am here today to enjoy this wonderful afternoon with you because of this marine. He did actually save my bacon. If it weren't for him, I'd be pushing up daisies not just once but twice. The first time, I wanted him to leave me to die and save his ever-loving ass, but the dumb ox he is—I'm damned sure happy today he disobeyed my orders—saved my butt."

The troops laughingly got a kick out of that line.

"We soon may be deployed as a company in the near future, and I think that any suggestions he makes to you, I want you to seriously listen to and consider. He's been there, done that, and the Corps didn't even give him a damn T-shirt for all the grief he's been through. As a final word, I thank you all for making this my day. I love you all!"

Then she walked off to the office with happy tears in her eyes.

Some of the junior ranks had been volunteered to do the cleanup, and they began as the troops went about their individual ways. The beer was gone, so the trailer only needed to have the left-over ice and water dumped, the food containers taken to the proper galley, and the trash bagged and placed in the dumpsters. Within twenty minutes, the area was spotless; not a soul was left in the area.

Back in their office, Phuoc was addressing Tolbane.

"Damn it all to hell, Travis. I don't know what I'm going to do with you. I don't know when some big-ass lug ever made me cry like this. I guess that's why I love you to pieces. Yes, before you can wise-crack or ask, you can get some pieces tonight if you play your cards right. Seriously, I never expected anything like this.

"I've been on the dark side way too long, big guy. No one ever did something for me like today. I'm overwhelmed, to say the least. I know you had help, but that doesn't change my feelings. I never knew a commander could ever have the sense of pride I felt today. I owe it all to you. Yes, the office PFC spilled the beans to me this afternoon. He needs to be a lance corporal, don't you think?"

"Great minds think alike. He does a great job in the office. He's a damn good worker. I knew you'd appreciate a promotion party. You deserve so much more than this, so it was the least I could do. By the way, you are my celebration. I need no other party to fulfill me. My life has really been full of adventure, danger, and love. Those are the gifts you've given me. I'd marry you right now if we were in any other career and let the babies come one right after another. I'd like just three, though."

"You have such a way with words, you big galoot. I feel the same way. Maybe someday, but we'll most likely never know when. I need to get out and get control of my emotions, so meet me at the steak house at 1830 hours. That's an order, marine!"

She kissed him on the cheek and left. She got in her car, drove a ways, pulled over, stopped, and had a good cry.

CHAPTER 29

The day finally arrived. Lieutenant Colonel Ngo was called to the Second Marine Division G-2/G-3 conference room for a classified briefing. She was still in her utility uniform from checking out the classes that were in progress at the time.

The new lance corporal in the office waved her out of the classroom.

"Ma'am"—it was how she liked to be addressed—"I just took a call from mainside. You're wanted at the G-2 just as soon as you can make it there. And quoted from some Colonel Dumfries, 'You best get your ass there ASAP, like, as in yesterday!' Sounds like the stuff is going to hit the fan real soon."

"Thanks for the warning. I think you hit the proverbial nail on the head. Let's get our butts back to the office. You're driving."

They double-timed to the office, where she gathered her gear, told Tolbane what was going on, and left. Upon arriving at G-2, most likely the same Colonel Dumfries who had called chewed her butt out for being in the utility uniform as opposed to the uniform of the day.

She replied, "Up yours. Next time, be specific about what uniform to wear when I'm performing my daily duties in which I may be required to perform like a marine in combat instead of an admin ass sitting behind a desk. Now, Colonel, shall we go to the conference room?"

She turned and casually strode to the conference room. The colonel stood there in disbelief like a blithering idiot. Evidently, he never bothered to find out what kind of woman he was confronting.

Upon entering the room, she could see several officers from lieutenant colonel to a two-star general. She was really impressed.

She had never been in such a local high-powered briefing before. Her instincts began working overtime at the sight of them. It looked like shit was really going to hit the fan this time for sure.

When all were seated and quiet, General Franks began his briefing.

"Marines, first off, welcome! I hope you are all comfortable. I will go over the mission briefly. Then on the way out at the completion of my briefing, a few of you will be given a top-secret copy of the operation order. Some of you will not receive a copy, as you do not have the need-to-know of all of the details of the OP or the intelligence evaluations contained in the order. Secondly, I begin my briefing.

"We have been following a situation in a South American country. There was an attempted coup, and the two individuals who led the attempt need to be extracted. Why? I have no idea why we would be charged with the extraction. My personal guess, not for publication, is, they may be CIA assets, and someone wants to test the new response concept headed by Lieutenant Colonel Ngo. This will be one hairy operation or a walk in the park. Our intelligence organizations have no info to process, only the known coordinates where the two are hiding out, except the coordinates are in the jungle a couple klicks or so inland from the shoreline. It seems that some obscure drug cartel or army is harboring them. Lieutenant Colonel Ngo has been charged to extract the two and ensure their safe transport to CONUS.

"All available information and conclusions are enclosed in the OP order for Operation North Star you will be provided with at the close of the briefing. It outlines the equipment, beans, bullets, and bandages needed, place, time, embark and debark times, and the landing and recovery of her provisional company from the operation area. There are also a lot of miscellaneous requirements. Our fervent hope is that the cartel does not know we are coming or, if they do, not when or in such force. Do we have any questions?"

"Yes, sir!"

The Colonel Dumfries who had reprimanded Ngo about her uniform threw up his hand.

"Yes, Colonel."

"Why do we have a noncombatant woman marine leading this operation and not a well-decorated combat veteran? It seems to me she has no experience in this field."

"Colonel, there are many things about the lieutenant colonel you will never have the opportunity to find out. If she had arrived in the uniform of the day, you would have noticed she has more bona fide decorations, including a Purple Heart, and has had more harrowing experiences than yourself."

The colonel's face turned red with anger from being put down. "Any other questions?"

There were no more questions from the floor, and the general dismissed the group, asking Ngo to remain a minute. The colonel stopped and said something to the general on the way out. He didn't look too happy at the general's answer. When the colonel left, the general motioned Ngo to approach.

After she placed her OP order in her valise, she approached the general, and he commented, "It seems you made a real impression on the colonel. He was upset about you showing up in the utility uniform and your remark to his reprimand. Good for you, Lieutenant Colonel. I don't particularly care for the man. I commend you."

"Thank you, General," she replied. "He rubbed me the wrong way with his manner."

"If I may call you Ngo, Ngo I have a bad feeling about this operation. If I could, I would cancel it. Higher-ups want to see your unit, a new corps concept. Prove they are correct in inserting your unit with high hopes of proving the concept is a success. Personally, between me and you, I would send a reinforced combat battalion. I do not know what may happen in the cartel's own jungle area, so I wish you good luck. Oh, on the way out, you needn't engage the colonel in joyful conversation! That's all, Ngo."

"Thank you, sir!" she said, smiling. "By your leave."

"Granted! Go with success, Ngo."

She came to attention, executed an about-face, and left the room, going straight to the G-2 office exit, making sure she avoided the colonel. She rushed to her waiting transportation as quickly as she could.

She climbed in and said, "Home, Jeeves!"

The lance corporal looked at her with puzzlement, shook his head, and started the vehicle.

"I'm sorry," she stated. "Master Gunnery Sergeant Tolbane's inane humor is rubbing off on me. I believe Jeeves refers to some limo driver in the movies."

The driver smiled and peeled out. Lieutenant Colonel Ngo grinned.

Arriving at the office, she would have to devour the OP order with Tolbane, then work on getting the troops briefed and figure out how to organize the troops into a viable combat company of three balanced and reinforced platoons with a company headquarters. Then she would have to set the order of march and whatever else was needed to brief the troops on. She knew they had a challenge ahead of them, but she intended to do her best to make this a success with Tolbane's help. If the general was correct, they would need all the planning and luck life could provide.

*****

Ngo and Tolbane spent several hours working on the OP order and making their plans into the early morning until they could not function rationally. They called it a night and went to their respective quarters.

CHAPTER 30

Both Ngo and Tolbane arrived at the office none the worse for wear from the previous night's planning session, but the office crew still noticed the lack of sleep showing on their faces. Ngo informed them that she and Tolbane would brief them on the night's session in about an hour. The four retired to their desks. Tolbane immediately fell asleep.

Ten minutes later, Ngo gently tossed her stapler, landing it on Tolbane's lap.

He jumped up, exclaiming, "What the fuck? Over!"

Ngo laughed her butt off.

"Oh, it's you!" Tolbane muttered. "Sorry I dozed off. I need a week of sleep."

"That's okay! You can buy the steaks tonight. Then we'll make up for what we didn't get to do last night. Right now, let's figure out exactly how much we'll brief the staff on. You need to get the rest of the staff to report to the office ASAP so we can get it over with."

Tolbane responded, "Aye, aye, ma'am."

Then he went on his way to round up the senior troops. He rounded up the instructors, senior officers, and staff NCOs and had them report to the office ASAP for the lieutenant colonel's briefing. They were all curious as to what was going on, as Tolbane wouldn't even give them a hint or a sniff.

When everyone was jammed into the office, Lieutenant Colonel Ngo came out and addressed them.

"Gentlemen and you too, Master Guns Tolbane, good morning to you all. Hope you all had a good night's sleep. Master Guns and I spent hours working on deployment plans for an operation outside of CONUS.[21] It seems that the proverbial shit has hit the fan for us. However, that's why we're here, to scoop up the shit and make sense of it.

"First, let's make sure every one of us has our wills in order. That is a priority for this OP, as we are going into I don't know what—could be hot—to rescue a couple of failed coup leaders protected by some drug cartel or army somewhere in a remote South American jungle.

"We have made a roster of who's in what platoon, what squad, what fire team, who's in the command group, RTOs, etc. and the order of march for our ingress into the abyss. The company commander and his staff have been assigned also. Later in the day, a typed list of assignments will be ready for your perusal on the company bulletin board. That's all for now, folks. And so ends this *Loony Tunes* episode."

After the dismissal, the troops went back to their duties, all curious as to what their future would be. The lieutenant colonel didn't seem too positive about the upcoming deployment in some far-off South American jungle. It seemed she thought it was going to be a big bag of worms in their estimation. Well, *Loony Tunes* or not, their Mickey Mouse duty was to do or die, so they went about their daily business and would worry about the roster when it was posted.

When the troops had left, Ngo called her staff of four into her office.

"Lieutenant, I want you with the command group. You'll handle the group's security. You three—Staff Sergeant, Sergeant, and Lance Corporal—will remain here. We need you to handle any admin crap that comes in plus handle any communication from us and any task needed as outlined in the communication. Master Guns, you'll handle getting the troops prepared for deployment, I presume. Dismissed!"

Everyone went to his desk and got back to work.

Tolbane asked, "If you have the list ready, I'll make copies, post it, and pass out a copy to the senior marines. Do you want me to answer their questions or refer them to you?"

---

[21] The continental United States.

"Here's the list. I think you can answer their questions as well as I can. Take your time. I'm leaving. Dine at our usual place at 1900 hours."

"You bet I'll be there, but not with bells on."

He went about his business. After posting the roster and speaking with the marine SNCOs and officers and giving them a copy, Tolbane retreated to his office. For some reason, he was getting bad vibes about the upcoming operation. He felt that way because every special operation he had been on since his last assignment in Viet Nam had turned to shit one way or another. He believed that Phuoc felt the same way. This one was supposed to be a cake walk.

He voiced aloud to no one in particular, "Drumroll. Cake walk my ass!"

Tolbane and Phuoc discussed their feelings about the operation over New York steaks, medium rare, with loaded baked potatoes and a tossed salad and a mild red wine. There were plenty of honey mustard and bacon bits for Tolbane's salad. They both reached the same conclusion about their premonitions. During their insertion and extraction, they must be very wary and must not relax their vigilance, make sure the troops were locked and loaded and aware of their surroundings, and hope they were wrong about their premonitions of an ambush.

*****

The big day finally arrived. Two-and-a-half-ton trucks arrived at their compound for their transportation. Loaded up, they were transported to Onslow Beach, where they would be taken to their ship by LCVPs, or Higgins boats. At least five of the troopers got seasick on the way.

Tolbane told one marine on his craft, "Suck it up, marine!"

When all were aboard, after the rope cargo net climb, the convoy lost no time in setting sail to their destination. Dramamine pills were dispensed to those who needed them for seasickness.

After a few days of journey at sea, they reached their debark station. The LCVPs were on station, and the marines got to use the rope cargo net once more. There was no opposition to their landing on the beach, and the company formed together in their order of march. Flankers to the north and south, the rear security, and the point men were in position.

The company commander gave the order to move out on the wide dirt trail, wide enough for two vehicles to pass, leading to their destination. The whole unit moved as one into the march until route step was given.

All the marines were vigilant, as per standing orders. So far, they moved as a well-oiled unit. Moving from the beach into the jungle, one of the main functions was to move as quietly as possible and listen for jungle noises. About an hour and forty-five minutes later, they came upon a large, fenced-in, seemingly deserted drug cartel compound, the gate standing wide open.

The point men were instructed to check out the compound to make sure it was deserted, except for the large building just inside the gate. They returned, verifying no one was in the camp, except for four people in the large building. The rest of the company moved in, dropped their gear, and relaxed, except for a rotating security.

Lieutenant Colonel Ngo and Tolbane cautiously knocked and entered the building. There were two unarmed civilians and two armed soldiers either protecting or guarding. The soldiers excused themselves to return to their unit when Phuoc and Tolbane entered. They left the compound and disappeared into the jungle.

The two remaining individuals introduced themselves as the coup leaders who were to be extracted to the States. Ngo called to a private, who brought rations and water to the two. Then she gave the word for all troops to chow down and rest up for the march back. After all the troops had chowed down, she had a meet with all the officers and staff NCOs. Her main point was that it had been too easy so far. She was worried about a possible ambush somewhere down the trail. They all agreed with her. They decided to wait and rest another hour before heading back to their rendezvous with the LCVPs on the beach.

Lieutenant Colonel Ngo radioed the ship of their estimated time of arrival back at the beach and to be on standby. The hour of rest passed, and the troops saddled up. The two coup leaders were put in with the command group for their protection, and once more, the unit moved out as quickly and quietly as possible. On the way inland from the beach, there were always some noises in the jungle, either close by or at a distance.

Ngo halted the group about twenty-five minutes or so into the march and had the company commander call his platoon leaders to the command group and brief them.

"Gentlemen," the captain began, "I don't know how many of you have noticed, but there is suddenly an absence of natural jungle noises around us, close or at a distance. I'm afraid our fears about an ambush may be answered shortly. Make sure the troops know that there is possibly an ambuscade not too far up the trail. Return to your troops and issue a warning. Everyone, be on alert. Everyone, unlock. Check to make sure there's a round in the chamber."

The leaders replied with "Aye, aye, sir!" and returned to their troops.

Lieutenant Colonel Ngo had the RTO contact the ship, and she issued a report on her suspicions to the ship's S-3. Then she instructed the RTO to notify the ship immediately if shit hit the fan and as to how far from their rendezvous they were and to stand by in case they needed the naval guns' support. She was not wrong.

Ten minutes into the march, shit did hit the fan when they were still about a little short of an hour away from the beach. Suddenly, they came under heavy fire from both sides of the jungle. The noise was maddening.

The first fusillade wounded the eight flankers, right and left, who then moved to the main body of troops. A lot of fire was concentrated on the command group with the two coup leaders being killed. Two of the command group's security, along with Tolbane, received two slight wounds. Lieutenant Colonel Ngo didn't fare as well. One round from the first enemy volley hit her on the left side of her head, tearing half of it off.

Returning fire with his TO 1911A1, Tolbane slung Phuoc's body over his wounded left arm's shoulder and hobbled on his wounded right leg to what cover he could find. In a matter of about five to ten minutes, the firefight was over. The marine fire superiority was too much for the drug cartel. They left twenty-five bodies lying in place, and many more were wounded. The group and their wounded all melted into the jungle without a sound.

Tolbane was found crying over Phuoc's body. He was in complete torment. The marines had seven KIAs and fifteen WIAs, and the two coup leaders were dead.

*****

The unit, after two more hours, finally made it to the beach and the waiting LCVPs, carrying their dead and wounded. It was a sad affair. Tolbane wouldn't allow anyone to carry his beloved Phuoc but himself. After the firefight, he discovered her body had taken three more rounds; all had been meant for him.

Wading up to his knees and limping from a thigh wound out to the LCVP, he carried her in his arms; tears were still in his eyes. He was devastated, to say the least. He had not been able to save her this time. He was as angry as he was sorrowful. He had a hard time and could not believe his one and only love was gone forever. He felt hate for the world around him who took her life.

Once aboard the ship, Lieutenant Colonel Ngo was taken to the ship's morgue, along with the other KIAs. Tolbane, with his upper-left arm and a light right thigh wound, was treated in the ship's sick bay and temporary hospital. He was in a very foul mood and was cursing every leader he knew of who had dispatched them on the operation, especially the general.

The more seriously wounded marines were dropped off at Guantánamo Bay, Cuba, for emergency care. The lightly wounded, including Tolbane, were taken to the US Naval Hospital at Camp Lejeune.

Tolbane was wheeled into a private room in a wheelchair. He had to stand up to crawl onto the hospital bed, which was painful to his right leg. He was immediately given an IV, and a nurse cleaned his wounds. A doctor entered after that to check the severity of the wounds and to check for signs of infections. There seemed to be none. He prescribed some pain pills and antibiotics for Tolbane and gave the nurse instructions on how to clean, treat, and bandage the two wounds to prevent infection.

It was the doctor's decision to keep Tolbane for a couple of days to monitor the wounds for signs of infection and because of Tolbane's sour demeanor. Tolbane, on top of his grief, was nearly going out of his mind lying in bed for two days when he needed to be free to find out what went wrong with the op. He felt like he was a criminal being denied his freedom. The thing bothering him a lot was the ambush in that godforsaken jungle and why that cartel was lying in wait for them. He knew he would never find out the truth about how and by whom they were compromised, but he could try like hell.

The day he was discharged from the hospital, he called the team HQ and spoke to Clyde, and one of the corporals drove his car to the hospital to pick him up. Against his protests, a nurse who didn't take crap from any patient put him in a wheelchair and wheeled him to the vehicle. He did thank her, though, and apologized for his behavior.

When he was comfortable in the car, he said to the corporal, "Home, James, and don't spare the speed!"

The corporal grinned at him and replied, "As you wish, sir! Next stop, Camp Geiger, Camp Lejeune, North Carolina. All aboard!"

And away they went.

CHAPTER 31

Tolbane, since leaving the hospital, he was kept there three days total, in and out, for observation, as his wounds were light but aggravating, and while recovering in his room from his minor wounds, he seemed to be in a state of malaise.

He forsook staying in his room to recover; he felt being at work would help him deal with Phuoc's death better. But he was lethargic in his actions and decisions at work. The death of Phuoc in the cowardly ambuscade they faced heavily weighed him down morning, noon, and night. He felt there was nothing at all to look forward to in the future for him.

Pursuing his duties, he was accomplishing barely enough to get the job done. What was even worse was, orders had come down from on high to disband the unit he had begun to love. Jason and his office crew handled the admin portions of the stand-down, the processing of the troops' transfer orders and leave time as the troops' orders arrived, arranging transportation for the troops, etc.; Tolbane had other duties to perform.

Tolbane had the responsibility of overseeing the physical aspects of the unit's stand-down and dissolution. The troops' gear and weapons had to be turned in. Quarters and classrooms had to be in good repair and immaculate. The firing range had to have targets removed, the berms had to be leveled out, and the area had to be left as pristine as possible. So many things had to be taken care of; at least he had a couple of weeks to get it done. He felt he was not adequate for the task at hand anymore, but he struggled on with his ghosts anyway.

Late one afternoon, sitting in his office, tired from lack of sleep at nights, his head hurting, he was staring at the desk Phuoc had sat at and led the unit from when he received a weird telephone call. A voice he could not recognize ordered him to go to the staff NCO club mainside at precisely 2000 hours. It would be to his benefit not to be late or refuse to be there, they said.

He was instructed to seat himself at a certain table and await a visitor who would update him on the ambush they had suffered in that godforsaken South American jungle, and then the caller hung up. Thinking about the call, he felt a slight elation, as maybe he would find out why Phuoc had to die, or it could be some kind of sick joke.

When the workday was over at 1630 hours, he hurried to the mess hall and devoured his food in Tolbane style—in other words, like a vacuum—which he had not done since the ambush. He went to his quarters, showered and shaved, checked his wounds and rebandaged them, and donned the uniform of the day after checking for Irish pennants (loose threads). He then timed his trip to the club so he would arrive in the parking area at about 1955 hours.

His timing was perfect, and he entered the club at 2000 hours on the dot. He went to the assigned table, where a cold bottle of Bud and a frosted glass and a dish of peanuts already awaited him. He had just poured a glass of ice-cold Bud and had taken a first swallow when an older man in civvies, about six feet tall, maybe close to fifty years old, and hair already turning gray, approached him and sat opposite him at his table.

As the man sat down, a waiter set an ice-cold Bud and a frosted glass in front of him.

What timing, thought Tolbane. *The guy must have some pull at the club.*

The man quaffed at a full glass and downed half of it before making any comment. Then he began.

"I know you are wondering what the fuck you're doing here, waiting on some old fart to explain himself to you. Am I right, Master Guns?"

"You got it, old man! I'm more than curious about what you have to say. I hope you can get my attention quickly, or I'm out of here before you can say scat."

Tolbane took a big swallow of his beer.

"First, I want your assurance that you will bear with me and hear me out before you become angry and want to kick my ass up onto my shoulder blades."

"Well, old man, you have it. I make no promises about after your narration. I will bide my time and listen to your story, so get it on."

"Secondly, I don't want you to jump up at attention, but I'm Major General Franks. I'm the one that sent your unit on the extraction operation in that foul and steamy South American jungle, the operation responsible for your lover's and a few others' deaths."

Tolbane's face reddened, and it became taut with anger. He wanted to jump over the table, grab him by the stacking swivel, jar the guy's butt plate off, and blacken his peep sights; but he kept his cool.

"Sorry for the rudeness, sir. The last thing I was expecting was a general officer. I thought it might be some clown prevaricating the situation. There are a lot of crazies out there that like to stir up a lot of crap just to get their jollies off."

"All is forgiven, Travis. I am well aware of those kind of clowns, as you call them. I have even nastier names for them. As I knew, I would need a little subterfuge to see you, hence the phone call. As far as I'm concerned, this meeting is off the record, has never occurred. We're only two marines shooting the breeze and spreading scuttlebutt and drinking beer while sitting at this table. Is that understood, Travis?"

"Yes, sir! My lips are sealed forever and a day. They will never sink a ship."

"I heard you had a weird sense of humor. I'm happy to now confirm that rumor. Okay, forget the military formalities now please! I knew about you and Lieutenant Colonel Ngo being lovers. In fact, I know more about her many covert operations in the Corps than you and many others will ever know. I really liked the way you two worked together on the ops you shared. It's hard to find people that blend with each other and function as one. I am sure she probably told you of a Colonel Dumfries getting on her about her uniform when she came to the briefing at G-2."

"Yes, she did. She thought he was an overgrown ass."

"Travis, he, not I, is the fucking lowlife animal that caused the compromise of the operation. Without him running his mouth, the operation would have gone off without a hitch. In getting those two coup leaders from the deserted cartel camp, there'd be no casualties, only success, in and out. I'm not the bad guy you may perceive me to be, Travis, if I may call you that. I guess I already did a couple of times.

"That day, at division G-2, the colonel briefed me about her rude comments to him after he chastised her for not wearing the uniform of the day to the briefing and the fact he didn't think any woman could or should ever be given the chance to lead any operation to a successful completion.

"He did not know Ngo as I did and her many accomplishments in some hairy undercover assignments in some godforsaken land that I personally knew about. Between you and I, personally speaking, I had the utmost confidence in her abilities to lead any operation to a successful conclusion."

"I thank you for your confidence in her. I know it was rightly deserved. Working with her seemed to be ordained. We made a good team. Now what about this asshole Colonel Dumfries, and how do I get my hands on his ass and make it grass?"

"Easy now, Travis. Let's go at this one logical step at a time. I sympathize with you wanting to kick his ass. I feel very much the same way. I'd like to stomp his face. We just can't do that, though. We have to be squeaky-clean. However, Travis, with your help, we both will have our day and justice for Ngo. So let me finish."

"Sorry! I just find it hard to control my emotions about her right now."

"Understood! Our Colonel Dumfries, who has been divorced for many years, has a Latin American girlfriend and lover he bangs on a regular basis. We found out she has ties to the drug cartel that ambushed your group. It seems he would always have diarrhea of the mouth around her about everything he was opposed to and things he was all right with to her in relation to our Corps, some of it highly classified.

"She would notify a contact in the Miami-Dade area of the colonel's thoughts, positions, and classified information. The contact would then forward the info to the drug cartel. The information he blabbed was also used for other breaches of the peace. That's how the compromise of the operation took its form. The wounds and deaths are all attributed to Colonel Dumfries's mouth."

"That scumbag son of a bitch. He deserves to die like the pig he is."

"I concur. However, you and I must keep our hands clean. The last thing we want to do is to screw up our Marine Corps careers, only screw up his. I know a way this can be done surreptitiously, and you and I will have our own private justice, a sweet revenge for Ngo and the Corps, and then we can move on with our lives.

"The success of this will be basically on your shoulders if you feel up to the task. After I explain the details and you do not want to be involved, we'll just part ways, and this meeting never happened. It didn't happen anyway."

"General, it makes no difference what the risks are. I'm in 100 percent like Flynn. Things can't be any worse for me than they are now. Whatever you have in mind, I'll make it happen—not just for me and you or the Corps but for Phuoc."

"I was sure you would feel that way. Listen closely while I outline what must happen to satisfy our vengeance. After that, we'll see to it you get proper consoling for your grief."

The general outlined his plan in detail. Then he handed Tolbane a small packet.

"Last of all, may God be with you, and may everything work out to perfection. A warning! If we ever meet again in the line of duty, remember, we do not—and I emphasize, we do not—know each other, except maybe by word of mouth from other marines about our exploits in the Corps. Please, as I leave, don't stand up. Just smile, nod, and wave. I'll do the same. We're just a couple of old fart marines hashing over old times.

"I do offer my sincere condolences to you over Lieutenant Colonel Ngo's needless death. I know she meant so very much to you, Travis. I want you to know that she'll be laid to rest in the Arlington

National Cemetery, but under her real name. I don't even know what that is. Sorry!"

The general finished his beer in silence, rose from the table, and left. Tolbane didn't know whether to shit or go blind. His spirit was alive once more at the chance to avenge Phuoc.

Tolbane finished the beer and had two more for the road. Contemplating the general's plan, he could not believe his good fortune this night. He did hope, though, that Major General Franks was on the level about the situation, because the plan would be so satisfying for him. The info was that the colonel would be home alone, relaxing and reading and enjoying a drink beside his fireplace, in two nights. That would give Tolbane ample opportunity to calm down his nerves, control his anger, and plan his words for the traitor's ears.

He had several points to make to the fucking sumbitch. He must make sure his words were understood by the ass, and when he left, Dumfries's human nature would take its course, and the world would be a better place. Most of all, Phuoc would be avenged, and the Marine Corps would be minus one mouthy, arrogant traitor.

*****

Finally, after stewing all of the second day, the time came for Tolbane to act. He took a couple of deep breaths and left his room. The colonel lived in a house on a few acres he owned on the way to MCAS Cherry Point, about five and a half miles from Jacksonville. It was a moonless, very dark, dreary, and dry night.

He pulled his car into a dirt lane in a wooded area close to the house. He was dressed in all black, but he wished his black outfit was that of a ninja, as it would have instilled fear in a victim. He slowly made his way to the house, being careful and not letting his footfalls make noise. He felt a little chilled and wished he had a black jacket to wear, as the weather had begun its fall cycle, and evenings cooled quickly.

He peered into a couple of windows until he found the subject reading a book in his recliner, all comfy, cozy, and warm next to a small fire in the fireplace, and what appeared to be a glass of whiskey on the little stand beside the recliner.

Tolbane slipped around to the front door, put on his gloves, and placed his right hand with his model 1911A1 behind his back. He rang the doorbell with his left, then placed it behind his back also, and he waited. After a couple of minutes, the colonel answered the door and looked hatefully at Tolbane.

"Who the hell are you? Oh, it's you, asshole. What the Billy Hell do you want with me here this time of night? Not one damn thing I can think of! You're not welcome here at all! I suggest you get your ass out of here before I call the county sheriff's department and have your ass locked up for trespassing!"

Tolbane brought his right arm around and pointed his 1911A1 at the colonel's head and stated very calmly, "I think you should think again, asshole. I do have business with you. It's best if we go in and sit by your cozy fire. I know I'll feel a lot warmer. Besides, we have a lot to talk about, don't we, you mouthy scumbag?

"There are several WIAs and a few KIAs from a certain operation that should be eating at your conscience 24-7. In your sociopathic mind, you could care less, I'm sure. Also, there's a question about your Latin American taco, the one I'm sure you eat regularly. Turn around and walk slowly back to your recliner and sit. No funny business. My trigger finger is pretty itchy at this point."

The colonel moved to and sat in his recliner and leaned back. Tolbane pulled an armchair up close but not too close to the colonel.

"It seems you became a regular Mickey Mouth about my beloved Corps's covert operations, and your comments traveled by telephone over many miles, ending up with a drug cartel in South America and a certain jungle ambush. More to come on that later. I've got a few things to speak about first. You're lucky I haven't blown your traitorous ass to kingdom come by now.

"Let me begin with a working relation: Lieutenant Colonel Ngo was the love of my life. You met her at the G-2 briefing and mouthed off to her about her uniform when she arrived to the briefing and to the briefing general when a certain operation was being announced. I knew her as Phuoc. We became lovers the first time I worked with her in Viet Nam. She was after a disgusting traitor, and she nabbed him, dead to rights.

"The next time we worked together, we rescued a US asset with a small firefight in some jungle. Then we resumed our affair later in Saigon, then moved into operational status. That op was compromised higher up the food chain, just like the one we were just on, and I was able to save her wounded life, even being wounded myself.

"Then a sergeant major, a platoon of marines, and I were detailed to protect her while she was still rehabbing from her wounds in Saigon from a small North Vietnamese and North Korean combined force. There were about thirty of them. We won, wiped them out big-time. Their bodies lay all over the place, and we had no casualties.

"She and I were in some hairy situations, but she had been on a lot more dangerous missions than I'll never know the details about. She was not this incompetent, helpless woman you objected to. You thought she could not lead the troops, even on a planned, benign operation. Well, I'm here to inform you, you REMF. In case you do not know what REMF means, it's rear-echelon motherfucker. That fits you to a tee.

"I have been given data on the many times you found a way to avoid combat duty or going on dangerous operations. Phuoc endured many of them and had the decorations to prove it—Silver Star, Bronze Star, Purple Heart, the CAR (Combat Action Ribbon), the Navy and Marine Corps Commendation ribbon to name five plus many more. Then you started the ball rolling with your shit-for-brains mouth that destroyed that magnificent woman, the love of my life."

"I never knew she was so experienced a marine with a lot of expertise. Maybe I should have asked the general right out why she was given the command of the operation."

"In Saigon, when we were betrayed and she was severely wounded, she begged and even ordered me to leave her to her fate and save myself. I disobeyed her orders, threw her over my shoulder, and carried her to our waiting *xich lo* while returning fire with a US

Embassy-issued handgun, then took her to an ARVN hospital, the closet one to us.

"Once again, last month, down in a godforsaken South American jungle, I carried her on my shoulder once more out of a hot situation. However, this time, she did not know it. She was missing half of her skull. The rest of it was spattered on the jungle floor. Her body took three more rounds while I carried her. Those rounds were meant for me. Even in her death, she protected me."

One lonely tear ran down each of Tolbane's cheeks.

"So, yeah, I guess maybe you should have asked questions instead of mouthing off like the ass you are. As we speak here and now, your red-hot tamale—you won't be muff-diving there anymore—and her contact down in Florida are being arrested by the FBI. They will be charged with espionage, treason, and murder. The death penalty will be on the table at their trial, and they will be found guilty and put to death. The death penalty will be on the table at your court-martial too."

Waving and pointing the 1911A1 at different parts of the colonel's body, Tolbane continued slowly and deliberately.

"I'm an easygoing dude. I don't get upset easily. I try to rationalize things that have gone bad and put them in the proper perspective. I do a lot of thinking, though, when something major happens to me. I couldn't figure out why someone would compromise our mission. I had no idea where to start looking for some scumbag. I moped around. Then I began to use the little gray cells like Hercule Poirot would or even Sherlock Holmes, eliminating the impossible and finding the truth in what is left.

"I dug here and there and finally got some leads. That's why I'm here. Just like Sherlock, I eliminated the impossible, and what was left, even though it seemed to be improbable, what was left was the truth, which is you. Did you know that Mike Hammer preferred an M1911A1 .45 APC just like mine? He offed a lot of bad guys with it. He also banged a few of them on the head with the butt of the weapon. I'll guess that those guys ended up with a dent in their skull in addition to a concussion.

"Guess what I'd like to do to you right now, Colonel Turd Ass. I'd like to shoot your kneecaps one at a time and watch you scream and thrash around, then shoot your elbows, maybe your wrists too, and maybe even your balls to follow that. I'd love to see you scream and holler a while.

"Then I'd like to put the muzzle in your mouth as far as it will go, then hold it for a long while and let you wonder for a time just when I will pull the trigger or if I ever will. I'd surely love making you wonder for a prolonged period of time before I end it for you and watch the back of your head explode your blood and bone, watch them splatter onto the wall, as Phuoc's did in the jungle.

"As I said, that's what I'd like to do to you. I have to look at myself in the mirror in the mornings. But lo and behold, dickhead, you're in luck tonight. I'm not a barbaric ass like the drug cartel people you supported. Instead, I'm going to give you two choices for the ending of this evening.

"Believe me, these choices do not come from me. They come from way higher up the food chain than you can imagine, like from someplace called Headquarters Marine Corps, Washington, DC, USA. I'm going to present these choices to you like any game show host would to a contestant. Phuoc didn't have any choice, no thanks to you, turd. Are you ready?

"Colonel Dumfries, behind curtain number 1. Drumroll. If I leave here and motion to those waiting in the woods, there will be the NCIS and MPs breaking down your door. Then after being jailed in a Marine Corps brig for a while—corrupt officers will not be treated very well there—you'll have your day in court.

"At your court-martial, I'm very sure at this time and place that you will be found guilty on all charges of treason and murder and sentenced to death by a firing squad. The Corps uses expert riflemen.

"Listen up, Colonel. Here comes the next option for you. We have behind curtain number 2 for you, Colonel Dumfries."

Tolbane pulled a small packet with a small dark-brown pill in it from the breast pocket of his black shirt.

"Drumroll. If you accept this happy pill in this packet and take it with your whiskey as prescribed, you'll be guaranteed a veteran's burial in one of the national cemeteries with an American flag-draped coffin, and your honor as a United States Marine field grade officer will still be intact. And no one, except those of us in this particular chain of command going way up, will ever know of your dastardly treachery or of the many wounded and the dead left in your wake. That includes all the other missions you compromised too.

"I'm serious! You have my word as a United States Marine master gunnery sergeant on it. It's all been taken care of. The choice is now all yours. If you choose the happy pill, you must take it when I go out the door, because the NCIS, the new designation for the NIS, and MPs will be coming in behind me. They would find a victim of a fatal heart attack vice a disgraced perpetrator of treachery. The choice is now yours, Colonel Asshole. Choose it wisely."

Colonel Dumfries, hanging his head, a little spittle drooling from his mouth, tears running down his cheeks, and nearly choking on his words, didn't waste much time making his decision.

"I guess I'll have to settle for curtain number 2, Master Guns. I truly am sorry the way it turned out. I thought I was home safe with the Latin woman. I never would have suspected her to spill the beans, as you've outlined. I surely do not want my friends, family, and the Corps to remember me as a filthy traitor. I want my honor to remain intact. I'll take the coward's way out. Sorrowfully, I choose curtain number 2. Give me the pill!"

Tolbane gladly handed him the packet with the dark-brown happy pill.

"One caution, Colonel. Swallow it whole. Do not chew it. Chewing it could fuck you up good. You'd die a miserable death. That's up to you also."

Tolbane got up from his chair, put it back in its place, and left the house, banging the door shut but not locking it to ensure someone could come in and find the body. He walked around to the side of the house and went to the window, looking in on the colonel.

Then he walked straight to his car after looking in the window and watching the scum take the happy pill with his whiskey. His eyes got big and began to roll around in their socket and dilate. Then he thrashed around a little, collapsing in his recliner, dead to the world.

Tolbane thought, *Ding-dong! The witch is dead. Which old witch? The wicked old witch. That's not right for this scumbag. That's a good thing from* The Wizard of Oz. *I need to rethink this. I got it! Ding-dong! The sumbitch is dead. Which old sumbitch? The wicked old sumbitch.*

A very big smile was on Tolbane's lips now. Phuoc had been avenged this night. The rat bastard was gone forever. It was a shame there was no house to fall on him. His feet sticking out from under the house would have been cool, to say the least. The colonel fell for the scam hook, line, and sinker. He was a real guilty guppy who swallowed the bait.

The FBI was going for the woman and the contact. However, he lied to the colonel. There never were members of the NCIS or MPs around waiting out there to make an arrest or to find a heart attack victim who died in his recliner, reading. They were never notified of Operation Fuck Him. Maybe tomorrow, someone would find his corpse.

He thought about it a bit. Then throwing his arms in the air in the victory position, he screamed his thoughts out loud.

"Yes, General, I carried out my end of the bargain. Vengeance is ours! How glorious it is!"

He was glad the area was rather isolated. He didn't need anyone seeing his victory sign or hearing his bloodcurdling scream. He wondered if anyone would be talking, after the body was found, about how a colonel in the United States Marine Corps could take his own life.

*****

The next day, at about 1030 hours, the lance corporal took a call from G-2 and relayed the info to the others in the office. It seemed that when Colonel Dumfries didn't show for duty at G-2 that morning or answer his phone, the G-2 chief went to his home for a wellness check. The chief found the front door unlocked, and when he entered the house, he found the colonel dead in his recliner. It seemed to be a natural death. When more information was known about the colonel's death, a bulletin would be published to all units.

As the office crew began talking about it, Tolbane chimed in.

"Wow! Who would have thought a man so young and strong would pass away like that? I wonder if he had a heart attack?"

The others made a few more comments. Then they all got back to work. Tolbane knew that once the colonel was autopsied and the tox screen came back later on, it would be known there was never a real heart attack.

"Semper fi, motherfucker!" he said to himself.

He sat at his desk and lifted his feet up on the desktop and thought about the good and bad times he and Phuoc had. He bowed his head, closed his eyes, and said a prayer to Phuoc. He hoped she was in a better place. He lifted his head, opened his eyes, and looked at her desk again.

A couple of tears ran down his cheeks. He wiped them with his handkerchief. Then he lowered his head and closed his eyes again. Soon, he was in la-la land, chasing nude Playboy Bunnies on a sunny beach.

CHAPTER 32

Twice a day, a courier would bring classified documents, ranging from confidential to top-secret, and pick up any classified materials not needed to be retained by the unit. Since the botched operation and the order to shut down the project, not many classified materials were needed. This day, the courier only had a couple to deliver, but he did have a letter addressed to Tolbane, which had the following in big red letters: "For your eyes only."

Tolbane went to his desk and opened the letter.

Travis Tolbane,

I congratulate you. You do very good work, my man. A lot of high-echelon dudes thank you very much, but unofficially, of course. They and I wish you could be promoted higher or even given a decoration for a very delicate operation. Sadly, it can't be done, because many lips must be sealed for eternity. I sincerely hope you have no aftereffects from you mission.

You need not worry about the colonel's autopsy or even the tox screen at all. It won't be coming back to bite someone on the butt. It's all been taken care of. He died of a massive heart attack period. A shame. He was so young too. The Corps will miss him my foot!

I promised you help with your sorrow and mental trauma. A Dr. Solstein, a forensic psychologist at the US Naval Hospital, will contact you in a couple of days by landline at your office. He'll set up an appointment for you. Don't miss it. I hate to have to say this, but it is an order that you meet with him for your own good.

Arrangements have been made to present Bronze Stars with V device and Purple Hearts to some members of your unit tomorrow morning for gallantry and trepidation during the ambush, including you. Have the troops—and your live body there too—in formation at 0900 hours for the presentations. Wish I could be there. Unfortunately, I have other duties to fry. We all have someone above us we have to please.

You've had some pretty hairy operations the last few years. Eventually, they all will take a toll on you, Travis. This is what I'm going to do for you. You will have a notation made in your SRB[22] that you will be nondeployable for training or combat missions for two years for your own physical well-being. That will take you almost to your retirement date.

Once the dissolution of your unit is complete, I think you will like your next assignment real well. What is it? I'll never tell!

Semper fi, marine, from an old drinking buddy.

---

[22] Service record book.

Tolbane was at a loss for words, something unusual for him. That major general was true to his words. He was glad for himself and at the same time happy that the troops would be rewarded for their bravery under fire. They were terrific in their response to incoming fire for the first time. He felt, after reading the letter, that he was in a win-win situation at last. No deployments for two years!

The appointment with the shrink should really help him with his mental anguish. His sorrow for Phuoc seemed to ease a bit each day. However, it still manifested some mental anguish a good deal of each day. Operation Fuck Him helped Tolbane in getting back on track somewhat. "God, how I miss her!" was always on his mind, and it felt like it was driving him so mad at times he would like to beat his head against the wall.

The next day, what was left of the company was presented their awards. Tolbane received another Bronze Star with V device and another Purple Heart and a small Bronze Star to place in his CAR. After the awards, Tolbane and the office crew had arranged for beer, a couple of grills, hamburgers, hot dogs, baked beans, buns, paper plates, and condiments to be brought to their site.

It was an unofficial wake for their fallen comrades. It was a solemn affair, not like the wild, grab-ass sessions they had before. A handful of the troops spoke a few words about the comrades they no longer had. When the beer was gone, the troops were given the rest of the day off. Liberty call began immediately after cleanup.

Two days later, Tolbane received a morning phone call from Dr. Solstein. The doctor sounded very professional and a bit cheery at the same time. He didn't go into much detail about the treatment Tolbane would receive. He gave Tolbane an appointment for the next day. It was 1400–1500 hours at the doctor's office at the US Naval Hospital. He also stated that the uniform of the day was not necessary; blue jeans and a tee would be fine.

Tolbane was so elated over the call he felt like jumping for joy, but he couldn't find her for love or money. He really needed to get some help for his depressed feelings. Help to him meant a clear mental state, but not forgetting his love, Phuoc.

*****

Tolbane arrived at the doctor's office at 1320 hours in blue jeans and a sweatshirt with a large eagle, globe, and anchor in gold on the front. He checked in with the receptionist and took a seat in the waiting area and scanned through some old magazines to while away the time. At 1400 hours on the dot, a nurse paged him and guided him to the doctor's office.

The redheaded doctor was about an inch taller than Tolbane and probably outweighed him by about thirty pounds of pure muscle. Tolbane had expected a couch in the room. A gray recliner was the only furniture in the office, except for the doctor's desk and chair. Looking around the room, he saw diplomas and pictures of the doctor with fairly important people on the walls and some kind of large poster that looked like a very long, dark tunnel.

The doctor shook his hand and made the introductions, then bade Tolbane to get comfortable in the recliner. They spoke for a few minutes about the weather, the base, Jacksonville, and a few nonimportant things. When the doctor felt he had established good rapport with his new patient, he eased Tolbane into relating all his memories of Phuoc from the first instant he met her.

Tolbane complied willingly. During his narration, his eyes teared up; and once in a while, a tear ran down his cheek. His voice would waver and get too soft and high-pitched at times, and his grief nearly overcame him. The doctor listened patiently and never moved or uttered a sound until Tolbane was through.

The doctor finally spoke after a few minutes of thinking.

"That was an amazing companionship, Tolbane. I can sympathize with you. When two people bond and function as one, it is a marvelous thing. You do need closure and peace of mind. If you are willing to trust me, I can resolve a lot of your anguish. I guarantee you will feel much saner after my treatment. Are you with me on this endeavor?"

"One hundred percent, Doctor. Free me from this mental prison I suffer in every day. I sometimes feel like I'm in solitary confinement. It's a real bitch and a half."

"Yes, it surely is a bitch and a half to you. I want you to raise the footrest, lie back, and relax like you would at home."

Tolbane complied, and the doctor put a pillow behind his head.

"The first thing I want you to do now is to look at the poster of the tunnel there on the wall. I want you to need to reach the other end of this long, dark tunnel. It's a very long and tiring walk. Now look at the tunnel and concentrate on it. I want you to imagine that you have now entered the tunnel, and it's a long way to the end, where you'll find your peace of mind.

"You've already walked a long way. Your legs are tiring, your body is tiring, and you are becoming very, very sleepy. Your eyes try to droop shut, but you are forcing them open. They are getting heavier, and you're tiring more and more. You just want anything to be able to sleep. As you plod on and become more fatigued, you just want to sleep. The more you walk, the more tired and sleepy you are becoming. Let yourself go, marine. Close your eyes and find the sleep you need now. Sleep now, a peaceful and deep sleep."

Tolbane's eyes finally closed. His head lowered with his chin on his chest, and he was deep in a state of sleep, breathing normally without his usual snoring. Dr. Solstein retrieved a long needle from his desk drawer. He moved to the back of Tolbane and jammed the needle into the back of his neck. Tolbane didn't move a muscle. He was now in a hypnotic state. The doctor smiled and returned the needle to its place in the desk. He walked back to Tolbane and spoke to him in a soft, quiet tone.

"Travis, you are now deep asleep, but I want you to listen to my calming voice and obey my every command. Now I want you to lift your head up from the pillow and open your eyes."

Tolbane responded by following the order.

"You will only follow my commands and no one else's. Do you understand, Travis Tolbane?"

Tolbane answered a slow "Yes."

"Now I want you to put down the leg rest and stand up."

Tolbane complied.

"Listen closely to me. You are an I-beam planted twenty feet in the ground, and ten feet of you is aboveground. Place your right arm straight out to your side."

Tolbane complied once more.

"It, too, is an I-beam welded to your body, and nothing can pull it down. Do you understand me?"

"Yes, I understand!"

Dr. Solstein grabbed Tolbane's right arm, lifted his feet off the ground, and hung for a few seconds on the arm. Tolbane's arm did not give the least bit. The doctor put his feet back on the ground and knew Tolbane was ready.

"Travis, your body and arm are no longer I-beams. Now I want you to sit back in the recliner. Now put up the leg rest, lay back, head on the pillow, and relax into a deeper state of sleep."

When Tolbane had lain back in the recliner and was in a deeper sleep, the doctor went to his desk, opened the top right-hand drawer, and took out a two-page letter from the general and reread it twice, his face turning red with anger both times.

It gave him instructions on how the general wanted Tolbane to be treated under hypnosis. He really didn't care to treat his patient the way the general wanted, but orders were orders. The general did not want Tolbane to forget the times he served with Lieutenant Colonel Ngo, the way they worked together, or the operations they were on. He did, however, want Tolbane to forget the name Phuoc, that she was an agent with the NCIS, his love for her, and that they had sexual intercourse. The only reason Dr. Solstein even considered something like this was because the general had convinced him that it was a matter of national security.

The doctor worked with Tolbane's subconscious for an hour and a half. Even though Tolbane was in a deep hypnotic state, the doctor had a lot of trouble getting past the patient's normal reaction not to do anything that was against his tenets. Finishing up, the doctor brought Tolbane back to consciousness.

"Travis Tolbane, listen to me carefully. When I ask you to awaken, I want you to feel refreshed, well-rested, and forget we had a hypnotic session together. We only had a question-and-answer session. When you awaken, I will ask a few questions, and you'll be out of here. Now I want you to wake up slowly when I say wake up! We'll then go on as if nothing has interrupted us. Wake up!"

Tolbane woke slowly as if nothing had happened. The doctor offered him a glass of water, which he drank heartily. The doctor questioned his patient thoroughly for fifteen minutes or so and was content that the session was a complete success. He still was not thrilled about the general's request.

Tolbane had no earthly idea who Phuoc was. He did know he served with a Lieutenant Colonel Ngo on several occasions. He did save her life once. He did carry her dead body back to their ship. Any marine would have done the same. Dr. Solstein hoped the general would be pleased with the outcome. He had instructions to call him as soon as Tolbane left his office.

CHAPTER 33

When Tolbane left the doctor's office, he really felt refreshed and didn't feel tired from lack of sleep or from hard work. He actually felt more alive than he had been for days—since the botched operation. It felt so very refreshing to be alive and to enjoy the world around him. He had the rest of the day to be ensconced in such a wonderful atmosphere. He walked briskly to his vehicle. He then drove straight to his favorite watering hole in J-Ville. He had about three beers, bought a couple of rounds, and went straight to his quarters.

The next morning, when Tolbane arrived at work, the unit staff all spoke about the loss of Lieutenant Colonel Ngo, but nothing was commented on about the closeness of Tolbane and Ngo, as directed. While Tolbane was at the doctor's office, the unit staff were warned by above to never mention the relationship between Tolbane and Ngo ever.

*****

One day, when the unit's stand-down was nearly at hand, Tolbane got a strange visitor. The man was dressed to the nines in what seemed to be a $1,500 gray suit with expensive, starched light-blue shirt and dark-blue tie and pointed-toe black shoes. He introduced himself as Mr. Mestophiles, commenting that it was okay for Tolbane to call him Mr. M.

"Master Guns," he began, "I see you have an entry in your service record book that you will not be available for any operation outside of CONUS, but that does not preclude you from local operations. We have a very serious problem at the Second Front. We—that includes personae higher up the food chain than I—feel you just might be the right person to handle that problem."

"Since I don't know what the problem is, I have no idea if I could be of any help to you," Tolbane replied.

"I'm about to enlighten you, my man. First, let me say, you come highly recommended by the powers that be, as you have a keen sense of right and wrong, a real straight shooter, and you can produce under fire. We have very few marines that come as highly recommended as you. I need to ask you one very large question before I continue. Do you think you are willing and able to answer my question?"

Tolbane, out of curiosity, agreed and stated, "I have nothing to hide or to be ashamed of. Ask anything you want!"

"Let me set the stage for it. You have performed under fire in open areas and never flinched and made your missions a success. The question is this. How do you feel you would perform in a firefight in close quarters?"

"In a close-quarter situation, there could be different events. Number one, if an event is spontaneous by a second party, there might not be time to resist. Number two, if I initiate the action, I should come out on top unless the adversary got me with a kill shot. I would do my best to study and understand the situation in either event before I exposed myself to any danger. Does that help any?"

Mr. M responded with, "I like your answer. I'm looking for an individual who can not only produce under fire but does not do it recklessly. I think you are my guy. I will be leaving now, but I'll be back at 0800 hours with reports for you to study. I believe you will understand better by reading the reports than by what I can relate to you at this time."

He arose, gave a half-assed salute, and stated, "Until tomorrow. Chao ong!"

He turned and left the office in quick time. Tolbane had a weird look on his face as he wondered what the hell he was in for now. It seemed to him that there must be some kind of mojo that guided him to all the real shit jobs.

*****

True to his word, Mr. M arrived at 0801 hours, carrying a thick folder labeled Jacksonville City Police and Camp Geiger MPs' reports on criminal assaults and robberies in the Second Front area, across from Camp Geiger.

"Master Guns, here are twenty-seven reports on the criminal activity in the Second Front area for the last three months. Read and take the appropriate action and be sure to have fun during your endeavor. Remember, a lot of troops are counting on you to clean up the area."

He was gone as quickly as he came.

Tolbane opened the folder and removed the reports. He checked the dates first and noticed they were in chronological order by date and time. He also noticed a document that broke down the incidents by the type of offense—assaults, robberies, sexual assaults, etc. He let the office staff know he would not be available for the next couple of hours. He settled in his desk chair, put his feet on the desk, and began reading the reports, taking notes and absorbing the pertinent data.

After about an hour, his eyelids began to droop; and soon, he was in la-la land once more, dreaming once again of naked Playboy Bunnies frolicking on the beach and sexually attacking him when they became aware of him staring at them with his eyes bulging and his tongue hanging out and a part of him at rigid attention. His revelry was interrupted a good hour and a half later when Mr. M returned and gently shoved his feet off the desk. The result was Tolbane jumping up and trying to swing at his rouser.

Mr. M thought it was funny and laughed a full, deep laugh at Tolbane's sight.

"You sure are funny, Master Gunny. I kind of thought you might doze off. Looks like you're about halfway through the reports. So tell me what you think of the situation so far!"

"To tell you the truth, I would never have guessed that this kind of shit is going on right across from our base here. Robberies, beatings, and rapes—it's unbelievable. I think these guys need to be neutralized by exposure, incarceration, or termination with extreme prejudice ASAP before some innocents are seriously harmed or killed.

"So far, it seems like only two guys are doing this. Do you know of or have you heard of a third dude being involved by trading places with one of the perps—or doing recon, for that matter? Could there be a boss telling these two what to do?"

"Right now, we have no real info on their modi operandi. There very well could be a third ass out there someplace, but we just haven't found anything to indicate a third being with the two. So far, we think they do their own recon. It's safe for them to do the recon themselves by taking off their masks.

"We'd like to keep this as quiet as possible. However, you're cleared to use any level of force, including deadly force, if it's needed to do the job. Protect your ever-loving ass first at all costs."

He reached over and shook Tolbane's hand.

"I know you need to formulate a plan, and I wish you good luck with it. I won't bother you until it's over. Take care of yourself. We don't need another hero or victim. This time, I will not return until something has happened, pro or con. So long."

"Thanks. I'll need all the luck I can muster, Mr. M. I'm thinking of a wild-ass plan to execute in one of the bars since they seem to hit the bars more often than spontaneous hits on the street."

Tolbane waved as the mysterious Mr. M departed his office. He immediately began to read the rest of the reports, absorbing the contents and devising his weird strategy as he read.

Later that day, Tolbane was at a steak house in Jacksonville, North Carolina, with a sixteen-ounce medium rare T-bone steak, a bottle of A.1. Sauce, a baked potato all the way, and a large mixed salad with strips of bacon on top and gobs of honey mustard on them. While inhaling the chow, he let his mind nitpick on the weird plan he had to get rid of the problem. He would have to improvise while implementing it, but that was okay. He finished his beer when he felt his plan would be the crème de la crème of criminal apprehensions. He slept well that night.

The next morning, he informed the unit staff of his plan and would need Lance Corporal Johns to work as a driver for a few days in a row. Then bringing his driver with him, he went to the ITR sick bay and spoke with a corpsman he knew there. The corpsman gave him some instructions on certain types of wounds and issued him some medical supplies. Now his last chore was to visit motor transport. He needed to have the use of an official USMC sedan.

Tolbane and his driver returned, and he explained his whole plan to the staff. Tolbane knew which bar he would use, and since a couple of the staff, Clyde and Styles, were interested in helping, he allowed them to enter the bar one at a time but not recognize each other and serve as backup if needed, if shit hit the fan. Everything was in place to put Operation Blow Their Mind in action.

*****

A USMC staff car pulled in front of one of the larger bars on the Second Front. The driver, Lance Corporal Johns, got out and helped the disabled veteran from the back seat. The veteran needed a walker—the driver recovered it from the trunk—due to severe leg wounds. He had a cast from just below the elbow to the wrist. The driver handed him a ten-dollar bill, and the veteran hobbled, holding on to his walker, into the bar.

He found himself a nice table where he could watch the door. He also noticed a couple of familiar guys among the fifteen customers. The bartender usually did not serve tables, but seeing the veteran's problem, he served him anyway to show his respect.

After a couple of hours, the veteran hit the jackpot. Two guys suddenly burst through the door wearing masks and carrying .38 revolvers. They announced it was a holdup, and everyone was instructed to take out their wallets and place their money on their table and line up against the wall. Everyone obeyed the orders, except the disabled veteran.

The one who seemed to be in charge looked at the veteran and said, "This means you too there, limp-along."

"Ha! Take a good look at me and my decrepit body!" the veteran replied. "Even with my walker, I can't stand very long on my shot-up legs. My left forearm is almost useless, and I only have the change from a ten spot my driver gave me that's on the table. If you take notice, I don't think I could be of any imminent danger to you."

"I guess you're right about the danger. We watched you arrive and the driver helping you and handing you a bill. I thank you for your service, and I'm going to let you keep your money."

"Thanks a bunch! Uncle Sam had me snooping and pooping in the wrong place, and I was the unlucky one from an AK-47."

"Okay, dude! I guess you can stay put where you are. Hey, number two, do something worthwhile and go empty the bar's till so we can get the hell out of here. And hurry your ass up, slowpoke."

The leader turned from the wounded veteran to move toward collecting the monies on the tables and bar. He did not see the disabled man reach behind his back and remove his Colt 1911 .45 ACP from his beltline, to his dismay.

Suddenly, the leader heard, "All right, motherfuckers, drop your weapons and cease and desist your activity now or face the consequences."

The leader was standing with his left shoulder toward Tolbane and made the mistake of trying to whorl around and fire at him. Tolbane was quicker, and his first round hit the leader's left arm, shattering his upper bone. The second caught the lower-right side of his stomach area as he was completing his turn. He fell on the spot, screaming and crying. The round he fired went over Tolbane's head and into the wall.

At the same time, the second ass behind the bar was shocked by the shooting; and by the time he leveled his weapon, Tolbane had put a round in his right shoulder area. He didn't get a shot off. He, too, was writhing on the floor, screaming. Tolbane handed a small slip of paper to the bartender, who was stat struck at the happenings, and directed him to call the phone number on the paper.

Then Tolbane stated, "Semper fi, motherfuckers. Eat the apple and fuck the Corps."

Tolbane and his two cohorts, Clyde and Styles, attempted to treat the two gangsters' wounds, but they didn't have the right equipment. However, they did try to stop the blood flow as much as possible until emergency services arrived. They arrived about three minutes before the Jacksonville Police and Marine Corps MPs. They immediately began treating the gangsters with IVs and oxygen while putting the two in separate ambulances, then rushing them to the nearest hospital.

The last one to arrive that evening was Mr. M. He congratulated Tolbane and his troops for the fine job they did on those two asses. By now, Lance Corporal Johns had arrived in the staff car. Mr. M took charge of the situation with the police and MPs.

His driver brought in a couple of bottles of Cutty Sark scotch whiskey. Mr. M gave them to Tolbane and told him to take the bottles and his crew to their unit's area. Everyone had to get drunk, or else. He would see them in the morning to debrief them. The four gladly followed orders as quickly as possible.

*****

The four awoke at about 0430 hours, lying around the office floor. Then with major hangovers, they had to race to their quarters to shower, shave, and get to chow and get to the office to suffer headaches and tremors all day. The suffering included the long and detailed debriefing by Mr. M. That afternoon found all of them asleep at their desks.

At about 1500 hours, Tolbane opened a bulky pocket folder Mr. M had given him with the directions not to open it until after 1400 hours that day. There was a letter and a lot of cash in the pocket. He gathered the guys, and he read the letter to them.

Master Gunnery Sergeant Tolbane,

I wish you and your crew could be publicly acclaimed for your performance last night. Alas and alack, it is not possible to do so. Your actions solved a lot of problems that had to be performed surreptitiously. Some are problems I can't speak of.

Once again, let me thank you all.

I am able to show the gratitude of several high-level individuals to you. Please find two thousand dollars each for your three helpers and five thousand dollars for yourself. It's the best I can do.

Once again, thanks for the good job.

Good shooting too!

Semper fi.

Mr. M

"Damn" was Tolbane's reaction.

Tolbane doled out the cash and thanked his cohorts from the night before. He gave the other two who did not help each a thousand dollars from his own award. Then Tolbane returned to his office and closed the door. He sat at his desk with his feet up as usual. He was not thinking about a nap since quitting time was near at hand.

Something was bothering him, and for the life of him, he couldn't think of what it was. He felt good about nailing those clowns the night before, but at the same time, he felt a sadness he could not explain. He put aside any concern about his next assignment, as he didn't even know what it was. He really felt elation and rejection simultaneously.

At 1605 hours, he decided it was time to quit for the day. He grabbed his piss cutter[23] and left for his quarters. On the way, he decided he would shower, put on his civvies, get a good, thick steak with all the trimmings, and then go to his favorite watering hole. Then he would say fuck it and get stinking-ass drunk. Maybe while sucking on a beer or two or three, he could figure out what was bothering him.

Two days later, Tolbane got a call to report to the doctor who had hypnotized him for a follow-up on his problem. After the visit

---

[23] Fore and aft cap.

with the doctor and being put under again, his problem was solved without him knowing about it. A slight memory of Phuoc had been trying to surface from his subconscious mind. Now her memory was ingrained so deep it would never bother him again.

CHAPTER 34

Tolbane left the doctor's office feeling refreshed and happy once again. It had been a long time since he was able to feel so fresh and alive. He felt he wanted to experience everything fun in the world all at the same time. Instead, he jumped into his car and settled for going to his favorite steak house and enjoying his usual fare and sating himself with two or three desserts after the steak and salad.

He thought this kind of funny, as he seldom ever ate desserts after a big sixteen-ounce steak and salad. But he persevered and managed to inhale a bowl of banana pudding and a slice of hot apple pie with a slice of American cheese and a large scoop of vanilla ice cream followed by a chocolate mousse. He felt really satisfied for a change, stomach too full, so he went to his quarters and to bed early for a change.

He awoke to the morning alarm feeling really refreshed and was ready for whatever challenges the day brought to him. He did the five Ss, went to breakfast, and carried on to the office.

Striding into the office, the lieutenant and the others stood and greeted him with a "Good morning, sir!"

Tolbane, being who he was, was slightly embarrassed by this reception. His rank did not rate being called sir, especially by a commissioned officer.

All he could think of was, "What's going on here?"

The lieutenant spoke up for the office staff.

"Master Guns, we want you to know that it has been a great experience for us to have worked with you and how we have come to respect you not only as a marine but as a man too. This is a sad moment for us, as we received orders for us to close up shop today. We are no longer a unit. We are to retire our colors at noon today.

We have to remove ourselves from the office by 1600 hours today and report mainside at 0800 hours in the morning for orders. We do this sadly."

Tolbane was stunned even more.

"I'm sorry to hear this, guys. I have really enjoyed working with you all. You work together as one and have a great rapport together, and you should be proud of your service. I'm sorry we have to part today. I had hoped we would have more time together here. Were you told what units we would be going to, Lieutenant?"

"I have to ask you, Master Guns, do you have the proverbial mouse in your pocket today?" the lieutenant humorously asked Tolbane.

Looking at the lieutenant in a puzzled manner, Tolbane asked, "Okay, what's up that I don't know about?"

"It's like this. When I took the phone call this morning, I asked about where each of us will be assigned. I was given the assignments for each of us, and I asked for yours. I was told that there were no orders for you at this time. I was shocked. I said, 'You mean he will be here by himself?' The reply was that you'll be bored, and you can talk to yourself and masturbate all you want. Sorry! I know that's not what you want to hear."

"For shit's sake! I'll go bug-shit sitting in here by myself. Damn!"

"I explained this to the guys here, and they think it's for the birds too. We want to do the handshakes now, as we have a lot of work to do packing up our files and whatnot. Here's my hand. We'll miss you!"

Tolbane shook hands with each of them and wished them well. He also gave each one a one-arm hug around their shoulders. Each of them seemed to have slightly damp eyes at the goodbye.

Tolbane sat alone in his office in a kind of daze. He only left it when the staff retired the unit's colors. The only time he was disturbed was when the lieutenant and the sergeant came in and packed up his and Lieutenant Colonel Ngo's files. When the staff were done packing up all the unit's files, they disappeared. Tolbane was now alone. He opened his office door, sat in his desk chair, and cocked his feet up on the desk and fell into a deep, coma-like sleep, no dreams.

He awoke around 1700 hours, his body stiff from his sleeping position. He walked through the abandoned office and went to his favorite steak house, still in uniform. He wanted to just get drunk, but since he was in uniform, he said screw it, went to his quarters, cleaned up, and hit the sack, not waking until about 0600 hours.

He woke feeling all alone and a little despondent. He had not realized how much he loved being in that special unit and having the opportunity to serve with a great staff.

He thought aloud, "I guess this must be the way orphaned kids feel. I wish I could help them."

After dressing in his uniform of the day, he went to chow and then to his dismal office. Arriving at what had been a viable office once upon a time, he decided he didn't need to sit in his own office space. He sat at the first desk on the left in front and tried to get comfortable. It wasn't easy. He didn't fall into dreamland; he just brooded and felt sorry for himself, especially having no idea as to what he would be doing in the future.

After about an hour and a half, he raised his voice and howled out, "Being alone sucks period!"

Not counting the weekend, he spent the next four working days feeling like a nonentity, just lonely and abandoned. Finally, late on Tuesday morning, the phone began to ring. He jumped up from his cramped-up slouch and grabbed it up quickly.

"Master Gunnery Sergeant Tolbane speaking!"

"Good morning! This is Captain Dirkson at Division S-1. I'm sure you're feeling alone and abandoned, but we need you to be patient for a couple more days. Okay?"

"I think I can do that for the Corps."

"Good. I'm not at liberty to say anything more to you. The powers that be never move swiftly when you need them to. Any questions for me?"

"I can't think of any. I do know how the powers that be move their asses. I thank you for your call. It is lonely in this run-down Quonset hut."

The captain terminated the call. Tolbane wondered aloud what the deuce that call was all about. He wondered why this stuff was getting weird. He smiled a bit when he thought about how many people it took to issue orders. His answer was, thirteen generals held the paper, and there was no one to find the general who was the signee. It was typical USMC procedure since 1775.

Tolbane then tried to get comfortable at the desk again and resigned himself to his solitude. As he sat cramped up at the desk, his mind suddenly had a plan for the day. He left the defunct office, went to his quarters, changed into civvies, and went to his favorite watering hole and got as drunk as a skunk.

*****

The next day, while nursing a giant hangover around 1000 hours, a Major Whitlock came barging into what was now known as Tolbane's Domain with a pissed look on his face. Without any greeting to Tolbane, the major demanded why he was not available to answer his phone all the previous afternoon.

Tolbane responded after jumping up from his seat, "Major, I was sent on a secret mission by the commanding officer of this unit."

"Why were you selected to go on a secret mission while your status is nondeployable?"

"I'm sorry. I can't answer that. You'd have to ask my commanding officer as to why I was chosen for this mission."

"Well, marine, just who is your commanding officer, and where is he?"

"Right here, sir! MGySgt. Travis Tolbane, commanding the abandoned, unmanned unit, at your service."

"What?" the major hollered while throwing his briefcase across the room. "Just what kind of scam are you trying to pull here, Tolbane?"

"Sir, with all due respect to you, where is the respect for myself and my rank after nearly thirty years in the Marine Corps? I've been sitting here all by myself for days without any inkling as to what my future will be the rest of my career in the Corps. I've felt abandoned and dismissed the whole time. I just got tired of being ignored by the command, and I went out and ordered myself to get stinking-ass drunk. I followed orders like a good marine. If anyone has any complaints about it, they can put it where the sun doesn't shine and move it in and out repeatedly.

"One more point while I'm at it, Major. You came bursting in here in a very disrespectful manner to me and my rank, demanding an answer to what you believe I was deliberately refusing to answer the phone for you. I have no duties to perform here. I have no orders to be available to answer your phone calls. If anything, you should apologize for busting in here like an asshole and for your temper tantrum. By the way, you need to cool it and go pick up your briefcase."

With that said, Tolbane sat back down at his desk.

"Something for you to remember, Major: those who give respect receive respect. Respect has to be earned to be returned. Quote Travis Tolbane evermore."

The major looked shocked at Tolbane's reply. He took a deep breath, let it out, and sat down at the next desk. He lowered his head, put his hands over his face, and sat like that for a few minutes before he composed himself and spoke to Tolbane.

"You're absolutely correct, Master Guns. I've been very disrespectful. I've been so overwhelmed and stressed out by my duties I've been forgetting to be human. I do apologize for my actions. They were very disrespectful to you. I've always wanted to be and have always been a grunt. Being with the infantry is my life.

"Alas and alack, I got transferred to Division S-1, not knowing a whit about the duties there. I'm just so overwhelmed at the amount of paperwork, the many duties I have, and the personal problems so many marines have that I must take care of. The job is overwhelming, and the paperwork is just putting me down. Sometimes, I just don't know what to do."

"Major, I accept your apologies, and I empathize with you. I have been in similar positions a few times. It's frustrating. So is the feeling of being alone and that no one gives a flying fuck about you. It is our lot in the Corps, though!

"If I was out of place in the manner I spoke, I apologize too. After our unit was sold down the drain by a traitorous lieutenant colonel in the USMC and the KIAs and WIAs we suffered, I was

232

demoralized. It was a horrendous loss to this unit that exists no more. And being alone and feeling abandoned has not helped me one iota."

"I sympathize with you too, Master Guns. I did some unauthorized looking into the incident myself. You should be proud of how your unit responded to the ambush, but it was not the ambush that hurt you all. I guess I should try to tell you why I tried to call you yesterday afternoon. But when nothing is going your way, it's just frustrating."

"I know the feeling well, Major. I sympathize too."

"I don't like the reason you were isolated here, but I had no choice, as it came rolling downhill. There is a problem with the E-9 billet you were selected to fill. The E-9 you were to relieve is really wishy-washy and a regular ass. One day, he wants to retire. The next day, he does not. I've been informed that if he doesn't make up his mind by Friday morning, he will be reassigned to a billet he definitely will not want, and you'll be moved to that billet posthaste.

"It's not often that this happens, but sometimes, you'd like to know what an individual knows that got him promoted above the rank of shitbird. Comparing your record and his, I wouldn't even make him a gunnery sergeant. He has had many problems with the troops at each command he's been at and reassigned several times. He must have a good aegis protecting his ass."

"I've had to serve under a couple like him. Too bad that unworthy promotions have to be in the mix. I'm sure some good-quality marines didn't get promoted because of those types."

"Well, Tolbane, it's been nice sitting here talking and relaxing, but I must cut this short. You need to have your gear here at about 1000 hours Friday morning. A staff car will come by to pick you up. The driver will have your orders and instruct you on how to get to your next duty station. That's all I'm authorized to tell you at this time."

He stood and took Tolbane's hand and shook it.

"I have to thank you for squaring me away. Semper fi and good luck!"

With that, he turned and left the hut. That meant that Tolbane would have to sell his car by Friday morning.

CHAPTER 35

Tolbane began his next assignment the next Monday at 0800 hours. He brought in a small box of personal items for his desk. He had a lance corporal to guide him to his office. He placed the box on the extra-large desk and sat down. He thought back to the past Friday morning.

He was surprised when the driver had his gear stowed in the staff car's trunk, handed him his orders, and said, "We're off to Norfolk, Virginia, Master Guns."

The driver started the car and drove off. Tolbane read his orders thoroughly three times before he could believe what he was reading. He was going to be the G-2 chief at Fleet Marine Force, Atlantic, Norfolk, Virginia.

Wow, he had thought. *I'll be up there with the big boys again. What an upgrade. I hope I can do the job to suit whoever will be in charge.*

A few minutes later, a gunnery sergeant came into the office, introduced himself as Gunnery Sergeant Hammond, and welcomed Tolbane to FMFLANT.

"Master Guns, the commanding general, the three-star general Tomison, and Master Sergeant Tobias are on an inspection trip down at Gitmo and send their best regards and welcome to the men's department of Norfolk, Virginia. In about five, I'll have the office staff in a loose formation in the inner office area for you to greet."

"Thank you, Gunny! I'll be there in five."

Five minutes later, Tolbane put a really mean scowl on his face and marched into the office area at attention to greet his office staff. He stood in front of them, looked from one to another, and spoke to them in the meanest damn manner he could muster.

"All right, listen up and listen tight. All I want to see around here is assholes and elbows, spit and polish."

He continued to scowl at the staff's moaning and groaning for another minute or two, then broke out laughing at them.

"I got you all good, didn't I? Well, folks, I'm MGySgt. Travis Tolbane, USMC, I think. I'm honored to be here and to work with what I've been told is one of the best intel crews in the entire Corps. I have no friggin' idea what I'm going to be doing here yet, so you all pretend I just disappeared, and continue to march as you've been doing.

"Before I forget," he chided with a full-faced grin, "I hear I have a class act to follow here!"

He got a few boos and raspberries from the crew as they went back to work.

"Damn," the gunny said. "You had me going for a minute too. I think you made a few brownie points with the crew. I could see it in their faces and the grins when you dismissed them. They've been walking on eggshells the last year. The guy you replaced was a real winner. He couldn't even relate to a sandbag."

"So I've been told, Gunny. I believe in having a crew that's a little loosey-goosey, who feels good about their working environment, and who loves to do their job. There will always be reciprocity when you respect them for who they are and what they do. For me, this 'Do your job, or I kick your ass' just doesn't work."

"I think the crew out there will love working for you, me included. You scored a lot of points with them. I'll bet you'll get more out of them than they've given for a while. I'm glad you're aboard. By the way, Master Guns, your reputation precedes you! It's unequaled by anyone I know. I've got to get back to work. You'll need a little time to get settled here. If you need anything, just holler."

"Gunny, I'm hollering!"

"What do you need?"

"What time and where do we eat lunch here? Do they serve seconds?"

"I've got the right sergeant to show you the chow hall when the time comes. She is one of our best analysts and knows everything going on around here, and truth and gossip too. She'll be here at lunchtime to escort you. After lunch, she'll brief you on what we've been doing here at FMFLANT. She'll get you on the right track or bust your balls. Ta-ta!"

He left the office. Tolbane knew he was going to like it here.

*****

Lunchtime came, and true to the gunny's word, marine sergeant Gloria Cruize entered Tolbane's office and stood at attention in front of his desk and introduced herself.

She then flatly stated with very little respect to Tolbane, "With all due respect to you, Master Gunnery Sergeant, I do not put up with sexual innuendo or sexual advances. I'm not here for any idle chitchat or whatever crap that's not job related. I don't kiss any man's butt regardless of his rank. Is that loud and clear, sir?"

"Loud and clear. Looks like we'll work good together. Besides, you're not my fucking type anyhow. Is that loud and clear, Sergeant?"

Somewhat stunned by Tolbane's answer, she kind of gulped and replied, "Yes, sir!"

"Good! Now get me to the chow hall. I'm starving."

She led Tolbane from the office and guided him to the senior staff NCO dining area and left, not too happy about being put in her place.

Returning from mess with a full gullet, Tolbane motioned for the gunny to come into his office.

"Gunny, being new here, I don't know what each person's job is. I do know one thing for sure. I do not put up with insolence. I will not deal with anyone who has a broomstick up their ass. I do not want Sgt. Gloria Cruize anywhere near me or my office. If she needs to brief me on something, she can find someone else to do it for her.

"You may inform her, invoking my name, of the situation. I don't patronize my personnel, nor do I fraternize with them—never have, never will. She could have explained her personal canon of ethics to me much better than she did. I really thought it was disrespectful. Thanks!"

At the end of the working day, Sergeant Cruize walked into Tolbane's office with the intention of apologizing.

Before she could open her mouth, Tolbane flatly stated, "What part of staying away from me don't you fucking understand, Sergeant Cruize? Remember, you set the tone for any work relationship we could have had here. You need to follow the gunny's order and leave before you get to the top of my shit list. Goodbye, Sergeant Cruize. Remember to have someone else brief me on your work."

Feeling very sad and dejected, Sergeant Cruize turned and slowly shuffled her way to the door and out, berating herself severely for being so stupid once again every step she took. It seemed she could not ever keep her mouth from overloading her ever-loving ass when courtesy counted. Maybe she would put in a transfer request to another unit.

*****

The general, Lieutenant General Tomison, and his staff returned on Tolbane's fourth day on the job. As Tolbane entered the G-2 office, he was immediately directed to the general's office for a meet and greet. The general greeted him with a smile and a handshake and indicated he had coffee and pastries, which pleased Tolbane.

Then the general outlined FMFLANT's role in the country's defense, as well as what Tolbane's job would be in that role and other expectations. Then they had some idle chitchat about various things for a few minutes. The general praised him for his introduction to the staff, then asked point-blank about the incident with Sergeant Cruize.

"I'll be frank, sir! Throughout my career, I've always rendered due respect to those senior, equal, and junior to me and did my best to earn their respect. I believe I have earned that respect back. She was to show me the chow hall, but she came strutting into my office like she had a broomstick up her butt and started berating me about sexual harassment and some other junk in what I considered disrespectful.

"I did my best to put her in her place. I personally cannot have a workplace relationship with anyone so disrespectful, sir! Additionally, I had been warned about her before she stepped one foot into my office."

The general replied, "It's a shame that one who is so talented has such an attitude. There have been problems with her about other guys too. It causes some strife in the office. I really don't know what to do about her. She's on the staff NCO promotion list. When her warrant for promotion to staff sergeant arrives, I have to decide whether or not to promote her. Any suggestions?"

"If I had to make a yes-or-no decision on her deportment in my office yesterday, I probably would not promote. I'm sure you'll make the right decision when the time comes, General. You have more information on her than I. If she is as good at her job as I've been told and an asset to this department, then maybe she should be promoted. Even so, she will remain persona non grata in my office for a time."

"That's okay with me. Now I have something pressing to attend to. We can continue or talk at another time."

"Yes, sir! By your leave, sir!"

"Granted!"

On the way out of the office, Tolbane stated, "Thank you for seeing me today, General. I looked forward to it."

He returned to his office and motioned to the gunny.

"You can tell Sergeant Cruize that she's on the promotion list for staff sergeant, and I won't interfere with her being promoted. I do hope I don't find her being disrespectful to anyone else in this office. How about yourself? Are you doing okay here?"

"Yes, I'm doing fine here. It's just about the best job I've ever had in the Corps, and I've had a few."

"I'm glad to hear that. What do you think of the office's overall performance in our mission?"

"This group produces every task to the best of its ability. It takes second seat to no other G-2 section in the Corps. I hope I'm not out of line, Master Guns, but Sergeant Cruize, despite her temperament and disposition, has been a big part of that success."

"Roger that. You're not out of line at all, and I appreciate those who convey truth and not bullshit. I don't care for those who try to dazzle me with their footwork. You can always speak your mind with me, and I'll do the same with you. You can be sure of one thing: that if I do have to have contact with Sergeant Cruize that's job related, I'll be respectful. Don't tell her that, though. From what I've seen and heard so far, she is an important part of this office."

"You got it, Master Guns. My lips are sealed. By the way, Master Sergeant Tobias has something personal to attend to today. He said he's looking forward to meeting you and working with you tomorrow."

"Thanks, Gunny! Check you later."

The gunny went back to his desk.

*****

The next morning, Tolbane was expecting to see Master Sergeant Tobias at his desk when he arrived at the office, but he wasn't in the office yet. Come noontime, he still hadn't arrived to work. When finally he showed up, it was nearly 1400 hours.

Entering the G-2 office, he strolled leisurely along the aisles, stopping at certain desks and joking with the office staff, obviously having a good time at each stop. He did not come near Tolbane's desk. Tolbane took note but did not say anything—yet.

After about fifteen minutes, he finally got to Tolbane's office. Tolbane was still quiet on the matter. Tobias entered, shook hands, and introduced himself, talking about how great it was to meet a real marine hero, then the weather and a bunch of superfluous verbiage. Finally, he got to the point.

"Hey, man, how come you're giving my girl out there some grief when you don't even know her?"

"First off, I don't know who your girl is. Second, I hope you don't mean you're having an affair with a marine in this office."

"Come on, you know who I mean. You couldn't wait to try to take her down, stop her promotion. Nobody knows what else you're trying to do to her!"

"If you're referring to Sergeant Cruize, I have not tried one iota to keep her from being promoted. As for what went on in my office with her, the general knows everything. Plus, you weren't there, and it's none of your business anyway. Got it?"

"Yeah, I got it."

"Good. Now I don't know how loosey-goosey things were run before I arrived here, but I know how things are going to be run while I'm here. I don't know what you did all day yesterday and most of today, and I don't even give a rat's ass. What I care about is that I'm responsible for everyone in this office, and I need to know of their whereabouts all of the time.

"I expect all personnel here to check in and out and where they'll be if needed. Just remember that there is a swinging door here, and your ass can go out of it as fast as you come in. One thing you should always be aware of: I don't play childish games. Now get the fuck out of my office, get to your desk, and do some damn work."

Tobias seemed to go out the door with a single bound; he went to his desk and sulked. As Tobias left, the general came in, lightly clapping his hands.

"Good show, Master Guns."

"Sorry you had to hear that conversation, sir. I thought it was deserved."

"I'm glad I was around to hear it. He and that E-9 who left us just did as they pleased. He needed to be taken down a notch. The gunny thought there might be some fireworks, so he gave me a shout. As good as this section is, thanks to a few, there has been a lack of discipline. Glad to have you aboard. I hope you don't mind if I call you Tolbane in the future. Do you?"

"I've been called worse, sir!"

"Well, I guess I need to get back to work, then, Tolbane."

With that, the general turned and returned to his office.

The gunny stuck his head in the door and commented, "Am I on the shit list?"

"Not today. You are the 937th one on my Christmas list."

"I guess I'll be the last one to get a present this Christmas, then."

The pen Tolbane threw at the gunny just missed as he closed the door behind him. Tolbane sat there and grinned. He needed to be quicker on the pen toss. For an instance, he thought that at some time or other, someone threw a stapler at himself.

About half an hour later, there was a knock on the door, and Tolbane cheerfully called them out to enter. Sergeant Cruize walked in at attention and stood before his desk.

"I'm sorry to enter here, Master Gunnery Sergeant, but the general asked me to bring this top-secret document to you ASAP!"

"Thank you, Sarge. Exigent circumstance does not count. Thank you! By the way, keep up the good work. I understand someone out on that office deck is saying that I won't let you be promoted to staff sergeant. That's a bunch of crap. Go ask the gunny what I said to him about it. Just continue to march. Dismissed."

She turned and left Tolbane's office, puzzled. Tolbane turned to the document to see what was important.

His eyes got big, and he said to himself, out loud as usual, and with a big grin, "You got to be shitting me!"

He couldn't believe it. Down in that godforsaken jungle where his last unit had been ambushed, the cartel had taken over the abandoned enclave once more and had recruited twice as many peons to man and rebuild from the shellacking his unit gave them. It seemed that two marine rifle companies, unit designations not cited, had snuck in and wiped them out nearly to a man.

The next morning, Tolbane came in forty-five minutes early and was asked to report to General Tomison's office immediately upon arrival. Already in the office was Tobias, the gunny, Cruize, and a couple of unnamed men in black suits. They were introduced as Mr. 1 and 2 by the general.

CHAPTER 36

His curiosity aroused, Tolbane asked General Tomison if this was in reference to the top-secret document Sergeant Cruize brought to him the previous afternoon. The general nodded.

"I've been updated by Mr. 1 and 2. In fact, they are just leaving. They have pressing duties to attend to."

Mr. 1 and 2 got up, shook hands, and left.

"Tolbane, these two don't know who I'm referring to, but I spoke to a certain general this morning. He has rescinded the 'no deployment for two years' order for me that was placed in your service record book. You are now deployable. Now let's get down to business.

"There were a few prisoners taken that were higher-ups in the cartel. Somehow or other, the subject of the disastrous raid your unit was on at that camp came up. You know who let the cat out of the bag and compromised your unit on that one. However, there may have been more than one individual involved in spilling the beans. That's why you are now deployable."

"I don't understand, General. How do I fit into this?"

"We need a top-notch interrogator to question these people. You are a top-notch interrogator, and you know more about what happened during the ambush there than any of us here does."

"So I guess I've been volunteered by yours truly to be in the frying pan on the fire again?"

The general grinned and commented, "I guess you are familiar with BOHICA. You might want to practice touching your toes. In all actuality, I don't believe you'll have any problems. I've decided that the gunny needs a little more time herding up a section before his E-8 warrant comes along—keep that to yourselves—so he will ramrod the section while you, the top, and Sergeant Cruize are down south. I'm sending a Corporal Duggin and a Lance Corporal Dienz with you for administrative support, note-taking, recording, and of course, gofering."

"I'm kind of glad you had that order nullified. I didn't ask for it. I'm a marine first, last, and always. And I'll go where I'm needed or ordered."

"That's my personal opinion of you. Now will there be any problem with these two coming with you?"

"General, we're marines first, and I believe we'll function as well as any marine team would. I have no problems with either coming with me. Besides, we may need each other's acumen before it's over."

"You two sitting there like the dog just bit you, do you have any problem going with Tolbane?"

They each answered one at a time that they were fine being deployed with him.

"Tolbane, I have no choice but to send you there even though something smells fishy to me. I'm also sending a reinforced rifle squad with you. A Staff Sergeant Denton will be in charge. I trust him completely, and so should you. There'll be twenty-five of you going all total. I understand that the prisoners are being guarded by a reinforced rifle squad, so I guess there will be about forty-five or so of you there just in case it goes south.

"You will have naval, air, and ship-to-shore support on call if they're needed. I'll have the operation orders typed up and in your office by late this afternoon. Any questions? No? Then I suggest you three retire to Tolbane's office and discuss this earnestly. Goodbye!"

He grinned as the three left his office.

When the three were comfortable in his office, each with a cup of coffee, Tolbane cleared the air to them from his standpoint.

"First of all, anything that's transpired in this office before stays in this office. Clear?"

The two answered in the affirmative.

"I don't like going back down there for any reason. It's just crummy terrain, the heat, the bugs, and the unpredictable cartels in the area, to name a few. I don't like talking about what happened down there with me. It's a long story starting with a test unit and ending with an ambush."

He related the forming of the special unit and its goal, the deployment of the unit, and how a ranking officer soiled the beans and got them ambushed. He found he could not talk about carrying his dead lieutenant colonel while being wounded himself without tearing up. The other two felt sorry for him.

"We kicked ass and took names, but our losses were horrendous to me. Have you any questions so far?"

The answers were negative.

"This is important to me and to you two. We should have M16s in addition to our issue handguns. It's better to be safe than sorry. I'm going to ask for a bunch of grenades and smoke, extra chow, and ammo. Maybe I can even get us a couple of corpsmen to hitch a ride."

Tobias raised his hand and asked a question he felt was relevant.

"Sorry to interrupt, but was this your only special ops?"

"I'm not at liberty to speak of certain things I've done, but I will say it wasn't my first dance by a long shot."

"Then I'm glad to be going with you. How about you, Sarge?"

"Suits me to a tee. I'm glad to be going with you too. I wouldn't miss it for the world."

Tobias turned to Cruize.

"Best you get back to your desk, Sarge. Lord knows what info may have come in."

She left Tolbane's office in a military manner.

"I purposely sent her away. Before you say anything, let me say my piece."

"You're on. Stage left!"

"First of all, I apologize to you for my unmilitary-like demeanor the last few months and for the couple of days goofing off. I needed to be put in my place. I then did some checking around and found out I was given the wrong scoop on Sergeant Cruise's promotion warrant. I also called some friends who knew of you. They told me to square away my ass and do my job, as I had an NCOIC that deserved his rank and his decorations and knew how to honcho an organization. So I'm looking forward to working with you! I've said my piece. Any comments, boss?"

"Glad to be aboard with you. We'll work well together, I'm sure. I want you to know, Sergeant Cruize was way out of order with me. She just needs to navigate a little different course. I've intended all along to get her to see her own follies. I'll help her in any way I can. Just don't tell her yet. Okay?"

"Okay, I can live with that. You just might be an okay guy after all!"

"Don't you have something to do?" Tolbane said with a grin.

"I'll just go check my desk."

Tolbane just laughed to himself.

*****

The OP plan and orders were delivered to Tolbane's office late that afternoon, as the general had promised. He needed to speak to his two analysts and the two admin people. He asked the top if there was a place where the five could get a good steak and have some privacy. Top knew of a restaurant that had a quiet back room for privacy and dining. Tolbane insisted the tab was on him, as it was his meeting. The four agreed heartily.

Once they were in the back room, Tolbane announced they would eat to their heart's content. Then and only then would it be time for business. During the meal, the four learned a lot about Tolbane's eating habits and his penchant for honey mustard and his vacuum-like suctioning of foodstuff. When the dining was complete, Tolbane informed them that they would have coffee until after the briefing was over. Then they would bring on the beer.

He carefully briefed the group on what had happened down there, giving the corporal and lance corporal a sanitized, short version, leaving out many details. He emphasized that their duty was only to obtain information on who might have been behind an ambuscade that had happened a few months before. Other matters would not be pursued unless the prisoners began to offer up other incidents or cartel infrastructure. Then he spoke to each and every one about his or her individual duty and responsibility.

His final comment was, "Waiter, bring on the beer!"

The group left for their quarters about an hour and a half later, a little tipsy.

*****

Tolbane's group was finally on their way. They were boarded on a C-130 making its milk run to Gitmo. It stopped north at Turner Field in Quantico, Virginia, then south MCAS Cherry Point, North Carolina, and MCAS New River, North Carolina, and finally, south toward Gitmo. They were met there by a lieutenant colonel from their intelligence section, billeted for the night, and flew out in an Osprey the next morning.

The Osprey set them down inside the old cartel enclave. The first thing they noticed was the intense heat and mugginess of the area, causing them to break out in sweat immediately. They were met by a 1st Lt. John Brown, who was in charge of the reinforced squad guarding the prisoners, and with their gear off-loaded the Osprey and left.

After the introductions were made, the group was taken to a shack passing as a living quarters. Then there was a meeting with Tolbane, the top, and his sergeant. The other group was represented by the lieutenant, a staff sergeant, and a sergeant.

Tolbane's first question was, "Are you able to tell us why the prisoners were not transported to Gitmo instead of being kept here at this place?"

"I asked the same question, and the best answer I received was the old adage we always hear. Ours is not to question why but to do or die or something to that friggin' effect."

"I'm not surprised at that kind of answer. I expected it. My next question is, how many prisoners do we have, Lieutenant?"

"We have three. One of them has a wound through his left bicep muscle. Not serious. Speaking of wounds, I've got one corpsman. Glad you brought two of them. My troops have some scrapes and bangs, more like what you'd get on the old type of school grounds. They need some TLC, I guess."

"They will be at your disposal, Lieutenant, for whatever TLC they need. What do you think of the captives, such as are they friendly/cooperative, neutral/nonpartisan, or hostel/antagonistic?"

"I believe I'd lean on somewhat friendly side. I've seen no tempers shown, at least so far. They seem to want to help us. It could be they want special treatment, but I guess you'll find that out soon enough."

"My next concern is security. I know from experience the bad dudes can mobilize a bunch of guys in a blink of an eye. They know this area like it was their own hand. I know from personal experience right here and down to the sea through the jungle.

"There are twenty-seven of us and twenty-three of you for a grand total of fifty. I'm sure your guys are tired of standing guard. Get with Staff Sergeant Denton and work out a guard schedule and take a good look at what you have covered. If you think it's needed, maybe even add a couple of posts. I would also suggest making sure everyone has plenty of ammo. We brought extra with us."

"That sounds good. I know my troops are tired of standing guard."

Staff Sergeant Denton spoke up.

"Do any of your guys have any recon experience?"

"I think maybe two of them have done a little recon in the past."

"I've got two I specifically asked for. We three have reconned together. If I may suggest, maybe the five of us can slip out tonight and snoop and poop a little. We'll look for any signs we might be watched. We'll be back in before dawn."

"What do you think, Master Guns?"

"I think it's a good idea. I know General Tomison has great confidence in Staff Sergeant Denton. I think without a doubt it should be a go."

"Okay, Staff Sergeant, get with my guy and work out the details. Go ahead and set it up now, and good luck."

Staff Sergeant Denton left the meeting.

"Okay, Master Guns, what else do you need to do your job?"

"I want the best room in the compound for our interrogation sessions. We'll need a desk, three chairs. One or the other of my two peons will be taking notes at each session. It would also be nice if some others could listen in some way or another. I would guess that the only incentive I could offer to the prisoners and produce to them would be extra chow. We brought a lot of extra MRE rations not knowing how long we'll be here in this heavenly paradise."

"Damn it to hell and back, Master Guns. You're a man after my own heart. Our OIC claimed he couldn't leave much for us. He was really worried about our situation. You're a lifesaver."

"Well, Lieutenant, in the Marine Corps green, we aim to please. So for now, I haven't anything more I can think of. My guys, do you have any questions for the lieutenant?"

There was none.

"Do you have anything more at this time, Lieutenant? If not, it's howdy doody chow time for us devil dogs to resupply and replenish our energy."

On the way back, Tolbane caught Sergeant Cruize's attention and motioned her to walk beside him.

"Now, Sarge, I don't want you to get your panties in a bunch, but I have a little project for you. Are you okay doing something different for a change?"

"I promise I won't get bunched up. I'm in this. Do whatever is needed of me."

"Good to hear. The troops that have been here from the start may know a lot as to what's been going on here. While you're innocently walking around to get the feel of the place, you might accidently come across some of the lieutenant's troops, and they might even be talkative to a young female sergeant of the marines rather than an old fart like me.

"You never know what could happen if that same lady happened to look in on the prisoners to see if they need anything. We need to have as much info as we can collect. Like the general, I'm not too sure about this mission. I can't put my finger on it, but something just doesn't compute upstairs."

He pointed to his brain-housing group as he commented.

"Master Guns, I need to learn how to relate to people instead of being uptight all the time. I think this op might be something I can learn by. Thanks for giving me this chance."

"You deserve it. I'm sure you will do fine."

Tolbane had been given a satellite phone with instructions to call the general at certain intervals. He reported what he could and listened to what the general was passing on to him.

Sergeant Cruize had been wandering around, doing her best to con information from the troops and prisoners. She saw Tolbane, and she went to update him on what little she had learned. Tolbane saw her approaching and decided to pull her chain a bit. As she was about to speak, he addressed her.

"Sergeant Cruize, why are you out of uniform at a time like this?"

"I don't know what to say!" she said as she tried looking herself over to see what was wrong. "I honestly don't see anything, but if you will show me, I'll correct it immediately."

"Good! Then I suggest you go find Staff Sergeant Denton to see if he can lend you one of his metal chevrons for you collar, Staff Sergeant Cruize."

"What? Can you repeat that?"

"Yes, ma'am. You need to get staff sergeant chevrons on immediately if not sooner, Staff Sergeant!"

"I'm a staff sergeant now?"

"The general just confirmed your promotion on our satellite call. Your precedence number is 345, Staff Sergeant."

She jumped toward Tolbane and hugged him. Then she caught herself and backed away from him.

"Oh god, I'm sorry!"

"Look, I have never had an inkling to hug a staff sergeant until now. Nothing to forgive. I must add that the restrictions to me and my office were for a sergeant, not a staff sergeant. Capisce?"

She jumped up and down, hugged him again, and went running off, looking for Staff Sergeant Denton, at the double time. Tolbane smiled watching her in her excitement.

"There is hope for her yet," he opined to himself.

Cruize found Staff Sergeant Denton asleep. She woke him, and he happened to have a couple of extra sets of metal chevrons in his shaving kit. He pinned one set of them on her collars, then in the highest tradition of the USMC, tacked[24] them on each bicep with his fist. She knew she would be bruised the next day, but to her, they would be happy bruises. Then she remembered that she forgot to relate to Tolbane what she had learned. She went to find him.

He saw her leave the hooch where Staff Sergeant Denton was racked out and called to her. When she approached him, he chided her.

"Before you say anything, I must warn you that when we get back, you're buying the beer, Staff Sergeant Cruize!"

"Yes, sir! I look forward to buying it all night if necessary!"

"Good marine. Now did you want to tell me something when a certain promotion got in the way of your report?"

He grinned.

"You bet, Master Guns. I did exactly what you asked of me. I did my best to be sociable to those I spoke with, and I think I managed to do it a little bit. I didn't learn much, but I think I laid some groundwork. In the next day or two, a couple of the guys may open up a little more to me.

"Overall, from the six guys I talked with, they seemed a little jumpy. I got the feeling they didn't like what was going on here either. They feel there should be at least a company of troops here. They were glad to see us arrive. It was a slight relief for them. The prisoners didn't have much to say, except that they didn't need anything. I think they didn't trust me."

"That's okay if they don't trust at this time. We can play that to our own tune. You did a good job. I appreciate it. To change the subject, Staff Sergeant, I want to help you, so what I say now I hope will help. You are now in a higher level of Marine Corps leadership. You must train yourself to be more patient and not quite so demanding.

---

[24] Tacking on chevrons means just hitting the promotee on the upper arms with a fist.

"If the troops think you're trying to be a feminist, they won't respect you. I see you're trying to do the right thing, and that's a good sign. Remember, I'm not your enemy. You can come to me with any problem you need advice on anytime. I'm there to help."

"Thank you, Master Guns. I felt bad about the way I approached you that first day. You did the right thing for me, dressing me down as you did. It made me think, and I'll never forget that. I also thank you for allowing my promotion."

"Hang loose for a minute. I'm going to call the general again."

He made his call, made his request to him and his reasoning, and got the general's answer.

"We're in luck. We'll be getting two rifle squads in the morning. It's getting dusk now. I guess we need to go to our quarters and get cleaned up as best we can, then get a good night's sleep."

"I'm with you there, boss. Oops!"

"That's okay. You can call me boss, because I'm the boss of bosses that always outbosses the big bosses' boss. See you in the AM."

He walked off. The new staff sergeant looked, puzzled, at him. The G-2 section had not yet seen the other side of Tolbane, his quips and nonsensical sayings, but it wouldn't be too much longer until they heard the Mike Hammer side of him.

Later, Tolbane asked his master sergeant to just wander around and keep things shipshape.

"I know you're very good at this, I hear. I need someone to keep up our standards and keep the troops from getting lax."

"You've got it, Tolbane. I'm not too good at your job, but I can handle troops."

CHAPTER 37

The next day was already getting hot and muggy by 0600 hours, as the sun was above the horizon. Everyone not on guard had shaved, except Staff Sergeant Cruize, and had cleaned up a bit and was ready to break open the rations for breakfast when two Ospreys landed, each with a squad of marines plus two extra machine gun teams for a total of thirty-one troops, making the compound's total eighty-one troops. Those on the ground appreciated the addition.

In addition to the weapons, ammo, and supplies, the general sent hot chow in sealed containers for breakfast. When word was passed on the chow, you could hear some hoops and howls from the troops already on the ground.

There was also a sealed packet for Staff Sergeant Cruize. It contained a congratulations from the general and two packs of a staff sergeant's metal chevrons. The note also stated her warrant was in her desk drawer, along with her cloth chevrons.

During the morning, Tolbane assisted the newly arrived riflemen in getting quarters in the run-down huts and meeting with the now platoon sergeant, the lieutenant, and later, around noontime, Staff Sergeant Denton. He and the lieutenant had a meeting with all sergeants and above. They worked out a guard schedule and even added two more posts.

Staff Sergeant Denton addressed the assembled group.

"Myself and four others did a close-in recon during the night. There was some moon, and it helped somewhat. We came across a couple of spots I'd like to check out during the day. The spots could be used to observe us. Otherwise, we found no trace of unfriendlies. What I'd like to do is take four or five grunts and check those spots in daylight. With the sun's light, we may find something else."

One of the sergeants spoke up.

"Staff Sergeant, I would like to go, and I've got three guys that have done this kind of stuff before. I know all three of them are qualified rifle experts on the rifle range, and they've fired in a hostile environment before."

The lieutenant looked at Denton and offered, "Staff Sergeant, it's your call!"

"It's fine by me. Welcome aboard, Sarge. Get your guys, extra ammo, rations, and water and meet me by the old gate on the south side. We'll start there and snoop and poop, ending up at what serves as a main gate."

"Sounds good to me. Oh, I just remembered we've got two radio operators with us. I'll bring one along, and the other one can monitor us in case the shit hits the fan."

"Good thinking, Sarge," Denton commented. "Go do your thing, and I'll meet you at the old, run-down gate in thirty minutes."

The sergeant waved and left. Denton excused himself and went to get his gear. The meeting lasted another half an hour and then broke up, everyone going to their assignments.

Staff Sergeant Cruize stopped Tolbane outside the hut to get a little advice.

"Master Guns, when Staff Sergeant Denton was talking about going out there this afternoon, I felt like I should go along for the experience. But for some reason, I kept quiet. Do you think it would be advisable for me to go out there with them sometime?"

"Okay, Ms. Grasshopper."

She looked at him funny, really confused.

"You do need the experience hopping grass, and I'm glad you kept quiet. I wouldn't have let you go, because we don't know what might be in the jungle out there. We'll be sending other patrols out there once we are sure things are not likely to get in the shit. I'll see to it you get to go too, but only as an observer, not in charge. I don't want to lose a brand spanking new staff sergeant out there."

"Thanks, boss. It's hard for me to say this. Maybe it'll make more sense to you than me. I love my job at G-2, but there are times I feel like I want to do and feel what it's like to be a marine out in the bush, something I can relate to when I'm reading messages and reports. Sometimes, I can't get the concept in my mind."

"I do understand your feelings and your desires. I was an admin clerk at one time, and I had similar feelings from time to time. There's just something special being in the bush with marines. You feel safe with them and that you belong there. I'll do my best to see you get the opportunity to find that feeling while hopping through the grass, grasshopper."

"You're really a trip, you know that?"

"At your service, ma'am! I aim to please. I even aim at the latrine."

She laughed heartily at that quip.

"To think I was going to hate you with all my heart and soul. I think now we are fortunate to have you. That last guy that was our G-2 chief was the pits. I need to get ready to sit in with one of the prisoners this afternoon. By your leave, sir!"

"Granted, Staff Sergeant Grasshopper. See you at our interview room."

*****

The prisoner Jose Chavez seemed to be at ease when he was brought into the makeshift interrogation room. He smiled and greeted the interrogators in his best broken English, which wasn't too bad. Across the table from him was Tolbane and Staff Sergeant Cruize, who was acting as an interpreter, and in the corner was Lance Corporal Dieny, taking notes. The two responded to the prisoner in a like manner. They passed the time of day, the torridly hot weather, lack of rain, and other nonessential topics.

When Tolbane felt they had established rapport with the man, he began the questioning in earnest. Treating the man as if he was just being interviewed, he began.

"Jose, several months ago, I was with a small marine unit that came down here to this enclave to take charge of some politicos. When we had them in custody, we were ambushed, and they, along with some of my fellow marines, were killed. Our operation had been compromised by one of our own. He has been punished and is of no consequence now. I have been told you have more information on our betrayal. Is that so?"

"Si, señor!"

"What can you tell us about the betrayal?"

"I would like to tell you, but first, I need protection from the cartel that owns this area. I don't want to die here."

"Jose, I can promise you safety from them. I can assure you, we will not be ambushed here again. No way, no how!"

Only Tolbane and the lieutenant knew they would fly out in Ospreys.

Prior to meeting with any of the prisoners, Tolbane had explained how the interviews would work to Staff Sergeant Cruize. She would interpret when necessary. Also, if the prisoner got a look of not understanding on his face, she was to feel free to explain the question to the individual. She explained to the man that his safety was a main concern, and he needn't be afraid.

"Master Guns, he understands now that you will protect him."

"Thanks! If you assist us, you may receive a small payment in American dollars. If you help us, you're safe with us. If you do not want to assist us, we must release you and ask that you leave the compound. The decision is yours!"

"Señor, after giving it some thought, I do not know a name. I was a—what you say?—ah, a gofer. But from time to time, I hear conversations while serving drinks, food, or running errands, hearing only little bits. The big honcho would be angry that some big shot in the marines did not get needed information to him on time. He was also mad because some lieutenant colonel committed suicide and could not pass on anything anymore like he did before they ambushed the Americans."

"I'm aware he betrayed us and committed suicide. Do you know anything else that could help us?"

"No, señor. I'm sorry, but that's all I know about your situation."

"Thank you for being forthcoming to me, Jose. You are safe with us. I may need to talk to you again, but you're free to roam the compound."

Jose was escorted out by a guard and turned loose.

Turning to Cruize, Tolbane stated, "When you terminate an interview or interrogation, always let them believe you may speak to them again. It could prey on their minds if they are guilty."

"Thanks for the tip! I'll remember that."

Tolbane refrained from telling her a joke about a tip.

"I see now the difference between an interview and an interrogation. I would have gone balls to the wall and blown it."

"Well, any other questions?"

"Yes! How did you know the rat committed suicide?"

"I'm going to trust you with this. Do not ever repeat this, because it is top-secret. I gave the rat, as you call him, the poison pill by direction from above. His death was reported as a heart attack and posted the same, not as a suicide. So you see, there is a bigger rat up the food chain somewhere. Jose doesn't know he gave us a valuable piece of information.

"Now let us get the next prisoner in. I want you to begin by explaining to him in Spanish about being safe with us. Get his hometown, province, why he's a member of a drug cartel, and whatever you think appropriate before you turn him over to me. Oh, no small talk this time. We want to see how he reacts to your beginning the interview."

The next prisoner Tolbane requested was brought in. This time, Corporal Duggin was taking notes. Cruize welcomed him in Spanish, and he got a big, lascivious grin on his face and looked her up and down. Even though he didn't respond to her greeting, she continued to question him. Tolbane noticed he was more interested in her than answering her questions. She finally turned it over to Tolbane.

"Look, asshole, I think you're bullshitting us. You have nothing for us, so I'm just going to send you on your way into the jungle. The next guy I'll turn loose will tell them how you cooperated with us and how you're to receive mucho American dollars for your information. Oh, and you don't get this woman!"

He turned to Cruize and said to her, "Go get the guard and turn him loose outside the gate."

Before Cruize could move, the prisoner was frightened and shouted, "No, not that, señor. I'll help you, but you must protect me. They'll cut off my cojones and shove them in my mouth before they kill me."

"All right, but you must be honest with us. What do you know about who is betraying our country?"

"One of our agents in Miami was relaying information to us for some time from some unknown source to me in Norfolk, Virginia. That's how we knew to ambush you. I remember you. I saw you wounded and carrying a woman over your shoulder and still shooting at us. You are a real hero, señor, not like our cowardly leaders."

"Thank you for the compliment. Please continue."

"I was one chosen to rotate security for the honcho. Once in a while, he would make calls on his satellite phone. I hear him talking to somebody called Gummy or something like that. The honcho always thought that the guy should be faster with his information. They would also argue with each other over how much pesos and when and how the payments would be paid. So help me, that's all I know."

"I believe you. You are now under our protection."

The session ended, and the prisoner was removed. Staff Sergeant Cruize had another question.

"How did you know to approach him that way?"

"It was easy. As we were approaching them while they were standing outside their hooch, this one was leering at you and eating you up with his eyes. He confirmed my assessment of him by his actions during your interrogation."

"Wow! You just think of everything."

"Don't get down on yourself. You've never been to interrogation training. That is only a beginning, because it must develop into an art. I have had a lot of experience, which helps my perception of an individual. As an analyst, you need to know the process of different methods of information collections, but you do not need to be proficient in each one, only how to process the information and evaluate the information that's collected."

"I dig it, boss. I feel you are waiting on me to say something on the last guy's information. Okay! I'm thinking about the name

Gummy. He said it sounded like Gummy. From what I've learned from the two guys, could he really mean Gunny?"

"Well-reasoned, grasshopper. It struck me right away he must be talking about a gunnery sergeant, because we're dealing with marines."

The information from the remaining prisoner confirmed the limited knowledge of the first two. Then the recon team came in with info on some tracks, probably a couple of days old, nothing pressing to worrying about at the time. Tolbane got word on the satellite phone that it would be at least two, maybe three, days before they could be extracted. He continued to send out recon teams with no sign of being observed by the cartels.

*****

On the morning of the third day, Tolbane, when he heard nothing about when they would be extracted, made a call. The Ospreys would start extraction at about 1500 hours, so he called Staff Sergeants Denton and Cruize and planned a recon.

"Denton, I promised the staff sergeant here the opportunity to find out what it's like to recon an area such as this is. It's for her own personal experience as well as to help her understand some reports that come over her desks. Since our recons have been benign, I thought we could do at least one last patrol just for her. If you would, Denton, get let's say about eight or nine guys you think need the experience, and we'll go out in about a half hour, okay?"

Denton replied, "We'll leave out the main gate in thirty. Don't be late."

Tolbane and Cruize got their gear, water, and ammo. He instructed Cruize how she should carry her weapon—loaded but not locked, trigger finger along the stock—and how the team would alternate the troops in a spaced-out line, every other team member facing a different direction with their weapon and moving as silently as possible.

Forty-five minutes after the team left the gate, they heard some noises, stopped in their tracks, and listened. Suddenly, eight cartel members came into view, as surprised as the marines. They pointed their weapons and began firing at Tolbane's group, the first round hitting Cruize in the lower abdominal area, missing any vitals. She was also the first to fire and took out two of them, then fell to the ground. The rest of the team took out the rest.

Tolbane and Denton rushed to Cruize, who was writhing in pain.

She looked at them and cried, "Did I do it right, boss?"

"You're damn right you did. I'm proud of you, kid!" Tolbane informed her.

The corpsman was now there and attending to her. It was easy for him, because she had passed out. Now Staff Sergeant Denton was on the radio, requesting cover for their immediate return to the enclave. Denton had a PFC cut two saplings and trim them. He had a couple of privates take off their tops and put the saplings through the sleeves, making a stretcher for Cruize. They began their movement to the enclave, reaching it without any further incidents.

As soon as they arrived, Tolbane got on the horn and ordered an immediate medevac and also issued a request to begin their extraction ASAP. He received an affirmative reply. The first Osprey was on station within thirty minutes, and Staff Sergeant Cruize was boarded immediately, then some of the troops, and they were whisked out quickly to a waiting aircraft carrier.

Tolbane was the last one to board the last Osprey. The hatch closed, and the craft was airborne, flying over the jungle. He wondered what the cartel would think when it was discovered the hated Janiques were no longer in the enclave. He didn't give a shit.

*****

Three days had elapsed since the incident. In his report to the general, Tolbane praised the deportment, the professionalism, and the willingness of the troops to do what was necessary to ensure the success of the mission. He made sure he inserted, "In the highest tradition of the United States Marine Corps." He especially praised the actions of Staff Sergeant Cruize and how she reacted, giving their team time to react to the sudden confrontation by the cartel group, even after being wounded, and her taking out two enemy.

Tolbane recommended that she be awarded the Bronze Star Medal with the V device for valor in addition to the Purple Heart award. In a private talk with the general on her behalf, he recommended that in the near future, Staff Sergeant Cruize could be recommended for officer candidate or warrant officers school.

The general thought it through for a minute and said, "I think warrant officers school would be the best. We wouldn't lose her annalistic abilities that way."

Tolbane agreed.

*****

Two days later, learning Staff Sergeant Cruize was doing better and could have visitors, Tolbane and General Tomison visited her in her hospital room. The room had a few vases of flowers sent from her office troops, and she was propped up in bed with a big pillow and a big grin on her face. She was really glad to see the two of them, especially Tolbane.

She was surprised when the general read her proclamations and awarded her the Bronze Star with V device and the Purple Heart. They congratulated her, and the general surprised her once more with the announcement that when she finished her rehab, she would be going to the first warrant officers class available. After that, General Tomison left knowing the two would probably want to talk.

Tolbane smiled at her and took her hand in his. She smiled back at him.

"Hey there, grasshopper, hopping around in bed. Now do you feel what it's like to be with the marines out there in the bush? You are one of them now, and it's forever, you know. You will never be a former marine. You're a marine for life."

"You're a fucking A boss. I had the experience of a lifetime because of you. I now know what it's like to be with them. I felt safe like you said, and I feel like I passed the test, and I am a marine."

"Yes, you passed the test. We were all concerned for you but proud as hell too. You did good, grasshopper."

"Tell me, boss, what in the hell is this grasshopper thing?"

"Watch the TV series *Kung Fu*, and you'll get the message. You haven't gotten to know my screwball side and inane sayings yet. Just so you know, we didn't hit it off the first meeting, but I knew you had the stuff. Just needed to learn patience and control.

"I don't want to deceive you. It wasn't just the general. I put a bug in his ear about warrant officers school for you, and he agreed. I really think you'll be a top-notch warrant officer in your field. In fact, I think you'll be the best, and I wish you that success. Your awards will draw respect too."

"Boss, grasshopper wants you to lean over here. I've always wondered what it would be like to hug a master gunnery sergeant."

He leaned over, and she gave him a tight hug and a kiss on the cheek with tears in her eyes.

"I don't know when I've ever been so happy to be alive, and all because I bitched you out. Fair winds and following seas, boss."

On the way out the door, Tolbane turned and spoke lovingly to her.

"If anyone, regardless of rank, gives you any grief about your awards without any awards from a hostile campaign themselves, let me know, grasshopper. I'll come and kick their ass!"

He was gone. He never saw her again. He did miss her.

CHAPTER 38

During the next few days, Tolbane had a lot of paperwork and other things to catch up on from his days away from his desk. Then he accompanied the general on an inspection of the G-2 operations at the G-2 of the Second Marine Division. Some of the procedures he had been responsible for implementing.

He had a kind of old home week with some of the personnel he had known from various assignments. He thought the whole time about Gummy/Gunny. An idea, as dumb as it sounded, was fomenting in his mind. He decided to approach the general about it.

"General Tomison, something has been bugging me something fierce. I don't have any evidence, but trying to find a gunny that could have had a lot of information that was passed on to the cartels has been futile. There is one, however, that is in the sphere of our operations, but I'm leery of making any accusation without proof."

"Okay, Tolbane, I trust your instincts. What are you trying to say?"

"If I had a suspect, would we be able to get his/her bank and financial records?"

"I'm not really sure. Let me call a colonel over at the NCIS that I know. I'll get back to you on it. I would think it would be easy."

"Thanks, General. If I'm right, we'll have solved several breeches of security and solve my mystery of the ambush."

The next morning, General Tomison motioned Tolbane to his office.

"I've got your answer. We submit a request to NIS, and they will request the civilian authorities to issue subpoenas for whatever files we'd need. So, Master Guns, just who do you have in mind that might be our culprit?"

"I hope I'm right, sir. It's Gunnery Sergeant Hammond, sir!"

"Look, Travis—if I may call you by your first name—don't worry if you are wrong. We need to check every possibility regardless of our feelings. Besides, he'll never know we've checked him out. It will be a couple of days before we have anything to check. Just be careful what you may say to him."

Tolbane had no more returned to his desk than Gunny Hammond entered. Tolbane pointed to a chair.

The gunny began.

"Looks like the general's on your ass a lot. I don't envy you."

"It's not really getting on my ass. The powers above seem to find more dumb questions to ask about the fiasco down south. It was a useless OP, to say the least. We didn't learn a damn thing we didn't already know, and it got us a WIA. I think the whole matter from upstairs is about getting an office worker, a woman marine to boot, wounded on a patrol. For some reason, they don't want to believe I was just furthering her training. They think we were trying to attack the cartel there."

"That sounds consistent with the guys upstairs. They always have to justify their existence some way or another."

"You got that right, Gunny. They can't seem to get it in their craw that the lieutenant colonel that had a heart attack was the guilty party that caused the ambush we got caught in."

"Was it a heart attack? I heard it was a suicide."

"I hadn't heard that. Probably because I was too busy with other things. It was a real pain in the ass to stand down a unit. It was a good thing I had an office staff that was good."

"I never had to do that. I guess that was a real pain in the ass to you. The mountains of paperwork involved I can't imagine. Well, I need to get back to my desk. Got more paperwork than I need right now."

"That's my problem too."

Later on, Tolbane, when he felt the gunny wouldn't hear, dialed the general's number and outlined the conversation with the gunny.

The general's reply was, "Looks like you may be onto something big, Travis."

*****

Two days later, at about midmorning, the general phoned Tolbane and asked him to meet at a really swank steak house for the evening meal. The meal was on the general.

Once seated at the steak house, the general informed Tolbane that he knew of his voracious appetite and his love of bacon and honey mustard and to dine till his heart was content.

"We'll talk business after you do your vacuum thing."

About the time Tolbane finished devouring his food, the CO from the NCIS entered carrying a thick manila folder and sat with them. He ordered beers around when the waiter approached. Served with three bottles of Bud and frosted glasses, Colonel Osgood began.

"I guess you hit the nail on the head, Master Guns. We got a real winner here. We'll cover the details later, so right now, I'll just mention the highlights."

Tolbane offered, "I'm all ears, sir."

"Not only does this guy have some large cash deposits on several occasions, but he's into several successful stocks. He's nearly a millionaire."

Tolbane and the general looked at the CO in disbelief.

"At this time, we have no idea where the cash is coming from, although it's suspected it comes from the cartel you are familiar with, Tolbane. How did you arrive at checking him out?"

Tolbane replied, "Well, sir, I'm a fan of mysteries, like Mike Hammer, Sam Spade, etc. My favorite is the man who said that when you eliminate the impossible, whatever remains, no matter how improbable, must be the truth. That was from a *Sherlock Holmes* mystery. I couldn't come up with any other gunny being privy to certain information and operations after talking to those guys down south. I thought he was a stand-up guy, but I had to make sure."

"Well, good job. Don't you think so, General?"

"Damn straight. Now we have to find a way to nail him."

"If I may offer a suggestion, I think it would be kind of cool to get him in a reverse sting. I think he would fall for it."

"What do you have in mind, Travis?" the general asked.

"I'm not sure. I haven't thought about it till this instant."

"Travis, you think on it. Meanwhile, let's call it a night."

Tolbane couldn't resist the urge.

"A night!"

"Well said," the CO agreed.

They left and went to their respected quarters. Tolbane tried to think of a sting operation on the way home. However, he was getting blanks.

Maybe the next day, he thought.

*****

Tolbane sat in his office, brooding all morning, trying to come up with a plan. Gunny Hammond came in and sat down.

"You've looked perplexed all day. The corps got you down?"

"No! My parents passed away years ago and left me some property worth a lot money. I got a call last night that some county officials want to claim it as some kind of eminent domain or some such crap and not paying me one red cent. I'm trying to figure a way to beat them at their own game."

The gunny was eating it up as Tolbane was pouring it on. Tolbane was getting good at fibbing to the gunny on the run. After a few more fibs on the subject, the gunny went back to his desk. Tolbane picked up his phone and dialed the general. He turned slightly in his chair so his lips couldn't be read.

"General, I believe I have an idea. I need to think it out some more. I'll let you know when I got a plan."

The general was okay with that.

Later that afternoon, Gunny Hammond was sitting in Tolbane's office when the general popped in.

"Chief, I need you to go down to G-4 with me about some new mount-out gear for the section."

"I'm on the way, General. See you later, Gunny."

Tolbane left with the gunny staring after them.

"Did you figure out anything yet?"

"You bet, General. I think he'll buy it hook, line, and sinker. I'm finding out he's a real guppy. Here's what I figure."

CHAPTER 39

The general, the day after Tolbane's phone call, announced a meeting of all the section's senior staff NCOs and NCOs in the conference room at 0800 hours the next day. He ensured that all of them would attend, as it was a matter of the utmost security importance for further forays down south.

At precisely 0800 hours, the general entered the conference room, and Tolbane called the attendees to attention. The general bade the group to sit and to make sure they had coffee and doughnuts. He then addressed them three minutes later.

"I have no idea what the deuce is going on with the grand people upstairs. As you all know, we've had two screwed-up forays to an abandoned cartel enclave in a classified location down south. It seems some mental midget decided that would be a good area for a recon team from the Second Reconnaissance Battalion at Camp Lejeune, North Carolina, to have a good training operation in a hostile area. Guess where? Yes, at our favorite location for fun and games where we lost marines and one of our own wounded.

"Right now, as far as I know, the team is about one klick southeast of the enclave in some heavy flora. It would seem their training was going well when a cartel member that had deserted stumbled into their midst. Lo and behold, what do you think he claims? You got it. He said he would give up the name of the last American marine traitor who is giving information to the cartel if he was guaranteed a safe haven in the States.

"I'll explain why I called you here for this meeting this morning. I do not want to send another group down there to question him. I've already exceeded my budget for that kind of operation. I have two choices. I can have him flown to Gitmo to be questioned and processed there, or he can be flown to a ship and brought here to Norfolk, Virginia.

"You each have a pad of paper and a pencil. I'd like you each to write what you think I should do with this guy. Now in either case, you must decide, do we need the name of the traitor immediately at Gitmo, or can it wait to get him here to find out?

"Take no more than five minutes to decide. Meanwhile, there's plenty of coffee and doughnuts to be drank and eaten. Time starts now."

Five minutes later, the general collected the papers. All had selected Gitmo and to nab the traitor ASAP.

"All right, troops, Gitmo it is. Now I have to work out whether the recon team will be extracted with him or not and how and when it will take place. Because of the terrain, the Ospreys may have to land in the deserted enclave. I thank you all for your participation this morning. You are dismissed. Tolbane, Top, and Gunny, I need to see you in my office right now for a few minutes."

When they were situated in the general's office, he settled in his desk chair, took in a deep breath, and let it out.

"Gentlemen, I still have another question or two. Master Guns, what do you make of this?"

"To be honest, sir, I'm really not sure. Could be a setup. As for the extraction, I was thinking that one of our Spanish interrogators could be put on an Osprey and get the info on takeoff from the enclave. The pilot could relay the answers. We'd have our answer a lot sooner that way. My only concern is the safety of using that old enclave again."

"Point taken! Top, what do you think?"

"Having been down there, I have the same safety concerns as Tolbane. I agree with him about the interrogator too."

"Okay! Gunny, what about you?"

"First, General, I thought the traitor had been caught. I didn't know there was another one to nab."

"Master Guns, explain to the gunny, if you would please!"

"Gunny, we didn't know for sure there was another guy, only rumors and the answers from the not-too-forthcoming prisoners we just brought back. There was one. There was not one! It was up in the air. We have no idea, of course, what this deserter will say. We have nothing concrete to go on at this time."

"Thanks! If there is one, I hope you can get him. When would we extract him?"

"Well, Gunny," the general answered, "there's a lot of training going on with the fleet and our marines, so it could be tomorrow or two or three days from now. It won't be a priority flight, however. Arrangements have to be made to have him checked medically aboard ship before being flown to Gitmo. We don't want to spread any tropical crap to our troops.

"I got a lot to work on, guys, so if you'll excuse me, I need to get to work. Thanks again for your input."

The men left the office, and the general picked up the phone.

When the number answered, he said "The hook is set" and hung up.

The gunny went straight to Tolbane's office with him. He had a lot of questions about what had been happening about this traitor situation. Tolbane lied fluently to him and reported the conversation to the general after the gunny left.

*****

Later that evening, somewhere in the naval base complex, a marine radio technician sat with headphones on and a recorder working. He was monitoring a satellite phone call to an unknown location. The conversation was interesting and referred to the extraction of a cartel deserter who would drop a dime on the caller. The caller was assured the Osprey would never get off the ground at the enclave, and there would be a bonus in the next check for the timely information.

The next day, satellite imagery showed cartel members moving into position around the old enclave area and concealing themselves. With a copy of the tape and photo images, General Tomison called Tolbane and the top to his office by phone.

When Tolbane was seated, the general grinned and said, "Well, Travis, you hit the nail on the damn head."

The general showed him the satellite imagery and played the tape for him.

"Well, Master Guns, do you want to do the honors as soon as the MPs get here?"

"General, it would please me greatly to do the honor and to do it in the name of Staff Sergeant Cruize."

"I thought you might feel that way. Permission granted! Let's go out to the office deck and bide our time for a few minutes."

They walked side by side to the gunny's desk. But Tolbane couldn't wait, so he asked the gunny to stand up.

When he stood, Tolbane stated to him, "This is special, just for Staff Sergeant Cruize."

Tolbane hauled off and gave him a good roundhouse right on the jaw, knocking the gunny asshole over tin cups.

Tolbane looked at the general and quipped, "He was resisting apprehension, General! I had no choice."

"Indeed, he was resisting arrest, Master Guns!"

The general raised his voice and said to the office crew, "Everyone in this room saw the filthy traitor resisting Master Gunnery Sergeant Tolbane's attempt for the apprehension of him, didn't you?"

In unison, the whole office crew called out, "Yes, sir!"

About that time, three large MPs came in.

The general pointed to the supine gunny and said, "There's your traitor, guys. Do not handle with care. Get his traitorous ass out of here ASAP!"

The MPs helped the gunny up and cuffed him. Two MPs each grabbed an underarm and began dragging him out with the third MP following them with a raised pistol. The whole office crew began clapping. Tolbane faced the crew and took a bow. Then he urged the general to do the same.

The general and Tolbane shook hands and smiled a victory smile at each other. Then the general motioned Tolbane to follow him to his office. He took a bottle of Cutty Sark and two glasses from his lower desk drawer and poured two one-half glasses full, and they celebrated after Tolbane made a toast.

"Here's to heat—not the heat that burns down the shanties but the heat that brings down the panties."

The general doubled over with laughter.

*****

The next year and a half Tolbane found to be uneventful for him. There were no special assignments for him. He was glad in a way. He had loved the adventure, but nearing his soon-to-be retirement, he felt it was time for the younger marines to live on the edge, not knowing one minute to the next what would happen as things went south on them.

It was strange for him. He kind of had a fear of a different nature. What would retired life be like? What would he do? Would he find a job somewhere he could enjoy? All these questions seemed to float around in his head daily.

He had leave time coming, so he decided to take a few days and go to Washington, DC. While there, he would visit some memorials and go through a few of the Smithsonian's many museums, visit some great steak houses, and then visit his monitor at Headquarters Marine Corps to see what kind of input they might have for those retiring.

*****

After five days, he finally went to see his monitor. He packed five sets of civilian clothes and three uniforms, three pairs of civilian shoes, two pairs of uniform shoes, and two pairs of pajamas. He loaded his suitcases in his car and left the base. He stopped at a convenience store and bought some snacks for the trip, filled his thermos, and got a separate large coffee; and then he was on his way.

As he had planned, he visited as many memorials as he could. The two he felt the most emotions for were the new Vietnam Veterans Memorial and the Korean War Memorial. The recently constructed

Vietnam Veterans Memorial, with its 58,467 names on the wall, was awesome.[25] He paid reverence to the names of three marines he knew. It made a trembling throughout his body and tears in his eyes.

The Korean War Memorial was so different. It was a group of statues representing a squad of soldiers in squad formation patrolling in bad weather. It was rumored that on a chilly, foggy night, one could hear the ghostly statues communicating with one another.

He really liked and felt educated by the several Smithsonian museums in the mall. He felt it was a once-in-a-lifetime experience, but it was physically tiring walking over long distances between museums and the hours of walking in them. As much as he enjoyed them, he wasn't sure he would do it again.

He had a nice suite in a four-star hotel. The cushiony bed was made for sleeping, along with the thick down pillows that swallowed his head at nights. He enjoyed doing a little reading at nights of a couple of books he had purchased. The hotel's eating facilities were good too. The best eating, though, was at some of the top steakhouses in DC, and the food on a river cruise was excellent.

Then his last day and the time to see his monitor came, and he knew that enjoying the easy life was over. For a change, he was really dreading going to see his monitor. He did realize that was really fear of the unknown after retirement. He knew absolutely nothing about surviving in a civilian world.

At 0630 hours, he breakfasted at the hotel's breakfast bar until 0730 hours. There was a multitude of the finest breakfast items one could imagine. He vacuumed up two large waffles; a ton of bacon, biscuits, and gravy; and two eggs over medium. He also drank two glasses of orange juice and two cups of coffee and then filled his thermos with his life's blood: coffee. He then checked out of the hotel and headed for Headquarters Marine Corps to see his monitor.

Tolbane felt lucky, as he found a parking place close to the entrance he needed. The sun was now on its way to its peak and was really shining brightly and bringing the day's heat with it. He took a deep breath, squared his shoulders, and entered the building.

---

[25] The present count of names on the wall is 58,467 heroes.

He had been in the building twice before but had no idea where he wanted to go. He saw a major about his height and a little stouter and inquired about where to find the 0-2 monitor. They looked at each other strangely.

Then the major said, "I know you. I can't forget that name or its face."

"Well, shit, I do know you too. You were the second lieutenant in charge of the MPs at our captive collection point at Chu Lai. Then you were with the MPs with us up at our Da Nang CP."

They shook hands and greeted each other as though they only parted yesterday.

"Look," the major offered, "we shouldn't be having old folks' week in the hallway. Follow me to the break room."

Once there, they got a cup of coffee and took seats. Then the major began.

"It's good to see you. It's a crying shame that we have no one around here with a sense of humor. The place is drab and boring. I can't believe you're a master gunnery sergeant now. Time really flies."

"It really does fly, doesn't it?" Tolbane replied. "Just think, I never thought I'd see you again, especially as a major. You've done well too, sir."

"Yes, I have. I'm also on the lieutenant colonel list. I'll most likely get my Silver Leaf next month. So, Master Guns, what brings you here?"

"I'm getting ready to retire, and I wondered, if I visited my monitor, they could set me a good date for my thirty-year retirement and give me some clues for my transition to civilian life. To be honest, I'm scared shitless about it. The Corps has been my life and my home for not quite thirty years, and I'm completely at sea about leaving it."

"It's reasonable you feel that way about it. I'm sure you'll do all right out there. You are good at facing your fears and overcoming them."

They talked and reminisced for a few more minutes. Then the conversation turned to things that happened in Chu Lai, Viet Nam, during the time Tolbane was there. The conversation turned

to a character named John Rawlings. Tolbane had caught him stealing merchandise from a mini PX in a CONEX box with pouring
monsoon rains pelting them. He tried to escape in a stolen jeep, but
Tolbane tackled him and shoved his face in the mud.

"The reason I mentioned him to you is that you caught him,
and he was only convicted of attempted theft—theft of personal
marine's items, theft of a jeep, and black marketing. What we didn't
know then was that he had cut up at least three prostitutes and buried them just outside of the little subhamlet of An Tam. Uncle Sam
is still looking for him. He disappeared after serving his six-month
brig time."[26]

"Wow, that's really something. This guy was a bigger wuss than
I thought. I remember him cussing me out and threatening me. He
couldn't take a joke seriously about getting his face mud-washed. I
should have rapped him an extra couple of times for prosperity."

"I heartily agree with that assessment."

"Yep! Double the punches, double the fun."

"I'm glad you're still the same old Tolbane. It's good to see you
again. I've got a meeting to attend shortly, so regrettably, I must cut
this short. You take care, and may God be with you."

"I feel the same, and the same best wishes be with you!"

They left their seats and went to the hallway, where the major
instructed Tolbane where to find his monitor. They shook hands,
and each went his way.

Tolbane and his monitor spoke for an hour, mostly about trends
in the various 0-2 fields and how the Corps was progressing. As far as
getting answers for his questions on retirement, he didn't learn much.
He enjoyed the talk, though. He did leave DC in a good mood. He
decided he would just take things as they came when he retired.

*****

Six months later, he was transferred to Marine Corps Base
Quantico, Virginia. Within two weeks there, he had his retirement

---

[26] Reference to book 2 of *The Jade Cross Trilogy, Before the Adventure.*

parade at Turner Field, Quantico's airstrip. A full regiment of marines paraded before him with the base band playing many march standards, finishing with the Marine Corps hymn.

At 0800 hours the next day, Tolbane picked up his orders, went to his car, and said goodbye to the Corps with tears in his eyes. Leaving the headquarters, he drove into the town of Quantico, whose entrance was on the base, and got the goodies he would need for his trip.

Leaving town, when he reached the main gate, he stopped and saluted the guard when he was waved through. He stopped in the town of Triangle, Virginia, at a gas station and changed into civilian clothes.

When he drove away from the gas station and started up US 1, the Shirley Highway, he had absolutely no idea where he should go, as he had no parents, no relatives to visit, and no home to go to. He had no earthly idea that his adventures had not yet ended. In a short time, he would confront his worst enemies with the lives of his friends and himself in mortal danger.

At this time, Tolbane knew nothing of two lovers' trek to obtain a bejeweled jade cross in the 1590s.[27] Tolbane was not aware that an enemy from Viet Nam was stalking him with hate and a desire to butcher him,[28] and he was not aware of the killing of his Vietnamese interpreter.

Tolbane didn't know that he, his lover Mai, and a friend would chase a madman from Nashville, Tennessee, to Honolulu, and then to Kowloon, Hong Kong, and on to Hoi An City, Democratic Republic of Viet Nam, and find what happened to the jade cross.[29]

---

[27] *The Jade Cross Trilogy* book 1, *Trek for the Cross.*
[28] *The Jade Cross Trilogy* book 2, *Before the Adventure.*
[29] *The Jade Cross Trilogy* book 3, *The Jade Cross.*

OTHER BOOKS BY THE AUTHOR

Trek for the Cross, book 1 of *The Jade Cross Trilogy*
Before the Adventure, book 2 of *The Jade Cross Trilogy*
The Jade Cross, book 3 of *The Jade Cross Trilogy*
Sherlock S. (pending)
Sherlock and Killer Investigates (pending)

THE JADE CROSS TRILOGY

Book 1: *Trek for the Cross*

At the end of the thirteenth century in Dai Viet, recently known as North Vietnam, a devotee of the secret No Name Society began an assignment to receive an object, which would take him to China. The devotee, Troung Van Ba, began the perilous trek to receive the jade cross from a Chinese master cutter, a Mr. Hu, along with a secret document related to the Chinese's intentions for Dai Viet—to invade or not.

Along the way, there were subhamlets where he would receive an update on the safety issues along his route. At one, he was assigned a beautiful young sixteen-year-old guide, Tran Thi Mot. Both were found taking an immediate dislike for each other. She was assigned to Van Ba as the route was changed, but he would never have chosen to work with a woman, a male Vietnamese thing.

In addition to enduring many hardships during the trek, robbers, murderers, and anti-No Name enemies wanting the icon for themselves were encountered; and battles were fought. Once the jade cross was obtained, they were joined along the way by two allies. Many hardships were encountered until the icon was placed in the hands of No Name's leader, Nguyen Hai.

During the trek, love evolved between the two protagonists. Van Ba and Mot could not have known that their trek and acquiring the jade cross would spur an adventure in the twentieth century, beginning and ending in Viet Nam.

Book 2: *Before the Adventure*

MGySgt. Travis Tolbane, USMC, served in Viet Nam twice during the conflict. He and his interpreter, Nguyen Ba, were on several operations during his first tour. He was lucky to have had Ba assigned to him on his second tour also. They became fast friends, being bonded for life due to several incidents during their military operations.

After one miserable operation during cold and driving monsoon rains, Tolbane caught a thief, a rogue marine private, attempting to steal merchandise from a mini PX situated in a CONEX box at a military enclave in the combat base in Chu Lai, Republic of Viet Nam. The thief cursed Tolbane, swearing revenge on him for pushing his face into mud. Tolbane did not have the least idea that this thief would be his bane during his after-military life, even costing him his first true love.

Then Tolbane settled in a small Tennessee town called Mount Juliet, Tennessee. He found a house there and a job as a mall security manager in Nashville. The thief became the overall boss of several smash-and-grab gangs in Middle Tennessee area and was headquartered in Nashville.

The thief, finding out that his sworn enemy, Travis Tolbane, was the security manager at a mall, engineered, along with his secretary and lover, Soapy, a havoc that would affect Tolbane, his friend Detective Parnell, who had served with him in Viet Nam on a couple of patrols, and mall employees. A blotched, fake shooting, then kidnapping and murder would take the life of Tolbane's love.

Neither Travis Tolbane nor his friend Sergeant Parnell knew that after the thief was taken down, their friendship would later lead to an adventure that began on a patrol in Viet Nam in mid-1966, near Hoi An City, and would end with the taking down of a vicious Vietnamese piquerist who had formed a bogus No Name cult in the States and who believed he was the reincarnation of an adored ancient Vietnamese general. He had a hatred for Tolbane and his live-in Vietnamese lover, the beautiful Mai. The whole incident would climax in Viet Nam.

Book 3: *The Jade Cross*

Going home from his job as the mall security manager at Perkins Mall in Nashville, Tennessee, for the day, Travis Tolbane, retired master gunnery sergeant, USMC, was ambushed by Vietnamese thugs. But it was only a close call. He was lucky that metro police were close at hand. Then shortly after that, on the same night, he discovered that his friend and former interpreter Ba had been murdered through a horrendous method known as death from a thousand cuts and had been staked out like a cross on his kitchen floor.

Various information and incidents led the group, now made up of four, to a Vietnamese priest who had been targeted also, who joined them in believing the attacks stemmed from a marine patrol in 1966 in which Tolbane and Parnell were a part of that found and buried a bejeweled jade cross. They also realized the incidents were according to a masked madman's cause.

He thought he was the reincarnation of Tran Hung Dao, a famous Vietnamese general from the end of the thirteenth century who was still revered. This drove him to recover an iconic jade cross, take the beautiful Mai for his lover, kill her lover and friends, whom he hated with a passion, and reunite all of Viet Nam under his power with Mai ruling beside him and his bogus No Name Society doing the dirty work.

Tolbane's friend Sergeant Parnell of the Metropolitan Nashville Police Department (MNPD) and Tolbane's Vietnamese lover Mai, stepsister to Ba, received several threats and attempts on their physical well-being over the period of several days. They then learned that another inactive marine acquaintance was brutalized in the same manner as Ba.

After a friend of Mai's was brutally beaten and raped, the four tracked and followed the masked madman to Hawaii and Hong Kong, where he left a trail of blood, and finally to Hoi An City in the Democratic Republic of Viet Nam, where he continued to spill blood.

Their quest for the jade cross and putting an end to the murderous, masked piquerist would be aided by a powerful Vietnamese ally who was once Tolbane's prisoner during the Vietnamese conflict. Will the four friends find a real No Name Society and, along with their ally, succeed in stopping the masked man's cause and find the precious, jeweled jade cross, or will Viet Nam be their ultimate fate?

ABOUT THE AUTHOR

The author, a retired marine, served a regular tour and two temporary assignments in the Republic of Viet Nam from December 1965 to January 1967 with the Third Marine Division as an interrogator/translator, for two months in 1969 with the Third Marine Amphibious Group, and for two months in 1970 in the Saigon Civil Assistance Group.

Since then, he has worked in nuclear security and retail security and has run computer operations for a chain store before retiring from the workforce. He has, for several years, volunteered at Veterans Service Organizations.

He has been bringing a field of flags to Wilson County Fairgrounds every Fourth of July weekend for the past few years. Proceeds go to Veterans Service Organizations in Lebanon, Tennessee, to aid in-need veterans and their families throughout the year.

Printed in the USA
CPSIA information can be obtained
at www.ICGtesting.com
LVHW090717071123
762826LV00001B/24